Another Night, Another Day

ALSO BY SARAH RAYNER

The Two Week Wait
One Moment, One Morning
Getting Even
The Other Half

Another Night, Another Day

SARAH RAYNER

St. Martin's Griffin
New York

ANOTHER NIGHT, ANOTHER DAY. Copyright © 2014 by Sarah Rayner. All rights reserved. Printed in the United States of America. For information, address St. Martin's Press, 175 Fifth Avenue, New York, N.Y. 10010.

www.stmartins.com

Library of Congress Cataloging-in-Publication Data

Rayner, Sarah.
    Another night, another day / Sarah Rayner. — First U.S. edition.
        p. cm.
    ISBN 978-1-250-05565-1 (trade paperback)
    ISBN 978-1-250-06609-1 (hardcover)
    ISBN 978-1-4668-5925-8 (e-book)
    1. Group psychotherapy—Fiction. 2. Life change events—Fiction.
3. Friendship—Fiction. I. Title.
    PR6118.A57A86 2015
    823'.92—dc23
                                                                    2014034007

St. Martin's Griffin books may be purchased for educational, business, or promotional use. For information on bulk purchases, please contact the Macmillan Corporate and Premium Sales Department at 1-800-221-7945, extension 5442, or write to specialmarkets@macmillan.com.

First published in Great Britain by Picador, an imprint of Pan Macmillan, a division of Macmillan Publishers Limited

First U.S. Edition: December 2014

10 9 8 7 6 5 4 3 2 1

Another Night, Another Day

Prologue

Johnnie struggles to open the heavy metal door of the clinic without dropping the stack of files he has clutched to his chest.

'Ah, Johnnie,' says Gillian, just as his duffle bag slides off his shoulder. 'Thank goodness I've caught you.' She is chatting with Danni, the receptionist.

Johnnie's heart sinks. The traffic into Lewes was nose to tail, his first session is due to start in less than five minutes, and he badly needs a cup of coffee.

'Could we catch up at lunch?' he ventures.

He can tell at once from her expression that they can't. Gillian is the senior therapist at Moreland's Place and it's occurred to Johnnie before today that for someone who works in the caring professions, there's something of the headmistress about her. Perhaps it's the tight grey bun and half-moon glasses; perhaps it's the robust Scots accent. Beside her Johnnie often feels like a naughty schoolboy, dishevelled in appearance and lacking in gravitas.

'Actually, now's fine.'

'Room 6 is free,' says Danni. 'I'll keep an eye on those if it helps?' She jerks her head towards Johnnie's files.

'Thanks.' Johnnie offloads his paperwork and follows his boss down the corridor.

Gillian closes the door to Room 6 behind them. It's blandly decorated in magnolia and beige and there are several like it at the clinic. They are used for private sessions with patients and staff meetings; one blends into another.

'Do sit down,' she says, waving towards a neat, bowl-shaped chair that offers little in the way of style or comfort.

Johnnie glances at the clock on the wall and hesitates, then perches on the edge of the seat. He racks his brain to think of what he might have done wrong. He's not very good at keeping up with his admin; last week he was supposed to submit case notes for eight patients and he only managed to complete five.

Gillian pulls up a chair opposite, adjusts her woollen shawl and clears her throat.

Johnnie braces himself, guilt mounting. I took those flowers, he remembers, and Gillian saw me leaving with them tucked under one arm. But the young woman checked out of her room without wanting them, and I thought my girlfriend could enjoy them at home. Surely it wasn't a crime?

'It's regarding one of our patients,' says Gillian. Her voice is gruff.

Johnnie's mind goes into overdrive. Who does she mean? Patients come and go from Moreland's all the time – they can have up to ten admissions each week – and that's just as inpatients. There are twenty-five beds and demand is high; as soon as they are empty, they're nearly always filled, and there are countless outpatients too.

'You mean one of mine?' he says.

Her face crumples, she casts her eyes downwards and Johnnie has an awful sense of foreboding.

'Well . . .' Her tone softens. 'It was someone from your eleven o'clock session.'

Again he glances at the clock. It's eleven o'clock right now.

Gillian leans forward and gives Johnnie's knee a squeeze and at once Johnnie understands the reason she was so keen to see him.

'I'm so sorry . . .' she says.

I
Clouds Gather

I

'Those socks look really stupid.'

'Shh, Luke.' Karen turns to her daughter. 'They're fine, sweetheart. Don't listen to him.' Though Luke has a point; like the rest of Molly's uniform, the socks are far too big for her. Karen smothers a smile – they mustn't mock; this is a huge moment for her little girl. 'Let's take a photograph,' she says, running her fingertips through Molly's curls in a futile attempt to smooth them. She pulls the front door shut. 'How about here on the doorstep?'

'I don't know why you're making such a fuss,' Luke sighs. He's nearly seven, so an old hand at this first-day-of-term malarkey, but for his sister it's all new. Though her chest is swelled with pride as she poses with her satchel and bottle-green fleece embroidered with the school badge, Karen can tell she is being brave. She is quiet and pale and has been sensitive since waking.

'Now Luke, stand next to Molly,' says Karen.

He bounds onto the front step and leans in close. 'Just be careful of the ogre in the girls' toilets.'

Molly's bottom lip quivers.

'I heard you,' Karen warns.

Luke smiles sweetly at his mother, then whispers, 'And the dragon under the stairs.'

'LUKE! Why must you be so mean? He's teasing you,' Karen assures her daughter. 'There are no dragons, sweetheart, I promise.'

Molly gulps. 'What about the ogre?'

'No ogres either.'

It's terrifying enough without her brother stirring, thinks Karen, as they start to walk. The school is nearby and Molly has often been to collect Luke with Karen. She's also used to spending three days a week with the childminder while Karen is at work. Nonetheless, she's leaving the safety of a familiar world, heading off to a strange wilderness of large classes full of children, lessons, lunch and assembly . . . Then there's playtime, with its potential for scraping elbows and knees on tarmac, or worse, being teased or bullied, not to mention endless alarming activities that didn't exist when Karen herself was growing up.

By the time they reach the school gates Karen's heart is racing and her palms are sticky; she doesn't know who's more nervous, her or Molly. She sees Miss Buckley, Molly's new form teacher, on the far side of the playground and heads over with the children. Nearby a small boy is sobbing, and as his mother bends to kiss him farewell he claws her shirt sleeve in his desperation not to be separated from her. Another child brushes off his mother's angst with a 'Bye, Mum' and a grin; her smudged make-up and blotchy cheeks betray she's finding this harder than he is.

'Hello,' says the teacher, and crouches to Molly's height. 'You're Molly, aren't you?'

Molly is too overwhelmed to speak. She gives a barely discernible nod.

I should leave, Karen tells herself. Fussing will only prolong the agony. 'Luke, you help Miss Buckley take care of your sister today, OK?'

'OK,' he offers, less disparaging now he's charged with responsibility.

'And Molly, I'll be back at lunchtime to collect you.' Karen girds herself. 'Good luck, darling.' She bends to give her daughter a hug, and senses Molly stiffen as she fights to be grown up.

Karen's heart twists, and as she makes her way across the playground, the woman with blotchy cheeks catches her eye and nods in understanding.

Five minutes later, Karen is back home. The house sits at the top of a street where all bar theirs and the neighbouring property are Victorian. The red-brick facade spoils the symmetry of the white-painted terrace, but the 1930s semi was the most she and her husband could afford when they bought it a decade earlier.

Years of living here with small children haven't helped, she observes, nearly tripping over a stray wellington as she steps into the hall. She picks the boot up, places it alongside its partner, heads into the kitchen and flicks on the kettle. As she waits for the water to boil she pauses to look around. The walls are covered in small fingerprints and spillages – every room could do with decorating, which means nothing gets done, because it seems a gargantuan task. Outside the window most of the pots in the patio garden are empty or contain plants wilted by frost; the narrow borders are weed-ridden from lack of care.

There's a rush of steam and bubbles and a click; Karen makes a cup of tea and leans back against the counter. Without the noise of the kettle the silence is striking – as though someone has come along and underlined it in red ink.

I wonder if the other mums are feeling this bereft? The first day is notoriously tough, thinks Karen. *And Molly seems so half-fledged and vulnerable, she's barely more than a baby . . .*

Then, like a truck at speed, it hits her.

Starting school is such an important milestone, she thinks. *Simon should be with us.*

* * *

A few streets away, Abby is standing in the bay window of her bedroom, looking out. Vegetation frames the view, lending it weight, as if it were an exhibit in a show. Between the fronds of a yew and the spiked leaves of holly she can see down into the dip of Preston Circus.

I'm going to miss this, she thinks.

The triangular roofs of railway workers' cottages are lined up like an army, some ancient and covered in lichen, others more recently renovated, gleaming silver-grey in the aftermath of a sudden downpour. The scruffiest are doubtless student dwellings; the rest more likely house people with children, keen to live near the park. From here pastel-coloured Victorian terraces climb up the slope of Hanover in diminishing rows, as if whoever laid out the city was an art tutor testing his pupils' ability to convey perspective. Beyond are the pale concrete blocks of Whitehawk Estate, and in the far distance, the gentle curve of the South Downs, chalky fields ploughed and ready for planting.

Abby sighs. 'Oh, Glenn,' she murmurs. 'Whatever happened to me and you, to us?'

She is not sure if she's sad, angry, or both. Either way, her husband is abdicating responsibility; at least that's how it feels. Fleetingly, Abby is tempted to absent herself instead. How about we don't put our home on the market, separate in a civilized fashion, she has an urge to say to him, as you're so keen to do? What if I were to drive into the blue yonder, leaving you to deal with all the shit? Then I could go back to photojournalism – focus on chasing stories, the challenge of deadlines, chatting with bright, sparky colleagues. My, how *easy* working on a local paper seems with hindsight . . . What if I were to say I couldn't cope – what would happen to Callum then? Would you pick up the pieces – take over our son's routine, give up your job? Because there's no way you could continue working in London and care for Callum. That's a full-time occupation in itself.

But of course Abby won't say this, and Glenn knows that.

I couldn't leave Callum, she thinks. I don't want to. I love him.

She looks around the room. A vast sleigh bed dominates the space, though these days Abby sleeps there alone. Glenn has been sleeping in the attic for months, yet his clothes remain in the wardrobe, which means he comes in every morning to get dressed, a reflection of the limbo they're in. Thrown over the chair is the shirt Abby wore yesterday – seeing it reminds her. There's a line of red, chafed flesh on the side of her neck, like a particularly vicious love bite, from when her top was tugged so hard the collar left a burn mark.

It's the aggression that Glenn can't handle, she thinks. That's why he's going.

Her eyes fall on their bedside table. On it is a picture of the three of them. There's her husband, unshaven, grinning – he appears quite the rebel. She is beside him; she was plumper then – these days she is sinew and bone. How she loved her fair hair like that, long and softly layered. She regrets cutting it, but needs must – she was sick of it being pulled. Between them is Callum, all white-blond moptop, rosy cheeks and big blue eyes – he was only a toddler at the time. It's winter; they're dressed in coats and scarves and gloves, enveloped in a hug, a bundle of love.

This house has seen so much – good times as well as bad. When they moved here she and Glenn had just got engaged – every inch is chock-full of memories. What a dreadful wrench it will be to leave.

Tears prick behind Abby's eyes. I can't cry, she thinks. I mustn't. If I start, I won't stop. I have to get on. She picks up the letter confirming the valuation of the house which Glenn left out as a pointed reminder the evening before – braces herself, and dials.

*   *   *

Several miles east over the pastel-coloured terraces and chalk downs, Michael is just setting off for work. *Welcome to Historic Rottingdean,* says the sign he passes on his way to the car, and not for the first time he hears his wife's voice: 'Rotten name, beautiful place.' But today he's not sure he agrees about the latter. Michael and Chrissie live in a modern pebble-dash bungalow off the main coast road, not in the village further inland with its pretty cottages, flint church and duck pond. When the sun is shining, the light bounces off the sea and the broad sweep of their crescent feels generous – it seems to provide more space for the residents to breathe and be themselves. But this morning a thick layer of pale-grey cloud causes their neighbour's snazzy Doric columns to appear kitsch. Mizzle hangs in the air; it clings to Michael's hair and makes it more apparent that he's thinning on top. This irks him; he likes to look good for the ladies – it could even be argued that this is essential in his business.

He quickens his pace. He's got to be at the shop before nine – the Dutch lorry is due. If it had been up to him, he'd have scheduled the delivery for later to avoid rush hour, but Jan, the driver, has other drop-offs to make. Across the road he can see several kids dressed in uniform making their way to the bus stop. The schools must be back, thinks Michael. The traffic will be even heavier.

He unlocks the MPV, puts his work bag on the passenger seat and the plastic carrier containing his lunch alongside it. The Tupperware container of sandwiches Chrissie has made for him slides out and onto the floor. As he's reaching to retrieve it, there's a ringing from inside his donkey jacket pocket. He is tempted to leave the call, but it might be Jan – with any luck the lorry will be held up and Michael can relax a little. He manages to answer seconds before his mobile switches to voicemail.

'Hello?'

'Blast,' he says to himself, seeing too late that it's Tim, the manager of Hotel sur Plage. He has to talk to his client. 'Good morning, Tim. What can I do for you?'

'Ah, Mike—' Michael winces: if anything, he prefers Mick or Mickey – 'have you left home yet?'

'I'm heading into Hove any second.'

'Splendid. Don't suppose you could swing by us on your way?'

'I'm afraid not – I've a delivery coming. Can I call you when I get in?'

'Oh, er, I suppose . . .' There's a moment's silence, then Tim says, 'It's only I'd like a chat, Mike, and it might be worth doing before you put in your order—'

What's the betting he wants to give me a steer on which stock to buy again, thinks Michael. He's such an interfering young man, always sticking his nose in with ideas, even though I've been arranging flowers since he was in nappies.

Michael is poised to ask Tim to elaborate when he realizes the call has been cut off. His Nokia has been playing up recently.

I must get a new mobile, he vows. This one's like me: nearly past its sell-by date.

He frowns as he checks the rear-view mirror and turns on the ignition. Was it his imagination, or was there an awkwardness in Tim's voice?

I'll ring from the landline the moment I'm at the shop, Michael decides. The hotel is his florist's biggest contract and it's important to keep them sweet, but he can't stop now.

2

The estate agent is on Abby's doorstep within an hour. Apparently there's a shortage of properties coming onto the market – he's eager to finalize details. 'I've people queuing up for places in Prestonville,' he says when Abby telephones. 'It's a real premium being near the station.'

Before he arrives, Abby dashes round tidying, but it's not enough time to make much impact – she finds it impossible to keep abreast as Callum creates mess at such a rate. Too soon she hears a knock at the door.

'I'm Ollie.' The agent puts out a hand. His grip is assured. Like all sales people, thinks Abby, I bet they're trained to do it. She takes in short ginger hair gelled into pine-cone spikes and a navy suit and is conscious she's wearing a faded velour tracksuit. Then – oh help – she sees the camera.

'You're not going to take pictures of the house, are you?'

'I was, yes.'

'I thought you were only measuring up.' Don't be stupid, Abby, she thinks, of course he'll need photos.

'I can take a couple so we can get it online and come back to do the rest another day if you'd prefer?'

'That would be good.'

He steps inside. 'Nice place you have here.'

The carpet on the stairs is best not scrutinized, so she directs his gaze upwards. 'The cornices are all original.'

As he examines the ceiling, Abby notices white flecks of dandruff on his jacket. Who am I to judge? she rebukes herself. I haven't even put a comb through my hair.

'Can I get you a coffee?'

'Mm, please.'

She leads him into the kitchen.

'These are attractive.' He runs a palm over the fitted cabinets. They're dated, Abby knows. She is thankful he can't see inside – she spilt almost an entire box of corn-flakes on one of the shelves in her haste to clear up breakfast.

'You don't mind if I take a picture in here?' says Ollie, raising his digital camera. 'It'll come out well – look.' He clicks to show her the image on the screen. The wide-angle lens makes the room appear huge.

He steps towards the window.

'The garden's a state.' She cringes. The grass hasn't been mown since last summer, and the people with the house backing onto theirs overlook their lawn. 'The best view is from the front. I'll show you upstairs.'

'It's a good space for a property this central.'

His enthusiasm only serves to emphasize the pain of Abby's loss. Doubtless he's assumed they're upgrading –

purchasing somewhere bigger, or moving further out of the city.

Ollie removes a bright-yellow object from his pocket. He stands back and points it at the far wall. There's a bleep.

'What's that?'

'It's an ultrasonic tape measure.'

'How does that work?' Abby moves closer to look, and sees Ollie glance at the red-raw mark on her neck. His consternation is palpable. 'Ah, kettle's boiled,' she says, thankful for the excuse to turn away.

'So why are you moving?' asks Ollie, a few moments later.

Abby's first inclination is to lie but she's likely to need Ollie's help finding somewhere new, and he must come across situations similar to theirs all the time. 'My husband and I are separating.' She's embarrassed to hear her voice crack.

'Ah.' A silence, and Ollie shifts his feet, awkward. 'Er, where next? Lounge?'

'Sure.'

As he turns to leave the room, he stops, stares.

'Blimey, what happened there?'

Abby feels her cheeks burning. The television on top of the fridge-freezer has been smashed, how could she have forgotten? Shards of broken glass splay out from the centre of the screen, as if it's been hit by a bullet. It happened only yesterday, and she knows her son will keenly miss being able to watch TV in the kitchen. Abby isn't sure it's worth replacing: a new set might meet the same fate. Nonetheless she must get rid of it. Callum's term starts full-time tomorrow; perhaps then she can get to the tip – the glass is a real hazard with a child around.

She senses Ollie gazing at the wound on her neck again, assimilating.

* * *

I've had far worse goodbyes than taking Molly to school for the first time, Karen reminds herself. Anyway, the start of January is notoriously dispiriting. Isn't it around now some DJ or other inevitably declares, 'It's the most depressing day of the year,' as if a nationwide announcement will help alleviate the gloom? Best keep myself busy – it's time the Christmas decorations came down. She scoops her hair into a makeshift bun using a nearby biro, and goes upstairs.

Getting the boxes out of the loft is an effort. Simon was such a big bear of a man he would have done it as a matter of course, but now she must manage alone. Even lowering the ladder is a test of her strength, then she has to drop the boxes through the hatch without anyone to catch them below. The fibres from the insulation make her cough, but at last she's standing in the living room covered in dust and sweat, mission accomplished.

What a shame to throw these away, she thinks as she begins taking the cards down from the mantelpiece. Putting the decorations up was so joyful – Molly squealing with excitement as they turned on the fairy lights, Luke pretending he wasn't bothered but clearly thrilled at the growing pile of presents. Even Toby, their cat, seemed to regress to kittenhood as he chased a piece of gold string around the room. The sense of anticipation gave them a lift, and on the whole she coped well – she bought gifts online to save money; the three of them made and iced a cake together; they joined her friends Anna and Lou to watch fireworks on the beach to celebrate the winter solstice; her mother, Shirley, came to stay for a few days and spoiled the children rotten. Still, sometimes Karen would catch herself standing with a plastered-on smile, trying to mask her upset. 'Fake it to make it,' Anna suggested. 'It's a good strategy for appearing more upbeat than you feel.'

In contrast, tidying up seems to say nothing other than *the fun is over,* thinks Karen. After all, what have I got to look forward to? The second anniversary of my husband's death in a few weeks' time? On the one hand it seems a century ago we were getting cards wishing Merry Christmas to the four of us; on the other as if it was only yesterday Simon was here to help with chores and DIY.

The trouble is that grief isn't linear, Karen has learned. It doesn't go in a neat line upwards, as if you were climbing a mountain. Then you could get to the top and say, 'I've done it, I've stopped being sad. Now I'm ready to meet people, to smile, laugh, drink, party. Bring it on!' Instead, grief sneaks up from behind, grabbing you by stealth, like a mugger. Sometimes it can be extremely frightening; certainly it robs you of a great deal.

The events she is able to brace herself for because she expects to feel miserable tend to be easier; then people rally round. Christmas Day was like that; Karen and the children had several invitations. And she has friends – Anna is one, Lou another – who are good at foreseeing occasions which might trigger upset and try to be there to support her. But the gaps in between, if she's not got her guard up, are when the mugger will strike. Without warning she'll pull a deck-chair out of the garden shed and it'll smell of Simon – how does that happen after nearly two years? Or she'll be the only single guest at a dinner party other than a friend-of-a-friend who's been invited as a pairing for her, although it's glaringly obvious they're ill-suited. Or it might be at night; she seldom got chilly with Simon there, but these days she is often freezing, even in summer. She'll pull the duvet round her tight as wrapping paper, yet nothing will stop her shivering.

One by one she unhooks the glass baubles from the tree with a shower of pine needles. The baubles are so worn that the mirror effect is peeling off. She wraps them in tissue paper and places them inside a box. That tinsel, she thinks, when I swathed it round these branches it appeared so festive and glittery; now it looks tacky. Why do I bother?

For the children, she reminds herself. That's why. Without them, I'm not sure how I would have kept going.

*. * *

Sod's law, the lorry doesn't turn up at nine, and when Michael tries Tim's mobile he fails to answer. Michael leaves a message with the hotel switchboard, and verifies his ancient Nokia is working by ringing from the landline. While he waits for the delivery, he focuses on the spartan supplies he has left; maybe he can make them presentable enough to do some trade, although early January is a bad time for flower selling.

Perhaps I should have closed up, taken this week off, he thinks. But he can't afford to: he has responsibilities – a mortgage to pay, a car to run, children at university; and his wife's income, such as it is, comes from her working occasionally at the shop, too.

At the back of the florist is a cool, dark room where Michael keeps stock when the store is shut, but once he gets the flowers into the light he sees they are past their best: gerberas folding back on themselves, petals sagging; freesias beginning to brown at the edges; hyacinths drooping under the weight of their blooms. The little he can salvage won't sell unless substantially discounted.

Eventually the deep throb of an engine heralds the lorry's arrival. The vehicle is enormous; Jan can't park it outside on the busy main road for more than a few minutes before other drivers start honking their horns and shouting. Michael mounts the steps of the truck and scans the shelves, assessing what will attract his customers. Roses are always a good fallback and though he prefers to buy them in London because the quality is better, these will do till he can get up to the market. Chrysanths usually go fast as they're cheap, but offer little in terms of repeat business because they last for ages. He spies daffs and tulips, trays of primula and winter pansies, all traditional favourites.

'I'll take these,' he says, once he's gathered a hoard. Next he ponders what he might create for the hotel. How frustrating he's not heard back from Tim. He'll have to make his purchasing decisions regardless – the Dutchman won't be back till next week.

'These are fantastic.' Jan shows Michael some amaryllis.

'Wow.' For a brief moment Michael is caught up in the sensation that made him want to run a flower shop in the first place. Eighteen-inch stems crowned by four giant red trumpets like loudhailers at a country show – he feels a rush of pleasure.

'Most people grow them in pots, but they make a superb cut flower, don't they?'

Michael checks the tag. 'Pricey, though.'

'I will do you this whole bucket for twenty pounds.'

'Can you add it to my account?'

Jan nods.

'OK. I'll take them.'

Michael rubs his hands together with excitement. I'll make an arrangement for reception at Hotel sur Plage that'll truly dazzle them, he vows.

Once Jan has gone, he takes off his donkey jacket so he can move more freely, and flicks on his ancient transistor. Just as he's getting started, he hears the familiar chords of 'White Man in Hammersmith Palais' by The Clash, one of his favourite singles. Grinning with pleasure, he turns the volume up full blast – it's not as if there are any customers in the shop – and sings 'Oo-ee-oo' along to the backing vocals as he slices the trunk-like amaryllis stems on a diagonal.

Funny to think an old punk could end up a florist, he thinks, pulling off the outer leaves of some brassica in time to the reggae beat. Wonder what Joe Strummer would make of a shop called 'Bloomin' Hove'? Might give him a laugh. After all, almost everyone settles down in the end – he spent his last days on a farm in Somerset. Didn't I read he got into planting trees to combat global warming?

Michael selects a few fronds of cedar – the spicy scent should work well on the hotel front desk. Whilst he twirls the arrangement to check every angle, he casts his mind back. At once he's in the mosh pit, pogoing alongside his mates, peroxide hair spiked up with sugar soap, elbows flapping like chicken wings to fend off fans who jumped too close . . . Yes, they did use to gob at whoever was performing, revolting in hindsight, but there was something so great about those days. The music was raw and simple, a channel for his youthful aggression and rebellion. I'm glad I was of an age to catch it, he thinks. Seventeen in 1977: perfect. A couple of years older and I'd have ended up into Yes and prog rock, like my brother. There was Bowie, but glam rock wasn't political, anarchic, whereas punk seemed to speak to lads like me from the suburbs. Croydon even had its own scene: The Damned were local, and there was a pub, the Greyhound, with gigs on every Sunday. That was another hallmark of punk – it was an anyone-can-do-it movement, you didn't need money or even musical skill to be part of it.

Michael sighs. This mentality seems to be missing now. He's tried to engage with his kids about what they're into, but he can't imagine his son or daughter picking up a guitar, even though he's urged Ryan, in particular, to give it a go. Instead his son seems more interested in playing computer games – or did when he lived at home – and try as he might, Michael can't pretend he's enthralled. Now Ryan is away studying and Michael's not sure what he gets up to. Sometimes it feels they're not just a generation apart, but on different planets.

The song finishes with a succession of rapid chords, and

the DJ announces he's doing a tribute to mark the ten years since Strummer's death this Christmas.

Blimey, The Clash on Radio 2, thinks Michael, shaking his head. In '77 that would have been an abomination. Next up is 'White Riot', and, inspired by the colour theme, he plucks some pale roses from a bucket and thrusts the stems between the amaryllis with a flourish.

Finally, his work is complete. He holds the arrangement at arm's length.

'What do you make of this, Joe?' he asks, looking up at the heavens.

Joe, he is convinced, approves.

3

Abby braces herself. He'll be back soon – it was just a half day today.

Minutes later, the key turns.

Straight away he hurls himself down the hall and head-butts her stomach, throwing her off balance.

'Whoa!' she says, struggling to grasp his shoulders and hold him upright. She is strong, but he is often stronger.

Several paces behind is Eva; she looks exhausted. That's the effect he has: those involved with him end up worn out, thin. Eventually most give up the fight, yet so far Eva is sticking with it, and Abby is grateful.

'How did it go?' she asks.

'All right.' Eva shrugs, then smiles. 'We managed a while in the park before he got agitated.'

'Well done, thank you. You must be hungry. Can I get you anything?'

Abby reaches to open the fridge and he is off, charging down the hall. Callum is such a live wire; he never stops, as if his veins are pumped full of electricity. Before she's had time to process what's happening, Abby is running after him. The front door isn't securely locked yet, and as he reaches to turn the handle, Abby darts beneath him and punches in the code.

Phew. In terms of passing traffic, at any rate, they are safe.

Then he's off again, into the living room, jumping on the armchair, Zebedee.

She dives for his ankles, knowing it's futile. With astonishing speed he leaps up and over her, past Eva, who's come to help, to BOING! BOING! on the sofa. No wonder the springs are going.

'Ouch!' Abby gets another headbutt.

He slides over the back of the settee and stands in front of the bay window like an escaped convict on watch for his captors, looking up the street one second, inside the room the next. He starts scratching, tugging at the skin on the backs of his hands. It's red raw and weeping, Abby notes, a sign he's especially upset today. Seeing this makes her heart bleed, too.

'Hey, hey, little man . . .' she murmurs, voice soft, concern for his state of mind mixed with fear he's going to headbutt the glass. 'Shall we try *Alvin and The Chipmunks*? How about *Alvin and The Chipmunks*?' She enunciates the words clearly and Eva reaches for the box.

The window isn't as interesting as this prospect, and – WHOOP! – he's over to the coffee table, snatching the remote and flicking on the telly.

'Come and sit on Mummy,' she says, and pats her lap.

Callum does as he's bid – a rarity – and, with no concept

of his seven-year-old weight or impact, lands on her bony thighs with a thud.

For a few moments, he is settled.

Abby exhales. It makes her manic too, being with him. It's catching, this inability to concentrate, to stay still: they ping from place to place, activity to activity, like a game of pinball. Even when Callum is out at school or with one of his carers, it's hard for Abby to slow down.

'I wish I understood more what goes on inside here,' she whispers, stroking his head. But as usual her son seems far away in his private world and doesn't answer. Conversation is only ever one-way. So instead she continues fondling his hair, hoping he remains seated long enough for her to catch her breath.

* * *

By midday Michael has still not heard back from Tim, so he asks Ali, the greengrocer next door, to keep an eye on the shop while he nips down to the seafront to deliver his handiwork. Michael walks into Hotel sur Plage and is poised to ask the lad on reception to let Tim know that he's here, when his heart misses a beat.

On the glass counter is a vast bouquet of deep-pink peonies. These are new blooms, poised to open; their fragrance is sweet and light as a sunny day. They are not remotely in season, so must have cost the earth.

Normally it would be down to Michael to remove the previous week's flowers and put new ones in their place. But on Boxing Day he supplied the hotel with an arrangement of ivy, moss and red and white roses; not this. He left a family gathering early to deliver it in person. Why the change?

At that moment Tim comes hurrying down the corridor, shiny leather loafers clicking on the marble. 'Ah, Mike, glad to see you! Happy New Year!'

'Nice flowers.' Michael jerks his head towards the counter.

'Beautiful, aren't they?' gushes Tim, then grasps that Michael is being sarcastic. 'Ah, yes, well, Mike, actually that's what I wanted to talk to you about . . . Hope you got my message on your mobile?'

Michael shakes his head.

'Couple of hours ago, must have been.'

'I've had my phone close by all morning.'

'It was your answer message – it clicked on after a few rings.'

Michael reaches into his pocket and retrieves his Nokia. To his surprise, through the scratches on the tiny screen he can make out the message icon. 'Must have missed it,' he says, confused as to how. Then he realizes. The radio. Oh shit.

'Er . . .' Now Tim appears nonplussed. 'I hope you didn't buy any flowers specially . . . ?' His voice trails off.

Of course I did, thinks Michael. 'Why?'

'The thing is, um, it's . . .' Michael sees colour rising up the young man's neck. Michael is not used to Tim fumbling; normally he's assertive to the point of bullishness. 'I might as well be honest. We're going to be getting another supplier to do the arrangements here from now on.'

Michael had a hunch something was amiss; still, he is

speechless. There's been no warning of this at all before today, no inkling from the management that they were unhappy, no moans or groans about his work, or mutterings to suggest he needed to watch his step, let alone a request for Bloomin' Hove to retender. Tim even asked him to make extra displays in the run-up to Christmas.

'It's just that . . . we've got this new—'

'You've found someone cheaper,' states Michael. 'Ah, well.' He struggles to think at speed. 'I'm sure I can do something about that.' Tim has beaten Michael's prices down repeatedly since he was promoted eighteen months ago, so Michael doesn't have much room to manoeuvre, but he can't give up without a fight. He's determined to see those amaryllis standing in their rightful place in the reception of Hotel sur Plage.

'I couldn't ask you to lower your costs,' says Tim.

Could have fooled me, thinks Michael. He waits, watching, strangely fascinated, as Tim's normally pale face continues to redden until he matches the peonies.

'Trouble is . . . It's, er—' Finally Tim blurts, ' – Lawrence's daughter.'

It takes Michael a few seconds to compute. 'As in *the* Lawrence, owner of this hotel?'

Tim can't meet his gaze. 'Mm.'

It's an axe to Michael's knees. 'I see.' Bile rises in his throat. I hate this man, he thinks. I've never liked him, now I fucking loathe him.

There's another silence and implications tumble like dominoes.

For any retailer to lose their biggest customer is invariably bad news, but at this time of year, for Bloomin' Hove, it's potentially catastrophic. The shop doesn't make much profit on the business from Hotel sur Plage, but it's the only contract Michael has: his anchor in a sea of crazily fluctuating income. Without it he will find it hard to pay this month's rent, and he has been running up credit with Jan and another supplier in the Big Smoke. But he's damned if Tim should glean any of this, and he's aware of the lad behind reception, pretending not to listen.

'Of course, we'll settle your outstanding invoices . . .'

'Right.' Michael nods.

The vase of sickly scented peonies, the bowl of mints to sweeten guests, the glass-topped counter polished to perfection – if Michael had a sledgehammer to hand, he'd smash them all to pieces.

Instead he turns and marches straight out of the building.

Outside, he stops. Suddenly he's desperately short of breath, heart beating so fast he feels it might burst through his ribcage. He grabs hold of the wrought-iron railing to steady himself.

His MPV is parked in a nearby loading bay, and after what seems a long while, the wind blowing along the promenade and the sound of waves crashing on the shingle calm him enough that he feels able to drive.

Through the car window he can see the giant red blooms rising up from their boxes, garish and defiant. His heart starts to thump again.

They're all trumpeting at him, jeering. 'So what are you going to do with us now? Sell us for a song at your sorry little shop?'

4

At lunchtime on the way back from school, Karen and Molly stop at the Co-op in Seven Dials. Karen is reaching for their usual wholemeal loaf when Molly asks, 'Aren't we going to get Grandma some bread?'

Karen's mother prefers sliced white, so over Christmas Karen has been buying that too.

'We're not seeing Grandma for a bit,' says Karen.

Her little girl looks worried. 'Has she gone back to Portugal?'

'Grandma doesn't live in Portugal any more,' Karen explains as they join the queue for the till. 'She's much closer to us now, remember? She's gone home to her flat, near Grandpa.'

'Why doesn't Grandma live with Grandpa?'

Lord, thinks Karen. Out of the mouths of babes. She considers how best to explain. 'Grandpa's not well, so he's in a special home where nurses can look after him.'

'So does Grandma live on her own?'

Karen feels a stab of guilt. 'Yes, sweetheart, she does.'

'Oh.' A small line forms between Molly's brows. 'Does that make her sad?'

Her daughter's question surprises Karen. It seems so grown up. 'Maybe,' she says, flummoxed.

'Like you're sad without Daddy?'

'Er . . .'

'If Grandma's sad, she should come and live with us,' announces Molly.

Just then they reach the till. Thank goodness Karen can focus on the cashier – she's utterly lost for words.

* * *

'Oh dear, not in?' says Ali, when Michael gets out of the MPV back at Bloomin' Hove.

'He was in all right.' Michael's voice is a growl.

'But—' Then Ali sees the boot full of amaryllis and his face falls.

I may as well tell him, decides Michael. If anyone will understand, it's Ali. His neighbour's trade has taken a nose-dive since the opening of a Tesco Metro a hundred yards down the road – luckily they've not much room for flowers.

'Fired.' He flings the trays of roses onto the pavement in frustration. He cut the stems short especially for the hotel restaurant – how on earth can he sell dozens of such blooms now?

One by one he lifts the precious arrangements from the vehicle and lays them by the door. As he struggles with the display he made for reception, he feels his skin prickling with resentment.

'Here, let me help you,' says Ali, and together they lower the amaryllis to the ground.

'Tim could have bloody tried the landline,' says Michael as he finishes explaining. 'I'm sure I would have heard that.'

'He should have made sure he spoke to you in person,' Ali nods.

'You know what he said before Christmas? "Off the record, Mike, it'd be smart to feature more traditional flowers in the arrangements you do for us. You're the creative one, of course, but I thought you might appreciate the steer, as the boss, you see, he's got a penchant for roses." What bullshit. If Lawrence is so wedded to roses, what the hell were giant peonies doing on reception?' Michael kicks an empty box.

'That Tim is a tosser.' Ali's family are from Rajasthan, but working alongside Michael has broadened his vocabulary. 'Why didn't he say to this Mr Lawrence he already has a supplier? You have been doing those arrangements for many years.'

'Over a decade. Wouldn't have occurred to him to stand up to Lawrence – pigs would sooner fly.'

'We all have businesses to run,' says Ali. 'But even if he did want to replace you, he could have given you some notice. To show such disrespect – it is not kind.'

Michael sighs. Twenty years ago no one would have dared treat me so badly, he thinks. I was a big shot locally then, though no one would guess it now. Once I had several outlets close to Hove Station . . . When did it all go wrong?

* * *

34

As Karen and Molly are leaving the Co-op, Karen catches sight of a figure walking ahead.

'That looks like Lou,' she says, recognizing her friend's spiked crop and parka. 'Do you want to run and see?'

Molly doesn't need asking twice. 'Lou! Lou!'

Lou turns round. Her anorak is unzipped over her domed belly. 'Molly!' She beams, clearly as delighted to see the little girl as Molly is to see her. 'Look at *you* in your uniform!'

Even from where she is standing with her bag of shopping, Karen can tell her daughter is thrilled to have the chance to show off.

'Hi,' says Karen, when she's caught them up. 'What are you doing here?' Lou lives in Kemptown, a couple of miles away.

'It's my day off and I've been to Pilates. There's a class in West Hill Hall for mothers-to-be.'

'You got time to come to ours for a quick catch-up?'

'Sure.'

Back at the house, Karen offers her friend a cup of tea.

'I'm fine with water,' Lou says, taking a seat at the pine kitchen table alongside Molly. 'Don't you worry, I've got some here.' She pulls a bottle from her bag.

How organized, thinks Karen. Lou's always so good at looking after her health. I must make more effort. I've put on weight since Simon died, and I was hardly slim in the first place. She riffles through the utensils looking for the tin opener to open some baked beans for her daughter's lunch, but can't seem to find it anywhere.

'So how was Christmas at your mother's?' she asks.

'Well, I'd been dreading it – you know we don't usually see eye to eye. My sister was horribly judgemental. Banged on about how selfish it was for me to have a child because I'm gay.'

'Oh, God.' Karen shakes her head.

'I'm used to it. The extraordinary thing is that Mum had a real turnaround. She even ended up defending me.'

Eventually Karen locates the tin opener in the wrong drawer. I seem to mislay things all the time, she thinks. As she empties the beans into a saucepan, Lou tells her the full story. When she's finished, she says, 'Enough about me. Was your Christmas OK?'

'Oh, fine,' says Karen brightly.

Lou gives her a sideways look.

Karen hesitates. She's not sure she's up to talking about this, plus she's conscious her daughter is present. 'I suppose I've been feeling a bit blue,' she says carefully. 'And today was a big day, you know, for Molly . . .'

'It can't be easy, seeing her starting school.' Lou cups her hands protectively over her belly.

She's got all this to come, thinks Karen, with a twinge of jealousy. I'd love to have the children's first few years over again. An image of Simon holding a newborn Molly flashes into her mind, but she pushes it away. 'No, it isn't . . .'

Her recent exchange with Molly has underlined that her daughter is likely to pick up on their conversation. True to form, Molly pipes up, 'Didn't you *want* me to go to school, Mummy?'

Karen laughs. 'Of course I did, sweetheart. It's only that Mummy will miss you.'

'But you'll still *see* me.'

'Of course I will.' Karen and Lou exchange glances. Then Karen says, 'Tell you what, Molly, would you like to watch a few minutes of CBeebies while Mummy and Lou have a chat? You can have your lunch on the coffee table in there if you like. Special treat.' She struggles to ignore the guilt she feels for allowing Molly to eat in front of the screen.

'OK!' Molly follows her into the living room.

'I don't know, sometimes I just really miss Simon,' Karen admits back in the kitchen.

'It's only natural.'

Karen sighs, reaching for the loaf and cutting two slices. However much Lou sympathizes, however perceptive she is, how can Karen explain that a voice inside her head is telling her that she should not be feeling this way? People keep saying time heals, she thinks, but my heart seems to break more with each passing day.

'What about your mum and dad?' says Lou. 'How did it go with them?'

Karen senses she's trying to be diplomatic by changing the subject, but this is another topic she finds hard.

Still, if I can't talk to Lou about it, who can I? she cajoles herself, putting the bread in the toaster. Lou must witness all sorts of upset as a counsellor, and she's seen me at my worst – she was there when Simon died. Karen pauses on her way to the fridge. 'You know they've just moved back here?'

Lou nods.

'Mum's had to sell their villa, which is such a pity. They'd been planning to spend their retirement in the Algarve, and we had some lovely holidays out there over the years.' Karen smiles as she recalls the whoops and laughter of Simon playing with the kids in the paddling pool; her father's cry of 'Coo-ee! Drinkie time!' that announced he was poised to pour their evening aperitifs; she can almost smell the Ambre Solaire . . . Then her smile fades as she considers her parents' current difficulties. 'Mum was finding it increasingly hard to cope with Dad's Alzheimer's virtually single-handed and living abroad.'

'I can imagine.'

'So now Dad's in this home in Worthing.'

'How's he finding it?'

'It's not really a case of how *he's* finding it. I'm not sure he knows quite where he is any more.'

'Does he still recognize you?'

'He rarely recognizes anyone. Not even Mum.' Again Karen sighs. Slowly but surely my father is disappearing, she thinks. He's only a shadow of the dad I once had. The gleam in his eyes he used to have on seeing me, the excitement on hearing my latest news – both have shrunk so they are barely perceptible. His concern for anyone else these days is sporadic, fleeting, and his ability to retain new facts and stories, or converse at length about people and places, has gone completely.

'That's tough for you.'

'Actually, I think it's worse for Mum than it is for Dad. He can't remember what he's lost, whereas she's acutely aware.'

Lou nods. 'So where's she living?'

'Goring. She's renting a flat to be near him.'

'I like that stretch of beach – it's great for water sports.'

Before she was pregnant, Lou was extremely active. I bet she's fitter than me even now, thinks Karen. Look at her, going to Pilates. 'I can't really see Mum windsurfing.' Karen laughs at the thought.

'I guess not.'

'She's had to leave all her friends, too.'

'Though I'd have thought she'd find kindred spirits in Goring?'

'You're right – it's full of retired folk, and she's making a real effort. Still, it must be so hard starting again at seventy-five. I've found it tough coping without Simon and I haven't had to move hundreds of miles. She didn't know anyone but us round here when she came, so I try to see her as much as I can.'

'Sounds like a brave lady,' says Lou.

'She is.'

'Reminds me of someone else I know.'

Karen brushes the compliment aside. 'I do worry. The flat she's in is tiny.' She pictures the basement flat: with its pink woodchip wallpaper and narrow single bed, turquoise bathroom suite and poorly fitted kitchen, it's a far cry from the big, bright villa her parents owned in the hills near Faro.

'Oh dear.'

'Along with the fees for the care home, she can't afford much.'

'That's awful. Your poor mum.'

'Tell me about it. Mum's having to spend the money they made selling the house on Dad. Heaven knows what she'll do if that runs out. I suppose we'll have to have her here.'

'God, are you sure?'

'The kids would love it. She came to stay over Christmas and she is great with them.' Karen pauses, recalling how on top of one another they were. Then she adds, 'It was nice having her,' as much to convince herself as her friend.

'Never mind Molly and Luke, how about you? Crikey, I could never live with my mother again.' Lou grimaces at the suggestion.

But Mum and I get on well, Karen tells herself. Still, it's not how she envisaged spending her forties: herself a widow, living with her mother.

'It would be fine,' she says, turning to take the pan off the heat and thus avoid Lou's gaze.

Just then Molly comes back into the room. 'Mummy, I'm hungry.'

'Yes, Molly, it's coming!' Karen snaps. At once she feels bad; it's not Molly's fault. Lou must think she's a dreadful mother.

'Er . . . Karen, something's burning,' says Lou. Smoke is billowing from the toaster on the adjacent worktop.

'Oh no!' She rushes to press the eject button, but it's too late: both slices of bread are charred and inedible. 'I'm sorry, Molly. We'll have to start again. It won't be long, I promise.' Tears prick behind Karen's eyes.

'I'm really hungry . . .' Molly's bottom lip begins to tremble.

Dear me, thinks Karen, checking the clock. It's way past when she normally eats. I should have seen this coming.

Lou gets to her feet. 'You sit down. I'll do it.'

'You mustn't.'

'Don't be ridiculous. I'm pregnant, not ill. I'm quite capable.'

And I'm not capable at all, thinks Karen sorrowfully. What's got into me that I can't make a couple of pieces of toast?

'Thanks,' she murmurs, taking a seat.

At once she is overwhelmed with exhaustion. Maybe it's going up and down to the loft so many times, or the distress of seeing Molly off to school and talking about her mum and dad, she isn't sure. But if someone were to say she could go to bed for the rest of the day, she feels she could sleep till next Christmas.

5

Eva has been gone ten minutes before Abby remembers they haven't done the weekly grocery shop. Having the estate agent round at short notice has thrown her off kilter.

'Damn,' she says under her breath. Taking Callum to the supermarket is far easier with two people, but she finished what little food was in the fridge making lunch. A proper stock-up can wait, but she'll have to go to the Co-op nearby to get supper.

Thankfully the walk is a familiar journey through quiet residential streets, so Callum is compliant and contained. Yet as they approach the automatic door of the store he starts to tug urgently at Abby's jacket and before she can stop him, he's on the pavement having a full-blown melt-down, banging his head on the ground, arms flailing.

This was a mistake, she thinks, kneeling to hold him as best she can to prevent him coming to harm. I should have asked Glenn to pop into the shop on his way home from work. But her husband is quick to gripe at her these days, and can't be relied upon to be back at a reasonable hour.

She tries to serve Callum's meals at set times – even if he won't eat properly, routine is important. Tempted as she is to go home, she can't. She has no choice but to ride this out.

'Hey, darling, hey, hey,' she soothes. Still Callum kicks and thrashes.

It's a scenario Abby weathers often: taking her son into crowded spaces has long proved an exhausting mix, as her energies are divided between looking after him and managing the distress of other people.

He has autism! she's tempted to declare loudly to the elderly lady who walks past them with an expression that looks like horror. Abby can imagine she's thinking that Callum shouldn't be having a tantrum at his age, and on such a filthy pavement too. She longs to explain that the Co-op might seem like a relatively small, ordinary supermarket to her, but for her son it's an assault on his senses. *He can't process so much information,* she wants to tell her, *and his brain is in overload. It's as if my little boy is being gunned down – bullets fire from every direction, showering him with messages. Wouldn't you be scared, too?*

To the mother with a pushchair whose heavy sigh seems directed at Abby for letting Callum get in her way, Abby longs to retort, *think about him, why don't you? I guess you're here with your perfectly 'normal' child, but imagine if while you were going round the aisles the chatter of customers, the clatter of trolleys and the beeping of tills actively hurt your ears. That's what it's like for my son: his brain can't properly filter what to you are just background noises. It's why he's wearing those things I expect you think are headphones –*

they're actually ear defenders, like people digging up the road use. Without them he's in pain. Yes, pain.

A young couple give Abby and Callum a wide berth as they stroll along the pavement. Abby yearns to make them understand that her son's world is so visually overwhelming he often jerks his head from side to side so as to block too much stimulation at any one time. *He's not some freak show. The lit-up signage on the storefront is so bright for my boy it's blinding.*

But there is no chance to say any of this because she's too preoccupied trying to stop Callum hurting himself. Instead she must put up with the unspoken condemnation of her mothering abilities, whilst ensuring Callum stops blocking access to a public thoroughfare as soon as possible. She's still struggling to soothe him, keeping her voice low and placatory whilst holding his wrists, when there is a cough behind her.

'Excuse me. Can I help?'

She turns her head to see a woman of roughly her own age with spiked hair and wearing a parka. The woman is pregnant, yet in spite of her large belly crouches down beside them, not so close as to be threatening.

'Looks like you could do with a hand.'

Abby would *love* a hand, but how can she explain to someone who's never met Callum how to manage him?

The woman says, 'Or maybe it would be better if I got your shopping – if that's why you're here – and you stay with him, until he settles down? Does he have ASD, or some such?' Abby's eyes widen. So she knows the term Autism

44

Spectrum Disorder – this woman seems to have some experience.

Abby nods.

'It won't be any trouble,' the woman urges, as if she can read Abby's mind. 'I've got to nip in anyway, get a few bits for myself.'

Normally Abby would never give money to a stranger, but there's something about this woman that radiates kindness and sympathy, and the idea that a heavily pregnant lady would run off with her cash seems most unlikely. 'Are you sure . . . ?'

'Quite sure. It's my day off, so I'm in no rush.'

'Then yes please,' says Abby, still kneeling with Callum, who, thank goodness, is quieting a little, 'it would be *brilliant* if you could get me a few things.' She adjusts her position so she can safeguard him with her legs, then pulls her purse from her pocket and fumbles for a ten-pound note.

'Could you get me some—' She stops. Buying food for her son is a challenge. He has bland tastes, yet his digestion seems to be affected by wheat and milk so she tries to avoid them. 'Er . . . rice and some sort of sauce – I don't mind what, one of the fresh ones for pasta, just make sure it hasn't got cheese in it – and teabags and a pint of soy milk?' It'll hardly be an exciting meal, but it'll have to do. It's a complicated list already.

She watches the woman head through the doors and into the store, and soon Callum calms enough for her to lift him from the flagstones and set him upright.

'That nice lady is helping us. We can stay here. *Stay here,*' she repeats, pointing. 'With Mummy.'

45

Callum moans. Maybe he's aware he isn't going to have to go inside; perhaps he's just exhausted. In either case, he is no longer resistant.

'Give me your hand,' says Abby, and holds out her palm. Astonishingly, Callum places his fingers in hers, and they stand side by side at the shop door. For a blissful few minutes they remain there, patiently waiting.

A while later the woman returns. 'Success,' she smiles, and passes over a bag. 'Hope I got everything OK.'

'I'm sure it's fine.' Abby can't look inside the carrier without letting go of Callum.

'And here's your change.'

'Fantastic, thank you. You couldn't slip it in my jacket pocket, could you?' The woman does as she's asked. 'This is terribly kind of you.'

'Honestly, it was no bother.'

'Well, it's made all the difference to us.'

The woman checks the oncoming traffic. 'Here comes a number 7, best be off.' She seems embarrassed to be thanked so profusely. 'Hope the rest of your day is good.' And she hurries away to the bus stop.

* * *

Even though Michael marks the prices of the bouquets so low he won't cover his costs, no one shows any interest in the arrangements he made for Hotel sur Plage all afternoon. They're too formal for most homes, he thinks, and this is a time for clearing out, not accumulating. As if to prove the point, a car drives past with a Christmas tree wedged in the boot, doubtless heading for the nearby recycling centre.

At five o'clock he cuts the stems of the amaryllis right down and rearranges the flowers into small, round posies in the hope that he'll broaden their appeal, though it galls him to do so. He even stays late in case he can lure someone to make a purchase en route home, but the crowds appear thinner than usual; maybe people are still on holiday.

It was the very customers I now depend on who scuppered my trade, he thinks. Down-from-Londoners.

In the late nineties, pushed out of the capital by escalating house prices, commuters started buying homes near the station in droves. It didn't take landlords long to spot an opportunity, and increase retail rents way beyond what Michael could comfortably afford. The arrival of a more affluent clientele sealed his fate; they seemed more interested in twee gift shops and trendy wine bars than shops that sold anything *useful*.

They call this 'gentrification'? thinks Michael. Pah! I bet Joe Strummer would have something to say about that.

First hit was his butcher; turned out new age-y types didn't eat red meat, or if they did, the last thing they wanted was to see pigs hanging from their back legs and trays of offal; they wanted it pre-sliced and packed up in polystyrene trays so they didn't have to confront where it came from. Next to flounder was his DIY store, and finally his greengrocer. The greengrocer sold the shop to Ali because he feared – rightly, as it transpired – it would get coshed by competition.

Leaving me with Bloomin' Hove, thinks Michael as he

pulls across the metal shutters with venom, a name that captures my sentiments exactly.

'Would you like one of these for Mrs A.?' he asks Ali en route to the car, offering him one of the posies.

'Are you sure?'

'Of course. And thanks for earlier.'

'Mrs A. will love them, so beautiful and bright.' Ali grins – 'You never know, it might mean I get an extra-special thank you!' – then winks.

Michael laughs, aware his friend wants to cheer him up, and he is pleased the amaryllis will give someone pleasure. Nonetheless, his dismay after all that has happened is acute – he feels humiliated, broken, as if he's been pummelled against the ropes in a boxing match by a much stronger contender.

'Where have you been?' asks Chrissie when he gets home. 'I was worried.' She gives him a peck on the cheek and returns to the kitchen where she's making supper, a gin and tonic by her side.

'Only at work.' He's poised to tell her about his encounter with Tim and has a sudden urge to say, 'We're up against it now, sweetheart, what would really help is if you got a job,' but he bites his tongue. In the run-up to Christmas he suggested she try in one of the shops or pubs nearby. 'Just something temporary, mind, while they're busy.' She'd brushed it away with a 'Not now, Mickey, the kids are only home for a short time.' Which is typical: although Chrissie's responses vary – 'I'll talk to them next week'; 'I'm not sure what use they'd make of my skills, love, they're so outdated' – his chivvying invariably comes to nothing.

Occasionally Michael feels his wife like a weight around his neck and wants to yell: *I've been doing this for thirty years, surely you can bloody well do something!* But instead he says, 'Come on, Chrissie, you're a beautiful woman, you'd be great behind a bar,' or whatever is appropriate, and she shrugs her shoulders and tells him he's biased.

'You are too soft on your lady wife,' Ali had said to him once. Mrs A. works alongside him in the grocery shop for several hours every day, and does the bookkeeping too.

Michael knows Ali has a point, but for all his punk heritage and gruff exterior, he doesn't want to push Chrissie into something that he senses terrifies her. 'I reckon she's lost confidence over the years,' he'd replied. 'It's been so long since she's worked for anyone but me.'

Anyway, he argues silently with Ali as he goes to the fridge and cracks open a beer, I wouldn't be keen on Chrissie working nights in a pub, not long term. He pads into the lounge, pulls the pouffe up to his favourite armchair and eases into the seat. Then he raises his voice to say, 'Mm, love, smells good, anything I can do in the kitchen?' knowing his wife will tell him she's perfectly able to cook supper on her own.

So it's not one-way, he reasons. She takes care of me too. Ali has even invented his own terms of endearment for Chrissie's repertoire of packed lunches.

'What's she put in your Tupperware box today, my friend? Salmon and cucumbria? Cheese and Piccadilly?'

It's a similar jibe every time, but it always makes the two men chuckle.

49

6

When Abby wakes the following Saturday, something feels different. It's early, but that's not unusual. She almost never sleeps beyond six as Callum is invariably up by then, though since she bought a light with a rotating sun and moon to help him understand there are set hours for waking and slumber, he's grasped he needs to stay in bed a while longer. So if it's not Callum, what is it? The orange glow of the street-light outside seems brighter, but it's not yet dawn, and there's a ghostly hush in the air, as if the volume button to the whole city has been turned down. She goes to the bay window, pulls back the curtains.

Snow!

It's still falling, large flakes of children's-book white. It's settled over the roofs of the pastel-coloured houses running up to the South Downs, where it blankets the fields in a vir-ginal hue. Close by it weighs down branches and coats garden walls and dustbin lids. Even the streets are bleached and brilliant, as yet unsullied by tyres, and there's not a single human footprint as far as Abby can see – only the twig-like imprints of a bird on their front lawn immediately below.

She claps her hands in excitement. This is quite a rarity on the south coast, a treat.

'Why don't you take Callum to the park, build a snowman?' she suggests to her husband after she's attempted to give Callum breakfast. 'He'd love that.' Saturday morning is supposed to be her time out, and tempted as she is to go with them, she needs a break more.

Glenn frowns, then says, 'No.'

It hurts to have the balloon of her enthusiasm pricked so swiftly. 'Come on, Glenn, give it a go.'

'No.'

'Why not?'

'I've had a shit week. I don't want to put myself through it.'

And mine's been a real blast, thinks Abby. She's glad Callum is out of earshot; she can hear him fast-forwarding and rewinding the VCR in the lounge. Other families have DVDs and downloads but her little boy is obsessed with specific songs and noises – video cassettes are more robust.

'He'll be fine.' Abby pictures Glenn and Callum together, gloved hands patting the snow to compact it.

'You know he's not good around other kids.'

'You could find a quiet space somewhere.'

'Can you imagine Preston Park today? Everyone screaming and throwing snowballs, tobogganing . . .'

But it could be fun, thinks Abby. 'It won't be that noisy everywhere. Anyway, snow dampens sound.'

Glenn's expression is rigid. 'Callum's not used to snow. He's bad at spontaneity.'

'So are you,' Abby mutters. Luckily Glenn doesn't hear or chooses to ignore her. It's a familiar pattern and her cheeks flush with irritation. *I take risks every single day with our son – why can't you do it for once?* she wants to spit. *How's he ever going to enjoy playing in the elements if that's your attitude?* 'Does it matter so much if other people think he's a bit of an oddball?' she says.

'He's not a "bit of an oddball", he's a social liability. He'll go up to some other kids' snowman and start eating it or laughing hysterically for no apparent reason. Or he'll overreact to a flying snowball or a sledge swooshing by or something – and before I know it, he'll be having a complete paddy.' Her husband escapes from the room.

There's truth in Glenn's observations, Abby is aware. But what a glass-half-empty view of the morning ahead! She is so upset her hands are trembling, so she wipes the table vigorously in a bid to calm herself down.

Maybe if Callum had not been our firstborn it would have been easier, she thinks, scooping crumbs into her palm. If we'd had a sibling to gauge him against, I would have known it wasn't normal for a kid to be so terrified of revving motorbikes and echoing swimming pools, and not to be able to travel in lifts or on escalators because they'd induce the most God-awful tantrums. I wouldn't have allowed my mother-in-law to say it was because I wasn't disciplining him enough, or Glenn to tell me Callum was just particularly boisterous. And if we'd known sooner, then maybe Glenn's distress would have been less profound.

He'd have had less time believing Callum was perfect, less time to romanticize his blue-eyed boy, less time to make him the vessel of his hopes and dreams.

As it was, Callum was two and a half when they'd got diagnosis; soon after he started nursery, denial proved no longer possible. Until then Abby hadn't been sure if he was simply slow to learn, but his first fortnight wasn't even over before the teacher had taken her on one side. 'He plays in a corner by himself an awful lot,' she'd said, voice full of concern. 'He avoids eye contact with me – in fact with everyone. And if I point at something – a bird or a dog – he has no interest in it.'

So Abby had returned to the doctor – who had been one of those reasoning that Callum was fine – and insisted on being referred to a consultant paediatrician, and at last, after a barrage of tests and hours of being observed by developmental specialists, they'd gained clarification: autism.

For Abby, diagnosis was vindication. Right from the start, when she'd had difficulty breastfeeding, she'd felt it was something she'd been doing wrong. So his changing from a relatively calm and placid baby to a child who was resistant to being touched wasn't because I repulse him, she'd realized. And when I tried to socialize with the NCT group and Callum had found being with so many other kids overwhelming and thrown toy bricks which had hit a little girl, that wasn't my fault, either. No – these were all symptoms of autism, she discovered, and she could forgive herself, to some degree at least. But for Glenn it was different – diagnosis shattered his vision of fatherhood, his future.

A few days after they'd got the news, the two of them sat down to talk it through. Glenn, a computer technician by profession, had spent many hours trawling the Internet, yet instead of tracking down support groups or websites offering insights, he seemed to find nothing useful anywhere.

'Looks like there will be loads of places we won't be able to take him – social settings he won't be able to handle and people he won't relate to,' he'd said.

Unlike her husband, Abby was relieved and grateful. 'But it means we can get help; we've a path we can follow.'

Yet Glenn had continued on his gloomy trajectory. 'Sounds as if he won't form relationships. He'll never get married or hold down a job.'

'How do you know? He's only two, for goodness sake.'

'I think it's best we're realistic.'

With hindsight Abby has more understanding of what Glenn was doing then; he was removing his rose-tinted spectacles so he could see the future with realism. But at the time it felt like he was determined to squash her optimism.

'So what if all of the fast-track immediate-gratification culture of the twenty-first century isn't open to him? Is that really such a loss? And maybe he won't get married; he might not understand how bank accounts work either, or buses, or shops. I agree it's a shame, but it's the hand he drew, and at least we know what the reason is. I think what we choose to believe about his options will make a big difference. If we make him feel he's not good enough the way he is, then it might well compound his behaviour.'

'Well, he's shown no signs of learning to speak so far. And

even if he does, apparently he won't begin to understand the subtleties of language. How are you going to feel about that?'

Of *course* I want to be able to communicate with my child, Abby had thought. What mother doesn't? How cruel to hone in on that. She'd gulped and declared, 'I'll work round it.'

And she had: gradually Abby had come to understand that the simplest metaphors and slang were beyond Callum's understanding, and likely to remain so. She'd learned to think carefully before she spoke; she wouldn't tell Callum her 'sides were splitting with laughter' or that he was 'making her heart burst with pride', nor would she be vague about what she wanted him to do. Instead of asking him to 'hang it up over there' she'd say, 'Callum: coat on hook,' and she encouraged his carers to follow her lead.

'We'll never fix him,' she'd said over a year later, when Glenn still seemed stuck in anger and grief. 'We need to get our heads around that.' But her husband never appeared to, and the two of them had polarized.

It's as if our way of waging war was at odds, thinks Abby. Glenn retrenched, hunkered down; I went out on the attack, guns blazing. And *that's* what happened to us; that we reacted so differently is the reason we've stopped working as a couple. That's the *true* tragedy – not that Callum has autism.

Footsteps overhead interrupt her thoughts; once again Glenn has removed himself from interaction. Abby wipes her hands and goes into the lounge.

'I guess if Daddy won't play with you, I will.'

Being with her son is like piloting an unpredictable plane, but this morning he proves responsive to her steer, and soon she is sitting opposite him cross-legged on the carpet.

'You're such a tease, aren't you?' she smiles at him. 'OK then, let's try this: *Pah*.' She leans forward and blows into his face as she makes the sound.

'Pah,' says Callum, blowing back.

Abby claps with delight. 'Good boy!'

She repeats the noise and her son's fringe lifts from his forehead in the small breeze. Once more he mirrors her. They do it again.

'I don't believe it.' She laughs in delight. 'You're saying the letter "p"!' She's poised to run and fetch Glenn to share the moment when Callum stops blowing and shifts onto his knees.

He's had enough, thinks Abby, disappointed. It's as if he knew I was enjoying it. She prepares to run after him. But instead he edges over and, like a pup wanting to suckle, burrows right into her. He wraps his arms around her back, rests his head on her belly and remains there, curled up in a crescent.

She looks down at him and feels a surge of love.

'What an incredible boy you are, coping with so many changing people and places when you can't say what you wish for. Your world seems so frustrating and frightening, you're amazing for getting through each day with all the mischief, giggles and smiles that you do.'

Then she stops and listens.

Even the sounds Callum is making are beautiful. Primal snuffles of content, more evocative than speech itself.

7

The next day is Sunday, and Karen and her mother are due to visit her father in Worthing.

'I'm afraid George isn't out of bed yet,' says the nurse who greets them at the care home. 'He refused point-blank.'

'Don't worry, we'll do that,' says Shirley, slipping off her tweed coat in preparation.

'They should have tried to get him up, Mum,' whispers Karen as they head down the corridor to her father's room.

'Maybe they haven't enough staff on a Sunday.'

No, it's because he's difficult, thinks Karen.

They tap on the door and when there's no sound from inside, they go in. George is fast asleep.

'The staff should raise the blinds if they want him to wake up,' mutters Karen, and walks directly to the window to do just that.

Shirley sits down on the edge of the single bed. The mattress creaks under her weight. 'George, darling. It's time to get up.'

'Go away!' George turns his head to see where the light is coming from. 'And shut those blinds!'

Karen joins her mother at his bedside. He could do with a shave, she notices; his white stubble is almost a beard. 'Dad, it's nearly midday.' Surely letting Dad stay in bed so long isn't good for him, she thinks, even if he does say that's where he wants to be? He has no routine and gets no exercise, which only makes him more infirm. Plus it dehumanizes him, leaving him alone all day. I'd treat a dog better.

'Who are you?' George rolls over, away from them, without waiting for her to answer.

'I'm Karen. Your daughter.' Part of her would like to admit defeat like the nurses, and leave. Then she and her mum could enjoy a cup of tea and a stroll – she's left Molly and Luke in Brighton with Simon's brother, Alan, and his wife for a few hours – and it's sunny outside, if cold. But her sense of duty is too strong.

'Let's get you up, Dad,' she says, gently easing back the covers.

George pulls them up again, huffing. 'I'm ill! Fuck off!'

'Darling . . .' Shirley shakes her head, exasperated. She and Karen are confident he is *not* poorly – he says this every morning. So Shirley takes over soothing and placating until eventually her husband relinquishes control of the duvet.

Karen snatches the opportunity. 'Would you like a drink, Dad? How about some water? You know you'll feel better if you do . . .' She reaches for a glass, fills it from a jug on his bedside table.

Scowling, he raises himself to take a sip. Shirley slips

58

pillows behind his head and the two of them ease him to sitting.

'Why don't you swivel round, pop your legs out of bed?' suggests Shirley. 'Then we can put on your shoes and socks.'

'I *don't* want to get up!' says George. 'Who are you? And who's *that* woman?' He points at Karen. 'You're fat.'

Ouch.

The insults Karen can just about endure, but the lack of recognition makes her want to cry out in pain. It seems he has not known who she is since he and Shirley left Portugal, as if his mind is like a bicycle chain, and the change of environment has caused it to slip and come off. That he's so disorientated appears to verify this, but Karen is loath to point this out to her mother. Shirley worries enough about George as it is.

'What are those?' He is pointing at his shoes, which Shirley is placing on the floor beside his swollen feet. 'Who are they for?'

He gets more confused lately, too. Everything has to be explained to him each time he does it – not once but several times. Getting him dressed is exhausting for anyone involved, let alone trying to persuade him to have a shower or take a walk round the garden, and he never ventures outside the grounds of the care home. He's unwilling, and here Karen and Shirley have given up coaxing. He's extremely hard to manage in public; he's inclined to insult strangers at the top of his voice: 'Your hair looks like a horrible old mop,' 'What a rude waitress you are,' 'Why are you wearing those ridiculous trousers?' – his insightfulness can be excruciating. Plus occasionally he gets aggressive, perilously close to violent.

Half an hour later, George is dressed and vertical. It takes ten more minutes to lead him with the aid of a Zimmer frame to the communal lounge, where they sit, a trio drinking weak tea, where only two of them know who all three of them are.

* * *

Michael is in the garden shed when a gentle rap on the door heralds the arrival of Chrissie with a cup of coffee.

'Thought this might warm you up.'

'Thanks, love,' he replies, barely glancing at her. He's down on all fours, mending one of their kitchen chairs with extra-strong adhesive and string. It's a relief to be able to concentrate on something unconnected with work: ever since his encounter with Tim, Michael has been doing his best to contain his anger, but having to be in the shop has made it hard.

'Brr!' His wife shivers. 'It's nippy. You sure you're OK?'

'Mm,' he grunts. How can he explain how much he likes being in here, regardless? Ryan and Kelly still have their own bedrooms in spite of being away at college, Chrissie has the rest of the bungalow, and Bloomin' Hove to some degree belongs to his customers, but this slatted wooden hut with one small window and a hazardous electricity supply is Michael's territory alone.

'Where do you want this?' she says, hovering. It's a good question: currently his bench is home to a disassembled hi-fi he's trying to mend because he has a vague notion he might take it to the shop so he can play some of his vinyl there. Could make the place less dispiriting.

'Er . . . just pop it down,' he says, indicating the floor close by.

'I don't know how you can ever find anything in here.' Chrissie eyes the disarray with an expression he knows well: a mixture of incredulity and affection.

But there's order amidst the chaos, Michael protests inwardly. Within easy reach above his workbench are his tools; years back he banged pairs of nails into a horizontal baton on which hang various hammers, pliers, chisels, screwdrivers, spanners and saws. Even the giant steel sledge-hammer he bought for knocking through a hatch from their small kitchen to the living-cum-dining-room has its own spot. Above are two shelves: one is stacked with glass jars – those filled with nails reflect a long-standing penchant for Chivers Olde English marmalade; those containing screws a liking for Branston pickle. Chrissie started soaking off the labels and saving the jars long before recycling was commonplace, and now he has a pleasing array separating out butterfly bolts from basin fixings, carpet tacks from clout nails, and much more. On the second shelf are larger items; some – different types of glue – go in plastic cartons left over from years of takeaway curry; plugs and light bulbs are housed in old shoeboxes.

Opposite the door is propped a 1950s Formica dresser now assigned to decorating equipment – paint, brushes, white spirit and filler, not forgetting a couple of rolls of wall-paper covered in pictures of cupcakes left over from Kelly's room. At right angles to the dresser hang tools for the garden and chammy leathers and an ancient minivac for washing the car.

'I like it in here as it is,' he says.

So what if my workbench is covered in splashes or the yellow stuffing of my armchair is being eaten by mice, he thinks. This is where I can relax and read my dog-eared *NME*s, where I can enjoy the rich bass of my analogue radio without anyone scoffing at the meagre selection of stations, and where I can come for a quick snifter of the Scotch I keep hidden in that old cake tin marked *Loose bolts* if Chrissie or the kids are getting on my wick. I'm not sure how I'd have got through the week without the occasional surreptitious swig.

'I know, love,' replies Chrissie, and bends to kiss the top of his head before closing the door and retreating back to the warmth of the house.

8

Abby is with Callum in the kitchen, clearing space so they can make biscuits. Through the ceiling she can hear the murmur of Glenn talking on the phone. He laughs, and she wonders who he's chatting to – it seems ages since Abby managed even to make him smile.

She turns to her son, trying to remain upbeat. 'Shall we start with the butter?' Yet he stares out of the French window, ignoring her.

This bit is best done without Callum anyway, she reasons, opening the cupboard and getting out the mixer. Using beaters is dangerous with no one to help keep an eye on him.

Then all of a sudden her eyes well up, and before she knows it, she is weeping.

Sharing a house with someone you're splitting up with is worse than living alone, she thinks. If only I had someone on hand to talk to; someone who understood Callum, like the woman who helped us out at the Co-op – what a tonic that would be . . . But it's so hard to connect with other parents – most mums with small children can only focus on adult conversation in fits and starts, and I can seldom focus on one at all. And there's the awkwardness of comparison; the milestones of their 'normal' children as opposed to the one-step-forward-two-steps-back of my boy.

For goodness sake, get a grip, she scolds herself. Weakness and self-pity won't help anyone. I must be strong. She wipes away tears with the back of her hand and turns her attention back to the task in hand.

A few minutes later Glenn strolls into the kitchen. 'What are you doing?' he asks, flicking on the kettle.

'Making biscuits,' says Abby, hoping he won't notice she's been crying. 'You can lend a hand if you like.'

'You're OK.'

'Of course we are,' she mutters under her breath. 'You carry on, leave us to it.'

'Have fun,' says Glenn once he's made a coffee, and he ducks back out of the room.

However busy he is, Glenn could easily work in here if he wanted, she thinks. We've got a wireless connection and he could set up his laptop at the other end of the table. Just being in the same room as Callum would show willing. She bites back a surge of anger. Since when did I agree to look after our child 24/7?

'Well, it's his loss, isn't it?' she says to Callum, unlocking the cupboard by the cooker. 'Hey, sweetheart, look, it's sugar. *Sugar.*' She grabs the packet.

Her son likes sugar, but he likes flour more. He sees the red-and-white-striped box beckoning and stretches up eagerly. 'Eeee!'

'Wait a minute, love.'

'Ah, ah.' Callum's fingers ping, impatient.

'No, this bit next.' Abby removes the bowl from the mixer and grabs a wooden spoon, determined to give this a try. 'Go ahead, that's good . . .' Together they tip in the sugar, and Abby stirs while Callum watches, mesmerized.

'Want a go?' She hands him the spoon.

Callum picks it up, gives the mix a cursory stir, then drops the spoon and leaves her side.

Abby finishes and turns back for the flour.

'OH NO! CALLUM!'

Somehow he has climbed onto the cooker and is standing on the hob, reaching into the cupboard . . .

He flips open the plastic lid, peers inside, scoops a handful of flour and stuffs it into his mouth – *Mm, delicious,* his expression declares. Then *POOF!* there's a splutter, and he coughs a white cloud. Before Abby can take in what is happening, he's down in one leap and off, running down the hall with the box in his hands. By the time she catches up with him, he's reached the first-floor landing.

'You . . . You little monkey . . .' she says, grabbing one of his ankles to waylay him and gathering him into her arms. Maybe because the packet is empty, he allows himself to drop, relaxed, onto her lap.

Abby pauses to catch her breath and they sit together on the top step. Then she looks back down. There's a powder trail all the way along the hall and up the stairs. On some steps it's only a thin film of dust; on others giant blobs spray out like stars. The carpet is peppered with footprints. Her son's face is a ghostly mask of white; there's even flour in his hair.

She shakes her head in disbelief. 'Well, I certainly experience things differently to other parents, don't I?' She laughs. 'You've created our very own art installation.'

* * *

After the stifling heat of the care home, it's a relief to be in the fresh air, thinks Karen.

'This cake is delicious,' she says. 'How's yours?'

'Good. Want to try?' Without waiting for an answer, her mother loads a large piece of gateau onto her fork and leans over the beach cafe table.

Karen eyes the layers of cream and chocolate sponge. Never mind her father's insult; she's earned this treat. She opens her mouth and Shirley feeds her directly from her own fork.

Mum's never been squeamish about sharing germs, reflects Karen as she savours the sweetness. For this she is glad. Shirley was a post-war child, used to making do and mending, and her no-nonsense approach ran through Karen's early years like an underground stream, invisible and nurturing. My mothering mirrors Mum's, she thinks. Molly and Luke share bathwater just as my brother and I did when we were small; they each have sections of our allotment where I encourage them to grow their own vegetables from seed just as we had in our garden . . .

Shirley interrupts her thoughts. 'I do worry about George in that home.'

Oh dear. Karen braces herself. Here we go. I should never have criticized the staff for not getting him up. It only fuels Mum's guilt. 'You had no choice, Mum. It was impossible for you to carry on the way you were.'

'I suppose you're right.' Shirley sounds uncertain, and her hazel eyes are troubled, but then she smiles. 'I do love being nearer you and the children.'

'And we love having you closer too.' Though having you down the hall might be a bit too close, Karen thinks, then flushes with guilt for even having the thought. Don't be so selfish, she reproaches herself. It would be great for Molly and Luke to have their grandmother on hand.

'I think it was the rosemary that made me realize,' says Shirley. 'Did I tell you that story?'

Karen shakes her head. 'What happened?'

'Your father went out with a bag of rubbish to the shed and he must have got confused and picked up the garden shears. In any event, he ended up decimating that bush I'd grown by the back door. And he was so proud of himself! "Got rid of that awful weed, Shirley!" he said. The air smelled of it for days. I was so upset; that was when I admitted defeat. Especially sad, when you consider rosemary is supposed to be the herb for remembrance. I should have brought some sprigs back with us, given them to you today . . .' Her voice trails off, and she puts down her fork.

For a few moments they sit in silence. The cafe itself is a charmless prefab building, so they've angled their chairs to face the sea. Straight ahead the light on the water is so bright it's dazzling; to their left is a stretch of neatly cut grass and beach huts which look to have been recently painted white; to their right a broad sweep of shingle, broken by a sculptural array of rocks and crags.

Eventually Karen says, 'Simon would have loved it here.'

'And George. Perhaps I should try and bring him . . .' But Shirley's tone lacks conviction. They both know George wouldn't manage it.

Again they fall quiet. The screech of seagulls and clatter of waves on stone mingle with the yelps of three teenagers trying to outdo each other balancing on the posts of one of the groynes.

'You know something else Simon would have liked?' Karen smiles. 'This cake. If anyone was partial to a giant slice of gateau, he was.'

Presently a waitress comes to collect their plates, shaking them both from reverie.

'Come on then, Mum, let's take that walk before I have to pick up the children,' says Karen, standing. 'We'd better work off those calories somehow.' And she holds out a hand so Shirley can steady herself as she rises from her seat.

9

It's 3 a.m., two days before Valentine's, and Michael is heading for London. He usually likes driving at this hour: the road is wide and empty and he knows the route well – the westerly sweep round the bypass; due north up the A23 with the shadowy downs behind him, slowing a touch to handle the bends past the garden centre where they've added a lane recently; the sign for Pease Pottage Services which always reminds him of 'Pease Porridge Hot' – a nursery rhyme he used to chant to Ryan and Kelly whenever they passed en route to his parents in Croydon. But tonight he is glum. Throughout January, trade lived down to his expectations. His credit card is up to the limit, and his current account is seriously overdrawn; he's been lying awake next to Chrissie night after night, silently panicking. Still, he urges himself, with any luck Bob can help when I get to the other end.

To buoy his spirits, he reaches for the zip-up case containing his CDs, fumbles through the plastic pages with one hand and slips *The Cure's Greatest Hits* into the stereo. Ryan scoffs at his inability to master downloads – 'If you got an

MP3 player, Dad, then you'd only need a lead to put it through the speakers in the car, it's easy' – but Michael still misses vinyl, so the thought of switching from CDs to digital is more than he can bear.

The strains of 'The Lovecats' remind him of Chrissie. He can still picture her with her backcombed red hair, sitting in an alcove of the Batcave nightclub, doing a funny little dance in tandem with her mate while all around them New Romantic types tried to look cool and mysterious. Hands curled like paws held up on either side of their cheeks, heads bobbing to the plinkety-plonk of the piano. He recalls going up and asking if they were professional dancers – talk about cheesy – and Chrissie leaning into her friend and giggling. She fancies me, he'd realized. Result! 'You're better than the girls in The Human League,' he'd said, directing his gaze at Chrissie. And that had been the start.

Fingers crossed I've still got a bit of that magic, he thinks, glancing at himself in the car mirror to check. In the dim light he can see crinkles round his eyes, the salt-and-pepper of his hair; even his eyebrows are threaded with thick strands of white. In the old days he only had to look at some women to make them blush. Not that Michael is excessively vain – he goes to a barber, not a salon, and wouldn't dream of buying moisturizer for his skin – but nonetheless he enjoys a bit of a flirt.

I hope they don't respond merely to humour an older fella, he thinks.

Soon he's in what would be the familiar territory of Croydon, had the entire infrastructure of Purley Way not substantially changed. Watching superstores take over is a transformation Michael wouldn't relish anywhere, but the effect on his home town has been catastrophic. One only has to look at the riots of 2011 to see the damage they do, he reckons. That unrest wasn't prompted by poor race relations and police brutality like the uprisings in Brixton and Tottenham during my youth; the rioters were thieves looting outlets for wide-screen TVs, phones and the latest trainers, then torching the properties afterwards. He shudders, recalling the horror of watching his old stomping ground become a war zone of flaming buildings and fleeing families. It made him want to weep to see so many small businesses suffer.

There's something wrong about the way megastores generate profit, he thinks, because at the same time that they encourage greed, they reduce customers' respect for the staff serving. When I started out, people appreciated floristry skills like mine; now they'd rather buy a cheap bouquet with their supermarket shopping.

The A23 weaves on through Streatham High Street and down Brixton Hill, then it's into Stockwell and Vauxhall with their mix of tower blocks and Georgian terraces. Finally, a sign welcomes him to his destination: *New Covent Garden Flower Market*. There's a queue for the car park, as Michael expected, but tomorrow will be worse. Buying stock for Valentine's Day is an art; on the 13th and 14th prices go crazy, yet if he had come here too far in advance, the flowers would be wilted by the day itself.

The bright fluorescent lights and the loud cries of sellers contrast with the dark and quiet of the suburbs so it takes him a moment to get his bearings. Beneath the corrugated roof of a vast shed are dozens of wholesale traders, each with their own patch. Everything is on a massive scale compared to a regular market; vendors boast trolley after trolley of cut flowers, foliage and bedding plants, not to mention sheets of cellophane and tissue paper, vases and ribbon in every style and colour, plus wires, floral foam, scissors . . .

Michael scratches his head, trying to work out the best way forward. He's sure there is everything he needs, but here cash is king. He's only got fifty quid, so although buying in bulk can help negotiate a better rate, he has little bargaining power.

No cause for alarm, he persuades himself as he collects a trolley; if I get everything else with my cash, then Bob can sort me out with some roses.

He makes his way slowly along the first aisle, appraising. At the back of one of the stands he spies some scarlet berries – long stems make them perfect for Valentine's arrangements. 'How much for a couple of trays of hypericum?' he asks the stallholder.

'Forty,' says the guy.

'I'll give you twenty.'

The trader shakes his head. 'I'll take a credit card?' he offers, eyeing Michael's thin clutch of notes.

'Thanks, but no.' Michael moves on to the next stand. Ah, gypsophila – now there's an idea. Never mind those pretentious florists who say the tiny white flowers are dated; his Valentine's Day purchasers will mainly be men who won't give a monkey's.

'What's your best price for the gyp?' he asks the young woman in a trader's apron bending over a bucket of tulips.

'Tenner,' she says, barely looking up.

Total rip-off, thinks Michael. I should have come yester-day. He recalls the Hotel sur Plage incident with a flash of resentment – after so many years in the business, it's unjust that he should be floundering.

Bite the bullet, he tells himself, or they'll go. The trip cost a fortune in petrol – he has to make it pay. 'I'll take three for twenty,' he says, and they do a deal.

It doesn't take long to get through the rest of his cash – a couple of wraps of white oriental lilies, some sweet-smelling eucalyptus, a tray of red anthuriums for the customers who prefer something more blatant, three rolls of brown paper, and it's gone.

He edges his trolley, now laden with purchases, across the hall. Bob has had his stall in the same spot – at the end of the furthest aisle – for the last thirty years.

I'm not looking forward to this negotiation, thinks Michael. Usually Covent Garden traders won't countenance any kind of loan, but Bob has been doing Michael a favour as they go back three decades. Convention is he should settle last month's bill before buying more, which lately he has not been able to do. Still, he tells himself, what choice do I have? And a few boxes of Bob's splendid red roses will help set me back on my feet . . .

But when he reaches the end of the aisle, his heart drops like a stone.

There's not a bucket or box or tray or wrap of flowers in sight.

Bob's stand is completely empty.

* * *

'Well, well. Fancy seeing you here.'

Abby is standing alone at the bar when she feels a finger run slowly down her spine. She starts and turns – it's Jake.

'How are you?' he murmurs, as if they were intimate only yesterday.

'I'm OK.' She drinks in black hair, bad teeth, a leather jacket, attitude.

'I'm down here on business, just for the night,' he says, raising an eyebrow. 'Fancy a drink?'

There it is, an invitation: *abandon yourself again to me.*

'I'll think about it,' she says.

'Well, don't think for too long.' And Jake turns to talk to another girl.

Abby wakes, disoriented. Between her legs is damp. Why on earth am I fantasizing about Jake after all this time? Maybe it's because the shops are rammed with romantic cards and gifts at this time of year, she thinks, though Jake was hardly a hearts and flowers kind of guy. Whatever the reason, it's disturbing. Being tempted to run away even seems to permeate my dreams. Yet it's not as if Jake made me happy: far from it. He was too wild, too unhinged – he almost sent me mad.

Jake was a reaction to the sweet, loving guy who'd been Abby's first boyfriend: with hindsight it's so clear. Abby had grown bored, sought someone more challenging when she was an art student in Manchester. And Lord, had she been challenged by Jake . . .

After Jake came her husband: each man a rebound from the last. They met at a party; Abby was attracted to Glenn at once. He looked almost piratical, yet when she got to know him he proved solid, sensible. He had a job he liked, was ambitious. She remembers he seemed to combine the two things she wanted most: sexual attraction and security. 'Move in with me,' he'd said, so she'd upped sticks and come to Brighton. And they'd been happy, blissfully so. She wasn't wrong about that, was she?

No, she thinks, I wasn't. We made love in the open air on the downs, we laughed at the foibles of other people, we were in sync about politics and the planet and what we wanted from life. We didn't simply love one another, we *liked* one another. It's just all this was before Callum.

She can hear their son thumping his legs against the end of his bed next door. Any second he'll be up, raring to go.

And if Glenn was a cross between her first two boy-friends, then Callum is a cross between the two of us, she observes, not for the first time. The way he pings from a high-energy Zebedee to an obsessive, like a trainspotter; that's me mixed with Glenn, for sure. Perhaps if we'd had a different child we'd have been OK, but I can't undo that and wouldn't want to. Still, who could have foreseen that finding the man to balance me would produce the child who pushed us apart?

* * *

Karen is lying in bed, but memories are flooding in so thick and fast she's barely slept at all.

The train to Victoria had left Burgess Hill. She and Simon had been in adjacent seats, facing forwards. Simon had brought a book to read, but they'd been chatting since leaving Brighton.

'My boss has moved my desk,' she'd been saying. 'He didn't even ask me.'

'Poor baby,' Simon had replied, and he'd been stroking her hand, when, suddenly, in a single moment, everything changed.

Simon had muttered something, clutched his chest, and with a thud he'd landed face down on the table. He was still, so eerily still . . . She'd been confused – shocked – frantic; it all happened so fast.

Within seconds she'd got to her feet and shouted his name. According to Lou, who'd been across the aisle, she'd been amazingly level-headed, though Karen has thought since that Lou might have skewed events in the retelling to help ease her sorrow and guilt.

It was a heart attack. A coronary so severe that Simon had probably died in seconds, or that's what they said after the post-mortem.

I shouldn't have ordered him that coffee, thinks Karen for the thousandth time. I should have listened when he said he had indigestion. We should have sat down on a bench in the concourse and waited for it to pass. We should never have boarded the train. I shouldn't have worried him by moaning. And when he collapsed, I should have tried to revive him, given him the kiss of life . . .

She's been over this again and again. Yet no matter how hard she beats herself up, no matter how many months have elapsed since that fateful morning, it seems she can never be absolved of her sense of wrongdoing.

76

She rolls over and checks the radio alarm. It's 06.45 on 12 February. Two days before Valentine's, and two years to the day since Simon's passing.

10

What a difficult start to the day, thinks Abby.

Callum's had his pants on, then off. His sweatshirt inside out, outside in and inside out again. His tracksuit bottoms were rejected as itchy, even though the label – as with all Callum's clothes – was cut out months ago. Then an identical pair – inexplicably – was accepted. Next came the rituals of touching and moving things round the bedroom. Persuading Callum to eat breakfast was impossible.

At 8.30 the carer arrives, but they don't get him into his coat until ten to nine. Abby is hurrying Eva and Callum out of the front door when the squeak of the garden gate heralds the arrival of visitors.

'We've . . . er . . . come to see the house?' A man about Glenn's age is coming up the path, holding a little boy's hand. Behind him is a woman with a small baby in a sling strapped to her chest. 'We're the Donaldsons.'

Oh no, thinks Abby. They're early.

There's a commotion as everyone crosses paths in the porch. Abby says, 'Ah yes, come on in,' at the same time as

Eva says, 'Sorry, don't mind us, we're on our way out.' As Mrs Donaldson makes way for them, the baby's papoose brushes against Callum's cheek and he recoils as if burnt, leaping onto the lawn.

Mrs Donaldson looks bewildered. 'The baby's not going to hurt you,' she says to him.

Uh-oh, red alert, thinks Abby, as Callum bats his arms and howls in distress. Luckily Eva picks up what's happening, shoots round the Donaldsons and coaxes, 'We're walking to school, Callum, walking to school.' She knows better than to offer overt comfort in the form of a hug or kiss; it's more important to reassure him his routine is not being changed.

Abby forces a smile and says, 'Hello and welcome,' encouraging the visitors into the hall with an expansive gesture. She shuts the door, praying Eva and Callum will be OK.

'This is Finn,' says the man, placing a paternal hand on top of his son's head.

'Hello, Finn,' says Abby, crouching to the child's level. 'How old are you?'

'Three.' Finn's father answers for him.

'Three and a *half*,' says Finn.

Abby laughs, and waits in the hall for a few moments to allow them to take in the space.

Mr Donaldson nods, 'Nice,' and Abby is pleased to see him look up at the cornice, but the woman is still frowning, stroking her baby's downy hair.

I bet she's wondering about Callum, thinks Abby, but she's keen to avoid getting caught up in an explanation. If the Donaldsons feel guilty or embarrassed, it might affect their view of her home. The agent has bigged them up: they are cash buyers.

They both seem taken by the kitchen – thank goodness Abby got rid of that broken TV screen – and when Finn pipes up, 'It's *much* nicer than the last house we saw, Daddy,' she warms further to the little boy.

They enthuse over the lounge, but as Abby leads them up to the first floor, the woman says, 'How odd – your stair carpet's paler in the middle than the outside; ours is the other way round from being trampled with dirt,' and Abby is torn. She could offer an account as to why: *Callum took a packet of flour and emptied it up the stairs. He was fascinated by the white powder and the trail was rather beautiful . . .* Yet she fears that without also explaining her son's condition, it will simply sound as if Callum is very badly behaved, especially compared to their own little boy. She could play it another way, and regale them with stories that are bound to shock them into sympathizing. She could show them the locks on all the food cupboards and the fridge, and explain that they're there not merely to stop her son sneaking biscuits – or even flour: he's just as likely to eat an entire tub of butter, fill the sink with honey or post dirty dinner plates into the bin. Or she could put a positive spin on her circumstances and enthuse about the joy of watching Callum on the trampoline, jumping higher and longer than any other seven-year-old, ever, and hearing his vocalizations evolve into chuckles of laughter.

But she is keen to avoid becoming The Woman With the Autistic Child – a label that irks her as much as the tags on

Callum's clothes irritate him. Once strangers see her that way, they rarely seem able to see her as much else. Right now it's important she's The Woman With the Beautiful House, so she keeps schtum and leads them up to the attic.

'I *love* this,' says the woman, turning to her husband. 'Wouldn't it be perfect for Finn when he's older?'

Finn's eyes open wide with excitement.

Abby shows them the main bedroom – where they gasp at the view from the bay – then Callum's room, which she has carefully tidied. Everything is going swimmingly until she opens the door to the bathroom.

They step inside – it's a good-sized room – and at once Finn says, 'What are those pictures for, Mummy?'

Beside the lavatory is Blu-Tacked a diagram of a boy with his trousers undone and an arrow indicating they should be pulled downwards; below is a similar picture with an arrow directing the boy to sit on the loo seat. Recently Abby and Eva have initiated a toilet-training programme with Callum, and they have printed out diagrams from the computer. Next to the loo roll is another picture to demonstrate how many sheets of paper should be used.

'They're for my little boy,' she says.

'Doesn't he use the loo?' asks Finn.

'Um – he's not very good at it.'

'Oh,' says Finn. 'He's very big not to do that.'

'He's getting better at it,' says Abby, though she's not sure he is.

The woman frowns once more; the man coughs. 'Now Finn, don't be rude,' he says. Abby is sure she can sense them thinking: *Good grief, is your son still in nappies?*

'It's OK,' she says, not wanting Finn to feel bad. By now she has no choice but to elaborate. She addresses Finn's parents. 'My son has autism.'

'What's autism?' asks Finn.

'Finn!' The woman speaks sharply. 'What did Daddy say?'

Abby can see that Finn is poised to cry. She thinks fast – her skills are honed on that score. Again she crouches down to Finn's height. It seems easier to explain to him. 'It means something happened inside my little boy's head before he was born, Finn, so that he's not as good at some things as you are, even though he's older than you, and using the loo is one of those things.'

'Ah,' nods Finn.

'And sometimes he does funny things too, like when someone touches him by mistake. That's why he jumped so high when you arrived, did you see?'

'Yes.'

'But he's very good at other things,' says Abby.

'Like jumping?' says Finn.

'Yes.' Abby smiles. 'You should see him on the trampoline!' Then, impulsively, she ruffles the lad's hair. How lovely to be able to touch a little boy in affection, she thinks, without fear of being batted away.

* * *

No point in moping, Karen says to herself. She's due in Worthing again shortly.

'Do you *have* to go and see your dad tomorrow?' Anna had said the night before. 'I don't wish to sound heartless, but it doesn't sound as if he remembers much when you visit. It's a lot to take on, when it's bound to be a tough day.'

'But I'm not just going for Dad – I'm going for Mum.'

'You're always putting other people's needs before your own.'

'If I'm going to have a shit day, it might as well be *really* shit.'

That had made Anna laugh. 'At least let me come with you to the cemetery.'

'I'll take you up on that.'

Maybe Anna had a point, Karen thinks, as she waves off Molly and Luke at the school gates. It's never easy seeing her father; the last time she and Shirley visited, the nurse told them George had become incontinent. 'Some people say there are many parallels between the phases of child development and Alzheimer's,' the nurse had explained. 'Just as a child learns to sit up, then crawl, speak and be potty-trained, so our patients . . . um . . . do the same, but in reverse.'

As fast as Molly is learning new things at school, Dad's mind is unravelling, Karen sighs. In many ways modern healthcare has failed both Simon and George. Their GP didn't diagnose Simon's heart condition; hardly his fault when her husband hadn't been for a check-up in years. Conversely, medicine has done almost too much for her father, for what quality of life does he have? In years gone by, another illness or disease would doubtless have claimed him by now. Instead he remains with them, but only just. Which is preferable, Karen wonders, to go in seconds like Simon, or from a protracted illness like Dad? Is watching her husband of fifty years go downhill any less awful for

83

Mum than the shock I had? At least I can try to move on, though I'm not very good at that . . .

You're getting maudlin again, she tells herself. To brighten her mood she opts for the coast road; the sea draws her closer like a magnet. As she approaches the row of shops near Hove station, a display outside a florist catches her eye. There's a basket of pansies hanging from one corner of the awning, swinging in the breeze. On a whim she pulls the car into a nearby loading bay and jumps out.

I *do* love pansies, she thinks, heart lifting as she examines them. There's something people-like about their faces, and these are such a happy golden-yellow, it's as if they're dancing in the sunlight. Mum could hang the basket by the entrance to her flat, it would cheer up the stairway. I'll have some anemones too – they'll be good to take to the grave later. She selects the best bunch from a bucket by the door.

Inside the shop is a man dressed in jeans and a donkey jacket. He's standing at the counter, putting together a small bouquet.

'I'd like these,' she says, handing over the anemones, 'and the hanging basket outside.'

'Can you give me a moment?' he says.

'Sure.' Karen can see he can't let go of the arrangement without it falling apart, so pauses to take in her surroundings. The floor is grey concrete, scuffed from years of use; white laminated chipboard shelves line the walls. On them rest an assortment of tin buckets; several are empty, some house one or two stems, a few are stuffed full of flowers not yet properly unwrapped. Above the till is a display of glass vases – presumably these are for sale, though who'd buy anything that dusty Karen isn't sure. The overall effect is distinctly tatty – not unlike Karen's own house and garden.

She can tell the man is concentrating on what he's doing, so she watches, curious, as he places a single red rose in a cluster of tiny white flowers. He has nice hands, she thinks. They're big, yet his fingers are long and elegant. And what he's making is pleasingly simple compared to the gaudy bouquets many florists seem to go for. He's taking great care, running scarlet ribbon down the blade of his scissors to form corkscrew twirls. Finally, he attaches the ribbon with a heart-shaped sticker.

With a lurch, Karen realizes what the posy must be for, just as he turns and smiles at her.

'Thank you for waiting. So, what do you think?' He holds out the bunch. 'Will it go down well with the ladies?'

'It's lovely,' says Karen, and to her surprise she finds herself blushing. He's nice-looking – his dark hair is threaded with silver, his features are strong, and the deep lines round his eyes and mouth hint at sensitivity. It's not often Karen encounters men she finds attractive, and he must be about Simon's age – or rather, the age Simon would be.

Before she can brace herself, grief hits her again.

Simon always remembered Valentine's, she thinks. But no one gives me flowers any more.

* * *

'Here, let me,' says Michael, picking up the hanging basket. 'Where do you want it? Boot OK?'

'Yes, please.' The woman nods, taking a seat behind the wheel of a battered Citroën. 'It should be unlocked.'

He lays the basket inside, wedging it as best he can between a large teddy bear and a set of jump leads.

She seemed nice, he thinks, as she drives away.

Reassured by his customer's enthusiasm, Michael makes several identical posies and drops them into some tin buckets which he places on the pavement. Not a bad job, he decides, stepping back to check. I managed to make those roses from Jan stretch pretty well, though they're nowhere near as good quality as Bob's, and blimey, they were pricey.

He lets out a long breath. He's still reeling after his trip to the market, but he can't put off this moment any longer. He goes back into the shop, slides the envelope out from under the till, tears it open and reads:

Dear Mr Harrison,

I'm writing to you today concerning your account at the above address. It has come to our attention that, contrary to the terms of our agreement of 1/6/2007, this account has not been settled for a period of nine months. Our terms clearly state outstanding debts must be cleared at the end of each month, and we enclose a copy of this contract along with the outstanding invoices.

If the total of £3850.00 is not settled <u>in full within 7 days from the date of this letter</u>, we will initiate legal proceedings . . .

The words start to swim before Michael's eyes. The contents are too much to absorb in one hit, so he slips the letter back under the till, vowing to reread it later.

86

II

I'm going to do those stairs before something else takes precedence, decides Abby, shutting the front door behind the Donaldsons.

She heads into the kitchen, unlocks the cupboard under the sink and locates a can of cleaner and a scouring brush. She fills a bucket with water and soon is on her hands and knees in the hall, scrubbing, scrubbing, scrubbing at the flour embedded in the carpet, creating an ocean of white foam. Then, quite without warning, she feels strangely light-headed and giddy, her limbs start tingling as if the nerve endings are on fire, and she goes hot and cold.

Everything is happening too fast, says a voice in her head. *It's all too soon.*

But the Donaldsons seem interested in the house, she tells herself. That's good, surely?

It's impossible to take in, let alone cope with, says the voice.

Don't be ridiculous, she thinks. Of course I can cope. What choice do I have?

She picks up the scrubbing brush again but her hands are shaking so violently she can barely hold it, so she stops and sits back on her haunches.

Her heart is palpitating, *ba-boom, ba-boom, ba-boom* . . . Yet the harder she struggles to control her thoughts, the more horrible her imaginings become. The idea of the Donaldsons here; of their little boy and girl running up and down this very stairway, putting their coats on in this hall, peeking through the letter box to see who's come to visit *them* . . .

Her stomach heaves and she dashes into the kitchen, reaching the sink just before she retches.

Yet her thoughts continue to race. I can't possibly leave this house. It's so near the shops . . . and the park Callum knows . . . we're in walking distance of his school . . . and I've fitted all the cupboards here with locks . . . Imagine having to start again somewhere else. I can't do it, I can't . . .

She reaches for a chair, manages to sit down.

If only I had someone to call, she thinks, bowing her head between her knees. But who? Mum and Dad are miles away, and what would I say, anyway? They don't seem to understand me that well, let alone Callum.

Eventually the sickness passes, but it takes an age for Abby to stop shaking enough to put away the cleaning equipment. It seems no sooner has she done so than her mobile rings, making her jump. What's got into her?

The number on screen reveals it's the estate agent.

'The Donaldsons have put in an offer,' says Ollie, and without preamble tells her the details.

Abby can barely think, let alone think rationally. 'That sounds a pretty decent price,' she hears herself say.

'I don't need to remind you that they're cash buyers,' he continues.

'Of course. This is great news, thank you,' she says, desperately trying to swallow her panic. 'Er . . . I need to speak to my husband. We'll come back to you.'

Slowly, she struggles to assimilate this news. *It's a few thousand less than we're asking, but an acceptable offer means we'll have to move really soon . . . Yet I've only found time to look at a handful of flats, and not one has been promising. They've all been so small, so dark, so far from everything . . .*

You're being too demanding, she tells herself. Then it dawns on her: maybe Glenn can handle this. He's the one who's keen to sell. But his mobile goes straight to voicemail.

'I wish you'd answer your phone,' she says, when she finally hears back. She fills him in on the offer.

'It's not enough,' he says at once.

'Sorry?'

'I want more – don't you? We both need as much as we can if we're each to buy somewhere decent.'

'No one ever pays the asking price.'

'And no one ever takes the first offer they're given. We've only had it on the market six weeks. Let's see if they'll bump it up. They're obviously keen.'

'*You* see if they'll bump it up,' says Abby. 'You're much better at negotiating than me.'

'I can't. You know calling from my work is extremely difficult.'

So it's down to me, thinks Abby, rage rising. Like every-thing else in this household. Why should I do the tricky bit, when I don't even want to move? She's about to say this, when she plays the conversation in fast forward. I refuse to phone the agent, Glenn and I row, I feel guilty, relent and end up calling anyway. At least her anger has made the panic subside. Nonetheless, she's too tired to fight.

'If that's what you want. Though I thought you were in a hurry to move on. This will delay it.'

'I am,' says Glenn. 'But this is business.'

'I see,' says Abby. Funny, she is tempted to add, and there I was thinking it was about our family.

*   *   *

Molly and Luke race ahead up the drive. Anna and Karen stroll at a more measured pace, taking in the stone memor-ials on either side. Karen is clutching the bunch of anemones, ready to lay on her husband's grave.

'I've always thought it a shame we don't do death with the same panache as the Victorians,' says Anna, tucking her arm through Karen's. 'Does that sound terribly morbid?'

Karen smiles at her friend. 'You always were more gothic than me. Just look at your outfit.'

Anna is dressed head to toe in black, whereas Karen is in her usual earth tones. It's been raining, but Anna's smart leather boots have high stiletto heels whereas Karen's an-cient rubber wedges have sensible grooves to provide grip.

'Point taken,' Anna smiles. Square tombs line either side of the path; almost all are topped by angels with palms held aloft and eyes cast heavenwards. 'Karen, please don't think me sacrilegious, but should I go before you, I'd really appreciate a nice big statue with proper wings and a serene expression.'

'I'll see what I can do.'

'Though you can skip euphemisms like *She fell asleep* or *She was called to rest*. Plain old *Died* is fine by me.'

Sadly missed, Karen reads. She identifies with the sentiment, but refrains from saying so.

Cobbles turn to tarmac and they walk on from the showiness of the nineteenth century to the simple crosses of the twentieth. '*In loving memory*,' says Anna. 'It's the same inscription time and again. Didn't they have any imagination?'

'You're such a wordsmith.' Perhaps it was a mistake to agree to her coming, thinks Karen. 'I'm not sure the First World War gave much opportunity for crafting.'

'Sorry.'

'Don't be.' Simon would have enjoyed our conversation, Karen reminds herself. He liked bantering with Anna. The last thing he would have wanted is me weeping every time I visit.

Before she lost her husband, Karen pictured graveyards as secluded places where mourners sat with only birdsong and church bells to interrupt their remembrance, but the cemetery where Simon is buried is wedged in between the busy Old Shoreham Road and the railway. Still, she wanted a grave to visit and this was the only place locally with available burial plots. At least a couple of crows are hopping about on the grass – that feels appropriate.

She and Anna pick their way along a narrow path, past a semicircle of memorials dedicated to those who've been recently cremated.

'Shame about the plastic flowers,' says Anna.

Karen presumes they've been laid by people without much money who wanted something that lasts, yet again refrains from comment.

'Mummy, look!' Up ahead, Molly is jumping up and down, pointing.

'Good Lord!' exclaims Anna when they reach her.

Giant 3D letters made from the heads of lurid blue carnations reveal that Jayden has died recently. The grave is covered in animals and teddy bears, snowmen in glass domes and tea lights in pastel colours, tiny chimes and spinning windmills. There are photos of him too, damp from recent rain. He looks barely more than a baby. Karen peers at the stone: *Aged 22 months,* and a lump comes into her throat.

'And please avoid anything like this,' Anna continues. 'I'm sorry, Karen, it's very sad, I know.'

'But the children love it.' Molly is crouching down, fingering the magpie collection with admiration.

'Darling, the day I use Molly as a guide to good taste is the day I've lost my marbles.'

Karen knows Anna is trying to cheer her up, but coming so soon after visiting her father, this is one dry comment too many. Normally she would let it go, but today she is already struggling. 'So what if it's over the top? I'm sure Jayden's parents will take most of this stuff away in due course. It's just their way of expressing grief.'

Her friend appears winded, but Karen continues: 'Who are you to say what's fitting and what's not?'

They walk on in silence, save for the *click click* of Anna's heels, up the gentle slope to Simon's grave.

'I'm sorry,' Anna murmurs.

Something in Karen refuses to leave it be. 'I hope this headstone meets with your approval,' she says viciously. A rectangle of marble is simply engraved with the dates of Simon's birth and death.

'I didn't mean to upset you.'

Karen's cheeks are burning. As she bends to help Molly place the anemones in the pot, she finds it hard to steady herself. 'I'd like you to leave.'

Moments after she's said this, Karen regrets it. Anna is my dearest friend, she thinks. She was there at my wedding and the birth of my children, she supported me hugely when Simon died . . . Yet already Anna is a way off, so Karen simply stands and watches as she walks back down the narrow path, high heels clicking, black designer coat flapping in the wind.

*   *   *

Michael fishes the letter from under the till and braces himself. It is signed *Bob Hawkins* in the presence of a witness. So it's official all right.

He checks the itemized list, alarm mounting. He can double-check the amount against his own receipts – which he's jammed into a box in the back room and not been able to face looking at for months – but he remembers almost every purchase, so it must be correct.

£3,800.

This is serious.

Perhaps I could offer Bob a few hundred pounds to appease him, borrow it somehow, he thinks. But if Bob's after nearly 4K, Jan will soon be demanding even more. Over the last few months I've bought my entire stock from the Covent Garden trader or the Dutchman. I can't begin to settle both debts. How will I pay the mortgage? The kids' college fees? Rent on this place? I'm behind with them all as it is.

He looks up at the ceiling as if some higher power might come to his rescue. But Michael has no belief in God – this latest injustice only confirms he is right. As he lowers his gaze, his eyes fall on the row of glass vases above the till. He rises from the stool, and, before he can stop himself, reaches for the largest. It is globe-shaped, valuable. A shower of dust makes him cough.

Then he lifts the vase high in both hands as if it were a basketball, and hurls it with all his might against the grey concrete floor.

12

'Mummy, why are you crying?' It's Luke, standing in the parallelogram of light created by the half-open door of the living room.

Dear me, thinks Karen. I put him to bed half an hour ago; he must have heard me all the way upstairs. Was I making that much noise?

'It's only I'm a bit sad, darling,' she says, struggling to come up with an answer that won't worry him.

'Sad about Daddy?'

'Yes.' And Grandpa, she thinks, but keeps that to herself. 'It's been an especially sad day today.'

Luke frowns. 'Shall I give you a cuddle?'

'That would be nice.' He nestles up to her on the sofa and strokes her hair with his small fingers. Soon the movement has lulled him into sleep. Karen carries him back upstairs to his room, and pauses over his bed, listening to the regular sound of his breathing.

I've lost Simon, she thinks. I'm losing my father. I can't lose Anna too.

Back in the living room, she picks up her mobile.

I'm so sorry. It was a crap day — just as you said it would be — but I should never have taken it out on you. I feel terrible. Forgive me, please. Love K x

And before she has time to worry about the wording, she presses *Send*.

*   *   *

'The usual?' asks the landlady.

Michael nods. 'Please.'

He watches as Linda pulls a pint of Speckled Hen. He can scarcely wait while the bronze nectar creeps up the glass, but he knows better than to rush her. Michael adopted the place years ago because of its decent spread of cask ales, and even though the Black Horse has been through several changes of ownership in that time, it remains one of the few local drinking establishments that feel like a proper pub, with low ceilings and wooden floors, stained-glass panels and a dartboard, and lighting so dim it's den-like no matter how bright it is outside.

Christ, I needed this, he thinks, and within moments he is placing his empty glass back on the countertop.

Linda raises an eyebrow. 'Looks like you could do with another.'

'Please.'

Along the bar is his neighbour, Ken. Ken is as much a fixture as the chalkboards and beermats, and is in his customary spot, his large backside spilling over the leather seat of a high stool. As Linda pulls the refill, Michael feels Ken's eyes upon him.

'Can I get you one?' he says automatically, before recollecting he can hardly afford his own.

'Thanks, mate.' Ken jerks his head at Linda, sufficient instruction for her to continue with a second pint of ale. 'Tough day?'

Michael nods. 'You could say that.' As he hands over a twenty-pound note, he's half inclined to offload onto the pair of them, but resists. Bad news travels fast, and it won't do his business any favours for his troubles to be made public. Although Ken and Linda are hardly high-flyers – as far as he's aware, Ken's career consists of very sporadic odd-jobbing – he feels humiliated. If I were to admit how close I am to losing what I've spent a lifetime building up, I might not be able to hold it together, he thinks. He's just wondering if that's why he can't face confiding in Chrissie either, when the numbing effect of alcohol hits his brain. Thankful for the reprieve, he shifts the conversation to a less traumatic subject – the previous weekend's football.

He's almost finished his second pint and Ken's glass has been empty for several minutes when Linda returns to their end of the bar. 'Another round, fellas?'

Ribbing Ken about Arsenal's poor performance has not entirely silenced Michael's inner demons, but they're no longer screaming quite so loud – he wants another drink to keep them at bay. He pauses for Ken to offer to buy him one, and when he doesn't, says yes anyway. As he'd hoped, Ken gives a jerk of his head and Linda opens up two taps, handing over both glasses. It's only after she's been standing

97

there a while that it dawns on Michael that Ken is expecting him to pay.

The nerve!

Normally he'd relent and cough up – he doesn't want to make Linda feel awkward – but Bob's letter means the cash in his wallet is going to have to last a while. Michael remains steadfast, yet Ken does nothing. He avoids Michael's gaze and merely stares at the two pints of ale before them.

It's like a scene from a spaghetti western, Michael thinks, with both of us holding out to see who will reach for his holster first.

Linda pointedly drums her nails on the counter and stares up at the ceiling. For a while longer Ken doesn't move, until eventually he edges his right hand, very slowly, in the direction of his hip. But he doesn't slip his fingers inside his trouser pocket; instead he pats the outside, feeling for the contents. Then he repeats the gesture on the left side and, with a shrug of his shoulders, turns to Michael and says, 'Sorry mate, I'm a bit short . . . could you . . . ?'

At once the demons return, protesting louder than ever. Michael feels his face flush and fury rise in his chest. He reaches for his wallet, pulls out the £10 note Linda's just given him as change, and slams it on top of the bar next to Ken, making him flinch.

'There you go,' he says. 'And while you're at it, have this one too,' and he plonks his pint down beside the other with such vehemence the beer sloshes over the counter. Then he leaves the pub, muttering 'tosser' as he goes.

He hurries across the high street, barely checking for

traffic, and sets a rapid pace up the hill to his bungalow. The cold air sobers him up, fast.

As he approaches Ken's house – a tiny cottage with a well-kept front garden full of cutesy statues and pots of miniature daffs (all his wife Della's work, Michael is sure) – he's half inclined to hurl a brick through one of the leaded windows. He pictures the metal buckling and smashed glass all over the living-room carpet with a burst of satisfaction, and for a brief moment feels empowered: the first sense he's had of being in control all day. If Ken were to come home to it he might suspect Michael, but he wouldn't be sure. And, God, it would be good for someone else to suffer today.

I've worked my arse off for decades, Michael thinks, and for what? – creditors biting at my heels like a pack of wolves.

Then he sees light coming through the gap between the curtains, and pictures Della sitting watching telly, just as Chrissie often does. As fast as the urge comes, it goes. He drops his hands, thrusts them into his pockets, and continues his journey home.

That it pays to work hard was a value instilled into Michael by his dad; he's tried to pass it on to his kids. But I've been hoodwinked, he thinks. In the last few years I've put in more hours than ever, and look where it's left me. Maybe if I'd cashed in a decade ago I'd still have options, but who the hell can I turn to now?

He feels caught in a game of chess where whatever move he makes next will put him in check. The thought that he might have to shut the shop, declare himself bankrupt and – at best – take up odd-jobbing like Ken, is not something he can countenance at the moment. Then again, he's not sure he can face Chrissie either. He simply wants to make everything go away. So instead of carrying on up the close, he takes a sharp right and heads for the corner shop. It's expensive and the selection is meagre, but needs must. Might help him sleep, too.

He has another flash of anger as he hands over the last of his cash. But once he's made his purchase, gone back outside and unscrewed the top, he feels slightly better.

I'll tell Chrissie tomorrow, he thinks, taking a swig.

And as he feels the warm liquid slip down his throat and hit the pit of his stomach, he closes his eyes in relief.

* * *

Abby falls onto the bed with exhaustion.

It's as if Callum can pick up changes in the air. He's been particularly hyper – it's nearly midnight and she's just got him to bed. Moreover, there's still no sign of Glenn. She's had a cursory text message explaining he's been caught at the office; he's not even called to find out if she's had any news from their agent about their house.

She leans over, turns off the light and closes her eyes.

But a while later, she's still lying there. Why on earth isn't her husband home? She checks the clock. If he's not back in the next few minutes, it means he'll have missed the last train . . . Briefly, Abby wonders if he's having an affair, and her stomach lurches. But she can't give headspace to that now – in less than five hours Callum will be awake. Then it'll be slam, bam, into the onslaught of the day, getting him dressed and breakfasted and off to school, going to the supermarket . . . And now she has to find a flat, fast, or they'll lose their buyers.

I *really* need to sleep, she thinks. I've got so much to do, and if I don't sleep, I won't be able to function.

She throws back the duvet, gets out of bed, pads to the bathroom and unlocks the cabinet. Right at the back, there's a packet of temazepam Glenn managed to persuade a locum GP to prescribe him when Callum was first diagnosed. The stress of that and his work had resulted in a period of insomnia. The packet is nearly full and though the pills are probably past their sell-by date, Abby is beyond caring. She drops one, then two, then – what the hell? – three tablets into her palm.

* * *

Michael's not aware of having drifted off, but he wakes with a jolt. His heart is thumping, his head pounding, his throat tight and parched. There's flickering light, talking . . . Eventually he works it out: it's the television. He's on the sofa.

He frowns, trying to piece together the night before. It's no good, he doesn't remember anything after he drank that whisky . . .

Then, with a shiver, he recalls the previous afternoon. The letter . . . His debts . . . The impact on his shop, his family . . . The repercussions hit him with hurricane force, and panic explodes in his brain.

Gradually, as if moving through syrup, he manages to get himself along the corridor. His legs are so heavy he can barely lift them, but after what feels like an age, he opens the door to the bedroom and leans, breathless and pouring with sweat, against the frame.

It's a coronary, he thinks. 'Chrissie . . . ?' But it seems his heart is still pumping.

At once his wife is awake. She sits up swiftly and turns on the bedside lamp. 'Oh love, what's the matter?'

The light is dazzling; it's one sensory input too many. Michael collapses and slides to the floor.

* * *

Karen is roused by a ringing. It's the landline, yet it's still dark outside. Her nerves jangle – no one would call at this time unless it was an emergency. Then she remembers the text she sent to Anna – her friend must have picked it up before leaving for work and is now responding. Relieved, she grabs the receiver.

'Hi!'

'Karen?' Before Shirley continues, Karen has an awful sense of what's coming. 'It's your father. I'm at the hospital.'

It's as if a hundred balls are being thrown at her at once. Karen reels; she can't catch a single one. How can Dad be taken ill so fast? Which hospital is he in? Which ward?

All this as Shirley says, 'They're not sure he's going to make it . . .' in a small voice.

This can't be happening, thinks Karen. Yet somehow she manages to articulate, 'I'll be there as soon as I can,' and barely has she put down the phone before she's galloping ahead, calculating what she should do about the children.

Take them? In the circumstances it doesn't seem right. There's only one person she feels able to ask to babysit at this hour. But . . . Oh Lord.

Karen reaches for her mobile, also on her bedside table. Ah, a text. Just the intro on screen is enough:

It's OK, love. Please don't feel bad – I was being insensitive.

It's all she needs to know. She calls; within half an hour Anna is round. In hushed tones they agree to leave the children sleeping.

'Feel free to use my bed to grab some more rest,' says Karen, rushing out of the door.

She drives along the A27 as fast as her ancient Citroen will allow.

What if he's dead by the time I get there, she thinks.

And she presses the accelerator to the floor, heedless of her own safety.

II

Winds of Change

13

You can tell it's a private clinic, thinks Michael, as he makes his way upstairs from the dining room. Look at these exotic flower arrangements – orange-tongued birds of paradise, cream calla lilies, towers of green orchids. I wonder who has the contract? Must be worth a fortune.

On the landing wall is a series of watercolour paintings of the countryside around Lewes – the dramatic chalk cliffs of Seven Sisters, a panoramic vista from high on the South Downs, rowing boats reflected in the water of the River Ouse. Michael supposes they've been chosen to convey peace and being at one with nature, but he still feels like he's been through a war.

He's not slept properly in weeks, so he asks a woman vacuuming the hall carpet where he can get a coffee, and she directs him to a kitchen. He presses the button that says *Espresso* and is watching the cardboard cup fill with black liquid when there's a whisper in his ear.

'If you're hoping for caffeine, I'd go downstairs.'

Michael turns to see a young man with a pierced eyebrow and a Mohican. 'Sorry?'

'The coffee in that machine is all caffeine-free.'

'What, even the espresso?'

'Yup. Promise you. Teabags too.' The young man jerks his head towards the boxes of Earl Grey, English Breakfast and Peppermint. 'You're new, aren't you? What programme are you on?'

Michael can't remember much of his arrival, let alone what he's supposed to be doing day to day. 'Sorry, mate, I'm not sure.'

The Mohican sniffs. 'Well, you'd know if you were an addict, for sure. You'd be detoxing if you've just arrived, and that's hell.' He shudders. 'Anyway, downstairs in reception the stuff in the machine is different – us addicts aren't allowed there.'

'Er . . .'

'Past the door with the coded lock, you must have seen that?'

Michael nods, though he's seen no such thing.

'Anyway, you want a blast of caffeine – that's where you'll find it.'

'Thanks. I think I'll give this coffee a miss then,' says Michael, and chucks his espresso down the sink.

*　*　*

'I need the loo,' says Abby. 'Do you have to accompany me there too?'

'Afraid I do.' The nurse winces, apologetic, but Abby

doesn't feel much sympathy. She doesn't feel much at all. Vague anxiety, misty unhappiness, but mainly she's numb.

'I want a pee,' she says when they reach the Ladies. 'I hope you're not coming inside?'

'No, but don't lock the door.'

Abby resists an urge to do exactly that. This woman following her around everywhere is getting on her nerves. She's not at all clear why she's doing it. If only the last few days weren't such a blur.

She's only been in the cubicle a couple of minutes when there's a tap on the door.

'You OK?'

'I'm fine.'

'It's just the group begins at eleven, and I think it could be really good for you to be there.' Abby can tell the nurse is trying to keep her voice soft and calm, but she sounds simpering instead.

'I'll come in a minute.'

'They like to start on time.'

'I'm peeing as fast as I can,' snaps Abby. She's no desire to join in the session – she's no desire for anything. Oh well, she thinks, emerging, it's not as if I've anything better to do. She allows herself to be led down the corridor and into the lounge, where she and the nurse sit down on a sofa.

An older guy in a suit appears at the door. Maybe he's the man who helped with my admission last night, thinks Abby, vaguely recalling his goatee beard. Her head is in such a muddle she isn't sure. He is followed by a middle-aged woman carrying a polka dot umbrella – through the window Abby sees it's started to rain.

I've got an umbrella a bit like that somewhere, thinks Abby. Though Lord knows where it is – I never have time to bother with using one these days.

'So this is where you'll be for group,' says the man with the goatee beard. 'If you'd like to take a seat, Johnnie is running it today, and he should be up in about ten minutes.' He turns to go.

The woman puts her damp brolly on the floor and tentatively arranges herself on the sofa next to Abby. She has long, wavy chestnut hair; it's fantastically thick, like a curtain.

She probably doesn't want to get her hair all wet, thinks Abby. In case it goes frizzy. I used to be like that about mine . . . How I miss my long hair. I want it back.

*   *   *

Karen has no idea what she expected the inside of Moreland's Place to be like, but it wasn't this. The lounge is more homely than she'd anticipated, and everything is on a generous scale, with sofas lining three of its four walls, armchairs angled out from the corners of the room and a giant flat-screened television. On the windowsill is a huge vase of fresh flowers and on a coffee table in the centre of the room is a box of man-size tissues and a bowl piled with fruit. The shelf beneath houses the latest editions of glossy monthlies and a copy of today's *Times*.

She checks round to see who else is in the room – presumably they will be in the session too. Directly opposite is a guy with salt-and-pepper hair, concentrating on filling in a form. He glances up as Karen sits down, and she thinks she might recognize him from somewhere, but can't place him. He's good-looking, but appears agitated, and instinctively she feels wary.

On the adjacent sofa is a blonde woman; Karen guesses she's somewhere between five and ten years younger than she is. She is pale and slender, with the toned limbs of someone used to exercise, hair cut into a short shaggy bob and not a scrap of make-up. She looks washed-out and drawn, but Karen can tell that she's pretty. Next to her is a nurse called Sangeeta, Karen gathers from her name badge.

She looks at the clock – only five minutes to go. This is all so unnerving – she's never done anything like this before. She remembers Molly on her first day at school; how proud she was, how excited. My little girl is braver than I am, she thinks.

An elderly Asian woman hobbles into the room with the aid of a walking stick. She has a cloud of white hair, and as she hitches up her turquoise sari to edge carefully into an armchair, Karen sees that one ankle is very swollen and feels her discomfort. Next is a young woman with glossy lips, eyelashes thick with mascara, tawny hair twirled into spirals, big breasts and a washboard-flat stomach. She's so glamorous Karen is immediately conscious of her own mis-shapen sweater and unwashed hair. I thought we'd all be here for similar reasons – how, Karen wonders, is she capable of looking that well turned out? Maybe she's been here for a while, and the treatment really works . . . For a moment Karen feels hopeful, then the sadness that's been weighing on her for weeks consumes her again and she has to gulp back tears. I can't imagine ever feeling better, she thinks. What have I got to feel better *for*? I suppose there's Molly and Luke, but I'm tired, so bone-tired.

She reaches for a handkerchief, and as she blows her nose she realizes the glamorous woman is looking at her and smiling. Karen blushes at being caught on the verge of weeping, but is relieved to have had some friendly contact. She smiles back as best she can.

Is she a film star? There must be famous people in here, thinks Karen, Moreland's is renowned for it.

'I'm Lillie.' The young woman stretches out her hand. Her nails are beautifully manicured.

'Karen,' says Karen.

Then she notices Lillie's fingers are shaking, and when she asks, 'Is it your first day?' her voice is tremulous and uncertain.

'Yes.'

'Ah.'

Karen isn't sure what the 'ah' means, but gathers that the fact she is a newcomer is significant.

'Have you been here before?'

'No,' Karen says. 'Never.'

Again the man opposite glances up at her. She senses he's about to say something but thinks better of it. He carries on filling in his form.

Next they are joined by an overweight young man with a ponytail who's still in his slippers – looks like he's staying here, concludes Karen – and a smartly dressed black guy who introduces himself as 'Troy' with an American accent.

Finally, at exactly eleven o'clock, a man with a spring in

his step and a floppy fringe comes into the room wheeling a large whiteboard, and carrying a stack of papers and a box of magic markers.

'Thanks, Sangeeta,' he nods at the nurse. 'You can leave now.' He adjusts the whiteboard so they can see it, puts the box and papers on the coffee table and closes the door. Then he turns to the group and beams in a way that seems to light up the entire space. 'I'm Johnnie.'

He looks about thirty, Karen decides, possibly even younger, though that might be because compared to the rest of us he seems so upbeat, full of energy.

'I'm a therapist and I'm running the group this morning. Let's start with a quick introduction as several of you are new today – Karen?' He bounds over and shakes her hand forcefully. 'Abby?' He does the same to the woman with the shaggy blonde bob. 'We met last night,' he says to her, but Abby appears confused. 'And Michael?' The man filling in the form has been writing furiously all this while, but at last he puts down his pad and pen.

* * *

I can't believe he's properly trained, thinks Michael, as he shakes the young man's hand. He barely seems older than Ryan. I bet he's still a student. And imagine shutting the door on a room full of anxious and miserable people! That girl over there – her hands are quivering like jumping beans – can this really be a good idea? Locking us in, controlling what we can and can't drink – reminds me of *One Flew Over The Cuckoo's Nest.*

113

'I'd like to invite all of you to start by saying a bit about how you're feeling right now,' Johnnie continues, pulling up a chair close to the whiteboard. 'Who wants to go first?'

I'd rather stick pins in my eyes, thinks Michael.

'Perhaps someone who's been in group before could start,' says Johnnie.

'OK, I'll go first.' To his surprise, it's the shaky young woman speaking. 'I'm Lillie—' She glances round at the group and smiles – he can tell she's done this before, ' – and I'm a bit wobbly today.'

She's mixed-race, Michael observes, and she's local. That's a proper Sussex accent there, if I'm not mistaken.

The therapist nods slowly. 'And what do you think that wobbliness might be about?'

'Well . . . They upped my lithium last night and I reckon I'm still getting used to it.'

Exactly, Michael says to himself. The psychiatrist I saw yesterday wants to put me on medication too, but see what it's doing to her? She's a nervous wreck.

'Though I know the morning is always my most difficult time—'

She has the most amazing cleavage, he thinks, and as Lillie continues speaking he finds himself unable to take in much of what she says.

He's roused from his reverie by an American, Troy, who speaks next: Michael gathers he is on sick leave from the army and due to return to service in Afghanistan at the end of the week. 'I'm dreading it,' he says.

A white-haired lady and a chap in slippers share a few

words, then there's a long silence. Expectation hangs in the air like a storm cloud.

Who is going to cave in? Michael wonders. The woman with the long reddish hair opposite, or the frail-looking one on the adjacent sofa? I'm damned if it's going to be me.

The woman opposite shifts in her seat and opens her mouth to speak, but then bursts into tears.

Michael looks at the floor, mortified.

But Johnnie simply leans forward and nudges the box of tissues towards her. He seems unfazed. 'Your feelings are welcome here, Karen.'

'Gosh.' Karen takes a tissue and blows her nose. 'I'm sorry, I'm sorry, I don't know where that came from . . .'

'No need to be sorry,' says Johnnie.

'I can't believe I've ended up here!' she wails, and starts to cry again, more forcefully. 'Oh no, I didn't mean that to come out like that. How rude of me, when I don't know any of you—'

'I don't know anyone either,' says Abby. Her voice is a whisper.

Michael supposes this is his cue to echo that neither does he, but he's too self-conscious to speak.

'That's how I felt when I arrived,' Lillie says to Karen.

' – and you've all been so brave and honest, and here I am crying my eyes out—' Karen gasps for breath.

'But it does get better, I promise,' says Lillie.

'Really?' Karen sounds deeply uncertain.

Michael wonders if he's met her before. Maybe she's a customer. Hove is only a few miles from Lewes; doubtless some patients are from there. He picks his cuticles as he tries to recall: he tends to be good with faces — or he used to be. Since he's been sleeping badly, his memory is shot.

'Yeah, you're at rock bottom,' says Troy. 'Nothing can ever feel that bad again.'

'Remember to speak in "I" statements if you can, Troy,' says Johnnie.

What the hell does he mean by that? thinks Michael. All these rules! He feels more tongue-tied than ever.

'Sorry.' Troy nods. 'I meant, when *I* arrived, post trauma, I was right at rock bottom.'

'Thanks,' says Johnnie.

'And from there the only way is up,' says Lillie.

Karen's face relaxes into a tiny, appreciative smile.

14

Johnnie goes to the board, draws a large circle and stands back.

'Today, as three of you are new, I thought we'd explore how the way we think can actually make our depression or anxiety worse,' he says.

I wish he'd stop smiling, thinks Michael. What's he got to be so happy about? I can't think of anything worse than spending all day talking about depression.

'This is one of the first steps in the therapeutic process – discovering your thoughts and behaviours and how they are linked. The second step is challenging that behaviour, but let's begin by looking at how we think. One way of doing that is by using the Vicious Flower diagram.'

'I've done this exercise before,' mutters Troy.

'Sorry about that,' says Johnnie, 'but every group is different because we've a different mix of people, which means I'm sure you'll get something new from what they have to contribute. Perhaps you can kick off by saying what goes in the middle?'

'"*Depression*",' says Troy, with a bored sigh, and Johnnie writes the word in the circle.

I don't get what on earth this navel-gazing has to do with flowers, thinks Michael.

'So, does someone want to tell me something they do when they get depressed?' Johnnie looks round the group.

'Stay in bed,' says the man in slippers.

You don't say, thinks Michael.

'Perfect,' says Johnnie, and draws an arc away from the circle captioned with the words '*stay in bed*'. 'And then what happens when we don't get up – how does that make us feel?'

'Shit,' says Troy.

'Exactly,' says Johnnie, and writes '*self-loathing*' in another arc, leading back to the circle.

'You should have written "*shit*",' says Michael. It pops out before he can stop himself.

'Thank you, Michael. I think for our purposes the meaning is the same,' says Johnnie.

Michael sees little pink spots rise in Johnnie's cheeks. They should put someone tougher in charge, if he can't deal with that, he thinks. Nonetheless, he feels a pang of remorse.

'Can someone else suggest something they might do when they're down?' Johnnie asks.

'Drink more alcohol?' offers Michael in a moment of generosity, and Johnnie draws a fresh arc away from the circle, and captions it.

'Thanks,' he says, and the pink spots fade. 'And what might this lead to?'

'A hangover,' says Lillie, and everyone laughs.

'More anxiety,' says Troy, and again Johnnie draws an arrow back to the circle.

Ah, thinks Michael, I get it. We're forming petals. How ironic, when flowers landed me in here.

They continue in this vein: Rita, the white-haired lady in the sari, confesses she stays at home more, which leads her extended family to invite her out less; Karen says she's stopped doing things she likes such as hosting parties and seeing friends, which makes her more miserable; Troy admits he gets angry and snarky then feels guilty; Colin, the young man in slippers, says he overeats and hates himself for doing so. Round and round they go, until they have a flower bursting with petals.

The only one who hasn't contributed is Abby, Michael notices. She's so pale and quiet, she's not said a word other than at the very start. I wonder what her story is? He sneaks a better look. She appears exhausted; she keeps closing her eyes as if she'd like to go to sleep.

Michael can sympathize. Perhaps he should offer to go and get them both a coffee from reception, try and perk them both up.

Johnnie is still speaking. 'So why do we do these things, if they're so self-destructive?'

Rita is busy making notes. She lifts her head and says, 'They're comforting?'

'In what way?'

'Well, staying in is easier than the alternative – the last thing I feel like when I'm miserable is being sociable.'

'Exactly,' says Johnnie.

'Johnnie?' As Lillie leans forward, Michael tells himself not to gawp. 'Are those what we call "*safety behaviours*" then?'

'Yes.'

'I don't understand why they're called safety behaviours if they actually do us harm.'

'Because they're things we do to feel safe,' Johnnie explains. 'And although it's important to remember they might make us feel comforted, the relief is temporary. In the long run they can make the cycle perpetuate.'

'Ah.' Lillie sits back, evidently pleased she's understood.

Oh dear, thinks Michael. He has just enough mental energy to work out the logic. As if giving up my business wasn't tough enough, now it sounds like I should give up drinking too.

*　*　*

I'm worried about Callum, thinks Abby. Who's got him ready, given him breakfast, helped him go to the loo? He should be at school by now, but I don't trust Glenn to have taken time off work, and Eva will never manage on her own. I'll bet no one here has a child who takes as much looking after as he does, or they'd never be able to chat like this. I've no idea what they're all on about anyway. And who's this young Hugh Grant lookalike with a floppy fringe? I believe he's called Johnnie, but I can't understand a word he's saying. How come everyone else seems able to grasp the point and contribute?

She closes her eyes, trying to shut everyone – everything

– out. If only it were that simple. No matter what she does, the thoughts are there, crowding, burning into her brain. However hard she tries to analyse them, to reason with herself, the cycle is the same. *You're a failure, a dreadful mother, a worthless human being. Unlovable, irresponsible, weak.*

Earlier that morning she asked for some drugs to slow down her mind – begged, more like – pride had no part to play. She just wanted to stop the suffocating torrent of abuse. Lately it's got so much worse – she can't stand it. But the psychiatrist had said, 'You'll still have temazepam in your system,' and given her such a low dose of sedative that the tablet barely touched the sides.

'So, with depression something is out of kilter,' Johnnie is saying. 'And the first step towards adjusting the balance is wanting to change these patterns. A lot of the time people don't want to change, but when we begin to understand how we're contributing to our own negative mood, the motivation for doing so emerges—'

Never can Abby recall feeling so unsure of what she's doing or why she is where she is. It's as if there's a glass wall separating her from the rest of the world, and she can't get her bearings, or relate to anyone or anything.

All of a sudden she knows what she must do: go home. Yes, yes, that's it. I need to leave, she thinks. Callum needs me. If I slip out quietly, no one will notice. The door's just over there. Johnnie has got his back to us, he's busy writing on the board . . .

She is halfway across the room when the therapist turns round.

'Abby, do you need to go?'

'Yes.' She can hardly hear her own voice, it's so subdued. 'I do,' she says, more forcefully, reaching for the door handle.

'I would prefer it if you could stay for the whole session. We have only a few minutes left.'

She opens the door.

'Um, well, hang on a moment—'

Abby ignores him and steps into the corridor.

'Excuse me,' she hears Johnnie say to the other group members. She starts to walk quickly but he comes after her and takes her gently by the shoulder. 'Abby, are you OK?'

The self-lacerating thoughts are back again.

'I have to go home,' she says, trying to regain the clarity she had mere seconds ago. She sets off again towards the staircase but has only gone a few paces when Johnnie catches her.

'Stop!' His voice is sharp.

'Is everything all right?' says a woman. It's that irritating nurse who was trailing round after Abby earlier. She's hurrying towards them, up the stairs.

'Ah, Sangeeta. Abby was just wanting to leave the group—' Johnnie smiles at Abby, though why she can't fathom.

'I've got to look after my son,' Abby explains. Surely once he understands this he will let her be?

'I don't think it's a good idea for you to go home,' says Johnnie. He jerks his head subtly at Sangeeta, but Abby sees it nonetheless.

'I'll handle this,' says Sangeeta. 'Abby, do you want to come and have a chat?'

'No,' says Abby. As if!

'I'd better get back to the group,' says Johnnie. 'I'll see you later, Abby.'

No, you won't, she thinks.

* * *

'Sorry about that,' says Johnnie, coming back into the room.

Wonder what went on there, Michael wonders. Bit alarming. Still, she won't get very far, that Abby, even if she wants to. Bet she doesn't realize the door downstairs is locked and you need to know the code to get out.

Johnnie picks up his marker again. 'Where was I?'

'You were talking about motivation,' says Troy, yawning.

I suppose I *could* do with some help with motivation, Michael thinks. Since the shop went bust, he's spent most days in front of the telly; Chrissie has been nagging him about it. It was when she heard him muttering that he couldn't see the point of doing anything any more that she insisted he go with her to the doctor.

'Ah yes. Thanks, Troy.' Johnnie wipes the Vicious Flower diagram off the board, and writes the words '*Goal Planning*' at the top. 'Next, we're going to do an exercise that might help with motivation.' He reaches for the A4 sheets he put on the table earlier. 'I've brought some handouts.' He walks over to Rita, who's sitting nearest to him, and gives her the stack. 'If you'd like to take a sheet and then pass the rest round, you can each have a go at completing the questions.'

Crikey, it's like being back at school, thinks Michael. Next we'll be allowed out to run around in the playground. With a teacher overseeing, of course.

15

'So, how did you find group?' asks Johnnie, as Karen takes a seat in the armchair opposite him. He invited her for a one-to-one chat after the session finished.

'A bit strange,' she says, glancing round the room he has led her to. It's magnolia and beige, with net curtains at the window. Aside from their two chairs, the only furniture is a small table, on which rests another box of tissues, a jug of water and some plastic cups, and there's also a clock on the wall. Apparently they have half an hour.

'Sometimes people do find it a bit odd when they start here, and I heard you say you've never done anything like this before.'

'No – I mean yes,' says Karen. She still feels dazed from struggling to absorb so much information, and her stomach is rumbling. I was looking forward to lunch, she thinks, but I suppose I'll have to wait.

'I'm sorry to spring this on you, but I wanted to take advantage of the fact we both had the time and I thought it would be good to make a start.'

'But why do I need this as well as the groups?' she asks.

'They're for us to catch up on how things are going for you personally; I like to look upon them as providing a space where we can talk about things which might feel a bit difficult to discuss in front of other patients. It'll be just me and you, and what you say here is confidential, unless I think you might harm yourself or someone else. I hope you find the sessions helpful.'

Karen nods. I've seen therapy sessions in films and on telly, she thinks. And Lou works with troubled schoolchildren, so I know something of the process from her. I suppose I could have talked to Lou about how I was feeling. But Lou's job is tough enough and her baby's due any moment. I didn't want to stress her further.

'So, Karen.' Johnnie interrupts her thoughts. 'Perhaps, to help me get a fuller picture, you could tell me a little about your background, and if there were any particular events or experiences that led you to spend some time here.'

Johnnie's fringe falls as he looks down at a file on his lap. That must contain my notes – they probably say I'm a total nutcase, worries Karen. And I don't know if he means to begin with my life story, or Simon's death, or the fact I can't stop crying . . .

'I'm not sure what you know about me already,' she says.

'Well, I know what you shared in group this morning.' But this wasn't what Karen was driving at, and Johnnie seems to pick this up. 'Other than that, all I have is a brief letter of referral from your GP, so you can assume I know very little and begin wherever you want.'

Help, thinks Karen. There's so much to say, but she's not

sure she's ready to reveal any of it. Still, most therapists seem keen to believe that problems tend to stem from childhood, so she plucks something that isn't too raw and seems apt. 'Well, I grew up in Reading, in Berkshire . . . and I'm one of two siblings . . . though my brother lives in Australia now, so we've not seen him in a long while . . . and my parents . . . um . . . my dad and mum were . . .' It's no good, the mere mention of her father triggers tears. I miss him so much, she thinks, remembering being his little girl once more. 'I shouldn't be doing this again.' She reaches for a tissue. 'Sorry. I didn't expect all this to come out quite so . . . so . . . fast.'

'Crying can be a really good thing,' says Johnnie.

Karen isn't so certain. Is it really productive to be weeping so much of the time?

'Maybe your tears are a sign that something's being released, or possibly shifting?'

'I suppose.' Considering how young he is, Johnnie seems astute. Karen lets out a long breath. 'My father died six weeks ago.'

It's as if she's at the hospital in Worthing all over again, running down the corridor, frantically looking for her mother, then finding her, ashen-faced and distraught, outside the Intensive Care Unit . . .

'He was in a care home,' Karen tells Johnnie. 'We don't know exactly what happened, but the nurse said she went to his room to give him his night-time pills and found him sitting in his chair, unable to move. She asked him if he was OK, and he couldn't reply. The thing about my dad was, if he was awake, he'd normally say *something*, even if it was "fuck off".' Karen laughs ruefully. 'He'd had a stroke.'

Johnnie nods in understanding.

'He never regained consciousness.' She dabs her eyes with a tissue. 'He lasted a week, in the end . . .' Although she'd been able to see her father, hold his hand, feel the warmth of his skin and listen to him breathing, he'd never woken up again.

'I'm so sorry for your loss,' says Johnnie.

'It's OK,' she says, then reproaches herself for using such a nondescript word. Is a death ever "OK"? And she doesn't want Johnnie to think she didn't love her dad. 'He was in his eighties, he'd had Alzheimer's for several years . . .'

'That must have been difficult.'

'Yes, it was . . . Though before, well . . . We were very close.' She looks up – Johnnie's expression is full of sympathy – and she's sobbing again. It's as if she's a soap bubble, held together only by tension; all it takes is a few kind words and *pop!* she bursts. The tears make it hard to speak. 'I . . . haven't managed it so well this time. I can't seem to keep it together, and, um, my friend Anna suggested I go to my GP and the doctor said . . . he said that it wasn't surprising I was finding things difficult, and, er . . . he suggested antidepressants, but I'm not happy taking medication . . . I don't want to not be myself any more – they might change my personality – and I don't want to get addicted . . .'

'I doubt very much that would happen,' says Johnnie. 'And some people do find them helpful.'

'Really?'

'They can help lift mood and, although I wouldn't

advocate their use on their own, it has been shown that, along with therapy, antidepressants can provide good results.'

'Oh.'

'You can always discuss it with Dr Kasdan – he's the psychiatrist here – if you decide you would like to explore it further. Why don't you see how you go over the next week or so coming to groups and seeing me, and review it then?'

'That sounds like a good idea.'

'Anyway, I interrupted. You were saying?'

Karen hesitates, struggling to pick up her thread. 'Yes, so, um, I decided that . . . Well, my friend suggested that maybe my health insurance might cover something else, you know, something like this, so I looked and I saw that yes, I had cover . . . so . . .'

'Perhaps we don't need to go into all these details now,' says Johnnie. 'Can I bring you back a moment to your father?'

'Oh, of course.' Karen is thrown. I must be boring him, she thinks, going into such minutiae.

'You said "this time" . . . "I haven't managed it as well, *this* time." Might I ask . . . have you experienced the loss of someone close to you before?'

'Yes.' She pauses, then says, 'My husband.'

'Your husband?' Johnnie is taken aback – Karen can tell. He hadn't expected her to be a widow. People don't. She's got used to this reaction, but still she finds it hard. She ends up holding back from going into detail to lessen their upset, and the fact that Johnnie is young makes her feel especially protective. She reaches for another tissue and says, 'He had a heart attack, out of the blue . . . It was just over two years ago . . .' Her voice cracks. Johnnie is a therapist, she reminds herself. He'll be able to handle it. 'My husband's name was Simon.'

'That must have been a terrible shock.'

'It was. But I seemed OK . . . I mean, I'm not saying it didn't affect me; obviously it did, horribly, it was a dreadful time, awful . . .' A flashback of Simon collapsing on the train makes her shudder. She gulps. 'But I managed: I had to, you know, because of the children, and I kept going. Yet now, with my dad, I can't seem to hold it together. The last few weeks – since he died – I've been crying all the time, every day, several times a day. And it's like . . . I don't know what's wrong with me. Some days I feel miserable, but other days I feel ghastly in a different way. It's as if someone else has taken over my body and I'm not my normal self at all.'

'Would you say these are physical symptoms?'

Karen frowns. 'It's hard to separate them. I get these headaches, as if someone's wrapped a metal band tight around my forehead – sometimes it feels so real I'm surprised I can't see it . . . like I've been wearing a hat, and when you take it off, it's left a mark, and you can still feel it.'

Johnnie nods. 'That's a good description.'

'But why now? Why could I handle Simon's death better, when it was so unexpected, and not my father's . . . when I should have known – I *did* know – it was coming? My dad was in his eighties; he'd been ill for ages.'

'Well, it sounds like you're experiencing depression. You've had a huge amount to deal with in a relatively short time, so to have some sort of reaction is completely natural.'

'It was such a stress for my mum looking after him . . . so, in a way this is a blessing, a relief for her . . . I wish I could see it that way, too, but now I can't stop worrying about her either, and what she's going to do . . . I guess she should move in with us, but I'm not sure I can cope with that right now, not when I'm such a wreck . . .' Karen stops and looks up, then says, 'Sorry.'

'There's no need to be sorry.'

'No, I guess not. Sorry.' Karen realizes what she's done and laughs.

Johnnie smiles. 'You seem to be beating yourself up a lot.'

'Oh?'

'It sounds as if you believe you should be feeling one way about your father's death, and because you're not, you're getting angry with yourself. I'm hearing the word "should" a lot in what you're saying – you *should* have foreseen your father's stroke, you *should* ask your mother to move in, you *shouldn't* be crying so much.'

'I suppose I do think a bit like that . . .'

'When something painful happens, we sometimes feel that we have failed in our response to it.' Johnnie glances at the clock. 'I'm afraid we've only a couple of minutes left, just so you are aware.'

'I can't understand why I seem *more* upset than when Simon died,' says Karen. 'Don't you think it's odd?'

'Well . . . it sounds to me as if you've probably experienced what is often called cumulative trauma. It can happen when you've been through one distressing event after another.'

'Is that why my reaction is so out of balance?'

'Perhaps it would help to look at it not as a balance like this—' Johnnie cups his palms before him on a level as if he were a weighing scale, ' – where one grief is heavier than the other.' He drops one hand down and the other up. 'Perhaps it's more like this—' He puts one cupped palm on top of the other, ' – where you could bear one heavy weight, but not two.' He drops both hands.

'Oh. I hadn't seen it like that . . .'

'I'm not saying it's entirely the case, but it might help you be kinder to yourself.'

Karen nods.

'I'm afraid we are going to have to stop now, but you might like to think about that a little before next time.'

'Sure.'

'And enjoy your lunch,' says Johnnie.

16

Oh no, thinks Michael, entering the dining room. Most of the chairs are taken; he's going to have to share a table with other patients. There's space beside Rita and she seemed harmless enough, but she's sitting with Troy, and Troy seems in as dark a mood as he is, so is probably best avoided. Michael looks around for Karen – he's more inclined to chat with her if he's got to talk to anyone, because she's new, too. But then he remembers that Johnnie waylaid her as they were leaving.

There are only two seats free in the corner by the French windows. The other chairs at the table are occupied by the guy with the Mohican who gave Michael the tip-off about the coffee machine, and another young man in glasses whose colourful tattoos appear to run right up both arms and across the back of his neck. Michael squeezes through to reach them and is just saying, 'Do you mind if I join you?' when there's a waft of scent and he feels hair brush against his arm.

'Hi guys!' It's Lillie. 'You OK with me sitting here?'

'Of course,' say the two men.

No surprises there, thinks Michael.

'Come on, Michael, park your bum with me,' says Lillie, patting the red-cushioned seat of the chair next to her.

Michael does as he's bid.

'Michael's new,' Lillie explains.

'We met this morning,' nods the Mohican. He stretches out an arm. 'I'm Karl.' Michael shakes his hand. 'And this is Lansky.' Lansky looks up from his plate – he's already been served with a burger and chips – and nods.

'That's an unusual name,' says Michael, then kicks himself for stating the obvious and adds, 'You probably get that all the time.'

'No,' says Lansky. 'It's what they call me in here. It's my surname – my first name's Paul, but there are two Pauls in ATP.'

'The addiction therapy programme,' explains Lillie, reading Michael's confused expression.

'So, what you in for?' asks Lansky.

'Oh, he's a Sad,' says Lillie.

'Whereas we're Bad,' Karl winks; his pierced eyebrow seems to emphasize the gesture.

'Very Bad,' Lillie nods. She turns to Michael. 'Karl was into cocaine.'

'And speed,' says Karl.

'With me, it's booze,' says Lansky.

I can tell, thinks Michael. Behind large, black-framed glasses, Lansky's cheeks are threaded with broken blood vessels.

There's a jug in the middle of the table. Lillie reaches to

133

fill up her glass with juice and says, 'In here, we like to say there are the Mads, Bads and Sads.'

Michael feels his face crack into a smile at the notion. 'So if we're the Sads and the Bads, who are the Mads . . . ?'

'Oh, there aren't too many of them in here at the moment,' says Karl. 'But they're – you know, the psychotic ones, the total nutters, people who've really lost it.'

'I lost it before coming in,' says Lillie. Her frankness is disarming, but Michael is rapidly learning that small talk is rare in Moreland's Place. 'I'm BP.' She smiles at him brightly.

'What's that?' asks Michael.

'Bipolar,' says Lansky, and takes a large bite of his burger. Ketchup squidges out and plops onto his plate.

Lillie looks up at a woman bringing in their food. The woman hands Michael a plate with a baked potato filled with tuna and sweetcorn; he now recollects ordering it earlier. 'You got mine, Sally?'

Bit strange to be on first-name terms with the staff as well as the other patients, thinks Michael. Though I guess it's good to be friendly.

'What was it?' asks Sally.

'Omelette,' Lillie replies. 'I have a wheat allergy,' she tells Michael. She lowers her voice to say this, as if it's a more personal revelation than her previous confession.

'So . . .' Michael isn't usually nosy, but this is fascinating. It's making him feel less weird, and he's been sensing himself as cut off from others for a long while. For the first time in months, he feels something faintly approaching cheeriness. 'When you say "lost it", how do you mean?'

'Oh, I tried to stab my sister,' says Lillie.

Michael nearly chokes on his baked potato.

'You must have seen it,' says Lansky. 'It was in all the papers.'

Just as he's saying this Michael cottons on. So *that's* where I know Lillie from, he realizes. Stone me! She and her sister present that TV programme my kids are into, *Street Dance Live*. I bloody hate it – it's the music I can't stand – but still. Imagine me, he thinks, pausing for a moment to swallow his mouthful, having lunch with some-one famous. Ryan and Kelly will be dead impressed.

'I had a psychotic episode,' says Lillie, adjusting her top so that once more Michael has to tell himself not to stare. 'But I'm all right now.'

Hence the meds, thinks Michael. Maybe for some patients they're not such a bad idea. 'What about your sister?'

'Oh, she's used to me,' Lillie smiles. 'And I did think she was the daughter of the devil at the time.'

'Mad, you see.' Lansky taps his temple, but he's grinning.

'So, you insurance or what?' asks Karl.

It takes Michael a moment to gather what he must be referring to. 'You mean, how am I paying to be here?'

'Yeah,' says Karl. 'She's private, obviously—' A jerk towards Lillie. 'So's Lansky here—'

'My dad's paying,' says Lansky. He looks sheepish.

'And my work have sponsored me. How about you?'

'Oh,' says Michael, still assimilating. 'I'm NHS.'

'*NHS?*' Lillie and Karl are agog.

Michael nods. I didn't realize it was that unusual, he thinks. Not that he's thought much about his admission. It's a blur.

'You lucky bugger,' says Karl.

First time anyone's called me lucky in a long time, thinks Michael. 'Why?'

'Costs a *fortune* to be in here otherwise.' Karl turns to Lillie. 'How much is it again?'

'You're an inpatient, aren't you?' says Lillie.

Michael nods, though he's no idea how long he's supposed to be here for.

'Like us then. Nearly a grand a night.'

For a second time, Michael has to stop himself from spluttering. He reaches for his glass and takes a sip of juice.

'So how come the NHS sent you here?' asks Karl.

'No beds anywhere else,' he says.

'Don't you remember?' says Lansky. 'That other guy – in a few weeks ago – Matt? Always had his nose in a book? Scrabble buff? He was NHS too.'

'Was he?' says Lillie.

'Yeah. They've been cutting beds in mental health wards, apparently. So now they ring round all the psychiatric hospitals, and if there aren't any spaces free, the overflow patients end up in clinics like here.'

'I didn't know that,' says Karl.

I don't get why they're so surprised, thinks Michael, there's a lot of pressure on public resources. Then he realizes the significance of what they're saying. 'So if a bed becomes available, will they move me, do you think?' He fights to control his panic. He's a keen supporter of the public sector, but he's just beginning to settle in, and the idea of being transferred to an NHS psychiatric ward fills him with dread. Images of straitjackets and patients chained to bedposts spring to mind. Don't be ridiculous, he tells himself. This isn't Victorian England. Still, he can't shake his horror at the prospect. There won't be original watercolour paintings on the walls, he's almost certain, but he can live without those. Worse by far is the idea that he might not have his own bedroom.

'No, now you're in here, you'll be fine. I'm sure it'll be way too complicated to shift you,' says Lansky.

Thank God for that, thinks Michael. Sharing a ward with people as nuts as I am – I can't imagine anything worse.

17

'Shall we go and sit in the little lounge?' suggests Sangeeta.

'Whatever.'

The nurse heads along the corridor to another door, flips a sign from *FREE* to *ENGAGED* and leads Abby into a space like the one the group was in, but smaller.

Aside from our bedrooms, is the whole building made up of magnolia and beige rooms like this? It's so confusing, thinks Abby.

'Have a seat.' Sangeeta gestures to the settee furthest from the exit. She sits down on the other one, by the door.

Abby remains standing. 'I'd prefer not to.' She's tempted to bolt again. It'd be hard to get past Sangeeta, but if she moves fast . . . Yet some tiny part of her is aware it might be wiser to stay. She jiggles from foot to foot. 'Why can't I leave?'

'If at all possible the therapists like people to try not to leave the groups halfway through,' says Sangeeta. 'Once one person goes, then others often follow suit, and it can be disruptive for those who want to participate.'

It wasn't halfway through, thinks Abby, and Sangeeta's missed the point. 'I didn't want to leave the group. I want to leave here.'

'Ah.' There's a pause. 'I don't think that's a good idea either.'

'Why?' Abby is in overdrive, continually searching for answers, yet every solution seems wrong as soon as she's come up with it. 'I've got to get home to be with my son.' She moves towards the door, but Sangeeta reaches across and takes hold of the handle. Anxiety rises in Abby again. 'I feel so awful, it's my head – I can't think straight, or focus – that's why I couldn't manage the group – and last night I hardly slept, people kept opening the bedroom door to check up on me – it kept waking me up . . .'

'If you like I can sit with you for a bit and we can do some deep breathing together?'

'No, thank you.'

'Are you sure? It might help you relax a bit and slow down your racing thoughts.'

'I've been trying to stop them for weeks.' Abby stifles an urge to scream. 'Have you got another one of those pills?' She racks her brain. It's no good, the name has gone. 'I think it began with a D . . . I was only given one.'

'Diazepam?'

'Well, can you check?' Abby is still jiggling her legs. 'Honestly, I can't bear this . . .'

'If I do that, will you promise to stay here?'

'All right.'

'And do you know who your one-to-one therapist is?'

'My what?'

'Your one-one-one therapist.'

'No idea.'

'Because you've only just been admitted I haven't been told,' says Sangeeta. 'I'll find that out too and be back very soon.'

Left alone, it takes enormous willpower for Abby to remain in the room. If it weren't for the lure of the diazepam, she'd scarper.

Moments later there's a knock and before she has a chance to say 'come in', the door opens. Her heart sinks – it's not Sangeeta with the medication, but another woman entirely.

'Hi,' she says. 'I'm Beth.'

Abby peers at her badge, suspicious. 'Have you brought my pills?'

'Don't worry, Sangeeta's sorting them out.' Something in her manner reassures Abby. Her anxiety drops a notch.

'I'm your one-to-one therapist.' Beth smiles at her. Her eyes are twinkly and her expression is more tender than Johnnie's; she's older too – considerably – and her voice is soothing. That she's a little plump makes her seem approachable, somehow; instinctively Abby senses she's in the presence of someone grounded, even comforting.

Those shoes she's wearing are cool, thinks Abby, admiring Beth's purple wedges. It's the first upbeat thought she's had all morning.

'Sangeeta said you were wanting to leave. I gathered you were upset, so I thought it might be a good moment to introduce myself,' Beth continues, taking a seat. 'Would you like to sit down, Abby? I don't know about you, but I prefer sitting to talk myself.'

'OK.' Abby perches on the edge of the sofa.

'I understand you've been feeling very anxious.'

'Yes.' Even the word gives Abby the urge to start jiggling her legs again.

'That's an awful feeling, I know. I've had it too.'

'You have?' Abby is taken aback to hear a therapist confess anything personal; all the doctors and specialists she's encountered over the years – and there have been a lot, if she goes back to her student days, and includes those who've been involved with Callum – have never brought up their own experiences.

'Oh yes,' Beth grimaces and shakes her head. 'It can completely take you over sometimes, can't it?'

Maybe I can trust this woman, just a little, thinks Abby. 'I wish they'd stop following me round,' she confesses. 'It's making my anxiety worse.'

'Who's been following you? People outside of here?'

'God, no!' Abby laughs. 'I'm not completely paranoid. In here. You know, the nurses.'

'You mean Sangeeta?'

'Yes. And last night too, it was bonkers. Even when I went to bed. They kept coming in, every few minutes, all night. How on earth was I supposed to get to sleep through that?'

'It's only because we've been trying to take care of you, Abby. We do it with a lot of our patients who, um—'

'Who what?'

'Who might be a danger to themselves.'

'Well, I'm not a danger to myself. Life's pretty shit, but I'm not going to do anything stupid.'

Beth says nothing for a few moments, then murmurs,

'OK . . .' and nods slowly. 'Would you like to say a bit more about how you're feeling right now?'

Abby frowns. It's a long time since anyone has asked so pointedly about her emotions. 'Stressed.' She shrugs. Where on earth should she start? 'It's been a pretty crazy time – my husband and I haven't been getting on.'

'I'm sorry to hear that.'

'We're separating, so now I've got to move. We thought we'd got a buyer for the house, but Glenn kept pushing them for the asking price, so it looks like we've lost them.' She comes to a halt. Even saying this makes her head spin. She can feel her legs juddering against the edge of the sofa. 'Oh yes, there's my son, too. He has autism.'

'That sounds like an awful lot to deal with.'

'Yeah, it is.'

'Have you had much support through all this?'

'I have a couple of carers who help with Callum—'

'He's your son?'

'Mm.'

'I shouldn't imagine they offer *you* that much opportunity to offload, do they?'

Beth saying this makes Abby appreciate how alone she's been. 'No. Not really.'

'Anyone else? Friends, family?'

'Er . . .' Who's she kidding, thinks Abby. I don't have any time for my friends. Certainly not lately. She considers her mum and dad. 'My parents live in the West Country and I've not seen them in a while. But anyway, we don't really have that sort of relationship. They tend to keep themselves to themselves.'

'So I imagine your anxiety has been building up a lot, over time.' Beth rests her elbows on her knees and leans forward.

Abby's racing thoughts slow a touch, so she's able to see more clearly. 'Yes. It's been much worse since the beginning of the year.' Maybe I ought to tell her I've felt like this before, she thinks, when I broke up with Jake. She adds, 'Seems I'm prone to anxiety.'

'What makes you say that?'

'It got really bad a while back . . .' Abby struggles to remember the exact timing. 'Though it was over ten years ago. I split up with my boyfriend just as I was doing my degree show.'

'That must have been horrible, both happening at once.'

She recalls Jake. What a dance he led her: on/off, on/off.

'I was awfully apprehensive doing my final exams, I remember. Got myself so wound up my mind froze for the first half-hour of one paper.' Beth laughs and shakes her head. 'That's what happens when we panic, we can't think straight.'

Once more Abby is struck by how open Beth seems. The therapist she saw briefly at college in Manchester was distant and robotic, spoke as if he was reading from a textbook. 'I was on Prozac for a bit,' she admits.

'Did you find that helped?'

'Oh yes.' More than the therapy, Abby recalls.

'Have you had any other anxious periods since then?'

'Not any really serious bouts, no.'

'Well, that's good.'

The last few years I've been so focused on Callum

I've thought of little else, thinks Abby. Maybe it's all been building up.

Beth is silent a while, then looks straight into Abby's eyes. 'I want to ask you something, Abby, and I hope you don't mind my being direct. When I take on someone new here, as I have with you, I do get some notes beforehand. They're very minimal – just what we've been passed on by the hospital, in your case, as I understand you were admitted at the weekend. Nonetheless, I read in yours that an empty packet of temazepam was found by your bed. Your husband seems to have been under the impression that you'd taken rather a lot of pills.'

Through the haze of the last few days, memories begin to resurface. Abby recalls Glenn returning home, late as usual – it must have been, when, Friday night? He'd come into her room – because Callum was crying or something, hadn't he said? She'd been really dopey, he'd been alarmed and insisted on taking her to A & E, where they'd given her something to make her vomit, even though she was half asleep . . .

Abby makes a connection. 'Is that why I've been sent here?'

Beth nods. 'Part of the reason you were admitted, yes. I think your husband was extremely worried about you. I gather he thought there had been a lot of tablets in the packet.'

'But I told him at the time, I only wanted to get to sleep.'

'Didn't you worry that taking so many might cause you harm?'

'I didn't take that many.'

'So you weren't intending to take an overdose?'

'No!' Did they really think she was trying to kill herself? Worse, did Glenn think so too?

'Well, luckily temazepam are relatively hard to poison yourself with. I'm not a doctor, but it takes a high dose to do so, from what I understand. Usually they just make you very, very sleepy.'

'I wasn't trying to poison myself.' Abby is getting wound up again. 'I'd never leave my son. I wouldn't take a whole load, however crap I felt. I kept trying to explain, I only took one or two to help me drift off.'

Once more Beth falls silent.

'I tried to tell Glenn and the people at A & E, but no one would listen to me . . . Glenn hasn't listened to me for months.' She tries to recall further details of that night, but it's no good. Maybe it was the drugs, maybe it's all the stress she's been under, probably both, but she can't remember much about arriving at Moreland's Place; only that Glenn brought her in the car the next morning, and that a guy in a suit filled in lots of forms.

Beth is still looking at Abby; her expression is perplexed. She's trying to piece me together, thinks Abby, as if I'm an item of broken crockery. I don't blame her; I'm having problems piecing myself together too.

All at once she realizes: *They've had me on – what's it called? – suicide watch.* That's why I'm being followed around. I have to explain more fully, clear this up. 'I think there's been a misunderstanding . . . I didn't take all those pills at once. Truly I didn't.'

Beth eyes her quizzically.

'OK. I *did* take more than one on occasion, but I've only ever had two or three at a time.'

'I see.' Beth rubs her forehead, as if it might help her sort out where the truth lies. 'Do you mind my asking how long you've been taking them for? It's purely that they can be very addictive.'

'Oh, a few weeks. But I didn't take them every night.'

'Ri–ight.'

'I told you, I've not been sleeping, and if I don't sleep there's no way I can cope with all I need to do.' Abby is frustrated. Why doesn't Beth believe her? She can feel anxiety mounting once more.

'Did your husband know you were using them?'

'No.' Abby blushes. They *were* his pills. Then she feels a surge of anger. 'He's hardly been around lately to find out.'

Beth nods, slowly. 'I think I've got the picture now. Thanks for sharing so much.' She nods again, more decisively. 'I'm sorry there's been this confusion.'

'Yeah, me too . . .' The apology makes Abby more forgiving. I suppose people were only trying their best. Except Glenn, she thinks. He seems to have shunted me off here, rather than offering to help. Not that I want his support, but how typical. I wish I'd been less out of it that night. I'd have been more resistant to being admitted.

As Abby wrestles with her thoughts there's another tap on the door.

'Yes?' says Beth.

This time it's Sangeeta. 'I got you this,' she says, and hands Abby a small white pill and a plastic cup of water. 'Dr Kasdan would prefer you to have one at a time, but he says we can authorize a further dose for you later today if you still feel bad.' Sangeeta gives her a half-smile.

The psychiatrist is probably convinced I'll OD if they give me more, thinks Abby. Still, perhaps Sangeeta's not so dreadful – she's only been doing her job, after all.

18

A middle-aged woman hurries, panting, into the lounge. Her badge reveals she is staff.

'I'm so sorry I'm late,' she says, flinging off a long cardigan and straightening her dress. 'I got held up.'

Was it with Abby? Michael wonders. She seemed in a bad way, and hasn't returned with the rest of the group after lunch.

The woman checks round. 'I think this is everyone.'

'What about Abby?' asks Lillie.

'She's not coming this afternoon,' says the woman.

'Is she OK?'

'You'll need to ask her, Lillie. So, I'm Beth and I'm going to be running this session. I've met most of you before . . . But you must be Michael?' She smiles at him. 'And Karen?' Karen nods. 'So . . . these afternoon sessions are when we try to apply the theories we talk about in the mornings to our own lives. They tend to be more experiential—' Beth seems to notice Michael's perplexed expression, ' – *practical*, if you like.'

Michael feels about eight years old.

'I understand from Johnnie that you've been discussing how when we're depressed we tend to follow the same negative cycles of thinking. We go over and over our problems, trying to solve them. Psychologists call this "ruminating". Does anyone here spend a lot of time beating themselves up for not dealing with their situation better? I know I do.'

She looks around at them. Michael peers at his shoes.

'Yeah, me,' volunteers Colin. 'I'm worried my girlfriend's going to leave me 'cos I'm still in here. I've spent so much time getting worked up about it, when I spoke to her on the phone yesterday I must have asked her about three times if she was going to dump me. Talk about paranoid.'

'I doubt she's going to dump you, Colin,' says Beth.

'Seriously, I reckon she might,' says Colin, twiddling his ponytail distractedly. 'I've been here a long time. Yesterday she got so pissed off with me she told me to snap out of it. If only it was that easy.'

Several members of the group nod in understanding.

'This is exactly what I mean.' Beth addresses them all. 'We spend so much time in this self-critical frame of mind that we get used to it.'

There's a low cough from the sofa opposite. It's Karen. 'I've been getting annoyed with myself for being so upset recently. Um, my dad died a couple of months ago . . .' Michael shifts in his seat, uneasy. Karen looks over at him and grinds to a halt.

'Do carry on, Karen,' urges Beth.

Karen blushes. 'I've been feeling guilty about the amount

I've been crying. I can't work out why I feel so miserable.'

'But it's quite normal to feel upset when your father dies,' offers Rita. 'It's only a measure of how much you loved him.'

'Thanks. It's a bit more complicated than that . . .' and Karen glances at Rita. The older woman seems genuinely concerned. 'But yes, I suppose you're right.'

'Those are good examples, Colin and Karen,' says Beth. 'The trouble with trying to get rid of our sadness or anxiety by churning over our worries is it can be like trying to dig ourselves out of quicksand – the more we struggle, the deeper we sink. Is that what you've been finding, Karen?'

'I guess so,' she says. 'Since Dad died, I have been getting really frustrated with myself and I seem to have felt worse, not better, as time goes on.'

'So are you saying it's good to feel sad or not?' Troy asks Beth.

'I'm not suggesting there's anything wrong with being *sad*. I appreciate this all sounds a bit convoluted, so let me describe it another way. You might guess—' Beth laughs and pats her thighs, ' – that I'm not the sporty type. Personally, I prefer chocolate to the gym.'

I can tell, thinks Michael.

'Still, it can be helpful to see the mind as like a muscle. You know how, if you're an athlete, you can train hard to be fit for certain tasks? Well, the mind is the same – I call it "Roger Federer's Right Arm Syndrome". A few years ago, when I was watching him play tennis – because whilst I'm not exactly athletic, I've always enjoyed watching tennis, for . . . um, obvious reasons—' she laughs again, ' – I noticed his right arm was much bigger than his left. "Doh," my husband said – he was quite scathing, "that's because he's right-handed." In other words, he's played so much with his right hand—'

'Oo-er, missus,' quips Colin.

Beth grins. She's better at handling ribbing than Johnnie, observes Michael.

'Perhaps I could have picked a better phrase. Anyway, his arms no longer match; they're out of balance, if you like. Not, of course, that I am criticizing Federer's physique, but I hope you get my point. Our moods are like this too – if we train our brains to operate negatively, they get used to doing it, so they get overdeveloped in that way of thinking.' She stands back. 'Make sense?'

'Kinda,' grunts Troy.

'But how can we retrain our brains?' asks Rita, pausing as she takes notes. 'It took me many years to get this way.'

'The thing about all our moods is that they're related to our thought processes,' says Beth. 'Being depressed involves thoughts, and thoughts can be changed.'

'I thought you said this was going to be a *practical* session,' says Troy. 'So far all we've done is listen to you.'

I wish he'd shut it, thinks Michael. I'm not enjoying this any more than he is, but at least I don't keep interrupting.

Yet again Beth seems unfazed. 'Fair point, Troy. Time is getting on, and I'm hoping this next exercise might help answer your question, Rita. So, everybody, it's stopped raining but you might like to bring another layer if you want one. We're going into the garden. Rita, we'll wait for you, so please don't feel rushed.'

Oh crikey, it really *is* playtime with teacher, thinks Michael.

* * *

Karen reaches beside the sofa for her jacket and stands to zip it up.

I like Beth's clothes, she thinks, as she watches the therapist pull a long cardigan over her dress. And those shoes are fab. I wonder where they're from?

'With this exercise, I'd like you to observe what's around you,' says Beth. As Rita adjusts her sari, then struggles to pick up her pad and pen as well as her walking stick, she adds, 'Don't worry about making notes, just pay attention once we leave this room.' There's much shuffling and muttering. 'The only rule is you aren't allowed to speak until we're back.'

Once they're all silent, Beth opens the door and leads them into the hall like a priest commencing a church service.

I'm glad we're going outside, I could do with some fresh air, thinks Karen. She's been doing her best to take in what Beth has been saying, but she's so drained after seeing Johnnie that her attention keeps slipping.

Paintings, she observes dutifully as they troop down the stairs. That's Seven Sisters, and I've a hunch that's Barcombe Mill.

Beth stops to tap in a code by the door to reception.

Gosh, I didn't know we were locked in, thinks Karen.

They follow Beth down another corridor, the silk of Rita's sari rustling as she makes her way slowly in their wake. Karen notices a photocopier and two women chatting beside it, then it's into a dining room.

Though this isn't where we ate lunch, thinks Karen. Here there are tables with benches, not chairs, and posters on the wall that say 'I can let go of shame', 'Whatever my weight today, I am a worthwhile person' and 'I am beautiful just as I am'.

Lillie whispers, 'Eating disorders. They have to dine separately,' in her ear.

'Ah.'

'SHHH!' says Colin loudly, and Lillie splutters with laughter.

'You be careful or I'll get you switched to that group,' she hisses.

'Ooh, vicious,' says Colin, patting his sizeable tummy.

The garden isn't anything remarkable. Why bring us here, Karen wonders.

Nonetheless she forces herself to concentrate. There's a wooden bench and rusting metal table on a patch of worn grass in the centre. The east wall is flanked by a flower bed containing a hydrangea with dried brown florets left over from last summer, clusters of daffodils and early tulips. Down the far end is a laurel hedge, what looks like a cherry tree poised to blossom with an empty birdfeeder hanging from its lowest branch, and a castor-oil plant. A high wooden fence cordons off neighbouring properties to the west.

After each group member has had the opportunity to

circle the lawn – including Rita with her walking stick – Beth indicates with a wave they should return indoors.

Upstairs they remove their coats and shrug at one another, unsure of the significance of the exercise.

'I bet this is some sort of memory test,' says Colin in a low voice, smoothing his hair back into its ponytail.

That's Karen's worry too. She has a suspicion it'll be like the party game she played when she was small, where you had to remember the objects on a tray after they'd been taken from the room. My memory is dreadful, she thinks. I'm bound to get everything wrong.

Beth picks up a marker, goes to the board and says, 'Now I'm going to draw a map of where we've just walked.' Rapidly she outlines the stairs, corridor, dining room and garden. It's neither to scale nor well executed, so accuracy can't be the point. 'Next, I want you to shout out what you've seen, and if everybody in the group remembers seeing it, it goes on the map, but not otherwise. Things that only one or two of you have seen don't go on. Got it?'

'BENCH!' shouts Colin at once.

'Who else saw the bench?' asks Beth, and the rest of the group raise their hands, so she marks it on her drawing.

'Table,' says Troy, and again it gets added.

'Fire extinguisher,' says Colin, but this time Karen and Lillie shake their heads. 'It was by the back door,' he cajoles, but Beth refuses to include it.

'Hydrangea,' says Karen. She's beginning to understand.

'What's that?' says Lillie.

'How can you not know what a hydrangea is?' Michael

says, but his tone is jokey, not mean. He seems to have lightened up a bit, thinks Karen.

'Anyone else see the hydrangea?' asks Beth.

'Me. It was in the flower bed, needs cutting back,' says Michael.

'No one else?'

The rest of the group shake their heads.

'Sorry, Karen,' says Beth.

So it continues. The watercolours get added, as do the women chatting by the photocopier, but not the posters in the dining room; and in the garden it seems Karen noticed almost all the plants, but completely overlooked a toolbox by the back door that the men thought impossible to miss. But there's more, so much more, that she failed to observe – the security camera at the bottom of the stairs, the sign on the door saying *Office Manager*, the rooms numbered 1 through 6, a half-eaten sandwich in the dining room, the stack of recycling bins by the garden gate; even, apparently, a large wooden shed.

How could I be so blind, Karen wonders, but it seems the rest of the group missed a lot too.

'Right, now we're going back outside to do it all again,' says Beth.

'No!' says Colin.

'Oh yes. I'm trying to show you how to challenge your normal patterns of thinking. Rita, if this is a bit much for you, please feel free to wait here. The rest of you, same route, in silence, and back upstairs. Coats, everyone . . .' And off they go.

This time, Karen is so tuned-in visually that she sees the

objects with ease that she previously missed. And every time she spots one of the items – the security camera, the *Office Manager* sign, the half-eaten sandwich, the toolbox, she feels a tiny burst of pleasure, as if a pathway has opened and joy has been released directly into her brain. She notices new items too. The banisters are beautifully carved as if entwined with ivy; there's a stack of Christmas decorations on a shelf by the photocopier; the wallpaper is peeling by the French windows of the dining room; in the garden there's a squirrel running along the wall – and the more she sees, the more delighted she feels.

All too soon they're back upstairs.

'So, how was that?' asks Beth. She's grinning.

'Wow,' says Colin. 'That was wild.'

'It's extraordinary, isn't it?' she says.

'Yes.' Lillie claps her hands. 'I *loved* that!'

'Notice it was the second time that the pleasure kicks in? This really puts us into the present, into the creative, intuitive part of the brain,' says Beth. 'By being careful to look at the world around us, it stops us thinking about the past or the future, and ruminating.'

'It was a bit like taking ecstasy,' says Colin.

'Shhh!' says Lillie.

But Beth isn't remotely concerned. 'I want to know how you're all feeling right now,' she says.

'I could smell the rain from earlier,' says Rita. 'It was lovely . . .'

'Me too,' nods Colin. 'So I'm nicely chilled.'

'I'm alert,' says Lillie.

'I suppose I don't feel quite as shit as I did earlier,' says Michael.

Karen looks around the room. Everyone – even Troy, who hitherto has done nothing but scowl – seems less morose.

I'm sure it won't last, she thinks, checking her own emotional state, and I don't really understand why, but what a relief it is to feel in good spirits again. I'd forgotten what it was like.

19

'Aren't you staying for Relaxation?' asks Lillie as Karen reaches for her jacket.

'I thought we finished at four and I'm afraid I have to pick up my kids,' says Karen.

'Pity. You don't want to miss it unless you have to. Best bit of the day, isn't it, Rita?'

'Oh yes,' says Rita. Slowly, she swivels round and lifts her legs up onto the sofa so she's stretched out along it.

'Johnnie's good at it too,' says Lillie.

Karen is wondering what being "good at Relaxation" means when Rita says, 'Lovely voice.'

'Here you are, then, Rita,' says Lillie, and reaches for Rita's woollen shawl. She spreads it over Rita's torso like a blanket. The elderly woman closes her eyes and smiles in gratitude.

'Maybe I'll stay next time.'

'You should, Karen,' says Johnnie, coming back into the room. In his wake are a couple of young men she doesn't recognize. One has a Mohican and a pierced eyebrow; the other is wearing large black-framed glasses and is heavily tattooed.

'Whatcha, boys,' Lillie greets them. She's scrambled onto one of the sofas to let down the blinds.

'People from all the groups in Moreland's participate,' Johnnie explains.

Lillie jumps onto the floor. 'Karl, Lansky, this is Karen.' She introduces them with a flourish.

'Hello.' Karen is curious to find out more about them, but it'll have to wait. 'I'm sorry I can't stay—'

'When are you back in, Karen?' asks Johnnie.

'Friday. I work the rest of the week.'

'See ya then.' Lillie flutters a butterfly farewell with her perfectly polished fingernails.

That's a shame, thinks Karen as she heads down the stairs. I could do with relaxing and I was enjoying their company. They're a nice crowd, and Lansky and Karl looked interesting too. Who'd have thought it, in Moreland's?

The receptionist waylays her as she's reaching for the front door handle.

'Excuse me, but you need to sign out.'

Karen backtracks to sign the book for the young woman, who, she gleans from her badge, is called Danni.

At that moment, a blast of cold air heralds an arrival, and Karen turns to see a woman catch her heel on the threshold and stagger forward. In one hand she has hold of a wheeled suitcase; in the other is a bottle of wine, which, judging from the splash of dark liquid that lands on the carpet, must be open.

'It's Elaine,' says the woman, heading straight to Danni.

She smells of cigarettes, Karen notices.

'I'm afraid you can't bring that in here,' says Danni, jerking her chin at the wine bottle.

'I'm not due to detox till tomorrow,' says Elaine.

'Still, you can't have it here.'

Karen gives Elaine a swift appraisal. She's sharp-featured, dressed in stretch jeans and a leather bomber jacket, and thin in a way that suggests she doesn't get much nourishment. I'm not sure I'd want to argue with her, thinks Karen. She decides to stay a moment, lest there's trouble.

'Why not? I've paid for the night.'

'Because we've a no drugs or alcohol rule.'

'I'll have it in my room – no one need see.'

Danni shakes her head. 'I'm sorry.'

'Aw, go on . . .'

Danni's mouth sets in a firm line. She's clearly had encounters like this before, Karen realizes, impressed by her composure.

'No.'

Elaine lurches towards the interior door.

'You won't get through there,' says Danni. 'It's locked.'

'Fuck you,' says Elaine.

Karen sees Danni reach under her desk. She must have pressed a buzzer, because at once there is the sound of running footsteps.

'Problem, Danni?' It's the goatee-bearded man in a suit who showed Karen round earlier.

'Elaine here wanted to check in with some wine,' says Danni. 'And I was explaining that we don't allow that.'

'Ah yes, I see.' He addresses the visitor. 'Hi, Elaine. I'm

Phil, the office manager. I know you're scheduled to be with us tonight, but I'm afraid we don't allow any alcohol in here.'

'But I'm not due to stop till tomorrow.'

'True, but . . .'

'I'll sit here and drink it, then.' Elaine flops down into one of the chairs. 'Cheers.' She raises the bottle to her lips.

'No, I'm afraid you can't do that either—' Phil moves towards her.

She flinches. 'Oi, don't touch me!'

He didn't so much as brush your sleeve, thinks Karen.

'All right, I'll go . . .' Elaine stands up and makes her way to the front door, leaving her suitcase in the middle of reception.

'Aren't you going to take your case?' asks Danni.

'I'll be back in a sec.'

Karen, Danni and Phil watch, transfixed, as Elaine makes her way down the steps at the entrance of the clinic, holding onto the handrail so she doesn't topple in her heels. She stops on the pavement directly outside, lifts the bottle once more to her mouth and drinks the contents, barely pausing for breath until the wine is finished. Then she bends over and carefully puts the bottle down on the bottom step and, swaying ever so slightly, walks back up to the front door.

'OK,' she says to Danni. 'I'm ready.'

* * *

Michael has been sitting for several minutes opposite a woman who's introduced herself as Gillian. Other than a 'yes' when she asked if his name was Michael, he hasn't said a word.

According to her badge she is a senior therapist. Well, *obviously* she's senior, thinks Michael; she's old. If Johnnie was too young for him to respect, this Scottish biddy with a grey bun, glasses and a paisley shawl is too far out the other side. It's not just that she seems to be from a different generation; Gillian also appears posh.

I can't see her getting hot and sweaty in a mosh pit, or going to a traders' market at the crack of sparrow's fart, he thinks. If I *have* to see a therapist, why couldn't I have had Beth, or whatever her name was? And to top it all, I've had to miss Relaxation. I could have done with a kip.

'I take it you don't feel like talking,' says Gillian after a few more minutes.

What is there to talk about, Michael thinks. Everything's gone tits up, end of. How's she going to help – bankroll me? I'd have been better off going to the Citizens' Advice.

Gillian catches his eye and gives Michael a tiny smile.

I suppose that's meant to encourage me, he thinks. If she knew how many smiles I've had today, she wouldn't bother.

'We've been yakking all day,' he mutters. Then he looks down and picks at his cuticles, avoiding her gaze.

'In the group sessions, I appreciate maybe you and the other patients have, but it's only us now. You might find it helps a wee bit to put your own feelings into words.'

'I don't get why everyone is so keen on talking.' Michael tugs at a particularly dry bit of skin.

'Do you mind if I ask you if you think keeping your problems to yourself will make them disappear?'

What does she know about my situation? wonders Michael. She has a file on her knee: bet it's full of all sorts. 'What's in there?'

'It's a letter from your GP,' says Gillian. 'You can see it if you want?'

'No thanks.' My doctor told me I'm clinically depressed, thinks Michael. Not sure what the difference between 'clinically' and plain old depressed is, but that's what got me admitted – apparently I was severely at risk. The notion of such personal information being down there in black and white makes Michael edgy, but to demand to see it might seem aggressive.

'I'll make a few notes as we talk, if you don't mind,' Gillian continues.

Michael shifts in his chair. He can't think what to say. Knowing she's going to write it all down is off-putting. 'I'm not into all this expressing myself,' he mumbles, finally. 'It's not me, you see. I know it's very trendy and stuff . . .' He falters, and is surprised when Gillian chuckles.

'Do I look trendy to you, Michael?' She fingers her paisley shawl.

He can't stop himself snorting. 'No, I suppose not.'

'The idea that putting our feelings into words can help us isn't particularly modern. It's actually ancient wisdom to suggest that if someone is sad or angry about a situation and we can get them to chat about it, it will probably release some emotions and make them feel better.'

She must be referring to the shop going under, thinks Michael. How else would she know I lose my temper, unless someone's told her? He has an urge to grab the file after all and check she's telling the truth about what's in there.

'More than two and a half thousand years ago Buddha talked about the benefits of labelling our experiences.'

Bloody hell, Buddhism, he thinks. If that isn't trendy, what is? She might be a Scot, but I bet she lives in Brighton, on Muesli Mountain, no doubt. Well, these sessions might work for some people, but I'm getting nothing out of it. Again he glances at the clock.

'Do you mind if I leave now?'

Gillian checks the time too. She nods. 'Aye, you can leave. We're down to see one another again on Friday. But two and a half thousand years, Michael. That's a while to establish that the talking cure works in practice. So perhaps next time we meet, you might like to try giving it a wee go?'

* * *

'Ah, Abby, welcome back,' says Johnnie. 'So, you're joining us for Relaxation?'

Abby nods. The extra tablet has helped – finally – reduce her panic. 'Sangeeta suggested I come.'

'Great,' says Johnnie. 'Can someone get Abby a mat?'

A glamorous young woman Abby vaguely recognizes from the eleven o'clock session is about to lie down, but instead scrambles to her feet and goes to a basket of exercise mats in the corner of the room. 'Here you are,' she says, handing over a dark-pink roll.

'Thanks.' Abby looks around to see what is expected of her. The sofas are already taken, but the coffee table has been moved to make room for the rest of them to lay out their mats on the floor. By the time Abby has edged in too, the space is crowded.

Abby stretches out on her back and watches as Johnnie dims the lights and shuts the door.

This is all very odd, she thinks. Then again, everything feels strange at the moment. She adjusts her shoulders, trying to slow the ceaseless churning of worries about Callum and the potential chaos at home by focusing on her surroundings. Still, she's uneasy being close to so many strangers. Ever since Callum learned to walk, crowds have brought nothing but trouble. A flurry of anxiety pierces her drug-induced calm.

She hears Johnnie open a CD case and slip a disc into the player. Then the gentle tinkle of music fills the room.

Chill, Abby, she says to herself. The more hyper you are, the longer they'll keep you here.

'Gradually start to bring yourself into your body . . .' says Johnnie.

Abby is tempted to turn her head to see what he is doing – where's he sitting? Is he reading from a book? – but forces herself to keep her eyes closed.

'Take a few moments to get in touch with the sensation of your breath.'

Abby senses her lungs rise . . . and fall . . . rise . . . and fall . . .

'When you are ready, bring your awareness to those places where your body is in contact with your mat or the sofa.'

Ah yes, thinks Abby. There are my heels . . . calves . . . thighs . . .

'And with each out breath, allow yourself to sink a little deeper.' Johnnie's voice is soft and soothing. 'Should your mind start to chatter or whirl, see your thoughts as mental events that come and go like clouds across a sky. Gently acknowledge those thoughts, then watch them float away . . .'

Abby is beginning to feel lighter and less agitated.

'And now, imagine your breath travelling down your body, through the right leg, to the toes of your right foot.'

Her breathing slows.

'Spend a moment being aware of the sensations in your foot, then, on an out breath, release any tension you may notice there . . .'

Within minutes, she is asleep.

20

'So how was it?' asks Anna as soon as Karen answers her call.

Karen yawns. 'Sorry, I must have nodded off after I put the kids to bed. Hang on.' She gently lifts up the cat, who's snoozing on her belly. Then she reaches for the TV remote to turn down the volume.

'Do you want to speak another time?'

'No, you're all right.'

'Excellent, 'cos I have to admit I'm very curious. I've always wondered what it must be like to go to Moreland's. You read so much about it in the press.'

Depends what you mean by 'press', thinks Karen, but then Anna has always been partial to celebrity gossip. She hoists herself onto her elbows to chat.

'I had a great day, actually. What I hadn't realized was they take a more holistic approach, so your mind isn't seen as a separate entity, as if you're cut off at the neck. We spent time in the garden, for instance.'

'Ooh, talking of gardening – you still OK to come to the allotment on Wednesday?'

'Sure,' says Karen. 'Have to be after work, though.'

'Great. Anyway, did you meet anyone famous?'

Karen laughs. 'Sorry, no.' *I'm sure I recognize Lillie*, she thinks, *but we're asked to respect one another's privacy.* 'I expect the celebs go to the London clinic. I gather it's far grander.'

'Oh.' Karen can tell Anna is disappointed. Doubtless she was hoping to experience a cross between a luxury spa packed with A-listers and Bedlam, albeit vicariously. 'I should hope it wasn't *too* basic. I hear it costs a fortune.'

'Don't get me wrong – it's very comfortable. I only mean it's surprisingly normal. The others on the programme I'm doing don't seem that different to you or me.'

'No madwomen in the attic, then?'

'Not a single Mrs Rochester that I saw.'

'Glad to hear it. Don't want you bumping into any axe-wielding psychopaths in the corridor.'

'Me neither. I'm sure some of the patients have more serious conditions, though – I didn't get to meet that many of them and some have clearly been going through stuff—'

'What kind of stuff?'

' – but then so have I.' Karen thinks of the episode with Elaine and the wine – Anna would appreciate that story, having lived with an alcoholic – but resists sharing. 'Well, nothing terribly dramatic, far as I can see, only the sort of thing lots of people go through – divorce, redundancy . . .' She hesitates. It was such an intense day; some of the revelations in the group later in the afternoon were very personal. Still, she can tell Anna about her own experiences, can't she?

'I'm glad you're finding it so helpful already,' says Anna, when she's filled her in on the session with Johnnie.

Karen detects a hint of suspicion in her friend's voice. Considering that Anna is the person Karen normally confides in, is she perhaps a touch jealous? I mustn't make her feel excluded, she reminds herself. 'I'm very grateful – it's all down to you that I'm there.'

She can almost hear Anna purr down the line. 'It wasn't just my doing, it was Simon's, too.' Karen's healthcare policy was a legacy from her husband; he set up their cover.

'I'm lucky, but it does make me worry about other people who don't have access to a similar level of support.'

'You need to stop worrying about everyone else and look after yourself.'

That wasn't what I meant, thinks Karen. 'From what I've heard, treatment for depression on the NHS is a postcode lottery, and the waiting list for therapy can be months. I hate to imagine what state I would have been in by then.'

'I don't think you should feel remotely guilty about being there. Simon paid into that policy for years.'

'Not that it did him any favours . . .'

They sigh in unison. 'Surely that's even more reason you're justified in using it now? Let's just be glad you've got this safety net.'

'You're right,' says Karen. 'And it sounds mad, but it gives me comfort, thinking that Simon helped with this. As if he's continuing to look after me from beyond the grave.'

'That's not remotely mad,' says Anna. 'Then again, I always did maintain you're the sanest person I know.'

* * *

There's a tap on Abby's bedroom door.

'Yeah, yeah, I'm alive,' she calls out. She'd hoped her chat with Beth would have made it clear she was not a danger to herself.

'Phone call for you,' Sangeeta announces through the door. 'You can take it in the nurses' office up here if you like.'

Damn, thinks Abby. I turned off my mobile for a reason. She gets up from the bed where she's been lying, wondering whether she can ask for another diazepam as she's sure the one she took earlier is wearing off, and opens the door. 'Do you know who it is?'

'I think it's your husband.'

Oh no, thinks Abby. Something's happened to Callum. Why else would Glenn call? She almost pushes Sangeeta out of the way in her rush down the corridor.

'He's on that line.' A male nurse gestures to the phone on the desk opposite.

'Thanks.' Abby grabs the receiver. 'Is everything OK?'

'Yes,' says Glenn. 'It's fine.'

The old Abby would have slid, relieved, into a chair, but this Abby seems to have no 'off' button. She jigs from foot to foot. 'How's Callum?'

'He's cool, actually.'

Really? thinks Abby. That sounds highly unlikely. Callum

is rarely 'cool', and even when he is Glenn never seems to acknowledge it.

'Yeah, we had a remarkably easy day, all things considered.'

You mean *considering I'm in here*, thinks Abby. *Shirking my responsibility.* Why don't you just say it? She swallows her irritation and says, 'So did you have to take the day off? I'm sorry . . .' Although I'm not truly sorry, she thinks. I feel bad that Callum's routine has been upset, but not that Glenn's had to miss work. It's about time he spent more than five minutes with his son.

'It wasn't a problem, honestly. You don't need to apologize.'

That's weird too, thinks Abby. Lately she's felt as though Glenn wants her to apologize for almost everything – even, on occasion, for existing at all.

'No, we're OK, trust me. I don't want you to worry about us. I wasn't calling to bother you or upset you about any-thing. I was, er . . . well . . .' He coughs. 'I was thinking it would be nice to bring Callum in to see you . . . But mainly, I wanted to find out how you are. Everything all right in there?' He sounds different, somehow, less antagonistic and uncompromising.

'I'm, um . . . OK, I guess.' She doesn't know where to start. It's been so long – months, possibly years, since her husband last asked how she was feeling, let alone showed any desire to have a more meaningful conversation. She almost wonders if the diazepam hasn't, in fact, worn off and she's having a drug-induced delusion.

'You had everyone very worried,' he says, his voice catch-ing. 'Me especially . . .'

And suddenly she realizes why he's calling, why he's done such an about-turn, why his voice sounds so tight and strange.

Of course. Glenn thinks I took an overdose, she remembers. God, my brain is addled! No wonder he seems so distraught. After all, that's what they say, isn't it: most people who kill themselves have attempted suicide before? So he's rung because he's concerned – frightened, even. Yes, that constriction in his throat is a sign. He's terrified I'll try to do it again, and next time I might succeed.

* * *

Michael is heading back to his room along the corridor when Abby comes out of the nurses' office at speed.

'Whoops!' he says as they collide, and steps back in embarrassment.

Abby rubs her shoulder.

'I'm so sorry. Are you OK?'

'Yes, I'm fine. Sorry. I'm a bit all over the place at the moment.'

Tell me about it, thinks Michael.

'Anyway, it was my fault. I wasn't looking where I was going.'

'Takes two to tango,' he says, then cringes at himself for using such a naff expression. It's not even in the right context, he thinks. To his consternation Abby turns to walk beside him down the corridor.

'I'm along here too,' she says. 'What room are you in?'

'This one,' he says, as they arrive at his door.

'Small world.' She opens the door opposite. 'This is me.' He's expecting her to turn and leave him, when she pauses on the threshold. 'How did you find today, then?'

The question stumps him. If he says he's loathed it, she might be insulted, given she's been part of it. But he can hardly say he's enjoyed himself; other than for a few minutes at lunch and in the session with Beth, he hasn't. 'Bit tricky . . .' he says eventually.

She nods. 'Let's hope it gets better, eh?'

'Yeah.'

'Anyway, sleep well.'

'Fat chance,' he says, then fears this sounds rude, so adds, 'I haven't slept properly for weeks.'

'No, me neither.'

Michael senses she's waiting for him to say something else, but he's at a loss. They both stand there, hovering. After a while he ventures, 'It doesn't help, the way they keep checking up on me all the time.'

'They do that to you too?' Abby lowers her voice and glances up and down the corridor. 'Still, at least they've stopped following me round. That was horrible.'

'I can imagine . . .' His voice trails off.

'Well, I hope you have a better night tonight.'

'Thank you.'

She gives a wry smile, and says, 'After all, tomorrow is another day,' before closing her bedroom door.

21

Abby peers through the glass door into reception. Glenn and Callum are already waiting so Danni buzzes her through at once.

'The little lounge upstairs is free,' says Danni, checking her file. 'Why don't you three use that?'

'Follow me,' Abby says, but Callum starts to keen in distress. He's not used to seeing me in this strange environment, she concludes, and when Glenn asks Callum to take his hand, Callum makes a bid to get away. It's only by working together that they finally cajole him into the room.

Funny to imagine that only forty-eight hours ago I was here with Sangeeta, Abby thinks, closing the door. I feel much calmer already – now my child is the wired one.

'Hey, hey,' says Abby, as Glenn sets Callum down. She crouches to her son's level. In a giant pair of ear defenders, his elfin features seem especially tiny; the overall effect is both comical and heart-wrenching. 'It's Mummy. Mummm . . . meeeee . . . Remember me?'

God, she thinks, it's been less than a week but how I've

missed you. She rests on her haunches and waits, hoping, yet she can't get him to so much as touch her, let alone give her the hug she craves. But at least he hasn't had a complete meltdown, and before too long he stops wailing and goes to clamber on one of the sofas.

Glenn sits down on the settee opposite. There's still something swashbuckling about my husband, she observes, seeing him afresh after being apart. He's so tall and dark, whereas Callum's so slight and fair. But there *is* an echo of Glenn's face in our son's if you look carefully – the dimple in his chin, the curl of his lips.

'So, is it going OK in here?' asks Glenn. No sooner has he said this than Callum reaches up and grabs a small vase from the window ledge behind the sofa. Then he picks out the flowers and throws them on the floor.

'Oh, Callum.' Abby leaps to retrieve them. But Callum pays no heed. He tips up the vase and – 'NO!'

He is about to drink the water when Glenn catches his arms. 'Hey, mate, can't you stop being autistic, just for a bit?' He spins Callum round to face him.

This is the kind of remark that Abby would often resent, yet this afternoon she laughs. Perhaps being at Moreland's is helping her understand where Glenn is coming from. Usually she is so caught up with her son she can't see the world without Callum in it. She is constantly vigilant, alert to where he is, what he's doing. The last couple of days she's had time to focus on herself for a change, even enjoy herself again, just a little.

'I think it's really helping me being here,' she says, as Glenn picks up the scattered blooms.

175

She'd like to add that it's been good to be around vases of flowers without fearing the water will be drunk, or the contents shredded. She'd like to tell Glenn what a luxury it was to have a bath the night before and be able to wallow in it. Above all she'd like to explain what a relief it is to talk to other adults. *I can crack a joke!* she wants to say. She's been hanging out with Lillie and Colin, watching telly and playing cards. But she fears Glenn will hear whatever she says as a criticism – he doesn't look after Callum enough, he makes Abby unhappy, that's why she's ended up here.

'You seem brighter,' he says.

'I am.' Though I'm a long way from better, she thinks. 'It'll still be a few weeks before the antidepressants kick in.'

'They've put you on medication? Is that a good idea after last week?'

'I told you on the phone, I didn't take an overdose.' Abby can hear the testiness in her voice. She'd prefer to be more measured, but she's distracted by Callum playing with the remote control, flicking the TV on and off. She fights to control her tone. 'I spoke to Dr Kasdan, the psychiatrist here, about antidepressants yesterday. He thought they would help me.'

'Oh.'

'What's the problem?'

'I'd have liked to go with you to see him.'

'I didn't think I had to ask your permission about what medication I'm on.'

'I wasn't expecting you to ask my permission.'

'Good. It wouldn't be appropriate, would it, given we're splitting up?'

'That doesn't mean I don't care about you, Abby.'

And there I was a few minutes ago believing we were beginning to understand one another, she thinks.

'Well, I am paying for this place,' Glenn mutters.

'*I beg your pardon?*'

'I said, if it wasn't for me you wouldn't be here,' says Glenn.

'That's not what you said.'

'OK, I apologize, I phrased it badly. I'm not paying personally, obviously.'

'No, your work insurance is coughing up. And in case it had escaped your notice, it's been pretty hard for me to work the last few years. Otherwise I might have had my own policy.' He's lucky to be *able* to work, thinks Abby. She can feel her attitude hardening.

'I know.'

Don't get into this now, Abby reminds herself. Callum may be wearing ear defenders, but who knows what he picks up?

'Come here, honey,' she says to her son, but he continues playing with the remote, his back turned.

Then, in a *whoosh*, the anxiety returns. She has to gasp for air; it's as if she can't get any oxygen into her lungs.

'You OK?' says Glenn. 'Your breathing's gone a bit weird . . .'

She gulps and nods, struggling to soothe herself as best she can even though she feels she is suffocating. *Be calm, be calm. It's only a physical reaction.* 'See your thoughts as mental events that come and go like clouds across a sky,' she reminds herself, but she's quaking from head to toe.

'Hey,' says Glenn. 'Callum, mate, careful. Let your mum have a bit of space, eh?'

Abby's vaguely aware she's batting her arms in distress. Glenn rises to his feet and guides her to the sofa. She wants to run away, scream, pray, take another diazepam – anything to stop this terrifying spiral.

Get me out of this crazy head of mine, she begs silently. Please, *please*, give me some peace.

* * *

Later that afternoon, Karen and her children are with Anna at the allotment, as arranged. The danger of frost has passed and the two women are keen to plant peas and beans. But the warmer weather means that brambles and dandelions are also beginning to take hold, so Shirley has driven over from Goring to help tackle them.

'Grandma,' says Molly, looking up from the small trenches she and Luke have been tasked with digging for mangetout, 'why haven't we ever been to your flat?'

Shirley raises her head from weeding to address her granddaughter. 'Ah well, Molly, it's not that I don't *want* you to come, it's only a bit small to have you round, that's all.'

'Grandma is renting her flat in Goring,' explains Karen, unsure if Molly will understand quite what this means. 'But maybe one day she'll have a place of her own.'

'Oh,' says Molly. She is silent a while, contemplating, then says, 'If it's too small inside, couldn't we sit in your garden?'

'I'm afraid I haven't got a garden.'

'You had a big garden in Portugal,' observes Luke.

'I know,' says Shirley. She looks wistful for a second, then smiles at her grandson. 'That's why I like coming here and helping you.'

'We've got a garden *and* an allotment,' Luke boasts.

'Ours isn't a very big garden, it's more of a patio,' says Karen, trying to soften her children's remarks. Poor Mum, she thinks.

'Why don't you come and live with us?' says Molly. 'Then you could help us all the time.'

'Er . . .' Shirley looks nonplussed. 'That's very sweet of you, Molly, but I don't really think you've got room . . .' She glances nervously at Karen.

Karen flushes, too taken aback to work out what to say.

A while later Anna comes to join Karen planting runner beans.

'That was a bit awkward,' she murmurs.

'Sorry?'

'When Molly asked your mum about moving in.'

'I know.' Karen glances to check that Shirley and the children aren't listening. They are immersed in conversation a distance away. 'It's funny how kids pick these things up. I've been wondering if I ought to ask what her plans are.'

Anna stops midway through making a small hole with her trowel to look at Karen. Her expression is one of concern. 'I hope you're not seriously planning on her coming to live with you?'

'Why not?'

'You're both still grieving over the death of your dad.'

'Yes, but—'

'I'm not sure you're thinking that straight yet. Either of you.'

'Maybe . . .'

'My dear friend, do I have to spell it out for you? You're already looking after two children on your own, on a limited income. I know you're getting stuff out of this Moreland's programme; I'm just afraid – I hope you don't mind my being frank – that it's a bit too soon.'

Karen smiles. 'If I minded you being frank I'd have dumped you long ago.'

'You've managed brilliantly since Simon died – Lord knows, I couldn't have coped half as well as you.'

'Thanks,' says Karen. Anna's not normally one for compliments; she's surprised.

'And you're a fantastic mum to Molly and Luke.'

'I've only done what any mother would.'

'I'm not sure that's true, but anyway. You've said to me yourself you've been really walloped by your dad's death. I'm worried about you. For goodness' sake – *you've* been worried about you. You're being treated for depression. The last thing you need is to take on something else.'

'But my mother isn't some*thing*, she's my mum—'

Karen recalls an anecdote Johnnie shared with the group at the end of his session on Monday. He'd been talking about motivation, and explaining how prioritizing one's own needs has a crucial part to play in meeting one's goals.

'Have you noticed when flight attendants run through the safety procedure before the take-off of a plane, they say something along the lines of: *If you're an adult accompanied by children, make sure you put on your own oxygen mask first, before you see to them?'* he'd said.

Everyone had nodded except Karen. She'd commented, 'I've always thought that was utterly counter-intuitive. I'd be desperate to sort my kids.'

'Yet the point is that if the plane is going down and oxygen is running out, then you'll *need* to have your mask on, in order to sort your children,' Johnnie had said. 'Can you see what this illustrates?'

Karen hadn't understood fully at the time, and it had taken Rita to interject: 'Until we look after ourselves, we can't properly look after anyone else?'

'I think I get what you're driving at,' Karen says slowly to Anna now. Still, she thinks, I don't wholeheartedly agree. From what I've seen, I get on much better with my mother than most grown-up daughters.

She pauses to listen to the animated exchange taking place on the far side of the allotment. She can't make out precisely what Molly and Luke are saying, but the contrast of their high-pitched and eager voices with her mother's more measured tone is reflective of the generations that separate them. They love being together so much, and that they are able to enjoy one another is a blessing, she thinks. If Mum wants to move in with us and Molly and Luke want her there, who am I to say no?

22

In spite of Abby's good wishes, Michael doesn't sleep well, not just on Monday, but every night that week. The days become easier as his routine grows more familiar, but still he prefers to keep himself to himself, and when he finds he is alone with Troy in the lounge on Friday morning, they sit in strained silence waiting for the group to start. Eventually the tension is broken by the arrival of Karen, back for the first time since Monday.

'Hello again,' she says, smiling at both of them and taking a seat. There's a short pause while she gets her file and pen out of a large cloth bag, then she turns to Troy. 'It's your last day today, right?'

Troy nods, and grimaces.

She's got a good memory, Michael observes, feeling bad for not asking this himself. Rather Troy than me, he thinks. It's the first time Michael has seen his own life as the better option than someone else's in a long while.

Karen continues, 'Do you mind if I ask how you ended up here in England?'

'Not at all,' says Troy. 'My unit is based in Italy, so it costs less to fly us to the UK for treatment than send us back to the US. Your clinics are way less expensive.'

That's rough, thinks Michael. I bet he'd rather have been treated at home. It's hard enough being here anyway, I'd hate to be so far from my family. No wonder he's been so negative.

Michael clears his throat, then says, 'Good luck, mate. I'll be thinking of you.'

'Thanks.' Troy nods.

He looks scared shitless, thinks Michael.

Next into the lounge is Rita, who makes slow progress to her favourite armchair. Then in come Lillie, Colin and Abby. Lillie is dressed in an eye-poppingly short skirt and angora jumper, Colin is *still* in his slippers, but Abby has changed from the worn tracksuit she's been wearing all week into jeans and a boldly striped top. She's got more colour in her cheeks, Michael thinks, as she takes a seat next to him and murmurs, 'Hello.' Not difficult, given how washed-out she was on arrival, but it's good to see her look-ing a little better. Finally they are joined by two people Michael doesn't recognize – a middle-aged man with a weather-beaten face and gnarled hands, and a young woman with a shock of bright-pink frizzy hair, who he'd guess is around his daughter's age.

'Hello,' says Lillie. 'I'm Lillie. And you are?' She reaches over and holds out her hand.

'Tash,' says the woman and jerks her head. 'Fuck off.'

'Oh.' Lillie recoils. 'Didn't mean to offend.'

'Sorry,' says Tash, and twitches again. 'Tourette's.'

'Ah. Not to worry, now I know. You're in good company with us lot. We've all sorts of conditions here.'

'Arsehole!' says Tash, blinking several times in quick succession. 'It's not Tourette's specifically that's brought me here – it's my mood swings. Hopefully my tics will diminish once I'm more settled.'

'Sure.' Lillie turns to the middle-aged man.

'Rick,' he says. His jaw is clenched and his throat is so tight he can barely say his own name. He looks ever so stressed, thinks Michael. Funny how it's easier to see in others.

'Morning, everyone.' It's Beth. She slips off her cardigan, introduces herself to Tash and Rick, then picks up a pen and goes straight to the whiteboard.

'Today our focus is on the connection between mental and physical health.' She yanks the top off the marker with her teeth and Michael settles back into the sofa. 'We'll be considering how looking after ourselves physically helps us stay well. It's important if you're to help your own recovery that you understand how our minds and bodies interact.' Beth draws a circle on the whiteboard. 'Who here is familiar with the Hot Cross Bun?'

'Fuck off,' says Tash.

'I've wanted to say that to Beth for months,' says Colin, and winks at Tash.

What on earth have hot cross buns to do with anything, thinks Michael. Some of the stuff these therapists come out with is crazier than we are.

Beth draws a cross in the circle, dividing it into four. 'Perhaps someone can say what goes at these intersections?' She holds the pen expectantly.

'Up there is Thoughts,' says Lillie, and Beth writes 'Thoughts' at twelve o'clock. 'Then to the right is Emotions, at the bottom Physical Sensations and Behaviour is on the left.'

'Perfect,' says Beth. 'As those of you who aren't familiar with the Hot Cross Bun will find out, this is one of the pivotal models we use in cognitive behavioural therapy or CBT.'

More initials, thinks Michael. It's so hard to keep track of what they all mean.

Beth continues, 'The word *cognitive* simply refers to our thoughts, and this kind of therapy looks at how our behaviour influences our thoughts, and vice versa. Who can explain the other links?'

'It's because our thoughts affect our emotions or moods which in turn affect our behaviour and the way our bodies react physically,' says Colin.

'Exactly. If we get into a negative way of thinking, we then start to feel bad emotionally. So if we believe something awful is going to happen, our brains pick up these messages and translate them into a physical response. Who here suffers from anxiety?'

There's a unanimous murmur of 'me'.

'And what physical sensations do you get?'

'I feel sick,' says Rita.

'My nerves tingle, all down here.' Abby holds out her arms and wiggles her fingertips.

'I get shaky,' says Rick. 'In fact, I'm shaky a lot of the time.'

'Me too,' says Lillie.

'My tics get worse,' says Tash.

There's a pause, and Michael decides he has nothing to contribute.

'I was particularly anxious on Monday when I came here for the first time,' says Karen. 'I think that's why I got so weepy. Does that make sense?'

'Sure,' says Beth. 'Anxiety and depression often go hand in hand.'

'I felt bad about it afterwards.' Karen glances round. 'I hope I didn't bring the rest of you down.'

'Not at all,' says Rita. 'It's good to know other people feel like I do.'

Beth writes the symptoms – including *weepy* – beneath the Hot Cross Bun, then turns to face the group again. 'This is why it's important to take care of our bodies. Obviously I don't expect you to be saints. Physical evidence suggests I'm partial to the odd bun myself. However, it does make sense not to give our systems even more to deal with when we're anxious than faulty thinking brings about already. Certain types of food and drink can exacerbate anxiety. What in particular might we try to reduce or avoid?'

'Alcohol,' says Troy.

'Coffee,' says Colin.

'Yes.' Beth pulls up a chair and sits down. 'It can be tempting to reach for more stimulants when you're feeling stressed so you can keep going, or else have a few drinks to help you wind down at the end of the day, but in excess neither is a good idea.'

'*Aah.*' Rick leans forward. He has grasped something, thinks Michael, though surely much of this is obvious. 'So do you think the fact I've got a bit of a coke habit might be contributing to my, um . . . levels of anxiety, and making me feel worse?'

Michael is stunned. No *wonder* Rick is shaky and looks like he's lived so hard. Michael had assumed he must be a builder or some such, and work outside.

Even Beth looks fazed. 'Er . . .'

'Wow. Coke,' says Troy, in his deep American drawl. 'That's not good.'

'What do you mean by a *habit*?' asks Lillie. ''Cos this is the group for people with mental health issues like depression and stuff, but if you're doing a lot of Charlie, maybe you should be in the addiction therapy programme rather than here. Don't you agree, Beth?'

'Hang on a minute, Lillie. Let Rick speak.' Beth appears disconcerted, thinks Michael. I reckon there's been an administrative cock-up.

'Not *that* kind of coke,' says Rick. 'I meant Coca-Cola.'

'Oh,' says Lillie, and everyone roars with laughter.

Beth smiles, visibly relieved, and waits for them to settle. 'Ah, but it is worth talking about, all the same. When you say you've a coke habit, Rick, how much Coca-Cola are you drinking?'

'I drink it every day.'

'Coca-Cola causes cancer,' says Rita.

'No, that's *Diet* Coke,' says Lillie.

'What would you say you get through each day?' asks Beth.

'Ooh . . .' Rick stares up at the ceiling while he calculates. 'A couple of bottles?'

'You mean the small ones? It might be an idea to cut down.'

'Oh *no*. I mean two this size.' Rick holds his hands one above the other, about eighteen inches apart. 'What are they? One and a half litres or something?'

Beth sits back, stunned. 'Goodness! So you're telling me you drink *three* litres of Coke – a *day*?'

'Yup.'

'There's a hell of a lot of caffeine in Coke,' says Troy.

'Maybe Rick can switch to caffeine-free,' says Karen.

'I'd give it up if I were you, Rick,' says Lillie. 'You could save yourself a *lot* of money. Are you paying to be here at Moreland's?'

'Ye–es . . .' Rick looks confused as to the connection. 'And it's rather more than I spend on Coca-Cola.'

'But imagine if your *anxiety* were to be eased a lot by cutting out Coke.'

'Ah.' Rick grins. 'That would be good.'

'Then you could save yourself the exorbitant fees of being a patient here, which would make you feel better emotionally too.'

Because behaviour and feelings are connected, thinks Michael. Perhaps there's some truth in this hot cross bun, after all.

23

'Henceforth my body is a temple.' Abby nods at her plate of fish and chips. 'Let's start as we mean to continue.'

'Good for our minds,' says Colin, who's ordered the same.

'That's oily fish, not cod in batter,' says Lillie.

Colin shunts a large forkful into his mouth and closes his eyes. 'So what if it's not exactly brain food? It's delicious.'

'Thank you ever so much, Sally,' says Lillie, as a plate piled high with salad is brought to her.

'Hark at you,' says Colin.

'Beth *would* be impressed,' says Abby.

'Teacher's pet,' says Colin.

'You're only jealous 'cos you fancy her,' says Lillie.

'I do not!' says Colin. 'She's far too old for me.' But his cheeks redden.

Abby is poised to push him further when she spies Karen hovering on the periphery of the dining room. Today is the first time Abby has seen her since Monday and they've not spoken outside of the groups yet. On first impression Karen seemed vulnerable, bursting into tears at the initial check-in, and Abby was too close to the edge herself to cope with someone else's misery. But the woman she saw in the session this morning seems less likely to rock her own fragile stability, and she gets to her feet so Karen can see her.

'Come and join us. There's plenty of room.'

'Thanks.' Karen smiles as she sits down at the table between Abby and Colin.

She has a kind face, thinks Abby. Not pretty, or beautiful – her features aren't regular enough for that – but her expression is warm and open, and as for that hair . . . Again Abby has a twinge of envy.

'So how are you finding your first week?' Lillie cuts straight to the question before Abby has a chance to ask.

'Well, it's only my second day,' says Karen.

'Ooh, remember that, Colin?' says Lillie. 'Your second day . . .'

'Seems *years* ago.' Colin rubs his chin as if he were a pensioner recalling his boyhood.

'How long have you both been here?' asks Karen.

'Since November,' says Colin.

'Gosh,' says Karen. Abby knows what she's thinking because she had a similar reaction when Colin volunteered this yesterday. *But that's months of being an inpatient and you're not better yet?*

'And he's *still* in his slippers.' Lillie winks.

'Have you . . . er . . . been outside?' asks Karen tentatively.

'In the garden, yes – with you, on Monday.'

'Haven't you ever left the clinic?'

'Can't be arsed,' says Colin.

Abby can tell Karen doesn't believe him either. He's in

190

danger of becoming institutionalized, she fears. No wonder his girlfriend is fed up.

'He gets his fresh air on the balcony,' says Lillie. 'Smoking.'

'Whereas *she*—' Colin tilts his head towards Lillie, ' – is in and out of here like a jack-in-the-box. So it's not a question of how long, but how often.'

'I'm a right tart.' Lillie wriggles and adjusts her miniskirt.

'This is the fifth time she's been banged up,' says Colin.

They're like Tweedledum and Tweedledee, thinks Abby. She is growing to like Colin and Lillie a lot – they're able to see humour in their circumstances, and it's catching. But she catches Karen frowning. 'Don't you worry. Not everyone here is as addicted to Moreland's as these two.'

'So do you think it works, then, the treatment here?' asks Karen.

'Ooh, *yes*,' says Lillie. 'They're absolutely brilliant.'

I know, I know, Abby yearns to say to Karen. *Total contradiction*. Though it'll have to keep. She doesn't want to push these two too far. She's grateful to them for taking her into their care.

'So do you mind my asking what brought you here?' Karen is addressing Abby.

Abby gulps.

All of a sudden her hands are trembling so much that a piece of cod falls from her fork. Help, she panics. I hoped I was through such awful anxiety – the last couple of days have been a false reprieve. She is forced to lay down her cutlery.

'I . . . er . . .' She has a surge of nausea and can feel the food she's just swallowed rising up in her throat.

'Oh, goodness, I'm sorry. You don't have to say if you don't want.' Karen's eyes are full of concern. She reaches over and gives Abby's hand a squeeze.

Abby swallows again. *I don't know why I thought I was immune from other people's interest*, she thinks.

'It's OK,' she says, even though the room is whirling and she's longing to run away and go and lie down on her bed.

I have to face this, she tells herself. I don't want to end up like Colin, in here for months – I need to get back to Callum. I need to show everyone that I can cope. And Karen seems to mean well, she really does.

Three expectant faces tilt towards her – she's not divulged much to Lillie or Colin either. Where on earth should she begin?

'I've had a dreadful few months.'

Karen sighs. 'Tell me about it.'

'It's been awful. My whole life feels like it's falling apart.' She surprises herself with the honesty of this admission.

There's a silence. Abby fears she's put something too huge and overwhelming out there. Still, at least the room seems to have stopped spinning. Perhaps if she breaks the situation down it will help her to explain. She grips the table to steady herself.

'My husband and I are separating. Our son Callum – he's seven – has autism. He's at the severe end of the spectrum.'

'My sister's son Nino has Asperger's,' says Lillie.

'Ah well, you'll know a bit about it, then. Callum doesn't speak, and he takes a lot of looking after – he goes to a special school, but all the same . . . and Glenn – my husband – can't seem to cope with it any more . . . Well, he never really has been able to.' She exhales. She can hear the breath leave her lungs, feel the release of tension. 'Which means I've got to start again, I guess. Find somewhere for Callum and me to live. Get a job. Re-establish who I am.' She shakes her head. ''Cos God knows who that is.'

She's aware Karen is still clasping her hand.

'I know what you mean,' Karen says. 'Not exactly, of course. But I have that sense too, of having to rebuild my life . . .'

Abby looks at her; Karen is biting her lip. She appears worried she's said too much. Even more telling, her eyes are filled with tears.

This is exactly what I was trying to avoid, thinks Abby. *Other people's stuff.* Although actually it doesn't seem that Karen's upset is going to knock her off balance. Quite the opposite.

She places her free hand on top of Karen's and gives it a squeeze.

I don't know who's comforting who, she thinks.

* * *

'So what are you doing now?' asks Abby. Colin and Lillie have made their excuses, keen to catch their favourite soap on TV before the afternoon session.

'I fancy a walk. Put into practice that mind-body stuff Beth was on about. Want to come?'

Abby shakes her head. 'I'm afraid I can't. I'm not allowed out without supervision.'

'Another time, then,' says Karen.

Abby pushes back her chair. 'That'd be nice.'

Goodness me, Karen says to herself when Abby has gone. She seems to have improved a lot since earlier in the week. I wouldn't know it was the same person.

'There's the perfect place to stroll down the road,' Danni tells her when Karen asks for a suggestion at reception. 'A nature reserve, called the Railway Land Project. The site was saved from development by local residents. Turn right out of the door and head straight. You can't miss it.'

Shame on me that I never knew this was here, thinks Karen when she gets there. All this open space, so close to the bustle of Lewes high street, and how long have I lived only a few miles away? It's over twenty-five years since she first came to Brighton as a student; first she fell in love with the seaside town, and then with Simon, so she never left. She pauses for a moment to inhale the fresh air and take in her surroundings, just as Beth recommended.

To the east Malling Down dominates the view, its chalk cliffs dwarfing a row of clapboard houses along the River Ouse; to the west is wet woodland; before her a stretch of reed beds. It's been an exceptionally cold, grey spring. There's been so little sunshine, winter has seemed to last forever. Yet today it feels as if the weather might be turning – birds are singing, trees are breaking into leaf, people are out riding bicycles and wheeling pushchairs.

A raised footpath allows Karen to avoid the marshy ground, and from her vantage point she can see a network of waterways loop and slice across the floodplain. Why are some channels straight and others curved, she wonders. What makes them follow a particular course? There's an old brick bridge over the broadest stream; it appears to have once carried the railway. So that must have been here long before residents reclaimed the land. Whereas nature doesn't carve straight lines, so those must be man-made drainage ditches . . .

Perhaps patterns of thinking are like streams, she muses. Rainwater starts eroding a channel in an almost random fashion, yet the more the channel deepens over time, the less the likelihood it will change direction. Is it possible losing Simon made me *used* to feeling sad? So now I'm stuck, thinking negatively as a matter of course, often on the verge of tears?

Certainly when her mother rang from the hospital with news of her father's stroke, Karen was thrust back to the morning of Simon's heart attack – and she has felt horribly jangled up ever since. She is haunted by the two men; one minute she'll imagine her father is booming 'Supper's ready!' up the stairs like he did when she was a little girl. The next she'll be convinced she's seen Simon outside in the garden, sawing wood.

They're the men she loved most on earth, and now they're both gone. Some days Karen is so flooded with sadness, she fears she'll never feel happy again.

I worry more since Dad died too, she realizes. I worry about Mum all alone over in Goring; I worry about Molly and her new school; about Luke not having a close male role model; I worry about work, money . . . *Ruminating*, isn't that what the therapists call it?

Though surely it's true – I *do* have less to feel joyful about without Simon at my side, and life *is* scarier, now I'm shouldering all these responsibilities on my own. Trying to change my mood isn't something I can do simply by clicking my fingers. If I could snap out of it, I would.

She pictures the other patients – Lillie, Colin, Troy, Abby and Michael . . . They seem to be finding it hard to lift their spirits, too. Can any of us really change the way we think? Isn't that what makes us who we are; what makes me Karen?

* * *

The therapist clears her throat.

'Did you think any more about talking?' she asks.

Michael had been hoping to avoid his lunchtime one-to-one, in spite of it being scheduled in, but Gillian came to find him and knocked on the door of his room.

He picks at a cuticle.

Gillian raises an eyebrow.

He pulls at a curl of skin.

Gillian crosses and uncrosses her legs. Adjusts her shawl. 'A bit.'

He knows she is waiting for him to elaborate. But why? All this talking, he thinks. I've never been anywhere people talk so much. The groups aren't so bad. Sometimes he says a little, when directly prompted by the therapist, or if something someone else says provokes him, but usually he keeps schtum. It's the rest of the time he minds, because many – indeed most – of the other patients talk to each other morning, noon, and, so it seems, night. Over breakfast, lunch and supper, watching TV, playing board games . . . Chit-chat, chit-chat, yack-yack-yack – they never stop. So-and-so-did-this and so-and-so-did-that and my-mother-was-awful-to-me and my-boyfriend's-walked-out and my-son's-a-nightmare and my-boss-wants-to-fire-me and my-meds-aren't-working and I'm-not-going-to-make-myself-sick-I-promise and can-I-have-that-magazine-when-you've-finished and you-must-eat-some-thing and I-used-to-drink-a-bottle-of-vodka-a-day . . . They're like bloody woodpeckers, hammering at a tree. So whenever he can get away with it, Michael retreats to his room, where he lies on his bed, watching TV. Not that different to home, in that regard.

Gillian raises an eyebrow again.

'I'm used to being on my own all day,' he offers, hoping that will suffice.

'Oh yes?'

'In a shop.' He yanks harder at the piece of skin.

'Ah.'

'I used to run a florist.'

'Used to?'

'It closed,' he says, and senses himself snap shut like a clamshell. However much Gillian might try to prise him open, she can't force him. Virtually everything has been taken from him: the right to remain silent is the only power he has.

*　*　*

Karen chooses a spot on the floor between Lillie and Tash to unroll her mat. Relaxation last thing on Friday, she thinks. This should set me up well for the weekend.

197

On the other side of Tash a woman is unzipping her high-heeled boots.

'Hi,' Karen smiles, then sees who it is: the woman who drank the bottle of wine on Monday – Elaine.

'Hiya,' says Elaine. Her skin is jaundiced; the whites of her eyes are yellowed.

She doesn't recognize me, Karen realizes. Not surprising, given the state she was in.

There are a large number of participants, and after much puffing and sighing and fidgeting and shifting they've finally managed to arrange themselves when there's a soft tap on the door. Karen hears Johnnie tiptoe over and turns her head to see who's there.

'Excuse me, guys, I had to go to the bathroom. Is there room for one more?' American accent: Troy. He looks round at the crowded space. 'I sure as hell could do with this today.'

'You're just in time,' whispers Johnnie. 'Could some of you down this end of the room possibly move up?'

'Of course,' says Abby, whose mat is closest to the door.

With further adjustments they create a gap, though those lying on mats are almost touching shoulder to shoulder, like sleepers on a railway line.

'Oi. You'd better not come that close to me,' Tash warns Elaine.

'Why not?' asks Elaine. 'I got BO?'

'No, no, it's not you. I've got Tourette's. So unless you want a clout, I suggest you stay at least hitting distance apart.'

Karen fears they're going to argue, but Elaine nods and edges her mat away.

Tash is very frank, thinks Karen. How mature for her age. She's poised to pay her a whispered compliment when, on her other side, Lillie starts to giggle.

'What?' hisses Karen.

But Lillie can't seem to stop. Oh dear. She'll upset Tash or, worse, provoke Elaine.

'Shh,' Karen urges.

'Sorry,' murmurs Lillie, wiping tears from her eyes. But within seconds she is giggling again.

'What's so funny?' snaps Elaine.

Eventually Lillie manages to catch her breath. 'I was just going to say, "*It's like a madhouse in here.*"' She pauses. 'Then I realized that's exactly what this is!' And she cracks up again.

Rita, stretched out on the sofa behind them, laughs along with her. 'Ooh, you are a funny girl, Lillie.'

Soon the rest of the group are laughing too – Elaine and Tash included.

'God, I needed that,' says Abby, leaning up on her elbows and clutching her belly. 'Thank you.'

Only Troy doesn't seem to find it quite so funny. No wonder he's not in a joking mood, thinks Karen. Imagine going from all this comfort and camaraderie straight to Afghanistan.

It takes a loud, 'Shush! Everyone, time to relax,' from Johnnie for the group to quieten.

But throughout the session Karen can feel Lillie's shoulders quivering with suppressed giggles next to her, and can't help but laugh to herself too.

24

'Oh hi,' says Lillie, popping her head round the door. 'I didn't realize you were in here.'

It's Saturday afternoon and Abby is with Callum in the main lounge of Moreland's, watching *Sleeping Beauty*. There are no group sessions at the weekend, so the room is free for inpatients to use.

'Did you want to watch telly?' says Abby. 'We can go somewhere else.' Though I hope we don't have to, she thinks, Callum's so well settled. Her son is sitting cross-legged on the carpet a couple of feet away, transfixed by the screen. Glenn dropped him off so they could be together, this time just the two of them.

'No, you're fine, carry on.' Lillie perches on the arm of one of the sofas.

'You look nice,' says Abby, detecting that Lillie has lavished even more care than usual on her appearance. Her tawny hair spirals like fusilli, her lips shine with deep-red gloss and her skin is smoothed to a flawless caramel. When she adjusts the broderie anglaise bodice of her dress, Abby gets a waft of apricot.

'I'm going home today,' she says.

'I'd no idea! Permanently?' Abby knows she should be pleased for her, but without Lillie there will be a hole at Moreland's. Who's she going to sit with at mealtimes, play at cards, chat to and laugh with? Being alone with Colin won't be the same.

'It's only for tonight. Dr Kasdan suggested I do a trial run, see if I can handle it.'

'Ah.'

'But I am feeling miles better, so I'm hoping to go properly at the end of next week.'

I wish I could leave soon, thinks Abby, drinking in the back of Callum's head with longing. But she's not yet had twenty-four hours without an anxiety attack, and Dr Kasdan has recommended that she remain an inpatient until she's on a more even keel.

Just then the Disney princess breaks into song. 'Forgive the film – my husband brought it in.' Abby drops her voice. 'Callum's got a crush on Aurora.'

'Don't blame him,' says Lillie. 'All that beautiful golden hair.'

'He keeps replaying this particular bit.' Aurora glides across the screen, skirt swirling as she trills 'Once Upon a Dream'.

'Ooh, hang on.' Lillie jumps up and hurries from the room. Seconds later she's back.

'Hey, Callum.' She crouches down next to him on the carpet.

Oh dear, thinks Abby. I'm not sure how he'll respond. I hope Lillie doesn't think he's going to be like her nephew, Nino. Children on the autistic spectrum react so individually. Though the fact that Callum is tolerating Lillie's invasion of his space is unusual.

'Here,' she says.

Abby can see Lillie is proffering a strip of stickers. A whole row of glorious, glittery princesses, each wearing a different-coloured gown.

Callum glances at the stickers. His eyes widen. He cocks his head and stares at them with even greater intensity.

Abby feels goosebumps all over. 'Wow, that's unusual, he really likes them.'

Lillie beams.

Callum hesitates, then, like a lizard unfurling its tongue to catch a fly, reaches out an arm, snatches the stickers and holds them close to his chest.

'It's OK,' Lillie says to him. 'You can keep them.'

'Are you sure?' says Abby.

'Of course.' Lillie scrambles to her feet. 'My sister gave them to me.'

'Then you can't give them away.'

'It's a pleasure, honestly.'

'Thank you so much.'

'I'd better be off. I'll see you tomorrow.'

'Good luck. Wave goodbye, Callum.' Abby waves to remind him of the gesture.

Callum flaps his hand – another honour – and when Lillie leaves the room he continues to examine each princess in turn, spellbound.

'So are you all locked in?' asks Chrissie as they're buzzed through the door from reception.

'Mm,' says Michael.

'That's not very nice.'

'No.'

'You're allowed out though, aren't you, Mickey?'

'I have to wait for the door to be opened, but yes.' This isn't strictly true; in fact Michael is only permitted to leave when a member of staff is available to accompany him, even if he merely wants to go to the corner of the street. Soon he may be authorized to venture out unsupervised, but then he'll have to go with another patient, and their bags and pockets will be searched on their return in case they've purchased alcohol or anything that could be used to self-harm.

Michael leads Chrissie up the stairs.

'What lovely flowers,' she says, and they both pause on the landing to admire the display.

'Hi-and-bye, guys,' says Lillie, bouncing past.

'Blimey,' whispers Chrissie when they reach the first floor. 'She was a bit glam.'

'Did you recognize her?'

'Should I?'

'She presents *Street Dance Live*.'

'So she does! You didn't tell me she was in here with you.'

Michael is pleased to have impressed his wife. 'No, we're not supposed to say. But given you saw her anyhow.'

'Is there anyone else famous staying? Go on, you can tell me. I won't tell a soul, I promise.'

Michael isn't so sure – discretion isn't high on the list of his wife's attributes – so it's lucky the answer is 'No'.

'I'll show you the communal lounge,' he says, but comes to a halt when he sees a small boy cross-legged on the floor in front of the television and Abby sitting on one of the sofas. 'Sorry, didn't mean to interrupt. We were just having a look at the room.'

'No worries,' says Abby.

'Very nice.' Chrissie steps past him into the middle of the space. 'Cosy, isn't it?'

'I suppose.' It's not how Michael would describe a place he associates with lessons and confessions.

'Compared to the NHS.'

'I've never been to an NHS mental hospital.'

'Well, neither have I,' says Chrissie, 'but I can't imagine they're like this. I was talking to Della about you being at Moreland's the other day—' Michael shudders. Della is Chrissie's friend and he hates her being aware he's here, but worse, she's Ken's wife, so doubtless he knows too. They're local; news will be spreading fast . . . Chrissie obviously sees his expression. 'Don't fret, I made her promise not to tell anyone, and she's my friend, we can trust her. Anyway, she was saying the psychiatric hospital up at Woodingdean is where you'd have been sent normally – Sunnyvale House, it's called – apparently it's awful. People locked in their rooms and all sorts.'

Michael wants to tell Chrissie not to gossip to Della, or anyone else. He's already asked her to keep his admission to Moreland's from the kids – to have them worry too would only underline how much he's failed them – but he doesn't feel he can issue this diktat in front of Abby. He wouldn't want her to think he's ashamed they're in the same boat.

'My goodness, look at all these magazines and papers . . . Ooh, and fruit—' Chrissie helps herself to a few grapes, ' – that telly's huge . . .' She turns full circle, slowly taking everything in. 'Aw, it's *Sleeping Beauty.*' She reaches to clutch Michael's arm. 'I used to love this film!' She stops to watch for a few moments and munch grapes as the princess sings 'Once Upon a Dream'. 'The prince is hiding behind those bushes, you'll see,' she says with her mouth full.

'My son's obsessed,' says Abby.

'Bless.' Chrissie smiles down at the boy. 'How old is he?'

'Seven.'

'Nice age.'

At that moment the song finishes and the prince and princess spring apart. The prince jumps back behind the foliage, Aurora dances alone once more. Michael is momentarily puzzled, then realizes the boy is rewinding the tape via a remote control.

'C'mon, Chrissie,' he says. 'I'll show you my room.'

'Bye,' his wife says to Abby. She follows him down the corridor. 'Everyone here seems very friendly.'

Based on what, thinks Michael, leading her into his room. A fleeting glimpse of Lillie and a few words with Abby? Chrissie's perspective is so different to his own, it's as if they're having entirely unrelated experiences.

He sits down on the bed. She parks herself close to him, then leans over and pushes the door to.

Help, he thinks, I hope she doesn't want sex. Michael hasn't felt like sex for several months, not since Christmas.

She picks up his hand. 'So how *are* you then, Mickey?'

His stomach turns over; it's her pet name for him. So this is what she wants – to talk. Normally he would avoid intimate conversation whenever possible. If they were at home he'd escape to his shed, but he can't do that here.

Strangely, tears have welled up behind his eyes. I've missed her, he thinks, as she strokes the back of his hand. It's been horrible, spending a week apart, amongst so many strangers. But he doesn't say so.

'Not too great,' he admits, after a while.

'You weren't too good before you came in here, love,' she points out. 'I told you how worried I've been.'

'I know.' He's trying so hard not to cry he can hardly speak.

'Have you talked to anyone yet? You know, one of the counsellors, or something?'

'Therapists,' he corrects her. 'No, not really . . .'

'Haven't you had any sessions? I thought they said you would.'

Michael can't remember what they said when he was admitted. 'I have . . . It's just . . .'

'Yes?'

'I don't find them very easy to talk to. Her, I mean.'

His wife laughs, but gently. 'Love, you don't find *anyone* easy to talk to.'

He looks sideways at her, struggles – but manages – to give her a half-smile. 'I feel terrible about this, Chrissie. Being here and everything. I'm so sorry.' At once he's overwhelmed with guilt. All the suffering he's brought upon her – the loss of his business – *their* business, given she worked at Bloomin' Hove too – the worry about the mortgage, the kids, how they'll survive . . . and now she must be worrying about him too. 'Great breadwinner I am,' he mutters.

'Let's not focus on your being a breadwinner now—'

'I'm a shit husband and dad.'

'You are *not* a shit husband or a shit dad. And you've been a perfectly good breadwinner for years. Let's just concentrate on getting you better. We can deal with the rest later.'

But how can I *not* worry, he wants to retort. 'I've lost everything,' he says.

'We've still got the house,' says Chrissie. 'Some people don't even have that.'

We won't have it much longer if I'm not working, he thinks. He was midway through negotiation with the receivers, trying to find alternative ways to raise capital, when he ended up here. Then he remembers something they discussed in the group earlier this week; *catastrophizing*. Maybe that's what I'm doing, he realizes. I'm taking my current situation and giving it a negative spin, turning it into a catastrophe. *One step at a time*, he remembers the therapist saying. *Don't believe that just because you're in a situation now, it'll always be that way: try to live in the present. If you anticipate everything that is going to go wrong, you're more likely to make things go wrong. Far better to be open to all the possibilities.*

It seems Chrissie can almost hear what he's thinking as she says, 'I think you should make the most of being here, I really do. Given what Della says, you're pretty lucky.'

'They could transfer me to the NHS . . .' He recalls the hospital in Woodingdean, a giant white block of a building in need of painting and with too-small windows – he's driven past it many times.

'Well, then, grab this opportunity while you can. *Talk* to people, Mickey. Have you spoken to the psychiatrist about medication?'

'Dr Kasdan, yes . . .' Michael went to the appointment he had scheduled earlier this week and nodded and agreed, reluctantly, to consider trying something the doctor called an *SSRI*, but he's not started taking any pills. The nurses keep urging him, saying how much they can help, but their enthusiasm only makes him more reluctant. He can't shake the image of Nurse Ratched in *One Flew Over The Cuckoo's Nest* doling out mind-numbing medication, and fears he'll end up much, much worse.

'Good.' His wife nods. 'When's your next chat with this – um – therapist? Is she really that awful? I'm sure you could ask to change if you truly don't like her.'

'I'm seeing her on Monday.' He pictures Gillian sitting opposite him in her paisley shawl. She appears so formidable with that bun and in those glasses! Then he remembers what she's been like running the group sessions – she led a couple this week. She was funny – dry – and some of her suggestions seem to have helped other patients a great deal. It was Gillian who spoke of catastrophizing, wasn't it? Maybe it's me, he acknowledges. And I'd rather have her than Johnnie. 'You're right, she's not so bad. I'll stick with her.'

'Excellent.' Chrissie gives him a hug. They clasp one another in silence for a while, breathing almost in unison; Michael can feel Chrissie's bosom pressing against his chest. Eventually he pulls away. Chrissie looks at him and does her best to smile. 'But you *must* talk to her, Mickey. If you won't do it for you, please, will you do it for me?'

25

'Oh my God!' Anna shrieks into her mobile. 'That's fantastic news!'

'What?' says Karen, trying to keep focused on driving.

Anna waves at her to be quiet. 'How much does he weigh?'

Karen's heart soars – *Lou's had her baby*. How wonderful, she thinks. Lou wanted this so much, and so did the man whom she found to father the child, Adam. He's gay and lives in Brighton too.

Sure enough, when she's rung off, Anna says, 'That was Adam calling from the hospital.' She turns to face Molly and Luke in the back. 'Lou's had her baby. It's a boy.'

'EEEEEEEEEEEEEEEEEEEE!'

Karen shakes her head and smiles. No one does excitement quite like my daughter, she thinks. This is turning into a truly lovely day.

'GOOD,' says Luke. Karen glances at his reflection in the mirror. His expression – a nod, a small yet contented smile – conveys that macho honour has been upheld.

'Can we see them now, Mummy? *Now?*' Molly is bouncing in her car seat.

Lord, thinks Karen. There'll be no peace until we do. But I thought we were heading home, and I'm tired – we've been gardening for hours. I have to be careful at the moment – that's what everyone's been telling me at Moreland's – so I mustn't overdo it.

She leans over to Anna. 'Would you like to go now too?' She mutters ventriloquist-style in a bid to keep the children from catching on.

'It would suit me perfectly,' says Anna, voice also low.

'*Pleeeaaaaaaaaaaaase,*' says Molly.

I haven't seen much of Lou lately, Karen reminds herself, and I'm keen to meet the baby. 'Did Adam say anything about visitors?'

'Only that Lou was exhausted. But we wouldn't need to stay long . . .' cajoles Anna.

Karen frowns, weighing it up. 'If we are going today, I'd much rather go straight there. Otherwise I'll be very late giving these two their tea.' And I'll run out of energy completely, she thinks. Yet being at the clinic has also reminded her that connections with friends are very important, and that clinches it. Karen raises her voice once more. 'You got those flowers, Molly?'

She can hear a rustle as Molly waves the bunch of tulips she picked at the allotment.

'Right then,' she says. 'Kemptown here we come.'

* * *

When Chrissie has gone, Michael returns to the lounge. Might as well start now, he decides, before I change my mind; with fewer people around, it's less daunting. Abby is still in there, but alone, stretched out on one of the sofas, flicking through a magazine.

'Hello again,' he says, lowering himself into an armchair.

Abby starts. 'Hi.'

I bet she's amazed I'm speaking to her, thinks Michael, immediately self-conscious. Other than in group sessions I've barely said a word to her since we bumped into each other in the corridor.

To his relief Abby opens the conversation. 'I hope you've been sleeping better?'

'Er, yes,' he lies. 'You?'

'Not really.' Abby sighs. 'I'd like to know your secret.'

Oh no, he thinks. I haven't got one. I should have been more honest. Unsure how to continue, he reaches to the coffee table for the paper, has a quick leaf through. But he could do that in his room, and anyway *The Times* has never been his rag. *Talk!* he hears Chrissie urge. He coughs, braces himself, then says, 'So was that your boy?'

Abby lets the magazine flop to her stomach to see him more easily. 'Yes, my husband – soon to be ex – has taken him home.'

'Nice-looking kid.'

'Thank you.'

'So you said in group he's autistic?'

'He has autism, yes.'

'Do you mind my asking exactly what that is? I've never really understood.'

'I don't mind,' says Abby, propping herself up on her elbows. 'And it's a good question, because there's no single thing that defines diagnosis. It's what they call a spectrum disorder, so it covers a range of conditions. But there are some common factors.' She curls up her fingers. 'A problem with spoken language, mannerisms such as hand-flapping, a fixation on parts of objects . . .' She unfurls her fingers one by one. 'Little or no eye contact, a lack of interest in other children and difficulties with playing and make-believe . . .' She stops. She's run out of digits, and her expression is hard to fathom. I bet she's been through this list countless times, thinks Michael. I shouldn't have brought the subject up. Yet Abby continues. 'It's like his senses are wired differently – imagine if smells were really loud, or noises made you feel sick – that's how overwhelming it seems to be for him sometimes.'

'That sounds a lot for a little boy to manage,' says Michael.

'Yeah, but not everything's like that. You might have noticed he was particularly fascinated by the same bit of *Sleeping Beauty* earlier? He loves that.'

'Is that why he was rewinding it?'

Abby nods.

'So will he get better?'

'Er . . . It's not something you outgrow, but he will change and develop, yes. Some adults with autism are able to live relatively independent lives, others will always need lots of support . . .' Her voice fades.

'He doesn't look like there's anything wrong with him,' says Michael. 'Well, not wrong, but . . .' Oh God, what a mess I'm making of this, he thinks. Why did I choose such a tricky subject? 'I mean, you can't tell he's disabled.'

'Actually, I prefer to call it a disorder.'

'Oh, sorry.' Michael's cheeks flush.

'It's fine,' says Abby. 'I'd much rather you asked about it than were too embarrassed, and you're right – it's hard because Callum doesn't look any different from other kids. I can't tell you the number of times I've had to cope with people assuming he's being naughty or slow or lazy or rude, when . . . frankly, he's just being Callum.'

'That must be frustrating.'

'It is.' Abby raises her eyes to the ceiling. 'There you are, trying to catch a child who's like, running round a cafe blowing out the tea lights on all the tables or something, which can be hard as, trust me, Callum is fast on his feet. Then you get some busybody mum or dad – I don't know why, but it's often the dads – telling you to control your son.' She shakes her head.

Life can be so unfair, thinks Michael, reminded of his dealings with Hotel sur Plage. 'People can be such pigs.'

'Yes, they can.' Again Abby sighs. 'So, that was your wife, was it, in just now?'

'Chrissie, yes.'

'She seemed nice.' Abby smiles.

Michael senses she's inviting him to reveal more. He pauses, wondering what to say about Chrissie, then shares the first thought that springs to mind. 'We've been together thirty years.' He has a tiny burst of pride. It's been ages since he's felt proud of anything he's accomplished.

Abby nods. 'That's a long time.'

Oops, how tactless. Abby only just said she and her husband are separating. *See,* he says to himself, *you're no good at this.* He adds, 'We've had our ups and downs, of course.' And this is one almighty down, he thinks.

'You wouldn't be human if you hadn't. Have you got any children?'

'Er, yes, Ryan and Kelly.' He feels another surge of pride, but hesitates. Given Abby's situation, it seems crass to enthuse.

'How old are they?'

'Ryan's twenty-one, Kelly's nineteen.' Michael tries to hold back, but the mere mention of their names means he can't help himself. He feels so bad about letting them down that he's tried to block off thinking about them, but now he can't resist. 'Would you like to see a photo?'

'Yeah.' Abby swivels so she's sitting upright. 'I'd love to.'

He stands to access his trouser pocket and pulls out his wallet, then unclips the popper and flicks it open. Behind the small plastic window designed for ID is a snap of the pair of them. It's a few years old, so faded and battered, but it captures them nonetheless. Ryan has inherited Michael's strong features and dark hair, whereas Kelly looks more like her mum, red-haired and delicate.

'That's Ryan on the right,' he says, stating the obvious, and hands Abby his wallet. She peers closely at the image.

What a fantastic holiday that was, Michael recalls. They were camping in Scotland, but were blessed with the weather. The kids caught the sun, which is why Ryan is tanned and Kelly so freckled in this photograph. Both of them are smiling at the camera; Kelly is beaming, unselfconscious, but Ryan's grin is slightly awkward – *Dad, do you have to?* it communicates. Nonetheless Michael treasures the photo. Whenever he so much as glances at it, he senses they're smiling at him.

* * *

'Wait, you two!' cries Karen, but Molly and Luke are excited and race on ahead. They push open the door of the ward and rush over to Lou's bedside.

'For you.' Molly thrusts the tulips at her, arms rigid.

The leaves are a touch slug-eaten, the petals are crushed and they're wrapped in silver foil, but Lou looks delighted. 'Thank you.'

As Karen approaches with Anna, she can see the baby at Lou's breast.

'Hold on a minute, poppet,' she says to her daughter. 'Sorry,' she says to Lou. 'Molly, can't you see, Lou isn't able to take those right now?'

'Oh,' says Molly.

'She's got the baby just there,' Karen explains. From Molly's height he is probably not visible, wrapped in a blanket. Karen gets a glimpse of dark hair and a scrunched-up face. 'Oh, Lou, he's gorgeous!'

'Can I see him?' says Molly.

Karen lifts up her daughter and Lou carefully edges down the cover to reveal his face more fully. His skin is all red and blotchy and his brow is damp, yet Karen can see her friend is overcome with love.

'He's got *lots* of hair!' says Molly, impressed.

'It's really dark,' says Luke.

'I can see red in it,' says Karen, now the baby is in more light. 'Though it's likely to fall out.'

Molly looks worried.

'It'll grow back,' Lou assures her. 'That's what happens with newborns.'

'You had very dark hair when you were a baby, and look at you now,' says Karen. Molly tosses her blonde curls; she's aware of her assets already, thinks Karen. 'You must be wrung out,' she says to Lou. 'Well done, you.'

'Now he's here, it's all been worth it.'

'He's beautiful,' says Anna, peering too.

'Thank you.'

'Look at his tiny fingers,' says Anna. 'They're so small and perfect. And those nails – wow, they're paper-thin, aren't they?' She inhales. 'Ah . . . He even smells new.'

Just then Adam arrives with two cups of tea.

Anna turns to him. 'Congratulations.'

Adam beams. 'Did you want me to get you some?' he asks, putting down the cups. 'The machine's down the corridor.'

'No, don't worry,' says Karen. 'We won't stay long – I need to give these two their supper. But they were desperate to see the baby.'

'Has he got a name yet?' asks Anna.

'We think so,' says Adam, and Lou nods. 'We're going to live with it for a few days, before we let everyone know.'

'Are you Lou's boyfriend?' asks Molly.

Karen shakes her head. 'I'm sorry. I've tried to explain.'

'No . . .' says Adam. Thankfully, neither he nor Lou seems fazed. 'But I am the baby's daddy.'

Molly frowns, perplexed.

'I blame Disney.' Karen drops her voice. 'She's determined to find a prince for everyone. I'll have another go at helping her understand.'

'It's OK,' says Adam.

'You know, I think he looks a bit like you,' says Anna. 'He has a similar hairline.'

Adam appears so chuffed it's as if he might burst. At once Karen thinks of Simon, how he was when Luke was born, here in this very hospital. She can picture him now: his big, bear-like presence such a contrast to the tiny, fragile bundle in his arms, his face shining with happiness.

26

'Hey,' says Lillie. 'When I was home at the weekend, I heard something really bonkers.'

'What?' Karen and Tash lean forward.

'There's a new family moved into the same apartment block as me and my sister and guess what their kids are called?' Lillie grins. 'You'll love this, Michael—'

Karen glances over. Michael looks unconvinced.

'Firstly, there's a girl; she's called Infinity.'

'Bit hippy,' says Rick.

'Oh dear,' says Karen. 'That's not terribly fair on the poor child, is it?'

'Hope she's good at maths,' says Tash.

'But—' Lillie splutters, ' – the best one is the son. You'll never guess what his name is—'

'What?'

'Box,' she says, deadpan.

'*Box?*'

'Yup. B-O-X. Box.'

Rick guffaws.

'You're kidding,' says Tash.

'Oh my goodness. Brighton parents can be a bit peculiar, can't they?' Rita, who lives in more conventional Worthing, looks concerned.

But Abby and I are Brighton parents, thinks Karen. Though she knows what Rita means.

Michael coughs. 'Good job they didn't call his sister Cardboard,' he says.

That's the first time I've heard him crack a joke, Karen notices, as their laughter fills the room.

'My, you sound like you're all having a good time,' says Johnnie, striding into the room and folding his long limbs onto a chair at the opposite end of the lounge. He beams. 'Welcome, everyone. I believe we've all met before.'

What a difference a week makes, thinks Karen, recalling her fear seven days earlier. Even so, when Johnnie says, 'Let's start with check-in and goal-setting,' she has a flurry of nerves.

'I went home at the weekend,' says Lillie. 'It was weird to be back after so long in here.' She scans the group. 'I hung out with my sister and played with my nephew Nino and I love doing that. The lithium dosage seems to be working so I'm more level – I didn't feel manic at all. It's good.' As she shakes out the spirals of her hair, Karen is reminded of her daughter. 'The only downside is my appetite has increased. I'm definitely putting on weight.' Lillie pinches the teeniest bit of flesh disparagingly. If only I had that amount of fat to worry about, thinks Karen. 'Anyway, my aim is to leave this Friday and become a day patient for a bit.'

'That's great to hear, Lillie. Who's next?'

Off they go: Rick has cut back on caffeine and has a thumping headache; Rita is still having panic attacks but vows to meditate more; Tash is feeling better knowing she has the safety net of being a day patient; Colin has finished with his girlfriend.

'Worrying about her dumping me was doing my head in,' he says. 'I've decided to focus on getting myself better first.'

There's a pause and Karen is poised to speak when Michael cuts in. 'I had a chat with my wife at the weekend – or rather, she had a chat with me.' He cracks a laugh. 'She suggested I should – how did she put it? "Talk to people, Mickey!"—' he adopts an exasperated voice, ' – so I'm trying hard to do that.'

'He's been doing pretty well.' Abby nods at him.

'I've got a one-to-one with Gillian after this, and I'm going to try and be a bit more, um, open.' He sits back on the sofa, clearly relieved to have got this speech over with. Karen catches his eye and smiles at him.

'My turn?' Abby asks. 'I'm OK . . . Better than last week, but I'm worried about being in here beyond, say, Friday. I'd like to go when Lillie does.'

'Ten days in here is no time,' says Colin.

'But I want to get home and look after my son.'

'I met him,' says Lillie. 'Lovely boy.'

'Try not to race ahead into the future, or judge yourself against others,' says Johnnie. 'How are you feeling right now?'

Abby jiggles her legs. 'Impatient, I guess.'

'And what's your goal – not for Friday, for today?'

'Hmm . . . Maybe *not* to think of the future, then?'

'It's almost impossible not to think of it *at all*. Though that sounds like a good aim.' There's a pause. 'That leaves you, Karen?'

'Oh . . . yes.' She'd been miles away. She lets out a long sigh. 'I was just thinking of Troy.'

The room falls quiet. As far as Karen is aware, Troy shared little of his experience in combat with any of them. Nonetheless surely everyone has seen Afghanistan often enough in the news to be able to picture him in some way: crouching down in the dust as a booby trap explodes feet away; sweltering in layers of protective clothing having not showered for days; sharing a sixteen-man tent in the middle of the wilderness; taking refuge from sniper fire behind a rock, even firing a machine gun himself.

'It made me realize I'm lucky to be here.' She glances round. They all look very serious. 'Sorry. I didn't mean to bring everyone down.'

'It can be hard when a member of the group leaves.'

'I suppose I connected with him because I think about death a lot . . .'

Johnnie nods.

'Perhaps my aim today should be not to.' Karen gives a half-hearted smile, though inside she is shaken. She is surprised to glance up and see Michael is gazing straight at her.

'He's a brave man going back,' he says.

*   *   *

There's a respectful pause, then Johnnie stands to pick up a marker. 'Thank you. A couple of things struck me just now.

Firstly, when I was listening to you, Abby, it occurred to me that this is an example of anxious thinking. Why is that?'

'Because it's future-focused,' says Lillie.

'Indeed. If you're feeling fearful, overwhelmed and that you can't cope, that's anxiety.'

Those are my symptoms, thinks Abby.

'On the other hand, if your thoughts tend towards regret and guilt about what's happened, broadly speaking, that's depression. Another thing I noticed — and it was subtle — is a touch of what is often called *people pleasing*. It came from you, Karen.'

'Oh, gosh.' Karen blushes.

'There's no need to feel bad.' Johnnie writes the two words on the board. 'Everyone does it. When you mentioned Troy, you apologized for bringing the group down, which was considerate. It's only that if we spend our time feeling responsible for others and putting their needs first, it can result in not getting our own needs met, and this is why it can be linked to depression.'

'You did it last week too,' Lillie says to Karen. 'You apologized to everyone for crying.'

'Did I? I'm so sorry.'

Lillie laughs. 'Stop apologizing!'

By now Karen is puce. Abby feels for her — Lillie's only teasing, but it can't be pleasant being held up as an example.

'If friends have told me once I'm always putting other people before myself, they've told me a hundred times,' says Karen. 'I did it at the weekend, too.'

Johnnie asks, 'Would you mind telling us what happened?'

'Though don't do it just to please him.' Colin chuckles.

'It was on Saturday afternoon. We were driving back from the allotment, and I was tired and looking forward to putting my feet up, when someone rang to say a friend – a good friend – had had a baby. And my kids were desperate to see the baby, and my other friend, who I was with, wanted to go too, so I agreed to drive us all to the hospital.'

'Even though you didn't want to go?'

Karen frowns. 'No, I *did* want to. It wasn't as if I was coerced. Not remotely. I'd probably have gone the next day if it had purely been up to me, but I didn't want to disappoint the children.'

'Still, it shows how somewhere, in your list of priorities, you're lower down than your children and your friend,' says Johnnie. 'You were driving?'

'Yes.'

'So actually, *you* were the most important person, as if you weren't up to making the journey, then you weren't obligated to make it.'

'Er . . .' Karen scrunches up her nose. 'It's difficult when you've got kids.'

I bet Johnnie hasn't got children, thinks Abby. 'I'm sure lots of mums would do as Karen did,' she says.

'Of course,' says Johnnie. 'But it's also important to learn to say no – even to children.'

'I do find it hard,' says Karen.

'If we always say yes to everything, it's exhausting, isn't it?'

Karen nods. 'I have been awfully tired lately.'

'Perhaps you need to put yourself first more often,' says Lillie.

'I don't let my children get their way the whole time, though. Otherwise they'd be horribly spoilt.'

I bet she's a great mum, thinks Abby. She seems kind and generous, but I reckon she's no fool.

'Setting boundaries is a vital step in taking responsibility for yourself and your life,' says Johnnie.

Sounds like he's reading from a textbook, thinks Abby, irritated. Just like the therapist I saw at college.

'But surely it's a good thing to help others,' interjects Rita.

'Sometimes I think we don't help one another enough,' says Tash.

'Exactly,' Abby mutters, hackles rising as she recalls how often people look away when she's having trouble with Callum.

'I'm always very grateful when people stop to help me.' The silk of Rita's sari rustles as she strokes her troublesome leg.

Tash nods, bright-pink hair serving to emphasize the gesture. 'If the world was full of everyone looking out for themselves, no one would ever lend Rita a hand to get on a bus.'

Rita and Tash smile at one another, pleased to be in agreement.

'Perhaps I wasn't being clear,' says Johnnie. 'I'm not saying we shouldn't help each other, not at all, and getting a response from someone if we're kind to them can be very rewarding too.'

Again Abby thinks of Callum. She'd love more response from him; often she craves it.

Johnnie continues, 'But putting other people first *continually* can be a sign we're depressed. If we *never* say no, or our boundaries aren't firm enough because we're always doing things for others, including our children, what is the danger?' He looks round at them all.

'We end up not knowing who we are?' says Lillie.

'Precisely. We lose our sense of self.'

Lillie nods. 'I read somewhere it's important for children to have boundaries so they learn about their mum's needs, too.'

Suddenly it strikes Abby. *They're talking about me!* she thinks. Yet they sound so smug and judgemental. It's one thing for Johnnie to be a know-all – he's in charge – but to be lectured by Lillie is galling. Anyone who can spend that long getting ready each day clearly doesn't have the kind of demands on them Karen and I do. Does she think I wouldn't *love* to say no more often so I could spend time nurturing myself? I used to enjoy experimenting with my hair and dressing up before Callum was born. People would say what quirky style I had, tell me I had a great figure. When I was at college I used to dance, go clubbing, I was quite the hedonist. Imagine what would happen if I started acting more selfishly now – the speed at which my son operates, he could break a couple of TV screens in the time it takes to paint my toenails. And there's already one parent being belligerent around the house; if I started saying no as much as Glenn does, all hell would break loose.

'When you're a mother it's not always possible to put yourself first,' she says tightly. 'It sounds as if you're saying there's something wrong with Karen making her children a priority, or me wanting to get home to look after my son as soon as I can. I don't think there's anything wrong with it at all.'

'But you can't look after anyone else properly until you can look after yourself,' says Lillie. 'You shouldn't let others define you.'

Abby's anger rises. 'It seems you're telling Karen and me how to parent. You know my little boy can't even say the word "no"? He understands it, but still, you haven't a clue how difficult these things are with him. Just because he accepted those stickers you gave him on Saturday, Lillie, you think he's always like that?'

'No, Abby, please, I wasn't—'

'I've spent the last seven years putting my son first – I'm his mother, for fuck's sake, and if I don't, who else is going to? Not the bloody authorities, let me assure you.'

Lillie's mouth falls open, but Abby doesn't care.

'When you have a child, they're like an extension of yourself. They're *part* of you. Unless you have kids, you can't possibly know that.' She looks pointedly at Johnnie, then Lillie.

Lillie grips the seat of the sofa. Her face drains of colour.

'It's OK,' says Rita, who is sitting on the adjacent armchair. She reaches over to squeeze Lillie's arm and drops her voice. 'She doesn't know.'

Know what? thinks Abby, as Colin jumps up and goes to crouch at Lillie's side.

'She doesn't, Lil,' he says.

Oh God, thinks Abby, what have I said? But before she can ask, Lillie has leapt to her feet and run from the room, black rivers of mascara streaming down her face.

27

Michael sits down in the chair opposite Gillian. 'My wife wants me to talk to you properly,' he says.

Gillian nods. There's a silence, then she asks, 'What about you, Michael, do you want to?'

'I'm not sure.' He pauses. 'Yes, I *do* want to. It's just I'm not sure if I can.'

Gillian clasps her hands together. 'It's difficult for you, Michael, I understand that. Sometimes the worst bit is getting started, then it becomes easier, as with a lot of things we're afraid of.'

Michael looks down at his cuticles. He sees a loose bit of skin that needs picking, but he stops himself. 'I don't know where to begin.' He shrugs.

'Well . . . How about you tell me about the circumstances that brought you in here?'

The last few weeks were so awful, I can't possibly unravel them into anything coherent, thinks Michael. He says nothing. He can hear the clock ticking on the wall.

Eventually Gillian coughs. 'I hope you don't mind me saying, but before . . . you mentioned a shop . . . ?'

It's as if he's been kicked in the gut, and next thing he knows, out the story spews. It still feels so raw it could be happening to him right there and then.

*

'Right. That's me done,' Michael says to Ali, clicking the padlock together to secure the grille across the window. He looks up at the Bloomin' Hove sign.

'Oh mate, I'm so sorry.' His friend's dark-brown eyes glisten with tears.

'Don't you start.' Once Ali goes, he'll go himself.

Michael steps forward and reaches out his arms to Ali. They thump one another on the back, once, twice, and break apart.

'You stay in touch,' says Ali.

'I will,' Michael says, although he doesn't know if he can bear to.

He climbs into his MPV, gives a quick wave and drives off.

It's a gloomy, overcast day; there's no breeze to carry away the clouds and the air is heavy. Back in Rottingdean, the bungalow feels pointedly empty. As Michael steps over the threshold, his footsteps echo on the parquet floor. He's not told Chrissie this is his last day yet; he decided to hand over the keys first, then say, so she isn't expecting him home this early. She must have gone out.

He goes into the living-cum-dining room; there's a letter

addressed to him lying in the middle of the polished oak table.

He opens the envelope, scans the contents. It takes a few seconds to process. He reads it again to make sure, but yes.

They want the car.

He stands there, letting the shock wash over him.

After a few moments, he pulls open the French windows, steps outside. The path is lined with daffodils leading down to the end of the garden and there, against the back wall – the shed.

His shed.

No sooner has he clapped eyes on it than it's as if the energy he's pent up from so many weeks sitting in front of the telly comes back in a flood of adrenalin and testosterone. He isn't fifty-three. He isn't tired and grey-haired and living in Rottingdean. He's seventeen. He's a peroxide punk, from Croydon. And he's livid.

FUCKING livid.

He throws open the door. *BAM!* The thin wooden walls shake. With robotic determination he reaches for his sledge-hammer; the very same sledgehammer he used to knock through the hatch from the kitchen to the dining area. Then, like a warrior wielding a weapon as if his life depended on it, he brings it down on one of the shelves. The chipboard isn't strong and neither is the bracket. Jars tumble with a tinkle of nails and screws.

BAM! He thwacks the shelf above. Boxes of electrical wires and plugs jump high into the air then thud onto the floor.

BAM! He hits the wall itself. Years of damp air and sea

salt have taken their toll – the wood is soft, like tissue paper.

BAM! He strikes his workbench – the wood is laminated, stronger. So he goes at it again – *BAM! BAM!* – and eventually it splits in two, jagged with splinters.

Far away he hears someone calling his name, but he simply turns to the rear wall.

The sledgehammer goes straight through the old Formica dresser; the doors ping from their rusted hinges. He turns his arm to use the sledgehammer as a hook, and in one movement scoops the pots of paint and white spirit and putty and filler from the inside of the cupboard, with a clatter of tin on tin, to join the chaos on the floor. The lid comes off some ancient white gloss; it gloops, sticky as honey, coating the broken shards of glass and a roll of wallpaper.

'MICHAEL!'

Michael spins round. There's a figure standing at the open door of the shed but he can barely see through the red mist.

He turns back, raises the sledgehammer above his head and – *BAM!* – brings it down.

The dresser is demolished. Good. He never liked it anyway.

'WHAT ARE YOU DOING?'

But Michael moves to face the third wall.

'MICKEY, STOP!'

Out of the corner of his eye he's vaguely aware of Chrissie, dressed in her coat and scarf. Just as he's about to bring the sledgehammer down once more, she grabs his right arm.

'NO!'

He bats her away with his elbow. She stumbles but just manages to steady herself. He's dimly aware she can't be badly hurt and is glad, but he's gladder still when she hurries off up the garden path. He carries on until he's razed the shed to the ground.

*

'So what happened then?' asks Gillian.

'Chrissie rang the police,' says Michael.

'I see.'

To his mortification, Michael finds himself too choked up to speak. 'She must have been very scared to call 999,' he says, after a while.

'Maybe,' says Gillian. 'But it was a good thing to do in the circumstances.'

'I've never raised a hand to my wife though, honestly. I wouldn't have hurt her.'

'Perhaps she was worried you'd hurt yourself.'

'I was just so far gone . . .'

'I understand.'

Do you? I can't imagine you ever getting that angry, thinks Michael. He glances up at Gillian; her face seems to have softened. Perhaps she isn't that much older than he is, after all; she just appears that way. 'You seem pretty patient to me,' he says.

Gillian gives a half-smile.

'You've waited a long time for me to say anything.'

She raises an eyebrow. There's an understated humour in that gesture, he thinks. I like it. 'Aye, well . . .'

'Chrissie says it's not helping that I bottle stuff up.'

'Do you think she's right?'

232

'I find it hard to talk about . . . er . . . my feelings.' Though it wasn't as hard as I thought it would be, he realizes. 'I guess when I do let it all out, it's quite spectacular, isn't it?' He laughs. 'I hope it was worth waiting for.'

'It was.'

Michael feels a small burst of satisfaction. 'Reckon that's why the doctor got me admitted here – he was concerned I'd trash all of Rottingdean.'

'Might I ask why you chose the shed, in particular?'

He is silent, casting his mind back. 'I'm not sure.'

'It's purely, from how you've described it, you were in the house when you opened the letter. So why not – I don't know – turn over the table or the sofa or break the TV in there? You must have been pretty fed up after watching so much television.'

Michael pictures the living-cum-dining room at their bungalow. He shakes his head. 'I couldn't do that. Not with all those family photographs watching me.' In his mind's eye he can see Chrissie's carefully dusted china ornaments, the plumped cushions on the sofa, the freshly vacuumed rug by the hearth. 'It's Chrissie's room.'

'It's not yours, too?'

'Yeah, but Chrissie works really hard to make the house nice . . .' Michael sighs. His wife's dedication both touches and dismays him. On the one hand he'd hate for her to let things slip; on the other it seems to underline his own shortcomings. 'I guess I went outside because . . .' He struggles to recall the sequence of events. 'When I read that letter, I was so angry . . . I've had run-ins with mates as a teenager, punched the wall, that sort of thing, in the past . . . But that afternoon – I can't remember ever feeling like that before. My skull was going to burst. I had to do something.'

Gillian nods.

'All those people, wanting a piece of my business. Tim and Lawrence from the hotel, Bob, even Jan . . .' He can feel sweat breaking out on the back of his neck at the memory. 'They shafted me.'

'It sounds as if you feel circumstances really conspired against you, Michael.' Gillian stops, then says, very deliberately, 'And I do appreciate it must have been horribly frustrating. But all these reactions you're talking about – the anger, the sense of injustice – are just thoughts, or that's where they start out. And thoughts can be changed. I'd venture to suggest if you look at what happened from a different perspective, you could see that you were very gallant.'

Michael shakes his head, confused.

'I mean, you didn't smash up the house, which would have upset Chrissie and your children much more, or the car, which some folk might have been tempted to do, to stop the receivers having it.'

'I suppose.'

'So the person who was going to suffer most as a result of your actions wasn't someone you owed money to, or even ultimately your family, was it?'

It was me, thinks Michael. I hadn't seen it like that. He nods slowly.

'Yeah . . . Chrissie was quite understanding about it, considering. Of course she was upset, but I'd have expected her to go completely mad.' He laughs. 'Guess she left that one to me.'

28

Abby taps on the door of the nurses' office.

'Sorry to interrupt,' she says to Sangeeta, who's busy on a computer. 'I was wondering if you've seen Lillie?'

'She's in the art room.'

Sure enough, Lillie is sitting at the large table in the studio, painting.

'Can I have a word?'

Lillie lifts her brush from the canvas and turns to Abby. Her make-up has been repaired – expertly applied eyeliner and mascara mask the obvious signs, but her cheeks are still swollen and blotchy. She has obviously been crying for a while, thinks Abby, filled with remorse.

'I'm really sorry about earlier. I didn't mean to upset you.' Abby holds her breath, fearing her apology is inadequate.

Lillie smiles. 'It's OK. You weren't to know you'd hit a nerve. And I was being out of order, or from your point of view it must have seemed that way. I'm just so keen for people to value themselves properly. Gillian would say I was "projecting"—' she mimics the therapist's Scottish accent, ' – and my real issue is valuing myself.'

Lillie resumes painting, and although Abby is curious to know what sparked her tears, she assumes it's not her place to ask. Still, she doesn't feel like leaving yet. She looks around the room. Works of art line the walls – patients have contributed everything from childlike daubs to painstakingly stitched samplers. Boxes of crayons, coloured pencils, felt tips and tubes of paint are piled on top of a large chest of drawers; the drawers themselves, according to the labels, contain sewing materials, wool, paper and plasticine. In the corner are a couple of easels. It reminds me of primary school, thinks Abby. Except for a large sign that says *NO SCISSORS* – even children would be trusted with those.

She turns her attention to Lillie's painting. In the centre is a large black hole, surrounded by circles which lighten gradually through maroon to a bright, blood red. Lillie is focused on adding what looks to be a bird to the top left corner.

'Do you mind if I watch?' asks Abby.

'Not at all.'

She pulls up a chair, taking care not to knock over the plastic cup of water Lillie is using to dilute her paints.

'Are those acrylics?' Abby peers at the chipped china plate being used as a palette. Round the outside are freshly squeezed blobs of red, yellow, blue and white; in the centre is a large swirl of scarlet.

'Yup. I'm not that good at this—' Lillie nods at her sheet of paper, ' – but I enjoy it.'

'Oh, I think it's lovely,' says Abby, and whilst the abstract picture is not something she would want hanging in her home, she means it, if for no other reason than that it seems to be giving Lillie pleasure. As Abby watches Lillie dab tiny dots of white with seemingly little forethought, she has a hankering to give it a go. *I can't remember when I last allowed my imagination to roam like that,* she muses. *Photo-journalism was a long way removed from such free creative expression, but years ago, when I was doing my degree, I used to paint all the time.*

They sit in companionable silence, save for the occasional swish of Lillie cleaning her brush in water, until Lillie says, 'I'm sorry I didn't explain earlier – I didn't feel up to sharing it in group, and I guess I've been trying to move on, to put it behind me. It's not something I've told that many people here. But you know I was admitted before?'

Abby nods.

Lillie drops her brush into the cup and turns to face her. 'I had trauma therapy.' She takes a deep breath of air into her lungs and lets it out slowly, exactly as they've been taught, to help calm herself. 'I know I've been in a few times, but when I came in here initially, they just got me back, stable, then let me go again. I say "just", but that was a big enough job – I was in a bad way. I wasn't sleeping at all and I was completely manic – drinking, not eating. I blew five grand in a single day in Churchill Square.'

Abby is agog. She'd find it hard to spend a tenth of that in one trip to the shopping centre.

Lillie continues, 'I didn't really let any of the staff here in then. But the second time, maybe it's because I trusted them more or maybe I was so desperate I was willing to try anything. Certainly I was terrified, as it was the second psychotic episode I'd had in less than a year. Anyway, as luck would have it, Gillian was allocated to be my therapist from the outset – she's the only one here qualified to do trauma therapy. So I ended up doing some really deep work with her, because we realized there was still loads of stuff that was fucked up in here.' She taps the side of her head.

Abby nods. I've an idea how that feels, she thinks. Though I've never been as bad as Lillie. 'I gather trauma therapy is very intense,' she says.

'You're telling me – you have to re-look at past events, so it's horrible . . .' Another deep breath. 'I find it hard to talk about even now . . . But when I was small, right from the age of about seven through to when I left home, I was abused by my stepfather and two of his friends. My mum worked shifts, and they used to come to the house when she was out.'

Abby is so shocked she can't think what to say. Eventually she blurts, 'How awful,' but the words seem hopelessly inadequate.

'I don't want to go into detail, but so you understand, what triggered me in the group was what you said about having kids. Because what finally brought everything to a stop was that I got pregnant.'

Abby flushes with guilt. 'Oh God, I really am so sorry.'

'You weren't to know,' repeats Lillie.

'No, but . . . I should have been more sensitive. What's that saying – *until we've walked a mile in someone else's shoes?* I can't remember exactly, but it's about not judging others, and I did. I assumed you were being preachy. I get a lot of it, what with Callum, and people who think they know all about autism . . .' This isn't about you, Abby, she reminds herself. 'Anyway, I can't apologize enough.'

Lillie shrugs. 'As I said, it's OK.'

'So can I ask, did you . . . er—' Abby hesitates, choosing her words carefully, ' – terminate the pregnancy?' Lillie's made no mention of having a child.

'I didn't, no. Even though my stepfather wanted me to. Even though I had no idea who the father was . . .' Yet another exhalation. 'I lost the baby. Maybe it was my body's way of saying I couldn't be a mum to this particular child . . .' Her eyes well up.

'Maybe,' Abby nods. 'Miscarriages happen for all sorts of reasons.'

'No . . .' Lillie's voice is small. 'The pregnancy ran full term. Everything seemed to be OK. Then the baby was still-born. So you see, I do have experience of having children, in a way . . .' She brushes away tears with the back of her hand.

Abby feels herself welling up too. This is even worse than I realized, she thinks. Poor Lillie. How I wish I could rewind the last few minutes of the morning's session.

'I was trying to express my feelings in this picture. It's something Beth suggested in group – you know how into creative outlets she is – and I do find it helps.'

Abby examines the painting again.

'That's my baby girl, there,' says Lillie, regaining her composure. She points at what Abby had assumed was a bird. The trail of dots in its wake suggests it has emerged from the dark core.

'She looks like an angel,' observes Abby.

They are both silent, staring, absorbing. After a while Abby asks, 'Do you think your bipolar illness could be connected to everything you've been through? Though, please—' she holds up a hand, ' – you don't have to answer if you don't want.'

Once more Lillie shrugs. 'I've no idea. My sister, Tamara – she was abused too, and she's fine . . . Well, not fine, obviously, but she's not bipolar. Who knows? Different people react differently to similar events, Gillian says. Although she did tell me damage from emotional trauma can result in actual physical changes inside the brain which can affect someone's response to stress and stuff. There was probably something in me, something chemical, that was misaligned already . . . But yes, maybe without all that *shit*—' she spits the word, ' – I might not have been so bad.'

'You're doing really well,' says Abby. She hesitates, then adds, 'I admire you. To be honest, I did already, but this only makes me even more.'

Lillie starts. 'Seriously?'

'Yes. And actually, the way that Callum responded to your stickers *is* unusual. I've never seen him engage that way with a complete stranger around. He doesn't react enthusiastically that often even with me.'

'Oh,' says Lillie. 'That must be hard for you.'

'Some days it is.' Abby hesitates. She doesn't want to sound too effusive; nonetheless it seems Lillie's not grasped what she's trying to convey. 'You have a gift, you know, Lillie. The way you connect with people, it's rare, and you take time to be welcoming and kind to everyone. I don't think I'd have got through my first few days without you.'

'Aw, Abby. Stop – you'll set me off again.' Lillie's bottom lip quivers. 'But thank you.' She hesitates. 'Can we have a hug?'

'Sure.' And as they embrace, Abby breathes in the sweet apricot of Lillie's scent.

29

'So how are you?' asks Johnnie, once Karen has settled into a chair opposite.

'Is Lillie OK? I feel really bad about what happened in group.'

Johnnie shifts in his seat. 'If you're concerned, perhaps have a word with her? I'm not at liberty to discuss Lillie's situation, I'm sorry.' He looks as if he wishes there was another way. 'Plus we're here to talk about you, Karen, and how you've been since our session last week.'

I'm doing it again, aren't I? she realizes. Focusing on other people.

She glances round the room. It's an exercise in neutrality. There's nothing to distract her; doubtless that's the point. 'I've been a bit up and down,' she says, then becomes aware that sounds as noncommittal as the decor. 'Though it's been good to come here and have somewhere to talk.' Other than this morning, she adds to herself. That made me uncomfortable. But she refrains from saying so. It might come across as criticism and instinctively she wants to shield Johnnie.

'I wondered if you've thought about what we discussed – in particular your feelings about your father?'

Ouch. Karen had hoped to avoid the subject for a bit. 'Yes.' She stares at the curtains, trying to gauge where she's up to, but merely finds herself thinking it's a shame they need to have nets when they block so much light.

'And?'

'I can see being sad might have become a bit of a pattern for me. Thoughts related to my husband do come up again and again . . .' In a flash she pictures Simon. He's stepped out of the shower, hair damp, skin beaded with droplets of water . . . 'I find it very hard not to think of him.' She gulps. 'Though I'm not sure I'd want to stop. It would feel like I'd forgotten him.'

Now Simon is rubbing his hair dry with a towel.

'The last thing I'm suggesting is that you squash those feelings,' says Johnnie. 'But maybe we can get you to a place where you can remember both Simon and your father without the depression.'

Just then, so unexpectedly it's as if Simon himself has planted the thought in her mind, Karen makes a connection. 'You know, I've been seeing the two situations as totally different because Dad was so much older and had been ill for a long time, but there are similarities in the circumstances of how they died . . . Both happened in February.' She glances back at the window. Through the nets she can discern it's a bright, sunny day. The morning of Simon's heart attack was anything but. Immediately she's on the train once more: there's a blast of cold air as the doors open at Preston Park; she sees passengers shaking rain from their umbrellas before boarding.

'Many people seem to find February a difficult time of year.'

'I never minded it particularly before, but I do now. This spring was particularly vile, wasn't it?' She stops to consider. 'As well as the timing, both events were such a shock. With Simon it's obvious why, but actually my dad's death was sudden too, because he had a stroke and never regained consciousness.' With a shudder she recalls the race across the downs in her tired old car.

'Yet, before, you said you expected your father to die.'

'I've blamed myself for not dealing with it better because I thought I knew it was coming, but I didn't. Alzheimer's often drifts on and on, and there weren't any specific warning signs.' Again she hesitates. 'Just like there weren't any for Simon.' It's too much: tears start to fall. I *wish* there had been some way of knowing, she thinks, reaching for a tissue. 'I never got to say goodbye to either of them . . .' she says in a small voice.

'If you'll allow me to suggest something,' says Johnnie gently, 'I wonder if perhaps your father's death could be triggering what are called *sensory* memories of experiences you've had before.'

Karen blows her nose. 'You've lost me.'

'Normally, we're not aware of sensory memories because they're connected to our senses and occur in a split second. But sometimes you can have another experience where those memories are triggered.' He leans forward, eager to explain. 'Have you ever had a particular scent suddenly remind you of something that happened years ago?'

She thinks of the deckchairs in the garden shed that still smell of Simon and another wave of grief hits her. 'Yes . . .'

'The thing about sensory memories is they're totally outside our conscious control. So you can't plan for them, but they're there, deeply embedded. And maybe with you, when you experienced another death at the same time of year, it set them off.'

'Gosh.' Karen sits back in her chair. 'I suppose that's possible. But what can I do about them?'

Johnnie runs his fingers through his fringe. 'The belief is that until the person works out that's what's going on, and the link, they get scared, or panicked, or whatever the emotion that comes up – again and again. But by making the connections conscious, we can begin to process some of these thoughts and feelings.'

'I see.'

'And you might find that simply having the insight helps.'

'Thank you. I believe it might.' Karen reaches over for the jug of water, pours herself a plastic cup and reflects while she takes a sip. 'There were differences in the experiences, though. Going back to what we were saying in this morning's group about support, when Simon died, in the immediate aftermath, everyone rallied round – I didn't even have to ask.' Realizations come fast, as if a series of lights is being switched on, one after the other. 'Like my childminder, Tracy. She offered to have the kids pretty much round the clock. Yet when Dad died, it wasn't the same. Not at all.'

'Did you ask Tracy to help?'

'No.'

'Why not?'

'Given he'd been ill for so long, I guess I thought it would seem over the top. After all, I'd had years to get used to the idea. Whereas before, I had my mum and my friends – Anna, in particular, and my other friend, Lou – everyone was really helpful.'

'And that's not been the case recently?'

'No . . .' Karen considers. 'It's not just I haven't asked for support because I'm bad at it, it's also that their situations have changed. Mum, obviously, she's lost my dad, and I feel I should be looking after her, not the other way round. Then there's Lou – she's been relishing her new baby. I didn't feel it was right to offload onto her.' Lou has had her share of difficulties, Karen thinks. This is a special time and she deserves to be happy.

'And your other friend, Anna?'

'Anna's been great, she's the reason I ended up coming here. Although . . .' Karen pictures her friend with her new partner, Rod. How the tables have turned. She and Simon used to worry about Anna living with an alcoholic; now she's half a contented couple . . .

Whoa, Karen realizes, *I'm jealous*. So it's pride that's stopped me confiding too. I've not wanted my friends to pity me.

She falls quiet. After a while Johnnie says, 'Do you think that having less support might have contributed to your depression? Might there be a connection between you looking after others, and not caring for yourself? Sometimes we become caregivers because we're avoiding our own issues.'

He's so spot-on she has an urge to applaud.

I wonder if that's why he chose to become a therapist, she speculates. Johnnie's not perfect, either. Buoyed by what she's piecing together, she decides to voice her misgiving. 'I did feel you pushed me a bit hard this morning, though I didn't say so.'

'Yet it would have been fine for you to protest. It would have been establishing a boundary – the very thing we were talking about.'

'Whereas actually Abby got angry for me.'

'Sometimes the things in therapy that provoke the biggest response are the things we could do with looking at most closely. We're back to triggers again.'

Johnnie's grin indicates he's not offended, Karen gleans. Perhaps I don't need to hold back after all. 'So the subject of boundaries triggered both me and Abby. How revealing . . .'

'You're keen to protect other people, but it's important to remember that you are a separate person from your friends – and your family, come to that – and you need to be cared for too.'

'I see.' Karen nods. But she fears it's not in her nature to be this way. It was different when Simon was around, as then he was the one who cared for me, she thinks. Learning to look after myself is going to be hard.

30

'Crikey, I could do with a drink,' says Elaine, flopping onto a sofa. 'Bloody hell, what a day.'

Abby knows where Elaine is coming from. The heated exchange in group that morning, the conversation with Lillie: it's been full-on for her, too. Supper is served early at Moreland's, and she's joined several other inpatients in the lounge. The evening stretches out before them.

Colin looks up from the book he is reading. 'So, what happened?'

'Step 4,' says Lansky, with a shudder.

Karl nods. 'Always a tough one.'

Abby is intrigued. The addiction therapy programme is based on twelve steps, and from what she's gathered, each step sounds tougher than the last. 'What's that?'

'I had to make a "searching and fearless moral inventory of myself",' says Elaine, indicating quote marks in the air. 'Which basically means I had to list all my faults.'

'Yikes,' says Colin, glancing at his tummy. 'Glad we don't have to do that.'

'Imagine having to write them down,' says Elaine. She unzips her high-heeled boots and kicks them off onto the floor.

'I tell you, it's tougher being a Bad than a Sad,' says Karl.

'A whole week without alcohol,' says Elaine, yawning. 'I don't think I've gone that long since I was about fourteen.'

'This is exactly the time I'd reach for a beer,' says Lansky, glancing at the clock.

'Don't!' Karl shakes his Mohican. 'You'll have me wanting to rack out a line.'

'I'll tell you what *I* want . . .' says Colin provocatively.

'A fag?' Elaine hurriedly sits up. 'Yes! I'll join you on the balcony.'

'A snog with Beth, more like,' interrupts Lillie, and smirks at Colin.

Colin grabs a cushion from the sofa and throws it at her. Lillie ducks. 'Ha! Missed!'

Before Abby has time to work out what's going on, Lansky and Colin are chasing Lillie round the room, keen for a pillow fight. Karl leaps over the coffee table – his Mohican narrowly avoids getting caught in the light-fitting – and soon the three lads have Lillie cornered. As they pummel her with cushions, she giggles and falls onto the nearest sofa.

'Stop it! Stop it!' she says, but Karl merely swings his cushion above his head with even more energy and brings it down with a thump.

'No, no!' Lillie cries. She's laughing, but Abby detects there's something about her laughter that is verging on the hysterical.

Perhaps this isn't a good idea, she realizes, remembering

the story Lillie confided earlier. By now Lillie is coughing and spluttering: whether in amusement or alarm, it's hard to tell.

'Hey, guys, lay off,' says Abby, and runs to grab Lansky's T-shirt in a bid to waylay him. The T-shirt stretches where she has hold of it, revealing pale skin and an array of colourful tattoos.

Colin seems to grasp the situation – he pauses – but Lansky and Karl are enjoying themselves too much to take heed. Maybe it's the adrenalin that used to fuel their addiction, thinks Abby.

It's at this point that Michael, who's been sitting quietly in an armchair focusing on the telly, gets to his feet. 'Oi. Maybe cool it?' His tone is serious.

At once Lansky and Karl stand away. Lillie stops coughing and laughing, sweeps back her hair and jumps up from the sofa.

Maybe I overreacted, thinks Abby, as Lillie adjusts her clothing and Michael returns to his seat in front of the television, but then Lillie catches her eye and gives Abby a tiny smile, and Abby detects she is grateful. Of course Lillie's good at keeping it together, Abby thinks. I've never watched her *Street Dance* programme, so it's easy to forget that she's a professional who has to handle the pressures of live TV.

Then, as if she's keen to show there are no hard feelings, Lillie claps her hands and grins at everyone.

'Never mind all this,' she says, hurling the cushions back into place on the sofa and reaching for the television remote control.

'Hey—' protests Michael as she presses the off button.

'Come on, Michael, you can live without Channel 4 News. It's way too depressing. And you—' she grabs Colin's shoulder as he's reaching for his cigarettes, ' – don't need any more fags today. You know it's only a safety behaviour.'

Colin pouts. 'But I *need* my coping mechanisms!'

'You don't say. Seriously. I've got a better idea. Back in a sec—' And she's off. Just like when she went to track down those stickers for Callum, thinks Abby. Sometimes Lillie's energy levels are astounding.

Lillie soon bounds back into the room, clutching her iPod and a pair of mini speakers. 'Right.' She plugs in the speakers and scrolls down the iPod screen. 'We're gonna dance.'

'Oh no, I haven't got the energy for your sort of dancing. One of my faults was laziness, don't you know?' Elaine yawns again and stretches back on the sofa.

'Nah, not *my* sort of dancing, if you don't want. *Any* sort,' says Lillie. 'Come on, everyone. Let's disco!' She clambers up on the back of the sofa behind Elaine so she can reach to lower the blinds. Elaine recoils as Lillie wobbles precariously, then the beat of Earth, Wind & Fire's 'Let's Groove Tonight' fills the room.

'You're too knackered to dance, do the lights then,' commands Lillie as she springs down again. She hurries to the switch by the door to demonstrate how Elaine should flick them on and off.

Wearily, Elaine stands up and does as she's told.

'We need more volume!' says Colin. He bops over to the iPod and whacks up the sound, singing along with the vocals.

Abby smiles, watching his ponytail sway from side to side in time to the music. Well, if Colin's prepared to give it a go, I will, she decides. He must be pretty unfit after so many months stuck in here. She kicks off her pumps. In seconds she and Colin are banging hips with each other, Seventies style.

Colin twirls and turns to face Abby, chanting the lyrics that declare how great she is looking, and as he wags his finger and blows her a kiss, Abby feels laughter bubbling up. At that moment she loves Colin for his sheer enthusiasm. He might be overweight and ten years her junior, but it makes her feel attractive, somehow, being in touch with her physicality like this.

I do love dancing, she thinks. I used to go clubbing in Manchester a lot, when I was Colin's age. And I was dancing at a party when I met Glenn . . . She has a pang of nostalgia, but the track soon lifts her up again.

Men are usually slower to take to the dance floor, Abby recalls, and Karl's Mohican and Lansky's tattoos suggest Seventies disco might not be their first choice of music. However, Lillie only has to crook her finger in their direction and they both get up to join her, one on each side.

Next up is Donna Summer.

'It's my own mix.' Lillie raises her voice so she can be heard over the rapid synth. 'Isn't it epic?'

There are only a few words to 'I Feel Love', so they're all able to mouth along. And as Abby swoops and twirls, she senses the carpet under her bare feet, the breeze from the open window in her hair and she can't stop smiling. Lillie is incredible, the way she can wiggle her torso like that, she observes. But who cares if she's better at shaking her booty than the rest of us? I'd forgotten how much *fun* this is. Everyone's worries seem to have vanished.

Only Michael is still sitting on the sofa.

Lillie gyrates over to him and holds out a hand. 'Join us,' she urges.

'It's not really my thing,' mutters Michael.

'Aw, don't be boring,' yells Abby. 'This is brilliant!'

Michael shakes his head. 'You're OK.'

'So what sort of stuff *do* you like?' asks Abby when the track finishes.

'Well, I was a punk.' Michael sounds defensive.

'You weren't!' says Lillie.

'I was,' says Michael. Abby senses it wouldn't be wise to mock him.

'Good man.' Karl gives him a playful punch.

'Come on, Michael—' Colin boings over to Michael like a jack-in-the-box. 'It's not my era, but I can manage the pogo.'

Colin looks so comical, jumping up and down with such ferocity that sweat pours from his brow, that laughter bubbles up in Abby again. And he's *still* in his slippers, she realizes, even after all that pillow fighting. Her cheeks are beginning to ache from grinning so hard.

'How about this one?' Lillie grabs her iPod and shuffles through the tracks. Within seconds she's hit play. Abby recognizes it within a couple of bars: 'Rock the Casbah'. Reluctantly Michael gets to his feet. 'I can manage this one, I suppose.'

He starts to dance, slowly at first, then gathering momentum. Elaine flicks the lights on and off at greater speed; by now she too is shimmying and waving her free arm, and when the chorus breaks out, Michael lets rip completely.

They continue for several more tracks. Wiggling and jigging or hopping and twirling, jiving and diving or strutting and swaying, every one of us has our own style, thinks Abby. And who'd have guessed Michael was such a good mover?

Suddenly there's a loud rap on the door.

'Oh shit,' says Lillie, and hurries to turn down the music.

Like children caught having a midnight feast, they scamper to sit down on the sofas, giggling and crashing into one another. Only Michael remains on his feet. The door opens.

It's Phil, the office manager.

They look up at him, wide-eyed and innocent.

'I don't want to spoil the party,' Phil says sternly, stepping into the centre of the room. 'But we're trying to have a staff meeting downstairs. Do you think you could keep it down a little?'

'Of course,' says Lillie, poker-faced. 'We didn't mean to—' Then she stops speaking and stares.

Abby follows her gaze. Michael is standing behind Phil, his face deadly serious. But above Phil's head he's cocking two fingers, and wiggling them like rabbit ears.

31

Abby is just putting down her knife and fork when Sangeeta waves from the door of the dining room.

'Your taxi's here.' The nurse has to raise her voice to make herself heard over the chatter. 'And Lillie, I saw your sister parking up outside, so I guess she's here to collect you too?'

Abby checks her watch. The car's early. It's fortunate she's finished her lunch. 'Oh well, better go, I suppose.' She pushes back her chair.

'You were going to give me your number,' says Karen, pausing midway through her lasagne to reach for her phone.

'So I was.'

Karen taps as Abby dictates. 'I'll call you in a bit, then you'll have mine.'

'Perfect.'

'And you must come round for coffee.' Karen has worked out Abby lives only five minutes' walk away.

'So, best be off,' says Lillie, yanking up the handle to her wheeled suitcase. 'Have a good weekend, Michael.' She gives his shoulder a squeeze with her free hand.

Michael pauses midway through a mouthful. 'I'll try.' Abby follows Lillie out to reception, lugging her bag.

'I can't wait to get out of here,' she says, and buzzes to ask Danni to unlock the coded door. It's Friday and the first time she's been home since her arrival.

'They must think you're doing well to allow you two nights away straight off,' says Lillie. 'Good luck.'

'Thanks.' Though Abby doesn't believe she'll need it. I'm back soon anyway, she thinks. She's looking forward to not being answerable to staff, sleeping in her own bed and cooking her own meals. Above all, she's keen to see Callum.

'I'm a bit scared of being on my own,' confesses Lillie in a low voice as Danni lets them through.

'You'll be fine. You were OK last weekend, weren't you?'

Lillie nods, but appears worried. 'It'll be good to see Tamara and Nino.'

At that moment her sister pulls open the front door of the clinic.

'Hi!' says Tamara. She has her child scooped up in one arm close to her chest. Both have the same corkscrew curls and golden skin – it's strange to see Lillie's familiar features echoed in Tamara's face.

'Hiya.' Lillie leans in to hug them both and gives her nephew a kiss. 'Ooh, hello, you scrumptious boy!' In the wake of her revelation earlier in the week, her affection for Nino brings a lump to Abby's throat. 'I just need to say goodbye to my friend – her taxi's waiting.'

Friend, notices Abby, pleased.

Lillie turns to her. 'So you're here all next week?'

'The plan is to stay Sunday night, then do Monday,

Wednesday and Friday as day care. Ease down gradually, that's what they recommended. How about you?'

'I'm in on Tuesday and Friday, so we'll overlap then.'

'Great.' Abby is tempted to ask for Lillie's number too, but decides against it. Yet again it had slipped her mind that Lillie is a celebrity. I bet she hates being pestered, she thinks.

* * *

It would be rude to leave before Karen has finished eating, thinks Michael. He feels a touch awkward that they've been left alone to make conversation.

Karen swallows a mouthful of lasagne. 'So was the florist you used to run in Rottingdean?'

The question startles him. He's mentioned where he lives to fellow patients, and that he had to close his shop, but no more.

'Er . . . No, it was in Hove.'

'Where, exactly? I live near there.'

'By the station,' he says. He can feel the colour rising in his cheeks.

'I drive past there all the time!' says Karen. She frowns, considering. 'You know, I think I bought some flowers from you not that long ago. Was it a green and blue frontage . . . and facing . . . what's the name of that street?' She lays down her fork and draws a map in the air to gauge her bearings.

'Cromwell Road,' says Michael.

'I did! Pansies. In a basket. For my mum.'

'You know . . . I might remember you,' he says slowly. I do, he realizes. I thought she was attractive. Which she is. The knowledge makes him flush more.

'You put the basket in the back of my car.' Karen smiles. 'It's funny, I thought I recognized you when we started, but couldn't place where from.'

'So I did.' Michael nods, but that Karen is privy to his past makes him feel exposed, vulnerable. He pictures the shelves of the florist lined with plastic buckets, the marks on the concrete floor. He can hear the 'ping' of the till, smell a dozen mingling blooms. But he masks his consternation. 'I hope your mother liked the pansies.'

'She did,' says Karen. 'Oh, *what* a shame you had to close up. I only came in that once, but whenever I drove past I used to look out for your displays. They always looked so pretty.'

'Thank you,' says Michael, unsure how else to respond. That she noticed the care he lavished is enough to make him want to sob, and he's grateful when he sees the office manager, Phil, making his way over to their table. Doubtless he wants to speak to Karen – so far Michael has had little to do with this neatly suited, goatee-bearded man, other than on the previous evening. Michael looks away guiltily, recalling how he poked fun at him.

'Excuse me interrupting while you're eating.'

Michael starts – Phil appears to be addressing him.

'When you've finished, could you pop round and see me, Michael? I need a word.'

'I've finished now.'

'Ah. Perhaps you'd like to follow me, then?'

'Sure,' says Michael, and gets to his feet.

* * *

As long as we don't get stuck in traffic, we should be there in twenty minutes, Abby calculates. She settles into the back seat of the taxi. It's a luxury to be chauffeured like this, not to be behind the wheel, watching the road whilst keeping an eye on her son in the rear-view mirror. No jams so far, she observes as the driver speeds through the Cuilfail Tunnel out of Lewes. Good. Although she told Glenn to expect her early evening, when it came to it she decided to forgo the afternoon group in order to have a couple of hours to herself before Callum returns from school. Whilst she is grateful that Glenn and various carers have taken over in her absence, she is like a cat marking its territory – she wants to reclaim the space as her own.

She leans her head against the window and watches as meadows swish by in a blur of green. *Home.* The prospect brings up a mix of apprehension and optimism.

'I don't believe I've ever learned so much in a short time span before – certainly about myself,' she'd admitted to Beth in her one-to-one that morning. 'It's the first opportunity I've had to focus on my needs in years. That's one upside of having a son like Callum – I've never had a moment to dwell on my problems. But the downside – I can see it now – is that everything built up inside me.'

'The mind is a bit like a pressure cooker,' Beth had said. 'We need to let off steam or else we can explode.'

'I've found it helpful to talk about everything – I feel so much better than when I came in. Still, I'm worried I'm heading back to everything that drove me here in the first place. Selling the house, separating from Glenn, looking after Callum . . .' Even saying the words had made Abby break into a sweat.

'It can be a difficult transition. How might you help yourself stay well?'

'Ask for support. It's true that Glenn often seems more able to say no, but the result is I hate him for it . . . So instead of resenting him, perhaps *I* should relinquish control?'

Beth had nodded. 'Sounds a sensible starting point – certainly that would give you time to enjoy more positive experiences. What would you like to do more of?'

'I don't know.' It had been hard to imagine having spare time.

'What have you enjoyed particularly about being here?'

Abby had smiled as she'd recalled Rick with his 'coke' addiction, Lillie in hysterics about the madhouse, and their recent disco. 'Laughing,' she'd said. 'And it's been brilliant to have such honest and open conversations.' She'd pictured Lillie in the art room. 'Mm, and maybe I'd like to try something creative again.' Then she'd frowned. 'Though I still can't see myself being able to sit around chatting or sketching – I've not found anywhere else to live.'

'But maybe you can see, having had some distance, that your current circumstances won't last forever?'

That morning Abby had concurred, but now this remark troubles her. It's true that one day, hopefully in the not *too* distant future, I'll be through the separation, but the need to care for Callum will remain, she thinks. And whether I'm catastrophizing or looking out for myself, it makes no odds what therapists would call it. Because the older and bigger he gets, the more chronic the stress of looking after him will become.

She sighs. It's not going to be easy to remain buoyant. 'Remember to focus on the positive,' she murmurs as the taxi heads up the hill towards the turn-off for west Brighton.

So . . . I need to sort out better respite options as well as asking Glenn for more support, she vows. After all, he has coped surprisingly well without me. It's been great that he seems to have bonded better with Callum while I've been gone. My time at Moreland's seems to be proving good for all of us.

*　*　*

Phil shuts the door of his office and pulls out a chair so Michael can sit down.

It's scruffier in here than the rest of the building, Michael observes. I suppose it's not maintained as well because fee-paying patients take priority over staff. I wonder how the people working here feel about that.

'I'll cut to the chase,' says Phil. At once Michael feels he must have done something wrong. His thoughts hurtle: maybe Phil saw me make rabbit ears – though how, I've no idea. 'An NHS bed has become available.'

It's like a blow to Michael's stomach.

'The good news is it's much nearer to where you live.'

'Oh?' Michael's head is spinning. He needs a moment to gather himself. But I was beginning to feel better, he wants to protest. You can't move me! I know the other patients, I was starting to make friends. We had a laugh last night, what with the dancing, and I slept for five hours straight afterwards – haven't done that since Christmas. I like it here, all things considered.

'It's in Woodingdean,' Phil continues, but Michael's panic is rising so fast he barely hears.

What about Gillian, he thinks. We'd just been getting somewhere. Do they know how hard it was for me, sharing that stuff with her? I'd been beginning to understand what a huge amount I've had hit me in the last few months. I wanted to talk to Dr Kasdan about trying antidepressants – other patients seem to think they're not so bad after all – but my appointment's not till Monday . . . I'm in favour of the NHS, but going somewhere new at this point seems a ludicrous decision, even cruel . . .

Gradually Phil's words permeate.

'Woodingdean . . . ?'

'Yes.' Phil smiles. 'You're in Rottingdean, aren't you?'

Michael nods. He starts to tremble. Inside he is screaming: *You mean you're transferring me to that giant white block where I won't know a soul? Chrissie's friend Della said it was grim inside and people get locked in their rooms* . . . Yet he can't speak.

'Sunnyvale House has a room free in the general ward.'

When Michael gets his voice back, he can only say, 'When have I got to go?'

Hopefully not till next week, he prays. Presumably no one gets admitted over the weekend.

Phil rotates his chair to check his computer screen. 'Really, we should check you out straight away – once an NHS bed is free, we're not supposed to have you here when you could be there. It's all down to costs, I'm afraid.' He sighs. 'Hundreds of beds have been cut in the NHS, you know. We take on overflow patients when there's no space, but now, as I say, a bed is free. I realize it's going to upset your continuity of care and I really am very sorry. Would it help if I were to call you a cab for later, so you can stay for this afternoon's session?'

If Michael weren't sitting down he fears he'd collapse. For some reason he'd allowed the knowledge that he might be transferred to the NHS to recede right to the back of his mind. *You all made me focus on the positive,* he longs to cry. *So many sessions, making me believe getting out of depression was merely a matter of changing my thoughts. I deliberately pushed that worry away!*

Michael stares at Phil. How can he have pretended, even for a second, that this is good news? At this moment he hates him.

I'm back where I started, he thinks. It's like Tim from the hotel all over again. Once more I've been shafted.

Yet he can't express any of this. He can only sit there, shell-shocked and shaking, like an animal in fear for its life.

III

Darkness Falls

32

Abby unlocks the front door and steps over the threshold. She drops her bag, picks up the pile of post on the doormat and goes into the kitchen. Her feet crunch on the lino floor: she looks down – there are cornflakes scattered everywhere. She makes a swift appraisal: the sink is piled high with washing-up, the surfaces need wiping and there's a faint pong coming from the rubbish bin.

Bang goes my relaxing couple of hours settling back in, she thinks, reaching for the broom. Typical. And there I was thinking Glenn was coping so well. He could have made more of an effort, given that I was due home.

Half an hour later, she's less rankled. Cleaning the kitchen didn't take that long, she says to herself, hoicking her bag with difficulty up the stairs. Maybe they left in a hurry. And Glenn wasn't expecting me till gone five, he probably planned on tidying later.

As she pauses on the landing to catch her breath, a picture on the wall catches her eye. It's a trio of monochrome photographs of the West Pier she mounted in a single frame many years earlier; she's not looked at it properly in a long while. In the first picture the pier rises like a black skeleton out of the sea; in the second the wrought-iron structure is half hidden by mist rolling in over the water; in the third only the top is visible, the rest swallowed by white.

They're rather beautiful, she realizes. *I'm sure being creative again would do more for my well-being than cleaning, but when would I find time? Maybe you should relinquish control*, she hears an inner voice say once again. *Isn't that what others do? They leave mess where they find it – certainly Glenn does. Perhaps rather than cursing him, I could learn from his example.*

She picks up her bag with a grimace and carries on up the stairs, but when she gently kicks open the door of her bedroom with one foot, anger rises in her yet again. The bed is unmade, and Glenn's dirty laundry is thrown over the chair in the corner.

I can't believe he's slept in here, she thinks, shocked.

Although they made no specific agreement, she'd assumed Glenn would continue using the attic. *Yes, the sleigh bed is bigger and more comfortable and his clothes are still in the wardrobe, but it seems disrespectful, given that he's not slept in the room for months. I bet he was going to change the sheets and pretend he'd been upstairs all along*, she fumes.

Like the mist in her photographs, a familiar sensation begins to creep over her. *Don't be swamped by it*, she tells herself, and sits down on the bed. *Deep breaths, Abby. In through your nose, out through your mouth* . . . Gradually she feels the anxiety subside.

As she inhales she notices a scent – unfamiliar, cloying. Maybe Glenn has a new aftershave. She leans down to the pillow. There is a distinct aroma of flowers. Perhaps it's a different washing powder.

Then she lifts her gaze.

On the bedside table – by the side of the bed she always sleeps on – is her favourite white porcelain mug. She picks it up, examines it more closely and her heart stops.

There it is on the rim, bright pink and pucker-marked, unmistakable.

Lipstick.

* * *

Dr Kasdan checks his paperwork and looks up. 'So how are you doing?'

It's a question Karen was expecting the psychiatrist to ask; she has the answer ready. 'I've been much less tearful. I reckon I'm starting to understand what's caused me to feel so down.'

'That's good to hear. What's been helping, do you think?'

'Well, the groups are great. Meeting other people who feel similar to me in one way or another is very comforting. I often get as much from what they say as when I share stuff myself.' She stops. I mustn't make light of my problems, she thinks. If I'm too effusive he'll conclude I'm better and can stop coming to the clinic. The security of being a day patient is keeping Karen grounded and able to function; without it she fears the slightest breeze might carry her back to where she was.

Just then Karen feels her mobile phone vibrating in her handbag. I hope it's nothing to do with the children, she thinks. She's tempted to answer, then reminds herself she only has a few minutes with the doctor – whoever it is will have to wait.

Dr Kasdan continues, 'I recall that we discussed anti-depressants before, but you wanted to hold off.'

Karen nods. 'I'd like to keep them as a fallback option, if you're agreed?'

'Sounds sensible.' The psychiatrist reaches for his pen. 'I'll recommend you continue coming twice a week for another month. We'll reappraise the situation in a fortnight.'

The prospect of having less support in the not-too-distant future is upsetting, but Karen reminds herself she has come a long way already. 'OK . . .' She rises from her chair. 'I'll see you then.'

Outside in the corridor, she reaches for her phone.

Abby, says the missed-call display.

*   *   *

'*It'll pass . . . It'll pass . . . It'll pass . . .*' Abby is murmuring like a mantra. Yet however hard she tries to remind herself that it's a physical reaction brought on by emotions she can't control, the power of panic is stronger. *Breathe . . . breathe . . .* What is it she's been told to do? Ah yes, a paper bag . . . She stumbles down the stairs from the bedroom, rummages in the drawer by the sink, fingers shaking and twitching, pulls out reams of carriers – all plastic.

She sits down. No, that's worse. She can feel her heart

thumping in her chest – *BA-BOOM, BA-BOOM* . . . She stands up. That makes her giddy. Perhaps walking? She paces across the kitchen, down the hall, and back again.

She tries to pluck out a single thought, make it form a line of logic, but her head is a jumble: Glenn's-been-having-sex-with-someone/who?/in-my-bed/*our*-bed/how-long-has-this-been-going-on?/just-when-I-thought-we-were-making-progress/was-it-a-one-off?/is-he-having-an-affair?/I-hope-to-God-he's-not-in-love-with-her/I-couldn't-bear-that/I-know-it's-over-between-us-but-ouch-it-hurts/all-those-late-nights-at-the-office/I-should-have-known/how-could-he?/the-*wanker*!/was-Callum-in-the-house?/what-about-Eva?/the-other-carers?/I-feel-so-stupid/the-humiliation/I'll-never-get-better-now/the-sheets-ugh!/I-must-wash-them/he's-still-my-husband/we're-not-even-for-mally-separated/why-here?/couldn't-he-go-somewhere-else?/is-he-trying-to-send-me-crazy?/I-*am*-mad/I-need-to-go-back-to-Moreland's/but-what-about-Callum?/I-can't-leave-my-son-here-now/he's-not-safe/I'm-not-safe/I-can't-cope/I-need-help/my-heart's-going-to-burst/someone-should-take-me-to-hospital/who-can-I-possibly-ask?

* * *

How strange, Karen frowns. I wouldn't have expected Abby to ring me yet; she knows I'm in Moreland's all afternoon. Perhaps she dialled me by accident. But then she sees there's a voice message.

'Karen, I'm really sorry to ring you but I didn't know who

*else to call. Something horrible has happened and I could
really do with talking to someone . . .'*

She presses call return and Abby picks up straight away.

'Oh Karen, thank you,' she says, and bursts into tears.

'Hey, hey.' Karen steps rapidly down the corridor in search
of a room where she can talk privately. 'I'm sorry I didn't get
back to you before – I was in with Dr Kasdan.'

'So you were.' Abby is breathless, gulping back sobs.
'Sorry. Did I interrupt your session?'

Karen sees the little lounge is free. 'It's fine, we're finished,' she says, taking a seat. 'What's happened?'

Out it pours in a garbled mess; nonetheless Karen gets
the gist. *I could murder this Glenn*, she thinks, though it
won't help to say so.

'Maybe I should come back to Moreland's,' says Abby
when she's reached the end. Her voice is barely audible.

Karen pauses for a second. 'I'm not so sure that's a good
idea,' she says slowly. 'It sounds like you're panicking, and
we know from the group sessions that it's not the time to
make a decision. I worry that if you come here without
sticking it out at home at all, you'll go right back to where
you've been, and you've come such a long way.'

'But I don't think I can cope.' Abby is still breathless.

Karen calculates fast. She'd been planning on staying for
Relaxation, so she's not due to collect Molly and Luke from
the childminder for another two hours. 'What number
house are you?' She already knows which street Abby lives
on.

'Eight.'

'I'll come round, we'll chat then.'

'But Glenn will be here at 4.30 with Callum and I'm not sure I can face him. Not yet.'

'Ah . . .' Karen is already heading out of the building. 'I'll be with you in half an hour. So I'll scoop you up and you can come back to ours.'

Abby is silent. Karen can hear her gasps coming short and shallow down the line.

'Abby, are you OK?'

'Yes, sorry, I was just thinking . . .'

'Don't think,' Karen orders. 'Say yes. We can work out what to do next over a cup of tea.'

More silence, then Abby says, 'A cup of tea. That would be nice.'

'I've got some cake . . .'

'SOME COW DRANK OUT OF MY FAVOURITE CUP!'

Karen winces. 'You can bring the cup and smash it against my garden wall if you like.'

Abby sniffs. 'I might just do that.'

'Good. Have you unpacked?'

'Not yet.'

'Well, don't bother,' says Karen. 'Bring your case to mine. You can always stay over if need be.'

'What about Callum?'

Oh, crikey, yes. Glenn should look after him, thinks Karen. With luck he will. 'We can always have him here later on tonight too,' she says recklessly. Though she worries how he'll interact with Molly and Luke, this is not the time to be precious. 'Let's see how we go once we've smashed a few cups and saucers, OK?'

'OK,' says Abby. Karen can hear that her breathing has slowed to a more normal level. 'And Karen, thank you.'

'It's nothing.' Karen waves the air as if Abby can see her. 'I'll be with you in a bit.'

Not until she's speeding along the A27 does she pause to consider: *Here I go, looking after someone else again.*

* * *

Abby strips the bed with an efficiency fuelled by rage. She bundles the sheets into her arms, grabs the offending mug and hurries down the stairs. She's sorely tempted to smash it as Karen suggested and leave the pieces on the kitchen table as a message to Glenn, but worries that Callum might get to the broken china first and hurt himself. Instead she scrawls a hasty note:

Came home early but gone to a friend's. Thanks for leaving the house in such a tip. I'll be in touch re Callum later.

She doesn't bother to sign it, simply props it up on the lipsticked mug in the middle of the table so Glenn can't be in any doubt that she's aware what's been going on in her absence. Then she charges back upstairs, picks up her bag again – it seems lighter now she's so enraged – and carries it back outside.

She locks the front door and goes to sit on the garden wall between the yew tree and the holly bush so she can see Karen's car coming down the road. Shouldn't be long now.

33

As the taxi pulls up at Sunnyvale House, Chrissie comes hurrying over to greet Michael. 'I'll walk and meet you there,' she'd said when he'd phoned with the news he was being discharged and ferried to the hospital. 'It's only a mile or so and I could do with a bit of fresh air.' Michael knew she was being diplomatic; she had no choice but to come on foot or by bus since their car was surrendered to the creditors.

She opens the door of the taxi. 'Hello, love.'

Michael slides himself out of the back seat and almost falls into his wife's embrace. His nerves were far too jangled to stay for the afternoon group at Moreland's; that would have involved saying goodbye to people he'd grown to like. Instead he went to his room to pack, and less than an hour later he's here, though he's no more able to process the transition than he was in Phil's office.

He glances up at the building over Chrissie's shoulder. The walls are not in fact white but pale grey; the windows are tiny and appear not to open, and high netting encloses the surrounding lawns. It looks more like a prison than a hospital.

The young man who comes out to welcome them seems far from warden-like, however. He introduces himself as Akono with a giant smile. Michael's got used to being beamed at lately; at least Akono seems to be expressing genuine warmth. 'Let me show you to Seaview,' he says, then seeing Michael's confused expression, adds, 'That's what we call the general men's ward. I'm afraid I'll have to take you through Meadows to get there. We'd not normally have to go this way, but we're doing work on the main entrance.' He leads Michael and Chrissie round to the side of the building.

Meadows, Michael gathers as Akono unlocks a series of doors, is a euphemism for the secure unit.

'You're a filthy lesbian!' someone shouts as they make their way down a corridor. Michael sees a wiry young man in pyjamas heading towards them. 'She's a filthy lesbian!' As they cross paths, the young man leers at Chrissie.

But she's holding my hand, thinks Michael.

Akono remains calm. 'Just ignore Jez and follow me. Calls me a nigger all the time at the moment, but it's only because he's unwell.'

Nice, thinks Michael. Then he recalls Tash with her Tourette's. Perhaps Jez is similar and can't help it.

They pass a big metal door with a grille through which Michael glimpses wall-to-wall grey foam. In the middle of the space the foam is raised into a platform to form a sort of bed.

'What's that?' he asks.

'Seclusion,' says Akono.

Padded cell, in other words, thinks Michael. Chrissie squeezes his hand.

'I'll show you your room first,' says Akono. 'Then you can leave your case before I take you to the lounge.'

'This isn't so bad,' says Chrissie as they step into a newly painted room with colour-coordinated shelving, drawers and a single bed. 'I thought you'd have to share. It's good you don't, isn't it, Mickey?'

'I like these blue rooms best,' says Akono.

'There are other colours?' asks Chrissie.

'Red and yellow and green, depending on the ward. This is the most relaxing, I think.'

I'm supposed to be grateful, thinks Michael, but the room reeks of disinfectant. 'Is there a bathroom?'

'The unit's down the hall,' says Akono.

Unit, thinks Michael. Previously he had an en-suite with a bath and shower.

He drops his suitcase and it lands with a thud; the floor is covered in lino, not carpet. Fleetingly he can hear Gillian's voice. *'Don't get caught up in negative thinking, Michael.'* He can imagine her persuading him he doesn't need fresh flowers and his own TV to get better. I'm trying my best to be positive, he argues, but this seems like a bad dream.

He moves around the space in an effort to adjust, goes to the window, looks out. Directly below is a ping-pong table; a couple of men are playing, he wouldn't mind a go at that. And there's a group of patients standing smoking – he's used to this from Moreland's. 'The Bads smoke *way* more than the Mads,' he remembers Lillie pointing out.

277

'OK,' he says to Akono. 'Perhaps you could show me the lounge?'

Michael is braced for minimalism, and sure enough, a CD player, television and stack of dog-eared board games appear to be the only niceties. True, in the corner is a kitchen area, but the counter is covered in used teabags, plastic spoons and spilled sugar, and the vinyl floor makes everything echo so that even their footsteps sound loud. The room is large but there are only a handful of men taking advantage of the space. Two of them are silently absorbed in a game of Scrabble, nearby a young lad about Ryan's age is scratching his arms and muttering something that sounds like 'Ugh! Dalmatians under my skin,' and an elderly man with hair like cobwebs has a wooden chair pulled right up close to the TV. He is watching the horse racing, and is the only one to acknowledge their presence with a nod of his head towards them.

It's hard to believe that a short while ago I was eating lunch with people I was beginning to see as friends, thinks Michael.

'So what happens next?' asks Chrissie as they step back into the corridor.

'You will be assessed by the ward doctor,' Akono says to Michael, flashing another enormous smile, but Michael can't process what's happening right then, let alone later, so says nothing. Akono turns to Chrissie. 'Now, we tend to find it best if patients are given the chance to settle in by them-selves.'

You're telling my wife to leave, thinks Michael. If that's

what you mean, why don't you say so? The prospect of being left alone makes him shudder.

'OK.' Chrissie nods. She's always been more compliant than I have, thinks Michael. Nonetheless as she leans in to give him a farewell hug, she mutters into his ear, 'Don't worry, love. We'll get you out of here as soon as we can, I promise.'

So she thinks it's as awful as I do in spite of Akono's cheeriness, he deduces. That makes it worse – it confirms his perception isn't warped. As Chrissie and Akono turn to head back through the locked ward, Michael is left with a Hobson's choice: to return to the bleakness of his bedroom or face the strangers in the lounge. With a lurch of fear he opts for the latter, feeling as if he's about to jump off a cliff.

* * *

'Nice house you have here,' says Abby, looking round the kitchen.

'Thank you,' says Karen. 'It's badly in need of decorating. In here especially.'

'I didn't notice.' Abby was more struck by the children's paintings displayed on the fridge, the shelves chock-full of spices and herbs, the half-drunk bottle of red wine next to the tea and coffee caddies. I wish I could leave stuff out like this, she thinks, instead of locking everything away.

'So, cake.' Karen stands on tiptoe to retrieve a large tin. 'Have to keep it out of the kids' reach,' she explains, sliding a chocolate gateau onto a plate.

Tell me about it, thinks Abby.

'Say when to stop,' says Karen, moving a knife slowly round like the hand of a clock.

Abby bites her lip, apologetic. 'I'm not sure I can manage to eat.'

'Ah yes. Weren't you one of those who said in group you lose your appetite when you're stressed? I'm the opposite. I eat too much when I'm happy and I eat even more when I'm sad.'

'Don't let me stop you.'

'Now I feel guilty.'

'You mustn't.'

'I've put on weight since Simon died . . .'

'You look great just as you are.' The combination of Karen's chestnut hair and green eyes is striking, thinks Abby, and she oozes warmth and generosity. 'OK, give me a small slice,' she concedes, realizing it will give Karen permission.

'Right. We've got an hour till I have to collect the children. Although you're welcome to stay longer if you want.'

Abby lets out a sigh of relief. 'Honestly, I don't know how to thank you, helping me out like this.'

Karen scoops a generous forkful of gateau into her mouth. 'You know, I met one of my really good friends, Lou, the day Simon died. The whole thing was so awful, but she was absolutely brilliant. I'd never have got through it without her, so I see it as karmic payback, if you like.'

That's such a positive way of looking at the world, reflects Abby. She's noticed Karen seems more upbeat than when she started at Moreland's. It's astonishing to think that only two weeks ago she couldn't stop crying. I was doing well too, she thinks. Till this afternoon . . . Once more she feels anxiety rising. She grips the side of the table.

'You OK?' Karen looks at her, concerned.

'I had a rush of panic,' she says after she's done some deep breathing. 'Sorry . . .'

'It's fine, honestly. I realized that's what was going on. I'm here for you, whatever.' Karen reaches over and gives Abby's hand a squeeze.

'Thanks.' Abby knows she's overdoing the gratitude but doesn't know what else to say. She's aware they've both fallen silent, but how can she explain that she's terrified of losing a sense of who she is again?

'Tell me what's on your mind,' says Karen gently.

Abby considers. Perhaps she could share these worries, and Karen won't judge her. She reaches for her fork, helps herself to a wodge of cake and – *yum* – is astonished to find it tastes delicious.

'You know, no one in my family ever talked to one another, not properly . . .' She glances up – Karen's eyes are wide, encouraging her to continue. 'We didn't articulate our feelings, not at all. And guess what I've also realized? Somehow I've ended up with a son who doesn't respond to me, and a husband who doesn't either. I must be doing something wrong.'

'It's not your fault,' says Karen. 'You didn't make your son autistic.'

'No, but—'

'And from what you've said before now about your husband, it's not your fault the relationship has broken down, either.'

'Isn't it?' Abby hasn't the energy to stop herself from crying. 'I've spent so much time care-giving over the last few years, it's no wonder our marriage couldn't take the strain.'

Karen goes to tear off a couple of pieces of kitchen roll which she hands to Abby. 'Strikes me Glenn didn't leave you much choice. You did what many decent people would do: you took over where he left gaps.'

'Mm.'

'You *mustn't* blame yourself, Abby. Honestly. I don't know Glenn, obviously. I haven't heard his side of the story. But I know from groups and stuff that you've done a huge amount of beating yourself up already. We all do it, don't we, those of us at Moreland's? It's one of the reasons so many of us end up with depression or anxiety. What makes me really cross is that probably Glenn's the one who should be having therapy, not you.'

Karen's cheeks are flushed, Abby notices. She seems angry on my behalf. It's funny how we identify with one another.

Suddenly, through all her whirling thoughts and upset, she has a moment of clarity.

'I knew he was having an affair,' she says.

'You *knew*?'

'I don't mean I really knew,' Abby explains. 'I mean I suspected deep down, though I didn't want to admit it to myself. Glenn withdrew from me ages ago. I don't think we've had sex since last autumn some time, and I've no idea how long it's been going on, but there've been signs . . . Like his staying late at the office . . . being so defensive . . .

never mind demanding that we split the house 50/50 when I do the lion's share of caring for our son. He probably wants somewhere bigger so he can continue seeing *her*, whoever she is.' Strangely, as she says this, Abby can sense her anxiety lifting a little – she'd expected the opposite. She stops to check if the relief lasts; it seems to. Then she says, 'Do you know what? I think that might be where some of my panic has been coming from.'

'Really?' Karen's eyes open even wider.

'It's as if I was blocking myself from admitting it.'

'You wouldn't be the first person to do that.'

'No . . .' Still, Abby feels a fool. 'It's been staring me in the face.'

'There you go again – don't be so hard on yourself,' Karen reminds her. 'If he has been seeing someone, he's the one who's been in the wrong, not you.'

Abby recalls conversations at the clinic. 'They say anxiety is often unexpressed emotion, don't they?'

Karen nods.

'Sometimes anger . . . or grief . . . or both?'

'Yes, so I gather.'

'I must have been in denial,' Abby admits, then laughs. 'De Nile, river in Egypt, so I heard.'

Karen laughs with her. 'We're getting better at therapy than the therapists themselves.'

Abby looks down at her plate, and is startled to see she's finished her sliver of cake. 'It's weird, but I do feel lighter having told you that.'

'Well, we can't have you losing weight when I'm getting

chubbier by the minute. Can I tempt you?' Once more Karen hovers the knife over the gateau, her expression inviting.

Abby nods. 'Go on, then.'

34

Michael enters the lounge as the racing draws to a close.

'Don't recognize you,' says the elderly man, turning from the screen to appraise him. 'You new?'

'Um, yes,' says Michael, and takes a seat next to the young lad who keeps scratching himself.

'*Finally.*' The lad jumps up to grab the remote control, flicks the TV onto *Top Gear*, and sits back down again so fast Michael is left breathless just watching him.

The old man shifts his chair to face the sofa, his cobweb hair catching in the slight breeze created by his movement. 'First-timer?'

'Sort of . . . I've come from Moreland's.'

'Ooh, get you.' One of the men playing Scrabble looks up from the table across the room. 'La-di-da.'

'Oi, I was there once,' says his opponent.

'I wasn't paying,' mutters Michael, riled by the implication he's wealthy enough to afford insurance, let alone the exorbitant fees.

'Brave chap coming to sit in here,' says the old man.

Michael already wishes he hadn't. What was he thinking? He's too concerned about his own survival to be able to converse much anyway. He glances nervously at the young lad next to him. Michael can hear him whispering what sounds like 'Woof! Woof!' as he scratches his arms.

'Don't worry, he's not going to eat you,' says the old man. 'Just a touch of psychosis – unusual one, Eddie's – he reckons he's infested by Dalmatians.' The old man holds out a hand to Michael. 'I'm Terry.'

Michael introduces himself.

The first Scrabble player looks up. 'Don't suppose you've got OCD, have you, Mike?'

'It's Michael, actually. And no. Why?'

'Kitchen area could do with a tidy,' says the second Scrabble man, and the two of them roar with laughter.

Michael squirms.

'Fancy a tab, Michael?' Terry reaches in his pocket for a packet. The first two fingers on his right hand are dark with nicotine stains.

'Don't smoke, I'm afraid.'

'Come for a blast of fresh air.'

Michael is tempted to run back to his room and hide, but is wary of being branded a coward. Plus the room stinks of bleach, and he's keen to get away from it.

'Go on then,' he says. Michael is grateful for Terry's warmth. He's seen friendships form in minutes at Moreland's, and instinct tells him he's going to need allies here – fast.

* * *

'It's him,' says Abby, seeing Glenn's picture come up on the screen as her mobile starts to ring.

'You going to answer?' asks Karen.

'No.'

They wait until the phone clicks onto voicemail; shortly there's the bleep of a message.

'Let's listen.' Abby puts it on loudspeaker.

'Er, as I can't get hold of you, I'm not sure what to do . . . I was going to ask Eva to stay late but I don't know where you are . . . I don't know which friend's you've gone to . . . Can you call me when you pick this up? And, um . . . sorry the house was such a mess. I didn't think you'd be back till later.'

Abby grimaces. 'I suppose I ought to go and get it over with.'

Part of her would like to stay in Karen's kitchen, eating cake. Another part of her is so fired up with fury she wants to scream. She's also afraid that if she doesn't act on anger, the sadness she senses lurking close behind, like a big cat creeping up on its prey, will pounce. She doesn't want to get tearful when she confronts her husband.

'I'm going to go,' she says. 'Sorry.'

'No need to apologize. It's fine. I've got to pick up the kids soon anyway. Would you like me to drop you off? You've got your bag and everything.'

'Thanks for the offer, but it's not that heavy, and I could do with the walk.' Abby picks up her bag and Karen follows her down the hall.

'Ring me,' says Karen, as Abby opens the door. 'Let me know you're OK?'

'Sure. Or I'll text or something.'

'And you can always come back here if you want. With Callum if you need to.'

'That's really kind. And seriously, Karen, I mean it, thank you.'

'Like I said, think of it as karmic payback. As my mum would say, "What goes around comes around."'

* * *

Outside on the lawn Terry lights a cigarette and inhales deeply, then blows a succession of smoke rings into the air. For a second Michael is taken back to his childhood. I used to watch my father do that, he recalls. He could make different shapes and all sorts. I'd forgotten how enthralling it was. Michael misses his dear old dad, dead a decade now, and he misses that sense of wonder too.

Terry flicks ash on the ground. 'How d'you find this place compared to Moreland's?'

Michael frowns. He doesn't want to diss Sunnyvale too much; it could backfire.

'Er . . . this is more clinical,' he says. Then he remembers that Akono was quite open about Seaview being preferable to Meadows; hopefully that observation won't cause offence. 'Have to admit the secure unit looked grim.'

Terry nods. 'Started out in there time before last. Sectioned, I was. Not so nice, you're right.'

So he's been in several times. 'What's brought you here?' asks Michael, hoping to shift the focus from himself.

'Recurrent depressive disorder, with a bit of borderline personality disorder thrown in.'

Michael doesn't know what this means; perhaps it'll soon become evident. The prospect makes him wary, but until then he might as well keep going. 'What are the staff like here?'

'Some good, some bad.' Terry shrugs. 'One or two are power crazy, you can imagine. Others are plain worn out – you can see why when the pay's shit and the hours are dire. Lots of them are agency workers anyway. But there are a few – like that guy Akono, saw he showed you round – he's OK. He does his damnedest, though it seems he's firefighting a lot of the time. You'll get to know pretty quick, and keep your head down, you'll be all right. None of them have much sway, other than the psychs.' He inhales again, though this time, to Michael's disappointment, exhales without forming a smoke ring. 'But I'm going to be out of here soon. Thank God.'

'Is it that bad?' Terry was beginning to give him a flicker of hope.

'Nah, it's OK – or I think so today at any rate – though I'm a bit up and down so I might think different tomorrow . . .' He takes another drag. 'Some might tell you otherwise, but you know what I reckon the worst problem in here is?'

Michael shakes his head.

'Boredom.'

'Oh?'

'There's TV if you can survive the ordeal. Daytime's not so bad, but I warn you, evenings there's nearly always someone wants to watch something else, so you'll have to fight to see anything you like.'

'Fight . . . ?' Michael recalls the desperation with which the young lad grabbed the remote control.

'Oh, I don't mean actually fight. People can look violent in here even when they're not. Medication takes care of that.'

Great, thinks Michael. So everyone *is* doped up, as I suspected. I'm buggered if they're going to do that to me.

'Though you can do art and stuff, if you like. OT, they call it – occupational therapy.'

'What sort of things?'

'All the usual classes: painting, pottery . . . And Matt – that chap playing Scrabble – think he was at Moreland's too, a while back – he's been running a book group.'

'Pottery?' Well I never, he thinks, *that* wasn't on offer at Moreland's.

'There's a kiln and a potter's wheel over in Riverside. That's the mother and baby unit, round there.' Terry gestures to the far side of the building. 'But you're allowed to go to classes whatever ward you're in. Teacher's good, I hear. They produce some very professional pieces.'

Somehow Michael doubts this, but he nods appreciatively nonetheless.

'Why, you interested?'

'Dunno.' I suppose I could make some vases, he thinks. Then Chrissie could put flowers in them.

It's so pathetic he could almost laugh.

* * *

'Would you mind looking after Callum for a bit?' Glenn asks Eva. 'Abby and I need to have a chat.'

'Of course.' Eva looks nervously at Abby. So she knows,

thinks Abby. How could Glenn put Eva in that position? And me too.

Anger courses through her. Nevertheless, it's better than anxiety. Abby is amazed how clear her head is. She feels like she could accomplish almost anything – sit an exam, bungee jump . . . If only she were doing one of those instead.

Callum seems to pick up the uneasy mood – or he's having a difficult day. Getting him settled is hard. He starts to pace around the living room.

'I think it's because he's not seen you in a while,' says Eva.

Of course, thinks Abby, and sadness rushes up, like milk boiling in a pan.

'Let's sit for a few minutes, shall we?' she says to her son, knowing he's unlikely to do so. But to her astonishment he drops down onto the sofa next to her, and for a while she holds him to her, stroking his hair. He seems to have missed me, she thinks. After a while he pulls away and Abby leaves Eva to take over.

Glenn is in the kitchen, tidying ineffectually. The mug is now washed and on the draining board. There's no sign of Abby's note.

She switches on the kettle and stands waiting; no inclination to sit. 'Well, who is she?'

Glenn swivels round. His face is drawn, his skin ashen. 'Sorry?'

'You heard me.'

He looks away from her gaze. 'No one you know.'

'Right. So there is someone.' Ha! That was easy. 'And – who is she?'

'She's someone I met through work . . . Her name's Cara.'

'She live near here?'

'No.'

'So I suppose you invited her over, then. Nice.'

Glenn is silent, avoiding her gaze.

'How long has it been going on?'

He glances up at her; she sees fear flash across his eyes. Perhaps he's wondering if he can get away with a lie.

'Tell me the truth. You owe me that.'

'Since last autumn.'

Abby feels sick. That's – what? – about nine months ago. Nine months he's been duping me. *Nine months.* That's before we put the house on the market, before Christmas, before I felt so bad. Karen's words echo in her mind: *Glenn's the one who should be having therapy, not you,* and she wants to punch him.

He allowed me to go to hell and back, she thinks. I felt I was going mad. I *did* go mad. And all the time I was unconsciously reacting to him. No wonder he was so worried I'd taken an overdose. No wonder he was prepared to claim on his policy so I could be in Moreland's, even though he moaned about it. Well, to hell with him. I'm going to stay there for *years* now, if I need to. I don't care if I bankrupt the insurance company. I don't care if I bankrupt him.

'I'm sorry, Abby, really I am.' Glenn moves towards her.

'Don't you DARE try and touch me!' She shakes her head, incredulous. It's a huge amount to take in and she can't digest it all at once. And what about this woman? Has she met Callum? Momentarily she's furious with this stranger, stealing her husband. No, she thinks, I'm not going to fall into that trap. Glenn is the one who pledged fidelity.

'I want you out,' she states.

'Out . . . ?' So it hasn't dawned on him this might be her reaction. How slow he is.

'Yes, *out.*'

'What about Callum?'

'Oh, for goodness' sake. It's only in the last fortnight you've begun to show the remotest interest in him. We're OK. We'll be fine.'

'But aren't you due back at Moreland's?'

'Not till Sunday. You can come back then to look after your son. Right now I don't give a monkey's where you go. You can go to hers, for all I care. I just want you gone. I need space.'

Half an hour later, Glenn has packed a bag. He taps on the living-room door and says he is leaving. Eva looks uncomfortable and Abby doesn't want to involve her any more than she has been already – especially in front of Callum – so leads the way to the front door.

'Get a solicitor,' she says to Glenn, surprising herself with the words.

'But the house . . . ?'

'What about it?'

'I thought we were going to sell this place first.'

'No, we're not. I don't want to leave. Never have done. You know that.'

The remaining colour drains from Glenn's face.

'As I said, you might want to get a solicitor.'

She shuts the door behind him and leans back against the wall. Astonishingly, although she is shaking, she doesn't feel a drop of anxiety. Sadness, yes, and anger. But the panic has vanished.

*　*　*

Michael is trying to have a bath, but nothing is going right. First, he had to ask for a key before he was allowed to use the unit. Then, when he entered, he found the room wet from the previous occupant. He was in the process of undressing when he noticed a small glass panel in the door – presumably so they can check he's not drowning himself, but the possibility of being overlooked is unnerving. Who's to say one of the more power-crazed members of staff won't come by merely to gawp?

He steps into the tub; the water is tepid, but it will have to do. He sits down and reaches for the soap; it's so slippery it slides from his fingers, then he can't locate it amongst his own limbs. Finally he manages to create enough lather to wash himself. Never has bathing been such a source of mental anguish.

He lies back, watches the water whiten around his body. The soap forms a skin on the surface.

What a bloody awful day it's been, he thinks. I'm not sure how I got through it. Adrenalin, mainly, I suppose. Being in the lounge earlier that evening was overwhelming. There were arguments – not just about the TV but also about a mobile that had gone missing – 'nicked', so the belligerent little fellow who owned it believed. Michael was accused not merely of stealing the phone but also of running off with Terry, apparently his lover. 'Get your hands off him!' Michael

294

had been ordered, and thwacked unnervingly hard. 'It's all in his head,' Terry had explained. 'I barely know the guy — we must have set him off by going for a cigarette together. He's obsessed with stealing.' There was also plenty of quick-witted banter and raucous laughter, yet Michael found himself yearning for the tempering effect of women.

Cowardice or not, enough's enough, he decides as he gets out of the bath and dries himself on a coarse blue towel.

Then he changes into his dressing gown, returns the key and retreats to his bedroom.

He can feel his mood sinking lower and lower with each passing minute. He's frightened by how fast it's falling. With any luck I can stay in here most of tomorrow, he thinks. I might get fed up with my own company, but I'd rather be bored rigid than re-enter the fray.

35

'Ooh, look at him!' says Karen. 'He's changed so much already!'

Lou unclips the baby carrier from the pram and edges into Karen's hallway.

'Let's sit in the living room. It's easier,' Karen suggests.

'Sure.' Lou follows her, puts the carrier down on the floor, then kneels beside her week-old baby and bends to sniff his nappy.

'Does he need changing?'

'Seems OK for the moment.'

'He's such a cutie!' The baby seems to furrow his brow ever so slightly at her words, and Karen coos at him. 'You're very alert, aren't you?'

'He's called Frankie,' says Lou. 'In memory of my dad.'

'That's lovely.'

'And he's a right flirt. Aren't you, my little man?'

'You're very brave bringing him all this way on the bus. Most first-time mums rarely venture out.'

'Yeah, well, most first-time mums don't live in an attic

barely big enough to swing a cat. Where are Molly and Luke?'

'Mum's taken them to the park. They've been ages. She has the patience of a saint, my mum. I guess they'll be back in a bit.'

Lou unzips the bag and reaches for a toy starfish. She shakes it close by Frankie and it rattles. 'How's your mum doing?' she asks Karen.

'You'll see when she gets back. Not so bad, considering, though I do worry she's lonely. I'd be interested to know what you think.'

'You know me and mothers.' Lou pulls a face. 'I'm not one to give advice.'

'I thought things between you two were better?'

'They are, you're right – mustn't complain. She seems to adore Frankie already.'

'My mum relishes spending time with Molly and Luke,' says Karen. 'I've heard it said grandchildren are the dessert of life.'

'There's something about having a baby that links us more to our parents, isn't there? I suppose it's because we begin to understand what it was like to be them.'

It's a shame my father wasn't well enough to appreciate being with my kids more over the last few years, reflects Karen. He was such a good dad when I was small, carving me wooden toys from scratch, always allowing me to win at draughts and chess, teaching me to ride a bike by running alongside, yelling encouragement. He'd have made a super granddad, if dementia hadn't depleted him so.

'What's up?' says Lou.

'Oh, thinking about my dad, that's all.'

'I've been thinking about my dad a lot as well.' Lou gives her a sympathetic smile.

At least Dad got to see Molly and Luke, Karen reminds herself. I should be more thankful. She catches herself; it's that 'should' word again . . . Then she remembers: 'Ooh, just to warn you, I've a friend who might pop round this morning – she's having a tough time, so I said she could.'

'Who's that?'

'No one you know.' Karen reaches for the starfish to shake it for Frankie. 'I met her—' She recalls she's not told Lou she's attending Moreland's. It's silly, given that Lou is a counsellor, but then I'd have to explain how awfully down I've been, and that'll be a long conversation, she reasons. So she fudges, 'We're on a course together, but she lives round here.'

'I didn't know you were doing a course . . . ?'

'Um, yes . . . Anyway, she's splitting up with her husband—' I mustn't say more or I'll be breaking Abby's confidence, Karen remembers. 'I'll let her explain.' It might be safer to head back to their original subject. 'You were asking about Mum. While she's out, I wanted to ask you something.'

'Oh?'

'I was wondering if I ought to invite her to move in here. She's still in that horrible flat in Goring.'

'Hmm. Well, you already know I couldn't live with my mother in a million years.' Lou recoils at the prospect, and Frankie scrunches up his face and begins to howl, as if in response. Lou reaches to unclip the fasteners of his seat. 'You need feeding,' she says, scooping him into her arms.

'You're such a natural,' Karen smiles. 'Why don't you pass him to me? Then you can sit on the sofa, and I'll hand him back.' Lou does as she suggests and Karen is delighted to have a few seconds cuddling him. Ah, the joy of newborn baby!

'You get on with your mum so well,' says Lou, once Frankie is suckling. 'All the same, how would you feel about her being here?'

'Burdened.' The word pops out before Karen can contain it. 'But Mum's always done such a lot for me . . .'

'She was living abroad when your children were small,' Lou points out.

'Yeah, but they had us to stay a lot. We had some wonderful holidays out there.' At least Dad was able to enjoy those with us, she recalls, even if his memory was slipping.

'I bet she loved it! You said yourself she enjoys being with Molly and Luke.'

Karen is uneasy being critical. 'She had a huge amount on, looking after my father. She managed virtually single-handed for many years.'

'Yes, sorry, I wasn't thinking – of course she did. I told you not to talk to me about mothers. I project too much of my own relationship. Great at being the objective counsellor, aren't I?'

If only Lou knew how much therapy I've had in the last fortnight, Karen thinks. I wasn't after more. 'I don't want to upset her – especially when she's just lost Dad . . . And I don't want to be unkind, or let her down . . .' She comes to a halt. I'm off *again*, she realizes, putting others' needs first. Now she's seen the pattern, it's showing up everywhere, like a dandelion seeding itself.

They're interrupted by the sound of people coming up the path.

Karen goes to the window. 'It's my friend.' Abby has a pushchair too; it's strange to see it occupied by a boy of Luke's age, and he appears to be wearing giant earphones like her father had in the 1970s. Karen has a flurry of panic about Frankie. He's so small and vulnerable. 'She's brought her son. I said she could but I gather he can be a bit hard to control. Are you OK with that?'

'Of course,' says Lou, as she eases her breast back into her bra and clips it up.

Nothing ever seems to throw her, thinks Karen, impressed. 'Back in a sec, then,' she says, and goes to open the front door.

* * *

'I'll wheel him inside in the chair,' says Abby.

'We're in the living room,' says Karen.

'Ah.' Abby notices the plural. She's worried how Callum will react to Karen's children – when she'd phoned, Karen had said they were out. She'd hurried to make it before they returned, but it took a while to get Callum out of the house. It often does, except when he fancies it – then he can bolt like an Olympic sprinter.

Abby tilts the pushchair to get it through the doorway

without scratching the paint and wheels Callum close to the television.

'Abby, this is my friend Lou,' says Karen. 'Lou, this is Abby and Callum.'

Abby has been fighting back tears all morning, so is disappointed to see a woman with a very small baby sitting on the sofa. She's patting the baby's back to wind him. I'm not sure I can cope with someone who doesn't understand my situation, Abby thinks. She's tempted to leave, but that would be rude. 'Do you mind if I put on a film for Callum?' She rummages in her bag.

'Go ahead.'

'I think we've met before,' says Karen's friend.

Abby looks up. There *is* something familiar about her.

'I did wonder, when Karen said your son has autism.'

Has autism, Abby notices, most people don't refer to it like that. Not unless they have some kind of experience – 'your son is autistic' is much more common. She speeds the film through to a section Callum likes. At once he leans forward to watch and Abby turns to give Karen's friend her full attention.

'You two were shopping . . . ?'

'Oh my goodness! You're the lady from the Co-op! Wow. And I see you've had your baby. Congratulations!' So *that's* why I didn't recognize her.

'Frankie,' says Lou with a proud smile. Her son gives a liquidy burp.

'You've met before?' asks Karen.

Instantly Abby's mood brightens, as if someone has let in the sunshine. She tells Karen the story, and finishes, 'In that situation some people can't get away fast enough, but mostly they just stand and stare. I know it's fascinating, but sometimes I get sick of being treated as if we're purely there for entertainment. But Lou was so helpful.'

'It was nothing.' Lou appears both embarrassed and chuffed.

'That is so spooky,' says Karen. 'You know Lou is the woman I was telling you about yesterday, Abby? The one I met the day Simon died on the train?'

'No way!'

Karen laughs. 'I did tell you what goes around comes around.'

What a tonic, thinks Abby. It's good to be reminded that not everyone is as selfish as Glenn, in the wake of recent revelations.

There's a tap on the window. Abby sees an elderly woman in a tweed coat, two children at her side.

Oh-oh, she thinks, bracing herself. Seconds later the children charge into the lounge.

'I'll go and put the kettle on,' says the woman and disappears down the hall. Abby deduces she must be Karen's mother. They have similar hazel eyes, she notices.

'Shh! Kids!' says Karen. 'Look who's here.'

'Lou!' her daughter gasps.

What gorgeous blonde curls, thinks Abby.

'It's the baby!'

'Quiet.' Karen puts her finger to her lips. 'He's about to drift off, see?'

The little girl tiptoes over to Lou's side. Her mouth opens into an 'O' of wonder.

'I've just fed him,' Lou tells her. 'So he's all woozy.'

'Molly, Luke, this is Abby,' says Karen.

'Hello,' says Abby.

'And this is her son, Callum.'

'Why's he in a pushchair?' says Luke.

Callum starts to moan as if in pain. Too many new people, thinks Abby, and a new house. It was ambitious to try this.

'Should I take the kids into the kitchen?' Karen offers.

'Let's give it a minute,' says Abby. The film might recapture Callum's attention, and it saddens her that he's so often separated from his peers.

'Molly, Luke – come and sit with me,' says Lou, 'and I'll explain. You need to stay very quiet, though.'

Karen's children obviously know her well, observes Abby; they plop down on either side of her without a quibble.

'Abby's little boy has a condition that means he has a hard time talking and understanding everything you say,' says Lou in an almost-whisper.

She's perceptive, thinks Abby. Imagine picking that up from just one encounter, let alone remembering several months on.

'Why's he wearing those things on his ears?' says Molly.

'Well, he's very sensitive to noise and sometimes he gets upset if people are too loud. That's why you have to be very gentle around him.' Lou glances at Abby. 'Is that right?'

Abby nods.

'So can we play with him?' asks Luke. 'We could introduce him to Toby.'

'Toby's the cat,' explains Karen.

'It might be easier for him to watch TV for a while,' says Abby.

'Doesn't he like cats?' asks Molly.

'It's not that exactly, just sometimes when Callum plays with friends he wants them to do it his way, and if they don't, he gets upset.'

'Is he ill?' asks Molly. She remains on the sofa, but cranes her neck in an attempt to see Callum's face.

'Not exactly, no. He has something called autism.'

'Can I catch it?'

'No. He was born with it. Actually, it affects boys much more than girls.'

'Can *I*?' Luke looks worried.

Abby doesn't know whether to be delighted by their honesty or disappointed by their suspicion.

'No,' says Lou.

'We're coming to his favourite song,' says Abby. 'Can we turn it up?'

Karen reaches for the remote and Aurora's trilling fills the room.

'I know this!' says Molly.

'Shh.' Lou nudges her.

Softly, Molly sings along to 'Once Upon a Dream' whilst Luke looks at her disparagingly. Callum bangs his fists on the arms of his pushchair with excitement.

'It's a while since I've heard that,' says Karen, as the prince and princess swirl to the end.

Abby is surprised to see her eyes are full of tears.

Karen comes over, crouches down and murmurs in her

ear, 'Molly used to love Princess Aurora *so* much . . . She's got a doll and everything . . .'

Abby's eyes brim. 'Callum adores Aurora.'

'Molly wanted to bury her doll with her father.'

It must be because the tears are so near the surface, Abby tells herself as she blinks them away. Then Callum starts to moan again. 'Sorry, we'll have to replay it, now he's got into it. Can I have the remote? Bear with us,' she says, as the picture jumps back a scene. She presses play and again Callum is caught up with excitement. This time Molly comes to sit next to him cross-legged on the floor. She watches him, then follows suit, banging her fists on her knees, sharing the thrill.

If only everyone connected with Callum as intuitively as Molly, thinks Abby.

Just then there's a rap on the door. 'I've made coffee.' It's Karen's mother. 'Do you want me to bring it through?'

'Oh gosh, Mum, thanks. Let me lend you a hand.' Karen scrambles to her feet and leaves the room.

Abby yearns to escape with her; she's still keen to talk. Isn't this how it often is? Of course Karen needs to help her mother but still, it's no wonder I end up bottling stuff up, she thinks. When I was at college I had lots of friends to chat to, but with my life the way it is, the opportunities for me to share with a kindred spirit seem so few and far between.

36

Michael is lying on his bed. All the energy he had yesterday has vanished – he's deflated, like a blow-up toy with a puncture, and feels just as useless. He can barely move he's so tired, yet throughout the night he slept little. He's bored, too – only the staff checking up on him has broken the monotony. In the dark someone came and shone a torch at him through the glass panel in the door; since it's been light two nurses have come to stare at him.

For a moment he longs to be back at Moreland's. The staff seemed less officious and the patients less intimidating. Sure, there were people he didn't see eye to eye with, but there was nobody he was scared of. He pictures Karen and Abby, Lillie and Colin, Lansky and Karl . . . Maybe I simply got used to them, he thinks, but they were a good bunch. At the end of the day, in spite of our different problems, we all just wanted to get better. It took me a while to grasp that, but I was finally getting there.

That office manager was a prick though, he reminds himself. It's thanks to Phil I'm here. So they weren't all saints, not by any means, and if Gillian genuinely cared about me, she wouldn't have let me be sent away.

Eventually there's a face at the glass he recognizes: Akono. The young man taps and comes in.

'It's time for lunch,' he says.

'I'm not hungry.'

'Delicious sandwiches in the lounge.' Akono gives a broad smile.

'Can't I have mine here?'

'It is not good for you to stay in here, my man. Come and join the others.'

It's 'the others' Michael wants to avoid.

'Terry's in there,' Akono cajoles.

Michael's surprised that Akono is aware they got on. Reluctantly, he pushes back the duvet.

'Why don't you put on some clothes?'

'Because then I'll have to change back into these.' He gestures at his T-shirt and pyjama bottoms. 'I'll wear my dressing gown.'

'It is not good to be in your dressing gown at lunchtime.'

'All right.' He stands up. 'But don't watch me getting dressed. I'm sick of being spied on.'

In the lounge, Terry is by the food trolley, so Michael heads over. He appraises the choice of sandwiches; the grub's worse too, he concludes.

Terry seems to read his disdain. 'They had to close the canteen recently. Cuts.'

'So you don't get hot food here?'

'Yeah, we get one cooked meal a day.'

There's a cough behind him. 'Want my advice? The

cheese is the best.' Michael turns and sees it's one of the Scrabble guys. 'Good strong cheddar.'

Then Michael clocks a woman wielding a clipboard – it's the same one who kept peering through his door. Once more she is checking up on them.

'Taken mine,' Terry says to her.

'Matt . . . ?' She glances at the Scrabble guy, then her list. 'Yup, you're OK.'

'This is Mike,' Matt says to her.

'Michael,' says Michael.

The woman frowns. 'I don't seem to have you down.'

'I arrived yesterday,' says Michael.

'I'm making sure everyone's had their morning medication.'

'I'm not on any medication.'

The woman raises her eyebrows. 'Not on a daytime dose? You take your meds at night, then?'

'I'm not on anything. I just said.'

'I'm not sure that's right . . .' She writes down his name. 'I'll have to speak to the psychiatrist.'

'Speak to whoever you want,' says Michael.

She sighs and moves on.

'Ooh, they won't like that,' says Matt, when she's out of earshot.

'Won't go down well, your not taking any meds,' agrees Terry.

'They can lump it.' Michael is tempted to add that he doesn't want to be doped up, but stops himself. He doesn't fancy riling Matt, in particular.

'They can help you feel better,' says Terry. 'Put you on more of an even keel.'

Michael shakes his head. 'I'm not keen.'

'Don't reckon they'll let you stay if you refuse to take anything,' says Matt.

'They'll decide you can't be that ill.' Terry nods. 'Probably discharge you, switch you to home treatment.'

Fine by me, Michael says to himself. Sooner I get out of here the better. 'How does that work?'

'You get to be in your own home and they send someone to visit you – mainly to chat, but also to help administer medication,' says Terry.

The phrase *help administer medication* scares Michael. He'd been coming round to giving antidepressants a go voluntarily, but this sounds as if pills will be forced upon him.

Later that afternoon, Michael is back in his room when he sees another face at the glass. A woman he's not seen before taps and comes in. She's tall and thin, with frizzy hair scraped back tight into a giant pompom. 'Have you a moment?'

Michael can hardly say he hasn't. 'Mm.' He sits up.

'I'm Leona.' I don't know why she bothers telling me her name, thinks Michael. I've met so many people in the last twenty-four hours, I haven't a hope of remembering it. 'Do you mind if I sit down?' She reaches for a chair, and the pompom waves comically as she moves. 'I'm a psychiatric nurse and I work on the crisis resolution team.'

'Surely everyone here is in crisis,' says Michael.

She nods. 'Fair point.' Then she says, 'The ward doc's off this weekend, so I've been seconded to gate-keep admissions here,' and he gleans he should pay attention. 'I gather you've not been on any medication, and I wondered if we could talk about that?'

'There's nothing to say.'

'OK . . .' She looks straight at him and holds his gaze. Her dark eyes have a spark. 'Let's examine it from another angle. If I was to ask you to illustrate your mood, how would you describe it?'

Michael leans forward and draws a straight line on the duvet cover. The sheet forms parallel ridges, as if he's dug a miniature road.

'That looks pretty level to me,' says Leona. 'But would you say that's a level that's generally up, or down?'

'Take a wild guess.'

'Touché.' Leona grins. 'I can't force you to try medication, obviously, but I do believe an SSRI might help you.'

'More bloody initials,' says Michael.

'Well, selective serotonin reuptake inhibitor is a bit of a mouthful. Would you like me to explain how they work?'

'They'll flatten me out and I'm like that already.'

'That's not what they do exactly. If you'll allow me—'

But Terry said medication removes the urge to fight, thinks Michael. Sounds ominously like doping to me. 'You're all right.'

'OK . . .' Again that direct gaze. 'If you're sure you'd rather not take them, that's your decision. It's just many patients find they help.'

'Lots of your patients here are a lot worse than me.'

Leona nods. 'That's probably true. We do have a high threshold for admission.'

He recalls the young lad he met the day before. 'Like Eddie, you mean? Yeah. I'm not barking.'

Leona shakes her head but he can see she's concealing a smile. 'Seriously though, patients experiencing hallucin-ations can be very distressing to witness, especially when you're not too great yourself. I gather you've come from Moreland's?'

'Yup.'

'How did you like it there?'

Whatever I say is bound to be misconstrued, thinks Michael. 'OK . . .'

'Sometimes we find people who've come from private health care have raised expectations. At Moreland's most of the patients are not as severely ill as those here. Many of the people you see at Sunnyvale have been hospitalized for their own safety.'

'Banged up,' says Michael.

'Actually most patients on this ward are voluntary. They can leave whenever they wish.'

'If they weren't zombies,' Michael mutters. He adds a T-junction at right angles to the road on his duvet cover.

'Speak up, Michael,' says Leona. 'I can take it.' She sep-arates the hair of her pompom into two parts, then tugs to tighten it as if preparing herself for battle.

OK, thinks Michael. You're on. He looks up, unblinking. 'Here all you're bothered about is keeping us drugged so we're easier for you to manage. How's that going to make me better?'

Leona holds his gaze. 'People here are not "drugged" to make the lives of staff easier, Michael, as much as their own. A lot of patients arrive here in a very distressed state and we work hard with every one of them to help get them as well as possible again. But we don't just give people medication. There are other things you can do here; classes and groups—'

'You mean pottery.' He raises his eyes to the ceiling.

Leona takes a deep breath. He senses he's trying her patience. 'You know, we'd love to have the sort of budgets Moreland's has to play with. But we don't. In all honesty, times are tough for the NHS. The number of consultants has been cut and beds have been reduced. Demand is very intense.'

'Fucking politicians.'

'You'd be surprised how many staff would concur with that.'

'I want to leave,' says Michael.

'Ah. Well, that was what I was coming on to.'

'I'm not that bad. I'm doing all right. I can manage.'

'I was about to suggest you might do better at home,' says Leona. 'I understand you've good family support.'

I'm not sure I want to be totally cut loose though, thinks Michael, back-pedalling. That's how I ended up at Moreland's in the first place.

'It wouldn't just be down to your family, though. You'd get regular visits—'

'You're going to come round and administer drugs. You can't kid me.' He leans back against the wall behind his bed with a satisfied huff.

'I'm not trying to kid you.' Leona's eyes spark again. 'Man, you've got me caught between a rock and a hard place. I'm trying to work out what's best for you, given the options available.'

He's definitely on the verge of pushing her too far. Don't be a troublemaker, he reminds himself, or they'll wrest decisions from your hands.

'Let me be frank with you, Michael,' Leona continues. 'Staff in here and on the crisis resolution home treatment team – we're not the enemy. On the whole we're a good bunch. But at least at home you won't have to deal with other patients – which I understand can be distressing. We can help devise a programme to manage your depression – plus you'll have members of my team popping in to see you. And I'm on the roster, so sometimes that person will be me. Imagine that – some men would give their eye teeth to see more of me. How does that sound?'

Michael narrows his eyes, appraising. Instinct tells him that Leona is being as straight as her position allows, but instinct hasn't served him well recently. Still, at least she doesn't seem thrown by a bit of banter, hasn't forced him to take medication (yet) and appears to respect his opinion. Regardless of his misgivings, it seems the better option. It's hardly as if his mood is lifting here.

'I'd like to go home,' he says.

37

'How was it being home last weekend?' asks Beth.

Such a lot seems to have happened that Abby can hardly believe it's only been five days since their last one-to-one.

Beth warned it would be hard going back, she thinks, and I didn't listen. No one gets in a state like I did, then sorts themselves out in a couple of weeks.

'It was awful,' she admits.

'Oh dear.'

'I found out my husband's been having an affair.'

Abby explains about the mug, the lipstick and the confrontation with Glenn.

When she's finished Beth says, 'How dreadful, Abby. I'm so sorry to hear that.'

'I haven't been able to shake off images of Glenn with this other woman since . . . Initially everything seemed unreal, I suppose, and I was so angry . . .' Abby starts to cry. 'But the last few days, I've been *really* miserable.' She wails, half aware she sounds about four years old. Though damn it, she thinks, I'm sick of being brave.

'It's hard losing someone,' says Beth, sliding the box of tissues towards her. 'You've been with your husband a long time, and you've got a child together.'

Abby grabs a hanky. 'Do you order these in bulk here?' she says, wiping her eyes.

Beth smiles.

'Sorry. I don't seem able to control myself.' Abby sighs. 'It's strange how it's only hit me lately, all this. I suppose it's because we've been sorting out a formal separation – selling the house makes it so final. Whereas really I lost Glenn, or rather, we became lost to one another, several years ago.'

'It strikes me you've been experiencing a lot of changes in a relatively short space of time.'

'I don't want to leave my home – it's the one thing I can rely upon,' Abby says.

'I can imagine it provides you and Callum with a sense of security.'

'Exactly . . . How dare he invite Cara there!' Abby's cheeks burn.

'And you've every right to be angry.'

'I am jealous,' Abby concedes.

'Even though you admit you knew your marriage was over, knowing someone we loved is with someone else is often hard – it intensifies the grief.'

'He's been seeing her for months behind my back!'

'So you feel betrayed?'

'Yes. I know we'd agreed to separate, but it's the lying that gets me – I wouldn't have lied to him. Not that I've ever had the chance to have an affair . . .' She stops to consider, and as fast as rage rose, it subsides. 'I can't help but worry it was my fault . . . I was so wrapped up in Callum. Do you think it was?' She looks up – she can tell from her expression Beth feels for her. The great thing about Beth is I'm in no doubt she's on my side, thinks Abby.

'It's rare that the break-up of a relationship is ever exclusively one person's fault – and from all you've told me, it certainly doesn't seem to be solely your responsibility. Do you see how it might not be helpful to blame yourself in that way?'

'You mean it's a thinking error?' says Abby. 'I suppose it could be . . . Anyway, I don't want him back. He drives me insane.' Abby laughs, aware of the significance of her words. 'He's half the reason I'm here.' Glenn's refusal to play with Callum, to do his share around the house, to negotiate on the sale . . . It's all part of the same pattern, she thinks. He's selfish, sometimes cruel. He didn't make any attempt to support me himself. And on top of all that he slept in my bed. *With Cara.* 'You know what? I don't even *like* him any more, let alone love him.'

I'm all over the place; in tears one minute and angry the next. Then she reminds herself: 'There is one good thing.'

'Oh yes?'

'Mm.' Abby checks to make sure. 'Maybe my medication is beginning to work. Anyway, it's weird. My panic has gone. Ever since I found out about Glenn's affair, it's like a fog has lifted. I can see more clearly again.'

* * *

316

Leona puts down a tatty bag bulging with papers and removes a file. 'It's a nice home you have here,' she says, striding around the living room.

Michael shuts the door so the two of them have some privacy. 'My wife takes a lot of trouble.'

'I can see.'

'That's Chrissie for you.'

'It's good she cares.'

Michael supposes it must be, but he can't get a sense that it matters. Even the fact that his wife has tidied up the wreckage in the back garden single-handed and salvaged what she could from his shed doesn't register much.

Leona peers at a photo in a silver frame on the mantelpiece. 'These your kids?'

'Yeah.'

'Nice-looking pair. Boy looks like you.'

Michael pays no heed to the compliment.

'What are they called?'

'Ryan and Kelly.'

'They live here too?'

'Not at the moment, no. They're at university.' Thank God, thinks Michael. I wouldn't know what to say to them at the moment.

Leona wanders over to the bookcase and Michael watches as she tilts her head to examine the spines of his CDs. She's so tall she can see the very top shelf.

'You've got some good stuff here.' She nods. 'Into New Wave, were you?'

'Punk.' There's a silence. Michael is aware he's not being forthcoming, but he appears to have lost the ability to elaborate. How on earth do people make conversation? Increasingly it seems he has almost nothing to say.

'May I?' Leona pauses before sitting on the brown velour settee.

Michael grunts.

'So how are you finding being at home? This is, what . . . your fourth day here?' Leona opens her file and slides a pen out from the metal clips.

'Bit strange.'

'In what way?'

'It doesn't feel normal.'

'Oh?'

He pauses. From the recesses of his mind, he pulls out a memory. It's a struggle and unpleasant, like untangling a knot of worms. 'Mind you, it didn't really feel normal before.'

'What, before you went into Moreland's?'

'I don't think it's seemed the same for a long time. I haven't said this to Chrissie, because I don't think she'd get it.' Completing sentences is hard. Michael begins to pick at his cuticles.

'Would you say you're sad?'

'Not exactly sad, no . . .'

'Numb?'

For a split second, he's grateful for Leona's help. 'It's more I can't feel anything about anything – even the things I used to like.'

'Such as your music?'

'Mm.' And the kids, he thinks. I can't seem to feel anything about them either.

318

'Detached, then?'

'Everything's sort of misty and unreal.' He holds out an arm. 'A long way away from me.'

'It sounds to me like you're still depressed, Michael.' Leona writes something in her file. 'How are things between you and Chrissie generally?'

'OK.' If only I could feel *something* for her, he thinks. I don't care what – even anger would do.

'It can be hard for people who aren't depressed to be around depressed people, that's all.'

'You mean it's hard for her to be around me?'

'I'm not saying it is definitely, just that it can be.'

'Not as hard as it is for me to be around me.'

'You've got a point there.'

Another worm wiggles through Michael's brain and emerges into words. 'It's like she thinks I *want* to be depressed.'

'And you don't. I understand that.'

'She keeps trying to help me be happy again.'

'That's good to hear.'

'No, it isn't.'

'Why not?'

'She'll put on some music she knows I used to like – The Clash or something . . .' Michael falls silent – he can hear the strains of 'Police and Thieves' as if it's playing once more. He pictures Chrissie the previous evening, ice clinking in her gin and tonic. 'Hey Mickey,' she'd said as she put down her glass and slipped a CD into the hi-fi. 'Listen to this . . .'

Then she'd turned up the volume and gone into the

kitchen, returning with a can of beer which she'd cracked open for him.

But I'm not sure I want this, he recalls thinking, both about the lager and the music. He didn't say so, though, he'd just stood there in the middle of the lounge, helpless.

'I'm so glad you're back,' she'd said, fetching her G & T to chink it with his can. 'I missed you, love. Come on, shall we dance?'

Chrissie had started swaying her hips, all the while smiling at him . . .

'And what did you do?' asks Leona.

Michael shrugs. How can he explain how horrible it was finding that something he knew he should enjoy didn't even begin to touch him? Nothing does; not in the boring, lonely, meaningless void he seems to inhabit. In the few days since he left Moreland's, he feels even further removed from other people.

Eventually he mutters, 'I wished she'd stop. She looked ridiculous.' Then he finds a bit of dry skin and pulls at it, hard.

Leona winces as she watches him, then says, 'Perhaps, from Chrissie's perspective, since she's not been depressed, it might seem like there's some untapped source in you that you've lost track of, and if she could just help you see how great some things are, you'll get it back.'

'She keeps encouraging me to be positive and hopeful, and I keep explaining I don't get whatever it is she's on about, so then she tries something else. So I explain *again*, and we go round in a great big circle, until eventually she gives up, and says clearly I want to stay miserable.'

'Is that what happened last night?'

'Yeah. After The Clash she put on a couple of other CDs. None of them worked.'

'Isn't it a sign she loves you a lot, though?'

'How?'

'Some women wouldn't play a load of punk for their husbands no matter how miserable they were.' Leona laughs but Michael ignores her. He moves onto another cuticle.

'So you're on her side now?'

'No. I'm on your side in this, if there are any sides to be taken. I want to help you understand one another a bit better.'

But don't you understand I wish she *didn't* love me so much? thinks Michael. Then I wouldn't feel obligated to keep trying.

Leona glances down at her file and scribbles something at speed. 'It's part of what I'm here for today – to make sure your situation at home isn't unbearable for you.'

Everything's unbearable, thinks Michael. But if I say so, they might put me back in that hospital, and that was even more intolerable than being here. 'It's fine,' he lies.

'OK . . . There's one other question I want to ask you, so I can make sure the crisis team has a proper handle on your needs.'

'Yes?'

'Have you had any suicidal thoughts at all?'

It's a trick, thinks Michael. If I say 'yes', she'll put me back in Sunnyvale. Or make me take pills. His thoughts are so scattered, he can't grasp anything properly. 'Not really,' he says.

Leona looks at him, holds his gaze. 'What does that mean?'

I'd better phrase it more clearly, he realizes. 'I'm OK. I'm fine. Chrissie and I are cool. I'd rather be here than in your shitty hospital.'

'. . . and medication?'

'No way.'

'What about if you had the opportunity to try medication here? Now you're back at home, perhaps you can see I'm not suggesting it so as to make the lives of staff easier at Sunnyvale, which is what you thought before.'

It's all too much for Michael to process. 'Let's talk about it next time.'

He sees the corners of Leona's mouth twitch, as if she's masking a smile. 'I guess I can live with that . . .' She flicks through her file, stops at a page, scans down with her pen, and says, 'You're a lucky man: I'm back on the roster to see you next Monday. We can chat about it then.'

'OK.' That's all he can manage. His brain is overloaded, and shuts down.

38

'Oh dear,' says Karen, seeing Abby's red eyes and blotchy cheeks. 'Tricky session?'

Abby nods.

'Come and sit yourself here.' She pats the space on the sofa between herself and Tash. There's not a lot of room, but Abby clearly needs comfort.

'It's OK, I'll move,' says Tash, and gets up. 'Too close.' She shifts to an armchair in the corner of the lounge.

'Oh, sorry.' Karen grimaces. Oops, that was tactless, she thinks. Sometimes it's hard to remember everyone's different triggers.

Abby settles down into the cushions and Karen lifts an arm to invite her to lean against her shoulder. Abby rests her head and Karen strokes her hair. 'You'll be OK . . .' she says. 'You've had a tough few days but you'll come up again.'

'Do you think so?' says Abby, in a small voice.

'Yes.' She observes Abby's bottom lip is jutting out; she's pouting, just as Molly does when she's upset. At once she is struck by a thought — Abby's own mother is far away, perhaps even unaware of what her daughter is going through. All Abby's mothering goes one way, thinks Karen – towards Callum. No wonder she brings out my own maternal instinct. I'm lucky, she thinks, heart swelling in silent appreciation. I might worry about Mum, and I might not be that good at caring for myself, but at least we can still look after one another.

'I keep thinking of Glenn and that Cara woman,' says Abby.

'I can imagine.' If I ever meet this Glenn, Karen thinks, I'm going to give him a piece of my mind.

Tash looks over from her armchair. 'He sounds a right shithead from what you said in group this morning.'

Abby lifts her head and Karen is pleased to see she is grinning. 'He's enough to make a saint swear, you're right there.'

'Fuck him then.' Tash nods. 'And her.'

'That's just it,' says Abby. 'I keep thinking of them . . . You know . . .' Karen feels a shudder go through Abby's body.

'I don't like women who shag other women's husbands,' says Tash.

Karen has to admire how bluntly she communicates her moral stance. Tash has relaxed a lot in a relatively short time – her tic is scarcely noticeable.

Abby pulls away from Karen so she can sit up straight. 'I bet Cara's more attractive than me.'

'Don't be daft,' says Tash.

'I used to think I was quite pretty.'

'You are!' Karen interjects.

'My hair's horrid this short—'

'I love your hair!' Karen can't believe what she's hearing. 'I'd do anything for hair that frames my face the way yours does – mine's like a great big thick curtain.'

'You could always dye it pink,' says Tash, shaking her cerise locks with a certain pride.

'It's typical, isn't it?' says Karen. 'Here we go again. Being positive for others instead of ourselves. Once you're through this – and you will get through it, Abby, I promise, though maybe you don't believe that now – you'll have men beating a path to your door. Don't you agree, Tash?'

Tash nods vigorously.

Karen makes a mental leap. 'You know what my friend Anna has been saying?'

'No?'

'She's been on at me for ages to try Internet dating. Perhaps we should do it together.'

'Sounds like a good idea,' says Tash.

'Oh God, I don't think I'm ready for that.' Abby looks startled Karen should even suggest such a thing.

I've been crass again, thinks Karen. 'No, no, of course not. I didn't mean right now – I'm not sure about it either. It's only when Anna split up with her last boyfriend, she started doing it right away. She said it was a good ego boost, and dating was like falling off a horse – the best way to get over a man was to get straight back on one.' Karen laughs. 'So to speak.'

Abby swivels to see her more squarely. 'Seriously, would you ever . . . um . . . look for someone else?'

'I don't know. I've no idea what sort of men you'd meet online.'

'I've done it,' says Tash. 'Yeah, you meet some right weirdos. But they're not all bad.'

'Is that how you met your current boyfriend?' asks Abby.

'Not this one, actually, no. But the one before I did, and I know plenty of people who've met their partners online.'

'My friend Anna's boyfriend is nice, but she's got less baggage. It can be tricky trying to attract someone as a single mum with two kids, never mind a widow.' Karen laughs. 'And soon I'm probably going to have Mum living with us too. Can you see the ad? *Two widows, two kids, one husband needed.*'

'I bet that Cara hasn't got children,' says Abby. 'Imagine me with Callum. If Glenn couldn't cope and he's his dad, who on earth would ever take us on?'

'Now, now both of you,' says Tash. 'I'm hearing all sorts of negativity here, and neither of you has even *been* online.'

'She's got us sussed,' says Abby.

Karen nods. Tash might be half my age, she thinks, but she makes me seem unworldly. And she's right – we should give it a go. After all, what have we got to lose?

* * *

Michael hears the rustle of cotton, feels the mattress dip as Chrissie edges close to him. Oh no, he thinks, as she starts to stroke his hair. Then she edges her fingertips gradually, lightly, down the nape of his neck.

I wish she wouldn't do that, he thinks, and sighs.

But she misreads the signal, slips a hand under his T-shirt, between his shoulder blades, gently massaging, and actually he's tense just there, and what she's doing almost helps. A tiny, tiny part of him wants to moan softly in gratification, roll over to face her properly, kiss her tenderly, stroke her too.

And yet a far bigger part of him resists. It's been so long since they've been intimate; too long. It's too difficult, too meaningful, too loaded – it – they – he – is sure not to work. The distance between them, so near in reality, feels impossibly, horribly far. He can feel her breath growing hotter, shorter, more urgent.

But he's weary; too weary for this. He can't do it. Not tonight.

So he rolls further over, curls away from her, back arched like a turtle shell, shutting her out.

39

There's a dog on the beach in Rottingdean, yapping as it runs in and out of the sea. Michael watches for a moment from his vantage point on the prom. The dog's owner is throwing a ball into the shallows – time and again the dog swims out to retrieve it, paddling eagerly, then returns with the ball in its mouth and puts it down, tail wagging, yapping until it is thrown again.

I don't – *can't* – give a fuck, thinks Michael.

He can't feel enjoyment like that; he can't feel even slightly happy, just for a second. The anger is gone, the tears – what few there were – are gone. Since he left Sunnyvale, all his experiences have flattened and blended together, so whilst he's aware different things are happening to him, they don't feel any different. This evening is the same; he's not sure what he's doing on the seafront on a Saturday night. He told Chrissie he was heading for the Black Horse but he has no yen to go there. He just wanted to get away from sitting at home surrounded by reminders of his failure

– the devastation in the back garden, the empty space in the drive, the deluge of mail from his creditors.

But besides getting rid of this sense of utter worthlessness, he has no desire to do anything. Somehow he has ended up here. The waves glisten in the fading light, but he's unaffected by their beauty.

I've lost myself, he thinks. I don't know where the me I used to be is any more. That Michael disappeared months ago.

It's as if he's vacated his own mind. He briefly glimpsed himself again when he was at Moreland's, but that was just an interlude, a taste of respite which only makes the void he's in more unbearable. And it was snatched away like everything else.

He continues walking along the prom until a vast pile of rocks hides the dog and its owner from view. He looks about: there's a couple strolling under the white chalk cliffs, but they're at least a hundred yards off and walking in the opposite direction, towards Peacehaven. Otherwise, the beach is empty. It's late, there's a chill in the air, and Rottingdean isn't Brighton: on this stretch of the coast there are no late-night revellers. For this, if nothing else, Michael is glad; he doesn't want to be disturbed.

He steps off the concrete path and onto the shingle. His shoes crunch against the pebbles; the gradient propels him towards the sea. Close to the water the stones are wet, shiny. He hears the dog yapping over the other side of the rocks, still audible above the crash of the waves. He wants to get away from it, this stupid, happy dog.

A yard or so further and Michael is in the water. He's still wearing his lace-up shoes, but so what? Now he's past his ankles; soon his jeans are drenched. It's very cold. He keeps going, pace slowed by his clothing; it feels heavy, yanked this way and that by the waves. The sea is choppy, with white horses running all the way to the horizon. But there's something consoling about sensing that the elements have power over him, that there *is* a force bigger than his own awful thoughts. He's been trying to escape them for an unendurable length of time. At last, he's found a way.

'I'm not myself,' he has an urge to say to Chrissie as he pushes on. 'That's why I'm doing this.' He's up to his thighs now, and he's freezing, teeth chattering like a clock-work toy.

Once he's in past his waist he starts to swim. The water gets colder the further he goes, but at least he's getting away from everything and everyone, his fuck-ups, his future.

It turns out to be hard moving in all his clothes, so he stops swimming and paddles so he can undo his shoes and kick them off. The jeans and sweatshirt he can manage – just – so he presses onwards with a mix of breaststroke and front crawl.

Eventually he swivels to look back at the shore. He can hardly make out the row of beach huts on the prom, they're so tiny.

Then, somewhere in the very furthest, smallest recesses of Michael's head, there's a faint echo of Gillian: *It's just a thought, and thoughts can be changed.*

But his jeans are weighing him down and he's tired, very tired, so when a large wave catches him as he swims round to face the ocean again, he has no energy to resist being pulled beneath the surface. It's only Gillian, and what does she know?

'MICKEY! MICKEY!' Now he hears Chrissie calling him.

He comes up gasping, spluttering for air. It's only his mind playing tricks again – trying to make him turn back when everything is hopeless. He'd never hear anyone on the shore from here.

And then it's too late: another wave drags him under.

IV

The Morning After

40

'No!' says Johnnie. The news is a punch to his gut. 'When?'

'At the weekend.' Gillian's voice catches.

'But it wasn't here, surely?' It's almost impossible for patients to harm themselves at Moreland's; there are safeguards in place throughout the building. No knives in the communal kitchen, no scissors in the art room, no razors in the patients' rooms – they have to ask if they want to shave, and are watched by nurses while they do so. The bedroom doors are kept unlocked at all times, and those patients who are thought likely to hurt themselves are checked on regularly.

Gillian shakes her head.

It's dreadful, yet Johnnie can feel his shoulders slump with relief. To have a suicide on the premises would make the situation even worse. There would be questions and finger-pointing, possibly an enquiry – who knows where that might lead. Most distressing would be the impact on other patients. Still, Johnnie feels terrible. I should have done more, he thinks.

Gillian seems to read his mind. 'I know you ran several of the relevant group sessions, but I don't want you to feel you're in any way to blame.'

'I should have realized how desperate things were,' he says.

Gillian glances through the window. 'Once someone is discharged, there's not much we can do . . . Unfortunately we can't keep people in here forever.' Her expression is so sad that Johnnie has a sense she wishes she could protect everyone from the struggles to be found in the world outside.

'But it's only been ten days—'

'I know. Unfortunately a lot can go wrong in a very short time when you're dealing with acute mental health issues.'

Johnnie knew he'd have to face a patient's suicide one day; he can even recall Gillian warning him he'd have to be prepared for it in his initial interview. Nonetheless it's one thing knowing something might happen, quite another having to cope with the reality. He's not had a chance to hear the full story, let alone absorb it, and he's got to guide vulnerable patients for the next hour and a half. He's at a loss as to what he should say to them. The prospect makes him panic.

Ironic, he thinks, all those months talking about anxiety; here I am thrust right into the agony of it.

'I realize you're running the next group,' says Gillian. 'I can't offer to take over the session – I've a patient at half past. But I could come with you to break the news. They'll hear of it anyway, if they haven't already, so in this instance we'd better take the lead. Would that help?'

Gillian is so much softer and kinder than she seemed when I first started, thinks Johnnie. 'Thank you. That would be good.'

'I won't say "My pleasure,"' says Gillian with a rueful laugh. She gets to her feet. 'We'll talk about it more at lunch. It's hit a lot of the staff hard, and we're going to need to process this too. Meanwhile, we'd better head on up. You ready?'

'Ready as I'll ever be,' says Johnnie.

* * *

It's 11.05: Karen is late. She parks her car (badly), flings money into the meter and charges up the steps into the clinic.

'Traffic was awful,' she says to Danni, signing in with a hasty scrawl.

'Lots of people have been having problems getting in.'

Karen waits to be buzzed through the coded door, then pounds upstairs – no time to make a cup of tea – and down the corridor.

The moment she enters the lounge, she knows something is wrong. Rita is in the armchair where she always sits, but she's hunched over and enfolded in a clumsy embrace by Colin, who's crouched at her feet. Abby is on one of the sofas jigging her legs, face drained of colour; Tash is next to her, jerking her head and yelping like a dog in distress. Only Rick, who's kneeling at the coffee table with a tabloid spread before him, so much as registers Karen's arrival.

'Hi,' he nods. But even the way he says this sounds strange. Too quiet, sober.

337

'Is everything all right?' she asks.

The silence, the tension, is horribly familiar.

*   *   *

I can't believe it, thinks Abby. How awful. We got on so well, I thought we were friends, or could have been. We're very different, but still, once I was out of here for good, I was planning to get in touch, find out how things are. I should have done it anyway. I should have called.

Her legs won't stop juddering; she feels sick.

I suppose I'm in shock, she says to herself, trying to get a handle on what's happened. But everyone around is in such a state too, it's shaking her up even more. She feels scarily ungrounded, spaced out, just as when she first came to Moreland's. I thought I was much better, she thinks, but I'm not. I'm as bad as ever. Maybe I'll never get well. Evidently being discharged is no sign that anyone's cured.

And now Karen has arrived. She doesn't seem to have a clue as to what's going on. God, someone tell her – I don't want it to be me – I'm frightened this will set her back too, and I couldn't bear it.

*   *   *

Rick slides the newspaper across the table.

Across the top of a double-page spread is the headline: *TV STAR IN SUICIDE TRAGEDY.*

Karen gasps.

Below is a picture of Lillie. Beside her is a woman Karen

recognizes as her sister. They are arm in arm, dressed in white minidresses and patent knee-high boots, beaming at the camera. Karen falls to her knees. She reads:

Tragedy hit the seaside town of Brighton yesterday when the body of much-loved TV presenter Lillie Laybourne was discovered in the early hours of the morning. Early reports indicate Lillie, 24, had taken an overdose of pills, and her death was caused by heart failure.

Sussex-born Lillie was best known as the host of *Street Dance Live*, which she co-presented with her sister Tamara, 26. The glamorous duo lived only a floor apart in a block of luxury flats on the seafront. It was Tamara who found Lillie yesterday. Their friend and neighbour Jack Lawrence, 61, revealed that Tamara was worried when Lillie failed to answer her mobile, and let herself into the flat to check on her sister. Tamara called emergency services, but it's understood that Lillie had passed away several hours previously.

'The two of them were very close,' Mr Lawrence said, 'and Lillie was devoted to Tamara's little boy, Nino.'

HORROR BENEATH
HAPPY-GO-LUCKY CHARM

On screen Lillie's warm and cheerful persona won her legions of fans of all ages. But whilst the public saw a bubbly brunette with a gift for boosting the confidence of young dancers competing in the prime-time show, it has emerged that behind the scenes Lillie was living with an agonizing mental condition. Only a few close friends and family members were aware that she suffered from bipolar illness, also known as manic depression, which meant her moods swung from dramatic highs to dreadful, debilitating lows.

It is believed that Lillie may have ceased taking the

medication she'd been prescribed to control her mood swings, according to a close friend, who preferred not to be named.

'Antipsychotic drugs and mood stabilizers often help patients like Lillie lead a relatively normal life,' explained leading consultant psychiatrist at the Maudsley Hospital, Dr Jiang Chung. 'About 1 in 3 of those with bipolar disorder will remain completely free of symptoms with the use of carefully monitored medication. But problems can arise when individuals are tempted to stop taking the maintenance dose. They may feel clear of symptoms and think they don't need it, or they may miss the euphoria of manic episodes. Research clearly indicates that stopping almost always results in relapse, especially if done abruptly. In the case of lithium discontinuation, mood can dip dramatically in a period of a few days, and the rate of suicide rises precipitously.'

NIGHTMARE CHILDHOOD

Sadly, it's only a few weeks since Lillie told this newspaper she was back on track after a very dark period. 'I had a particularly difficult childhood – my parents split when I was 15 and I haven't seen my father since,' she told our Celebrity Reporter Jayne Whitehead. 'But with the support of my sister and friends, and help from a wonderful team of professionals, I've faced my demons and I'm pleased to say I've finally laid them to rest.'

It's also believed that being in the public eye exposed the fragile presenter to scrutiny which she found hard. Two years ago she was photographed leaving Moreland's Place in Lewes, a local clinic specializing in the treatment of psychiatric disorders.

Mr Lawrence said, 'I knew Lillie had been a patient at Moreland's, but I had no idea she was so unhappy. She moved into this block when she was 17, and often popped in for a cuppa. Last time I saw her she was laughing and full of life – she'd just come back from a shopping spree and dropped by to show me all her new clothes.' He choked back tears as he added, 'She was a delightful girl and those who loved her can't believe one minute she was here, and the next, she's gone. We will all miss her hugely.'

Karen doesn't stop until she's finished the piece. Then she peers at the smaller pictures. There's a blurred shot of Lillie and Tamara as little girls, another of Lillie glammed-up with a recent winner of *Street Dance Live,* one of Lillie cuddling her baby nephew Nino, and finally Lillie in a mackintosh exiting the clinic, shielding her head with a paper in a bid not to be recognized.

Karen leaves the newspaper open on the coffee table and takes a seat on the sofa next to Abby. Wordlessly, she reaches for Abby's hand and they interlock fingers. Then for several minutes the two women sit, eyes cast down, hands clasped.

41

Michael senses her breath first, warm against his cheek. Even in this soporific state, he knows who it is.

'Mickey . . .' she is whispering into his ear. 'Mickey . . .'

He feels her take his hand; her palm is soft and smooth.

'It's me, Chrissie.'

He opens his eyelids, a crack. He can't bear to see too much, unsure of what he's going to find.

'Oh Mickey, thank God you're back.'

Where is he? He's not entirely convinced he's alive.

Gradually her face comes into focus; it's on a level with his own. His wife is almost unrecognizable: her sandy hair flat and unwashed, her eyes red-rimmed, and beneath faint freckles her skin is grey.

'*Why?*' Her voice is pleading.

He has the vaguest sense of remorse, but what it relates to he can't fathom. He has an urge to explain, 'I'm not myself' – he has a recollection he's wanted to say that to her before – but the words won't come out. Finally, after a huge effort, he manages to mouth, 'Sorry . . .' He feels his eyelids droop.

Chrissie says, 'They've given you a sedative, love.'

He turns his head on the pillow, trying to see beyond her. Even this small movement is hard. Behind the armchair she is sitting on he makes out another bed with a white metal frame. There's a hump beneath the blanket; someone else is there, back turned.

So he's not at home.

A smattering of memories returns. The beach . . . The sea . . .

'Michael?'

He jumps awake at the sound of his name and opens his eyes. Everything is blurry, but gradually a figure comes into focus. A tall, skinny woman with her hair scraped tight off her face is standing beside him.

'It's Leona, I'm the psychiatric nurse. Remember me?'

Michael frowns, trying to piece together what's going on. He manages to say, 'Where am I?'

'Sussex Hospital,' says Leona.

'How long have I been here?'

'You were brought into A & E on Saturday night, and transferred to this ward yesterday.'

But I don't know what day it is today, thinks Michael.

Leona looks down at him. 'You were very lucky.'

I don't feel lucky, thinks Michael. He doesn't know what he feels.

'Do you remember what happened?'

'The sea . . .' says Michael. He can recall swimming and getting colder and colder. After that . . . He tries to dredge up the memory. Nothing.

Leona sits down. 'It seems as if you were trying to take your own life, Michael.'

He can sense shame beginning to creep through his veins.

'If you can, I'd really like to talk a bit more about that night. I want to help, you see, we all want to help.' Leona glances down to the end of the bed. Michael lifts his head a little and sees Chrissie standing there, twisting her hands. 'Last week we chatted about how you've been feeling lately. I came to your house to see you?'

'Mm.' Last week . . . ? It's no good, Michael's lost all sense of time, he hasn't a clue how it fits together.

'I know you've been very down, and I'm terribly sorry I didn't appreciate how bad things had got.'

Down? thinks Michael. No, she's not grasped it.

'It seems you took a real nosedive in the few days since then.'

He longs to be able to communicate, but he seems to occupy a meaningless fog where he's lonely and discon-nected from everything – even the things he knows he should love, like Chrissie, don't make him feel anything. He's been stuck there for what seems an eternity.

I couldn't bear it any more, he recalls dimly, so I took myself out to sea . . . Every second I experienced in my head was torture – still is – and you're bringing me back to it, waking me up and wanting to talk about it. *Shut up*, he wants to say. But he can't, and Leona sits there, waiting.

Eventually he offers her a morsel to fend her off. 'I don't feel myself.'

'Can you explain a bit more?'

344

'I feel I've disappeared.' And you can't help someone who's disappeared, he argues. Not when that's what they reckon has happened, whilst they're sitting right in front of you. The Man With No Personality, that's me.

'There are medicines we can prescribe that may well help give you a sense of your old self back.' Leona glances again at Chrissie and she nods.

They're in cahoots, thinks Michael. They're going to drug me, keep me in this God-awful place. He can hear the man a few feet away groaning and he can smell piss. He shakes his head. 'Pills will make me lose my personality even more.'

'No, they won't, Michael,' says Chrissie. She moves to stand behind Leona's chair.

They're going to coerce me into submission, thinks Michael.

'Leona and the crisis team think antidepressants could really help you. I don't know what you've got against them. I thought you'd been taking them since you were at More-land's, I didn't know you hadn't—' She starts to cry.

Oh, leave me alone, thinks Michael, *please*.

'I *wish* you'd give them a go, Mickey.' This comes out as a howl. 'The kids want you to as well.'

'The kids?' Do Ryan and Kelly know he's here?

'I had to tell them,' she says.

But still he's adrift. 'I can't remember what happened.'

Chrissie pulls a tissue from the sleeve of her top and dabs her eyes. Then she turns to the nurse. 'Is it OK if I tell him?'

Leona nods.

'A woman on the beach saw you wading out, love. Apparently she was with her dog.'

Ah yes, thinks Michael. Through the fog he can just make out that memory. 'It was yapping . . . They were on the other side of the rocks.'

'Yes, that was the lady. Bless her . . .' Chrissie goes quiet. Then she composes herself again. 'She was a way off, but she could make out you had your clothes on. So she watched you, and when you started swimming straight out to sea, she got very worried.' Chrissie starts to cry again. 'Thank God.'

'She didn't rescue me, did she?'

'No, she'd never have reached you – she called 999 and—' Chrissie gulps, ' – they sent the lifeboat from Brighton. The men pulled you from the water and then you were transferred from the beach by helicopter to here. Apparently you'd only just gone under – the crew saw it happen . . .' She stops again. She's shaking, Michael notices, violently. 'I keep thinking what might have happened if they hadn't seen . . . They'd never have saved you.'

Shame burns through Michael's veins like fire: all these people, trying to keep him alive, when he has no personality worth saving.

A couple of minutes more and they'd have been too late, he thinks. I wish they had been. And now Chrissie's having all her horrible sad feelings and directing them at me, like spray from a hose, and I don't know what to do. I can't even stand being in my own mind, let alone dealing with someone else's.

Leona leans forward. 'Michael, do you remember when we met before, and I asked if you could describe your mood? You drew that line, yes?'

Michael nods.

346

'You told me you couldn't see what medication could do for you, and you didn't want levelling off as you were flat already.'

'Mm.'

'I'd like you to give it a shot, Michael. No one wants to take tablets. Believe me, I know. I see people like you – some better, some worse, some about the same – a lot.'

No one's like me, thinks Michael. They couldn't possibly be. Being in my mind is like existing in a hell on earth. I'm only here because of some damn dog.

'It's my job to try and help you. A lot of folks *hate* the idea of pills, just like you. However, when you get sick, sometimes you require treatment to get better. At the moment, you're like someone who's had a heart attack, but who's refusing to allow anyone to give you the kiss of life.'

Her expression is serious, but Michael can't grasp what she's trying to say.

She continues, 'You've been feeling down for months and months, and managing without medication, I know. But you got to the point where you attempted to end your own life. Isn't it worth giving antidepressants a go?'

'You want to turn me into a zombie . . .' he mutters.

Leona shakes her head. 'That's the last thing we want. At the end of the day, it's your choice. And it's only a trial – if you try them and you don't like them, you can stop.'

There's a low cough from Chrissie. 'Is it because you're too proud, love?' she ventures. 'Maybe think of them like blood pressure tablets, something like that. I don't think you'd refuse them, if doctors said you needed them. There's no shame in taking medicine.'

Michael's head is hurting; he can't argue any more. 'OK,' he relents. 'I'll take your bloody pills.'

'Darling, thank you!' says Chrissie, and bends to kiss him. Michael is aware he used to like being kissed, but now it does nothing for him.

Leona nods. 'It's a good idea, trust me. One day you'll feel much better than you do today, I truly believe that, though I know you can't imagine it. The antidepressants will take a few weeks to work, but I'm very hopeful they're the best way forward.'

'Hurry up and get them so I can go back to sleep,' he says.

Leona raises an eyebrow. 'Great. I'll sort your prescription.'

Once she's gone Chrissie slips into the chair. 'The kids have come back home, Mickey, and we really want to help.'

'Ryan and Kelly . . . ?' He closes his eyes to shut out the guilt.

'Yes, they came to see you earlier, but you were dozing. They're so relieved you're all right . . . They both break up soon anyway, so it made sense for them to finish uni a bit early, and it'll be nice to have them around, won't it?' She strokes his arm. 'We're going to get through this. Truly we are.'

'Mm.'

It'll take weeks for the medication to work, Leona said, yet Michael has been dragging himself through the most miserable, endless wasteland for months and months already. It's as if in the distance, across a strait of water, he saw the promising glimmer of a different land, and just for a while, when he ventured into the sea, he thought he'd finally be able to reach that better place. But he's arrived at the other

side, and found it's merely another miserable, endless wasteland. And now his whole family is involved. How can he
explain that he doesn't think he can go through this any
longer?

* * *

Gradually, as Karen clutches Abby's hand, she feels her
friend calm down and the jigging of her legs subside. The
two women are still sitting this way when Gillian comes into
the lounge.

Normally Karen finds it hard to read what Gillian is
thinking – the tight bun and half-moon glasses lend her an
impenetrable air – yet today her face is taut with anguish. A
few paces behind Gillian is Johnnie, but the spring in his
step and the broad smile have gone, and as he reaches for
one of the chairs, he glances at the newspaper on the table
and Karen sees the pain in his eyes. Despite her own shock
and upset, she empathizes. To be expected to take responsibility for other people – many of whom are in a precarious
mental state already – must be ghastly.

Gillian moves a chair to the end of the room by the
whiteboard, drops down into it and closes her eyes. It seems
the therapist is bracing herself, but she stays like that such
a long while, breathing in and out, that Karen begins to
grow concerned she may be too upset to lead the session.
Eventually Gillian lifts her head and looks around at them
in turn.

'So, I expect you have heard the very sad news about
Lillie.'

There's a universal acknowledgement that yes, they have.

'I've come to let you each know that, as best we can, the staff here will do everything in our power to support you through this. We appreciate this is a big shock for many of you, as it is for us. Many of you knew Lillie well and I believe considered her your friend—' there's a wail of grief from Colin, ' – and were deeply fond of her.'

Gillian's lip quivers and she pauses. Karen gives Abby's hand a squeeze; Abby squeezes back.

'In a while I'm going to hand over to Johnnie and there will be space to share your feelings in the group about what's happened, but first I thought we could start today by remembering Lillie with a few minutes' silence, if you're all agreed?'

They nod assent, and Tash's yelping diminishes to an occasional whimper, then stops. And as they sit there in a silence broken only by the *tick tick tick* of the clock on the wall, Karen is thrust back to another moment, on another Monday morning, more than two years earlier. Then, as now, she was left reeling, unable to comprehend what's happened, or why, or where she should go from here.

* * *

'Friend', thinks Abby. The last time I saw her, Lillie called me her *friend*. And to think I so nearly asked for her number, but thought she must get pissed off with people hounding her. I should have taken that word for what it signified and pushed for her address or email – *something*. I could have been a shoulder for her to lean on, I could have said I understood, and if she'd told me she'd been skipping her meds, I could have encouraged her to keep taking them . . . Even a text might have helped.

Instead my own difficulties took precedence, and now it's too late.

Perhaps I'm kidding myself, she thinks. Even if I had called, who's to say Lillie would have answered, or confessed how she was feeling? Evidently she didn't tell her sister or Gillian or Colin or anyone else how desperate she was, and she was much closer to them.

Still, she reasons, shouldn't those of us who've experienced similar lows look out for each other? All of us in this room let Lillie down to some degree; we failed one of our own. Only three days ago she and I were due to overlap in day care. I considered asking staff if she was OK when she didn't turn up on Friday – but I thought they wouldn't tell me. How precarious her situation was. If only I – we – had been aware of just how bad things were, perhaps she would be sitting in this room today.

V

A Glimmer of Light

42

After a while, Leona returns to Michael's bedside.

'Success.' She brandishes a white paper bag. 'I also managed to discuss your situation with the psychiatrist, Dr Kasdan.'

'I thought he worked at Moreland's . . .' Michael is perplexed.

'He does. But he's a consultant and works three days there and two days here. Luckily he's in this afternoon, which was helpful, as he remembers you.'

'That's good,' says Chrissie. 'I'd been worried all this inconsistency in staff wasn't helping.'

'We do try,' says Leona.

'Oh, er . . . I didn't mean you, love . . .'

'No offence taken.' Leona turns to Michael. 'Dr Kasdan and I agreed it would be good to start you on these. It's a common antidepressant which a lot of patients react well to.' She opens the paper bag, removes a box and lays it on the bedcover.

'What about side effects?' he asks.

'I'd prefer you not to get too caught up in those. It's easy to obsess when you're in a vulnerable state. They're detailed in the leaflet inside the pack.'

'You're scared I'll change my mind.'

Leona looks squarely at him. 'Yeah, I suppose I am. You've been on quite a journey, from what I've witnessed, my friend – and it's not even a fortnight since we met. It depends how you see it, right? You're thinking, *Leona's not telling me about side effects as they're so awful.*'

'Er—'

'Whereas I'm thinking, *I don't want to focus on the negatives, as I believe these bad boys—*' Leona taps the box, ' *– could help this man.* Not on their own, as I've said before, but alongside a programme of exercise and guidance in managing depression and with the support of his family.'

'Ah.' He just about gets what she's driving at.

'For some strange reason, I don't want you bumping yourself off. And nor, I suspect, does your wife here. I reckon she'd be mighty sorry to lose you, too.'

Chrissie gives a half-smile.

'But my worry about you, Michael, is you're on the edge. You quit the tablets before they have any effect, and who's to say you won't take a walk back into that lovely warm ocean out there you find so inviting?' She flings an arm in the direction of a nearby window. 'Yet I *know* that we can get you through this. I'd like to see you make the most of this programme – I reckon you could get stuff from it.'

'How do you know?'

'It seems you and I share a trait,' continues Leona. 'We tell it like it is. So, you can get yourself in a right palaver about side effects if you want. Or you can go with my advice.' She glances at Chrissie, then back at Michael. 'Which is it to be?'

'You said they take weeks to work—'

Leona holds up a hand. 'I know it feels an eternity when you're in a bad place. Nothing lasts forever and the pain you're in *will* pass. But I understand you can't ignore it just now, so I've a suggestion I hope will make that time less excruciating for you.'

'You going to remove my head?'

Leona guffaws. Her laugh is like she is – an unrestrained hoot. She shakes her head at Chrissie. 'Like it. We'll pop it in the freezer. But seriously, thought we'd try these in the interim.' She removes a second box from the bag. 'Diazepam – commonly known as Valium. Addictive, so not a long-term solution, but they should help you relax and sleep while we wait for the antidepressants to take effect.'

Michael eyes the two packets. 'I can't believe those are going to sort me out on their own.'

'They're not.' Leona's dark eyes flash. 'You do any therapy in Moreland's?'

'Yes . . .' says Michael. Not that he can remember much of it.

'Well, the other thing we're going to do – you and me, but mainly you – is work on changing what goes on in here.' She taps the side of her head. 'Did you talk about that?'

'Yeah, kind of . . .'

'Great. So, here's how I reckon you see where you are at the moment: *I'm on another planet, and no one understands what I'm going through.* Is that more or less right?'

Michael can't help but nod.

'Whereas actually, truth is, they do. *I* do. OK, so I don't get every nuance and horrible thought, but I get the gist. You don't think I do, because your only reference point is your-self. Tell me, is this the first big depression you've had?'

Michael struggles to work it out. It's hard to remember, but he can't recall feeling this bad in the past. Certainly he's not tried to kill himself before. He'd not forget that.

'It seems to me it is,' interrupts Chrissie. 'We've been together for years and I've never seen him like this till recently.' She looks at Michael. 'It's ever since your business went under, isn't it, love?'

Mention of his bankruptcy makes Michael want to hurl back the bedcovers, jump out of bed and run away.

'Figures,' says Leona. 'Can't tell you how often I see people – not being sexist here, but it tends to be fellas, quite often older men too – whose self-esteem is so bound up with their work that when the job goes – BOOM – so does their self-esteem.'

'Really?' says Chrissie. 'I find that kind of comforting.'

'Yeah, well.' Leona jerks her head towards Michael. 'We've just got to help our Michael here see that.' She gives him a wink. 'I know it's a lot to take in. And it's even worse if you've never felt this way before, because the shock of the descent into depression is so traumatic. You are in a dark, dark land—'

That's right, thinks Michael. That's exactly where I am. Hell on earth.

' – with a population of millions.'

Really? wonders Michael. I thought there was no one here but me.

'I doubt if you'll believe me, but others *have* been where you are right now, and they've got out the other side,' Leona continues, 'a few of them with my help. I'd like to try and show you the way forward. Though I can't do it on my own, so you'll have to at least *try* to trust me.'

Michael is suspicious. The idea that someone – anyone – might lead him through the wilderness is hard to believe. After all, he's been wandering for months, and he's met other people – some of whom have endeavoured to guide him – yet he's still lost.

'It's up to you how you choose to react to what I'm saying to you. You can tell yourself the next few weeks are going to be just as dire as the last however-long-it's-been. Or, instead of that, you could begin to consider the possibility you *might* have been through the worst.'

'Ri-ight . . .' Michael's brain is hurting again.

'Which means that from here on – although sometimes you'll go one step forward, two steps back – you'll gradually get better.'

'Ah.'

'You should listen to Leona, Mickey,' ventures Chrissie.

Once again Michael recalls Gillian's words. *It's just a thought, and thoughts can be changed* . . . But this time, instead of silencing her voice, he takes heed, and, if only for a few moments, gleans comfort. It's as though he's glimpsed a tiny, tiny spark of hope after it's been totally eclipsed for months on end, and something has shifted.

There is a glimmer of light in his world once more.

43

'Budge up, Dad,' says Ryan, dropping onto the brown velour sofa with a *boof* that makes the springs creak.

Michael shifts along. He's half watching the local TV news, but his head is so woolly with diazepam that he has the volume muted to allow himself to drift off. Suddenly, a face he recognizes flashes across the screen.

It's Lillie. Immediately he sits upright.

The camera cuts to a young woman with spiralled hair and honey-coloured skin. She is being interviewed by a reporter and, from her expression, is trying not to cry.

Ryan reaches swiftly for the remote and flicks over to another channel.

'Hey!' says Michael. 'I want to see that.'

'Not sure it's a good idea, Dad,' says Ryan.

'Why? What's happened?'

'It's only that TV presenter from *Street Dance Live*—'

'Exactly. Turn it back now.'

Reluctantly, Ryan does as he is bid.

'Give it some volume,' says Michael. 'I want to hear.'

'Why you so interested in her all of a sudden? You hate that show.'

'Shut up, son, let's listen.'

'We're having a small funeral for close friends and family,' the woman who resembles Lillie is saying. 'And although we really appreciate the public support we've been getting, my sister's death was a dreadful shock.'

'*Funeral?*' says Michael. He turns to Ryan. His son is scarlet. 'Lillie's *dead?*' He can't take it in. Lillie was perfectly healthy when I saw her, he thinks. It doesn't make sense.

'They reckon she . . . er . . . killed herself,' says Ryan hoarsely. 'That's, um, Tamara, her sister.'

Michael refocuses on the screen. 'I want to thank you all,' Tamara is saying, and she looks straight into the camera. Michael feels she's speaking directly to him – her features are so disconcertingly like Lillie's. 'Whilst I appreciate fans want to pay tribute, I live in this block of flats with my son—' she glances up at the building behind her, ' – and so much attention is hard to bear. I'd like to ask, please, if people would allow us to grieve in peace.'

The camera pans back to a white-fronted apartment block Michael knows is on the seafront overlooking Brighton Marina. He used to pass it every day on his journey to work. It must be less than three miles from where he and Ryan are sitting.

Propped up against the wrought-iron railings and the steps to the front door, attached with ribbons to lamp posts and bollards, are hundreds of bunches of flowers. Michael can make out a few mixed blooms and single red roses, but mainly there are lilies – tiger lilies and stargazers, calla lilies and peace lilies, as well as cream, yellow, pink, orange and scarlet varieties he couldn't name specifically. A couple of dozen young people – teenagers, mainly – are sitting amongst the floral tributes. One has 'LILLIE' daubed across his face in red, others are listening to music, a couple are weeping. To his dismay he too starts to cry.

It takes several seconds for Ryan, riveted to the screen, to notice. 'Oh dear, Dad . . . I said not to watch . . .' Michael can sense his son is fazed.

Just then there's a bang of the front door and Chrissie, who's been out for a while, blusters into the room. Straight away she zones in on what they're watching.

'It's so sad. I read what happened in the paper.' She turns to Michael. 'I wasn't sure about telling you—' Then she sees his tears. 'Oh, love, I'm sorry.' She sits down next to him, hugging him close to her.

'Have you got a hanky?' Michael mutters.

Chrissie fumbles in her handbag. 'Here.'

'Thanks.' Michael blows his nose. He glances at Ryan, guilty and humiliated at once. 'Sorry.'

'You're all right.' Ryan pats his knee. It feels weird for Michael to be comforted by his son; it's always been the other way round. So far he and Ryan have hedged round the subject of his suicide attempt – he left it to Chrissie to explain.

Michael hesitates. He's unsure whether it's OK to reveal he knew Lillie, but surely now it can't matter? 'She was at that clinic in Lewes, same time as me,' he says in a low voice.

'No way!' Ryan leans forward. 'Really, Dad?'

'Moreland's. Yeah.'

'Wow. Jeezus.' Ryan sits back. Michael can't tell if he's impressed, fascinated or horrified. 'You mean you *knew* her?'

'Kind of . . .'

'You spoke to her?'

'Yes.' Michael attempts to recall the details. If only his mind weren't so fuzzy. 'We were in group sessions together.'

'Did you know she was so . . . um . . .'

'. . . depressed?' says Michael helpfully. It's a relief to have the word in the open. 'No.' He can't recollect Lillie being anything other than ebullient. 'She didn't come across that way. She's—' his voice catches, ' – she *was* – a nice girl. Friendly. Funny.' Great tits, too, he recalls, but has the sense to keep this observation to himself. 'Is that how she seemed on that programme you and your sister watch?'

'*Street Dance Live*. Yeah, she was cool. But that was the telly. She might have been different when you met her.'

Michael shakes his head. I thought she was happy, he thinks.

'And the dances she did – they were *hot*.'

Michael nods, recalling the disco night. Lillie was quite something to behold, but she was more, so much more, than a pretty face.

'I don't really understand this street dancing thing,' says Chrissie. 'It always looks a bit odd to me.'

'The thing is, you often kind of teach yourself. Tricks 'n stuff.' Ryan looks from his mum to his dad, and back again. 'I could show you both a few moves if you like.'

'Eh? You can do it?' says Michael.

'Kinda. Here. Let's push this back. Up you get.' Ryan

rises, holds out a hand and yanks his father to his feet. Together they move back the sofa.

'Careful of the carpet,' says Chrissie.

Ryan tugs down his sweatshirt, adjusts his tracksuit bottoms and checks the laces of his trainers. He glances from side to side, judging whether the space is adequate. Then, abruptly, he jumps in the air and lands on his hands, kicking high with his legs at right angles. He switches from one hand and the opposite foot and back again. The sequence, though jerky, demonstrates athleticism, balance and grace. There's no doubt it takes more skill than pogoing.

'It's sort of more break-dancing, that move,' says Ryan.

'I never knew you could do that,' says Michael.

'Guess there's quite a bit of stuff we don't know about each other, Dad.' Ryan yanks at his shirt again, awkward. 'But I'm not *that* good, not like Lillie was.' He flops down into the sofa, then turns to his mother. 'Hey, Mum, sorry, I forgot to ask. How d'you get on at the pub?'

Chrissie gives a broad smile. 'I got it.'

'Whoa, that's great, Ma!' Ryan slaps his knees.

'Got what?' asks Michael.

'A job,' says Chrissie.

Michael can't keep up. One moment he's trying to grasp that someone he thought was happy was in fact as desperate as he's been, and has taken her own life. The next he's discovering his son's hidden talents. And now it seems his wife has found herself work. Even more bizarre than this series of events is his own reaction – his emotions have lurched from shock to tears to pride to astonishment in a matter of minutes. But compared to a no-man's-land where he couldn't feel anything, it's terra firma; he's back on planet Earth.

* * *

'This whole thing with Lillie has really got to me,' says Abby, reaching for yet another tissue.

'That's quite understandable,' says Beth. 'Suicide brings up a lot for those left behind.'

Abby nods. 'We've been talking about it all this week – no one had any idea that Lillie felt so bad.'

'Perhaps your feelings are especially intense as Lillie doesn't seem to have communicated her intention to anyone beforehand? When something like this happens, we can find ourselves being very self-critical or blaming of others. Sometimes it brings up anger or our own despair.'

Abby casts her mind back. 'We got on very well . . . I liked Lillie a lot. We had some good conversations . . .' She recalls their heart-to-heart in the art room. 'It probably seems silly, given we only met recently, but I really miss her.'

'That doesn't seem silly at all. Sometimes we can form bonds very fast, especially when we're open and vulnerable.'

I'd been missing close friendships, thinks Abby, and Lillie helped me realize their value again. 'She looked after me when I arrived . . .'

'Lillie was very kind and sweet that way.' Beth sighs. She must be sad too, thinks Abby. Lillie contributed a lot to the whole clinic. This week's groups have seemed eerily empty.

'She told me about what happened to her . . . She'd coped with such a lot, yet she never seemed to grumble or get maudlin . . .' But the pain must still have been there, Abby realizes, beneath the surface. Waiting to strike. 'I'm worried I led her to revisit that trauma and perhaps it made her worse.'

'From what I understand, the main thing that made her worse was probably stopping lithium,' says Beth. 'Might I ask, given you got close to her, if maybe you identified with Lillie a little? Sometimes we are drawn to others whose experiences seem to resonate in some way with our own.'

Abby frowns. She'd not thought of this before. 'I've never been suicidal. Even though you all reckoned I was when I came in here . . . But this . . . I don't know . . . It has really made me think.' She fumbles for the right words, then realizes how this might be construed. 'Not that I want to kill myself or anything. Still, I have felt very anxious and wobbly again. It's like, if Lillie wasn't better, even though it seemed to us – and all of you, I gather – that she was, will I ever get properly well myself?' She can feel panic rising with the admission. 'Sometimes I think I'm a bit like her, my moods swing a lot – and I've been quite hedonistic sometimes . . .' She recalls the effect Jake had on her all those years ago. 'Yeah, I can be almost manic.'

'Breathe out,' says Beth.

Abby exhales.

'You were holding your breath.' Beth smiles. 'OK, before we go any further, I'd like you to close your eyes . . .' Abby does so. 'Now I'd like you to lay those thoughts and memories about Lillie aside, and bring yourself gently into the space you find here through your senses. Feel the carpet beneath your feet, your arms resting in your lap, your thighs and bottom being supported by the chair . . . Listen to the sounds about you, the ticking of the clock, the birds outside, that car revving its engine . . . What else can you hear?'

'A lawnmower. Someone's cutting the grass . . .' Gradually Abby feels the whirring in her brain slow. Life goes on, she reminds herself, as she and Beth breathe in and out.

'Next, when you're ready, gently open your eyes, cast your gaze around the room, notice the pictures on the wall, the carpets, the ceiling, the coffee table . . . And me sitting opposite you . . .' Beth's expression is tender. 'Better?'

Abby nods. 'Yes. Thanks.'

'Good.' Beth sits back in her chair. 'I wonder if you'll allow me to tell you something of my own experience? When you said you've been feeling wobbly, it reminded me.'

'Sure.'

'Well, last weekend I was lucky enough to visit the lighthouse at Portland Bill. Do you know it?'

'We studied Chesil Beach in geography at school,' Abby recalls. 'And my family are from the West Country.'

'So you'll know that the geology is fascinating – Portland is only connected to the mainland by a thin strip of land. Sometimes I find it refreshing to experience a different landscape, and the coast is much more bleak and rugged than round here. Anyway, I digress. In the early evening there I was, standing on the beach, watching the sun setting into the ocean, and the waves were coming one after another, crashing onto the shore a few feet away. As I was standing there, the lamp of the lighthouse on the clifftop was going on, then off, then on again. I was mesmerized – nearly an hour later, I was still in the same spot. I noticed that as night was falling, the waves were getting bigger and bigger, and I felt increasingly small and vulnerable. But then I turned my eyes to the lighthouse again. Its lamp was still flashing – as if the waves were no bigger at all, and everything was under control. I found this very comforting.

'Afterwards, it struck me that life is like the ocean – there are calm times and stormy times, and there will always be waves crashing onto the shore. Yet no matter how big the waves get, there will always be the flash of a lighthouse. Sometimes we get so caught up in the frightening waves, we forget to turn and see something that secures us; that reminds us storms do pass.'

'I had forgotten to do that. Thanks, that's really helpful.'

'I want you to remember that you're *not* Lillie, Abby, even if you identified with her in some ways. You're a separate person with your own thoughts, feelings and experiences. You said yourself you've never been suicidal; not only in this session but before – you were most insistent about that. You've done really well in the time that you've been here, and it's completely natural that this has affected you – you wouldn't be human if you didn't feel rocked by it. I've been sad about what's happened myself. . . .' Beth gulps. 'But just because you've felt shaken doesn't mean you're headed to the place you were before, or the place that Lillie was. It's quite possible to have a dip that doesn't last as long as the one that brought you in here so you bounce back quicker.'

'I suppose . . .'

'Next time you feel wobbly, I want you to try to remember that lighthouse. Picture it flashing on and off, and trust that you are safe, and the waves won't carry you away.'

44

'Ooh, Michael, good to see you getting some fresh air.' It's Leona, coming up the path.

'I'm only taking out the rubbish,' says Michael, dropping a black bag into the wheelie bin.

'Still, symbolic, getting rid of your trash.' Leona guffaws. 'You going to invite me in or what? I'm desperate for a cuppa.'

'Come in.' Michael can sense himself smiling. He's pleased it's her turn to visit this afternoon – he's not been on her roster for a week and some other members of the crisis team irritate him.

Leona follows him into the kitchen and stands looking out of the window while they wait for the water to boil. Michael follows her gaze and cringes. His wife did her best, but the back garden remains an area of devastation. There's a concrete slab on the lawn where the shed used to be, and what Chrissie managed to salvage of his stuff is piled up under a tarpaulin.

It's not just an eyesore – if someone got over the wall they could make off with a stash, he thinks. Perhaps Ryan can help me build something makeshift to store it in. The task is too much to tackle alone. But together . . .

'How've you been getting on, then?' says Leona. It's over three weeks since Michael swam out to sea.

'Up and down.'

'I guess anything that involves use of the word "up" could be categorized as some sort of improvement?'

Michael scowls. He's wary of sounding too positive. 'I'm much worse in the morning.'

'Lots of people say that. Trick is to rise and shine, even if you don't feel like it.'

'Didn't have much choice today – Chrissie and I had to talk to the receivers, see if we can put off the sale of this place.'

'And can you?'

'Maybe . . . Helps that I live with her and the kids are still based here – in any event we've a year's grace. We could be all right, if we can raise the capital another way. Though God knows that won't be easy.'

'Hey, well done for talking to them. I bet it was really daunting.'

That's an understatement, thinks Michael. I hardly slept last night.

He reaches for the tea caddy and two mugs.

'You can leave the bag in. I like it almost orange,' says Leona, so he just adds milk and hands hers over. 'No, I don't take sugar, thanks for asking,' she grins. 'Cheers.'

'Do you want to sit in the lounge?' Michael is conscious Leona is once more looking out of the window. 'Ryan's mate brought round his Xbox, but I can tell them to stop.' From the kitchen they can hear whoops and yelps over the sound of gunfire.

'You're OK, I'm fine in here. I fancy standing – seem to have spent most of the day in the car.' Leona blows on her tea to cool it. 'So, I know you don't like my asking about this stuff, but I have to. Last time I saw you, you said you felt less flat.'

'I said I *might* be less flat.'

'Sure. But it did seem you were beginning to feel more intensely again.'

Michael would like to explain he's not yet felt any *joy*, but that'll sound ridiculous, he decides. He doesn't want Leona to think he's expecting miracles. Eventually he admits, 'I think I'm a bit jealous of Chrissie . . .' Though that sounds mad too. Who on earth gets jealous of their spouse?

'Oh?'

'She's got that job, remember?'

Leona nods.

'So I should be pleased – it's great she's bringing a bit of money in, and I hate us having to rely solely on benefit . . .' Now he's concerned he'll seem churlish, but he's gone too far to retract what he's started to say. 'I don't like it when she goes out to work.' This hardly communicates the sickness he feels in the pit of his stomach that he's no longer able to provide for his family. For nearly thirty years he's been the breadwinner – he spent his childhood watching his father in the same role. Now he's letting them all down, his dad included.

Nonetheless he's relieved to have offloaded. It's weird,

the way anxiety is often worse than actually putting an admission out there. Especially with Leona.

'I reckon that's a totally normal reaction,' she says, nodding vehemently. 'It'd be lovely if emotions came back symmetrically, so your ability to feel sadness and happiness were restored at the same rate, but that's not the way depression seems to operate. You've had so much rubbish come up over the last few months, negativity is bound to dominate. And jealousy's understandable in your situation, but it doesn't mean you can't be pleased or maybe even a bit proud of Chrissie too.'

'Really?' says Michael. He hadn't considered having several emotions at once. It seems astonishing to be having any at all.

'And you needn't beat yourself up if you don't feel more positive right away. Those feelings could come later. In fact, if you berate yourself for feeling jealous, you'll end up hating yourself even more. You're sensitive, man – probably a darn sight more sensitive than me.'

That's odd, he thinks, I've never seen myself that way. 'Guess I have been a bit tearful lately,' he admits gruffly. Mostly he tries to do it when no one is around.

'See.' Leona knocks his elbow in jest. 'You're a softie, just like I said.'

At once Michael is reminded of Ali – he used to say that too. Michael wonders what's happened to his friend. I miss him, he thinks.

'Pretty much every human being could find a reason to hate themselves if they thought about everything as much as you do. We can be total arseholes, us humans, but we can also be angels sometimes.' Leona's head bobs as she talks. She's so tall her pompom could be used to dust the ceiling, thinks Michael, and finds himself smiling as he envisages unsuspecting spiders being caught in her afro.

'See, you want to smile at what I'm saying, I can tell,' she says, clearly pleased. It would be cruel to say it's her hairdo that's amusing him.

He has an impulse to confess further. 'See that pile of stuff out there?' He points at the tarpaulin.

Leona nods.

'I smashed up our garden shed, you know.' He can feel himself flush at the admission. 'S'pose it was my shed, really. That's what Gillian pointed out.'

'Gillian? Oh yes, the therapist at Moreland's – you've mentioned her before.'

'I still feel terrible about it.'

'Why? It's done now.'

That such a small heap should be all that remains of so much that was useful is criminal, and he's appalled that he got so angry Chrissie was forced to call the police. He explains this to Leona.

'Sounds like you've got some shame going on there,' nods Leona. Michael vaguely remembers them talking about shame in the groups at Moreland's. He never quite grasped what anyone meant; the way they used the word seemed odd. 'But we've all behaved badly at some point in our lives. I'll wager even Mother Teresa wasn't a saint the whole time. Just because we've temporarily screwed up doesn't necessarily mean we're *inherently* bad people. Our actions could be the result of stress.'

'I suppose I was pretty wound up.'

'Everyone can be found wanting sometimes – even us psychiatric nurses.'

I wonder if any of the staff at Moreland's feel bad about Lillie, thinks Michael. But Leona's eyes are sparking; clearly she's not finished making her point. She's feisty, he says to himself. Reckon that's why I like her. Plus she doesn't soft-soap me.

'Don't tell anyone,' she drops her voice, 'but I got some points for speeding last week.'

Michael smothers another smile. As if anyone I know would be remotely interested, he thinks.

'Obviously I don't approve of driving too fast, especially in built-up areas. But I've not got used to those twenty-mile-an-hour zones, and forgot 'cos I was in a hurry to get to a patient I was concerned about.'

Michael is losing her thread. 'So you're saying it was OK I smashed up the shed?'

'Not *OK*.' Leona shakes her head. '*Understandable*.'

'Ah.'

'Anger is a normal human emotion – a part of life. Think about it – even animals get riled.'

'What, like say, cats?'

'Exactly!' She appears poised to give him a high five before thinking better of it. 'Strange puss comes into your garden, your pet hisses and arches his back and fluffs himself out in order to safeguard his territory. The other cat has made yours feel threatened and vulnerable.'

Like the shysters who shafted me, thinks Michael.

374

'What makes us feel particularly bad is when we believe we're acting out of proportion to what's happening.'

'I certainly managed that,' mutters Michael.

'Depends on your perspective,' Leona shrugs. 'Actually, I kind of agree with your Gillian, from what you've said of her reaction. It's important to express your feelings. If you'd not taken your rage out on the shed, maybe you'd have done something worse. Though the best thing you can do is talk to others.'

Typical, thinks Michael. You therapist types want us to talk the whole time.

And Leona's still going. 'Some people worry if they talk about what they're feeling, it'll heighten their emotions and they'll lose control. In fact, from what I've seen, the reverse is true. Talking *releases* emotions. Though it's important to pick someone you can trust. Which is why it's a good idea for you to chat to an awesome chick like me.' She grins and sets down her mug. 'That wasn't a bad cup of tea. Right you are then, best be off.' Michael has a twinge of disappointment. 'But before I go, I'll leave you with one final Leona insight.'

Any second she's going to wag her finger at me, he thinks. Not that he really minds.

'Anger isn't all bad. It can provide us with the motivation to do things that otherwise we wouldn't. Like go into politics or do a great painting or write a book . . .' She rearranges her hair so it's pulled tight once more in preparation for her departure. 'Or play in a rock band . . . I dunno, you can pick your own examples.'

She could be referring to punk, thinks Michael. So much

375

of that music was fuelled by anger. He recalls the mosh pit, the sense of release it gave him, the camaraderie and excitement.

And suddenly there it is: beautiful and unexpected, like a kingfisher emerging from the water with its catch – a burst of joy.

45

'Hi, Mum.' Karen grabs her mobile from the countertop. 'I can't talk now. I'm about to get the kids' supper. Was it anything urgent?'

'No,' says Shirley. 'I just wanted a chat, and to let you know about your father's estate. You can ring me back later.'

Oh God, thinks Karen. I can't face more talking tonight. Today was her last full day at Moreland's. She learned from her insurance company that they wouldn't cover much more treatment, so after discussion with Dr Kasdan she decided to stop day care and focus on seeing Johnnie for therapy once a week. She hopes to stay in touch not just with Abby but with Tash and Colin too, so she took their numbers, though as they're both much younger she doesn't expect they'll really want to maintain contact.

I need time to acknowledge that an important period of my life has ended, she thinks. Yet at once she feels guilty for not supporting her mother as well as she should. Then she notices it: *should.* OK, so I won't offer to call her back, she decides, and says, 'I can't chat later, Mum, I'm sorry.'

'Oh.'

Her mother sounds disappointed so Karen relents a little. 'Perhaps you can tell me a bit about it now, and we'll speak properly tomorrow?'

'All right,' says Shirley, though Karen still feels it isn't. 'I went to see your father's solicitor today. And the long and the short of it is . . .'

Karen's stomach turns over. This is when Mum asks to move in here, she thinks. Oh help.

'. . . because he – um – died – um, sooner than we expected—'

I really can't deal with this now, Karen thinks. I wish I'd never answered the phone.

' – well, it's good news actually.'

'Gosh.' Karen is startled. Her mother isn't gloomy by nature, but because of George's condition, for years she has tended to be the bearer of bad tidings. 'What's the situation, then?'

'There's a bit more money left than I thought.'

'Ah.' For all the insight she's gained on the hazards of being too future-focused, Karen can't stop herself racing ahead. Mum's going to suggest I buy a bigger house with her, she thinks. Years of unremitting responsibility stretch out ahead of her. She feels a familiar weight descending: the sense of being overwhelmed, of not being able to manage. *Don't undo the good stuff that's happened to me*, she pleads silently. I've only just left day care. It was tough to make the break, but she didn't want to get dependent upon it.

'Anyway, I wanted to let you know, I've decided to stay in Goring for the time being.'

Karen isn't sure she's heard correctly. 'Really? Are you sure, Mum?'

'Yes. I'd like to remain here while I have a proper think about what I want to do next.'

Karen's head is spinning, but she realizes it's important to focus on what her mother is actually saying, rather than what she feared she was about to say. 'You mean you're going to keep renting that flat?'

'Maybe. Maybe not. I could make it much nicer, if I put in some effort.'

Karen pictures the woodchip wallpaper and narrow single bed and winces. 'Is that worth it, with a rented property?'

'I don't mean I'd change it a whole lot, but I could get a nicer bed, for a start.' Karen can hear her mother getting prickly.

'Of course you could, Mum. I'd love to help you make your place more homely. We could get some rugs to cover up that carpet, some prettier bedding . . .'

'Yes, thank you, darling. I appreciate the offer.'

Karen gleans that her mother isn't keen. Doubtless Mum wants to make her own mark on the flat, she thinks. I suppose it's good she's keen to remain independent. Still, Karen is faintly hurt.

'I've got some stuff in storage that would improve it,' says Shirley. 'I don't want to rush into anything, obviously. But then I might have a look at buying somewhere.'

Here we go. Karen braces herself. 'In Brighton . . . ?'

'No, I don't think so. I don't think Brighton is terribly me.' Karen is so stunned she has to grip the edge of the worktop to steady herself. 'It's all a bit busy and noisy. I got used to

379

having space, in Portugal. Whereas the houses near you are so bunched up together, everyone lives on top of one another.'

Don't be rude about my neighbourhood, thinks Karen. She's tempted to voice her disgruntlement, but bites her tongue.

'I like it better here in Goring. And I'd hate to be a burden to you.'

'You wouldn't be a burden. Far from it.'

'I don't want to sound selfish or ungrateful, and please don't take this the wrong way. I loved your father – we had many happy decades together. So I'm not saying this out of disrespect to him. But caring for him over the last few years . . . well, it's been bloody awful.' Karen starts – Shirley almost never swears. 'His illness was such a drawn-out process, it took so much out of me, and in the end I felt I'd lost the man I loved.'

'Oh, Mum. I'm so sorry.' At once Karen wishes her mother was with her, so she could wrap her arms around her.

Shirley's voice cracks. 'Yes, well. I think in some ways I was lonelier with your father still alive than I am now.'

'I understand.'

'Since he died, at least I'm free to remember him the way he was when he was well.'

'That's good.' Karen is conscious she's coming out with mere platitudes. This is how people were when Simon died, she recalls.

'I'll be honest and admit I feel released by the lack of responsibility, freer. So I'm going to think about it carefully, but I can afford to rent a while longer. Then I should have enough capital to get myself a little flat of my own, so I just wanted to check if that's OK with you. I mean, maybe you'd prefer to have some of your father's money . . . um, now?'

Good Lord! The notion that she would be keen to get her hands on any inheritance is so far from the direction she thought this conversation was heading that Karen is at a loss for words. 'I didn't expect to have any of Dad's money,' she says when she gets her voice back. 'To be frank, I didn't think there would be any left after you—'

'Ah, I see.'

Oh dear, thinks Karen, I'm bodging this. It's because I'm so tired. 'It's purely I realized you'd need some for yourself, and I hadn't got any further than that.'

'That's OK, then. It's only I didn't want you to be upset.'

Upset? thinks Karen. As fast as the weight descended, it's lifting. Anna was right. All those months ago she said having Mum here would be too much for me. Maybe in a few years' time it would be fine, but not now; not when I've struggled so hard to get on an even keel.

'I might get a bit lonely, I know, but I've already made some friends, so it won't be too bad. Anyway, there are worse things than being lonely.'

Gosh, do you find that? Karen frowns. The way my heart aches for Simon I can't think of any.

Shirley says, 'Insofar as one can ever know, I'm hopeful I could enjoy a few more years looking after myself. So I'd like to try and manage on my own. I don't want to go straight from having someone dependent on me to depending on someone else – even you, darling. I'm still pretty fit and reasonably healthy, touch wood—' Karen reaches for the table too, ' – because if George's illness taught me anything, it's to make the most of our independence before we lose it.'

The more her mother offloads, the lighter Karen feels; she's like a helium balloon, floating up and away.

'I appreciate you could do with a hand with the children, so maybe you were hoping I might move in? I hope you don't mind . . .'

'No, no, not at all!' Oops, Karen thinks. Mustn't sound too gleeful. 'You must do what's right for you,' she says soberly. 'And of course you're welcome to spend as much time with the kids as you like.'

'Well, I do enjoy that, as you know.'

'So do they.'

'I'm sorry I've kept you – we've been chatting longer than you had time for. Forgive me. But I wanted you to understand where I'm coming from and not be terribly disappointed. You're not, are you, darling?'

No, thinks Karen. It means I can do what everyone's been urging: focus on healing myself.

46

'Hi,' says Abby, opening the door. It's strange to find her husband on the front step, after he's let himself in for so many years.

'Hi.' Glenn seems awkward, possibly even nervous. 'So, you OK to go for a coffee, like we said?'

'Hold on a sec.' Abby pops her head round the living-room door to check Callum is settled with Eva. She's surprised when Glenn steps behind her and into the lounge.

'Hello, Callum. It's Daddy.' Callum is focused on wheeling a toy car to and fro on the floor, so Glenn goes round and ducks his head in front of his son to make sure he sees him.

'Say "Hello, Daddy".' Eva waves at Glenn.

'Aaee.' Callum flaps his hand.

That's new, thinks Abby. When he lived here Glenn would rarely bother to address our son directly unless he needed to.

'You look really well,' says Glenn, as they head down the road.

'You mean fat.' Abby smiles to show she's not offended.

'You'll never be fat,' says Glenn.

'Women all know "well" is a euphemism for putting on weight,' she tells him. And it's true she has gone up a dress size – possibly it's a side effect of her medication, though it could also be because she's no longer so wired. She's pleased, regardless. Over the last couple of years she'd been feeling scrawny and unfeminine; now she's beginning to perceive herself as an attractive woman once more. *Ironic, given I've not had sex in ages,* she thinks, *and my soon-to-be ex is still sleeping with someone else.*

'Where do you want to go?' asks Glenn. He's being quite the gentleman, Abby notices. *Perhaps he feels guilty.* Then she reminds herself not to think the worst of him. *Maybe he's simply being nice.*

Either way, it's a beautiful day and she is keen to be outside. 'Why don't we get a takeaway coffee and sit on the lawn in Montpelier Terrace?' she suggests. There's a crescent of green space not far from the cafe which serves the best local coffee.

'Sounds good to me.'

She glances at Glenn as they wait at the counter. He looks tired, she thinks. *Perhaps it's all that sex with Cara.* Then again, commuting never did anyone's complexion any favours and he's always worked hard. And lately he's had to look after Callum much more.

'How are you doing?' asks Glenn, once they're settled on the grass far enough from other people to speak privately.

'Better.' She stops to consider. 'Yeah, much better. I've

been feeling less wobbly, overall. Though I had a bad dip a few weeks ago—'

'Sorry to hear that.'

Abby brushes off his concern. 'I'm back on a more even keel now. It was mainly because one of the other patients who I'd got really close to . . . um . . . died—'

'You mean Lillie Laybourne?'

'Er . . .' There's been enough speculation and prurience in the press; to add to the gossip seems tasteless, disrespect-ful. 'Anyway,' Abby sidesteps, 'I've talked about that a lot in my one-to-one sessions, and I'm finding it easier to separate myself from other people's issues.' She catches Glenn's eye and he looks away. He knows what I'm implying, she thinks. Good. She's acclimatized to the knowledge of his affair, but still isn't ready to forgive and forget.

I was treated badly, she argues to herself. He lied to me for months. Then again, how we deal with emotions is often influenced by our family, and neither of us had the kind of upbringing where we talked much about how we felt.

Now she seems to be coming out the other side, Abby is almost glad she had a breakdown. To be losing so much in one hit, that was what triggered it, she can see that now. And whilst it was sheer hell to live through – she hopes not to repeat the experience, ever – it has fine-tuned her self-awareness.

Only the day before Beth had asked, 'Do you think your panic attacks were your unconscious crying out for help, saying you couldn't manage?'

'Are you suggesting I got admitted to hospital so Glenn had to step up to the mark?'

Beth had nodded. 'Not deliberately, but indirectly, maybe.'

'I suppose deep down I have been furious about his ab-
senteeism from fatherhood,' Abby had agreed. 'Mm . . . It is
possible some of that anger came out as anxiety.'

'Yes, and perhaps your sadness emerged that way too.'

She'd nodded in acknowledgement. 'Having Callum wasn't
the version of motherhood I envisaged.' A lump had come
to her throat.

'Sometimes the process of letting go is long and difficult,'
Beth had said gently.

'I suppose seeing himself as Callum's dad has been hard
for Glenn, too.'

'Yet from what you've told me, in many ways Glenn has
risen to the challenge posed by your absence. After all, he
could have *not* done as much as he has; he could have put
Callum into temporary care.'

'You mean run off with Cara and left him?' Abby had
recoiled at the suggestion.

'He wouldn't be the first parent to let a child down.'

Now, as Abby looks at Glenn sprawled on the grass, limbs
floppy, skin drawn and eyes red with exhaustion, she can
see that Beth was right, and, in spite of all her resentments,
has a rush of affection for him. 'I'm grateful you took so
much time off work to look after Callum,' she says.

'That's OK.' He plucks at the lawn.

Abby tilts back her head, enjoying the warmth of the sun
on her cheeks for a moment, then says, 'And I also wanted
to thank you for helping me get this treatment at Moreland's.'

Glenn is still picking at the grass. Now it's his turn to be evasive, she thinks. *My praise has disarmed him. I've berated him so much over the years, perhaps it's no wonder.*

'Seriously, I was in a right state when I checked in – I'd never have got there on my own, and, well—' she leans forward, ' – I think I've learned a lot as a result.' *So has Glenn,* she thinks, and adds, 'I'm pleased you seem to have connected with Callum, too.'

There's a long silence, but Glenn doesn't appear awkward. He stops plucking the grass and looks into the distance.

'It's funny, but it's like your being away has given all three of us a new beginning,' he says eventually.

At once Abby feels compelled to touch him. She reaches over and gives his hand a squeeze. It's a gesture that reminds her of Karen; a sign of friendship, because Abby has saved her most fulsome thanks till last. She still can't quite believe it's true. She takes a deep breath and ventures, 'My solicitor said you might be willing to let us stay in the house . . . ?'

'Yes.'

'That's very kind.'

'Well . . . I would like some money from it, somehow. Maybe you could remortgage or something, to give me a bit . . . ? But . . . er . . . I've been thinking I could move in with Cara . . .' Abby can tell he is apprehensive about mentioning his girlfriend's name. 'If you're OK with that?' She's taken aback he's even asking her – Glenn reads her bewilderment. 'It's only I'd like to have Callum there, you know, at weekends, and you're his mum so you need to be happy with it.'

No, I didn't know you'd like to have him, thinks Abby. *But* it's great to hear. She can't quite believe this either. 'How's Cara about that?' Having another woman's child in your home is challenging enough, she thinks, let alone Callum.

Glenn shrugs. 'She says she's up for it.'

'Saying and doing aren't quite the same.'

'No.' Glenn frowns. 'But she knows it's important to me.'

Well, well, thinks Abby, this is a turnaround. Glenn wasn't exaggerating when he talked of a new beginning.

'I was thinking if Callum and I do stay, I could take in a lodger,' says Abby. 'To help financially.'

'Sounds a good idea.' Glenn nods. 'Why don't we see if we can thrash out the rudiments of an agreement between the two of us? Going through lawyers will cost an arm and a leg.'

Abby smiles to herself. Always has been slow to part with money, Glenn. Even so, it makes sense to her, too.

We can stay in the house, she thinks, at last allowing herself to accept it. My beloved home. I won't have to look at any more dispiriting flats in unsuitable locations; I won't have to put locks on all the cupboards somewhere new; I won't have to sell off half our furniture. I'll still be able to enjoy my view over the city, I'll still be near the Co-op and the decent cafe. I'll still have Karen as a neighbour.

It's not as if life will be without its challenges, and as Callum grows and becomes physically stronger, Abby knows that many issues will get worse. Nonetheless, here, now, she is grateful; more grateful than she can possibly express.

'Thank you,' she says softly.

'No, thank *you*,' says Glenn. 'You did a lot when I should have been doing more. I really am sorry about that.'

Why couldn't he have said that before? thinks Abby. His apology has come too late to save their marriage, but nonetheless she is glad of it.

They've finished their coffees; Abby senses their conversation coming to a close. Sure enough, Glenn says he ought to go, gets to his feet and dusts the grass off his trousers.

As she watches him walk away, her heart is full of sorrow.

I miss the way we balanced and complemented each other, she thinks. I miss the man I loved, the times we shared. I miss his sleeping form in bed beside me. I'm sad we couldn't pull through and be there for our son together, and that it took my breakdown for us to have this breakthrough. But who knows? At least apart we'll each have some respite from caring, so maybe we'll do better for Callum now that we're separated than we did as a couple. No one is perfect, myself included.

The time for recrimination is past.

47

'What do you think?' asks Michael.

Leona leans over his shoulder and reads the handwritten letter on the table.

'Nice one,' she says when she's finished. 'Didn't gather you knew her.'

'We were in Moreland's at the same time,' Michael explains. 'So we met there, did some groups together, that's all.'

'Still, you probably got to know her better than a lot of people,' says Leona. 'Those groups can be very intimate.'

'I suppose so. But it's more the timing of when she . . .' Michael stops. He doesn't wish to get drawn back into that experience – not when he's trying to share something positive. 'I realize, what happened to her, er . . . well, it could have been me.'

Leona nods. 'But it wasn't.' She pauses. 'I hope you're glad?' She looks at him quizzically, pompom tilted.

Michael nods. He's still not comfortable gushing. 'I've no idea why she did it – she seemed so happy when I met her, and that wasn't long before she died.'

'We can never be inside someone else's head, no matter how much we try. Often it's hard to recall what it was like inside our own minds when we look back with hindsight. Bet you find it tricky to remember how dire you felt a couple of months ago. Well, I hope you do.' She grins.

Leona is someone whose smile never seems to irritate me, thinks Michael. And she's right. The darkness of that particular night is gradually fading.

Then Leona's face falls. 'You know, I come across suicide more than I'd like to in my line of work. Often I find it hard to understand, same as everyone else left behind. Frequently people preach about the selfishness of suicide, but it's a choice we all have. And who are we to judge? Lillie may have wanted that release more than she wanted to carry on living – no one has the right to say that was wrong of her.' She stands up fully and stretches. 'But I like to believe that sometimes we can make more sense of someone's death if we see it in the context of what that person contributed to others. Even a short life can have a huge impact.'

'That's a good way to look at it,' says Michael. He recalls Lillie, the way she welcomed new arrivals at the clinic, the way she was prepared to face the responsibility of checking-in first, the way she identified with others and made everyone laugh. Not forgetting the way she moved; her enthusiasm, her energy. He'll never forget the evening they all danced together. If it hadn't been for Lillie, he'd have stayed sitting on the sofa, excluded by self-consciousness. She drew him in, encouraged him to be part of things. 'Yeah. I reckon she'd have liked that. And perhaps she'd given all she could.'

'And now you're helping others.' Leona taps the letter. 'I bet you'd never have done anything like this prior to your stroll into the sea, would you?'

'Probably not.' Michael frowns. 'Although I've a lot more time on my hands these days.'

'Oh, it's more than that, surely? It's as though losing everything has given you the opportunity to explore possibilities you'd never have thought yourself capable of before.'

Michael squirms. She's crediting me with more than I deserve, he thinks. 'It's only a bloody letter,' he mutters.

'A letter, my arse – it's an *idea*. Fingers crossed her sister agrees. Do you want me to drop it off? I drive past those flats en route to my next patient.'

'No, you're all right,' says Michael. 'I was heading into Brighton myself.'

* * *

'So, I guess today is the day we say goodbye,' says Karen. It's hard to imagine this will be the last time she'll sit in a chair at the clinic with Johnnie opposite her – eight more weeks have passed since she left day care; now she's finishing one-to-one therapy too.

Johnnie nods. 'Yes.'

Karen looks at him, with his floppy fringe and boyish face. It's hard to believe he's helped her so much but, along with the groups, the sessions they've shared have made a real difference. She's glad she held off on taking antidepressants, because in the end it was talking – connecting with others who were also vulnerable – that she, personally, needed. So she no longer cries several times a day, she no longer feels bone-tired, she no longer worries quite so much, or wonders why she bothers with everything. She's even starting to remember the good times with her father again, regaining a sense of the man he was, just as her mother seems to be doing, too. Nonetheless, this is hard.

'I hate goodbyes,' she admits.

Johnnie crosses and uncrosses his legs. She senses he's uncomfortable too.

'Though at least I now know why.' She doesn't have to explain: they're both aware of the reasons.

'There's a kind of shattering that happens with death – we often lose our sense of who we are and what our lives are about, and reconstruction is needed. But first we need to accept that a part of us is broken,' says Johnnie.

'Yes . . .'

'Every time we brush up against our own mortality it does remind us to take life seriously.'

'I've had more than the odd brush,' she reminds him, then laughs. 'Feels more like I've been gone through with a nit comb. Golly, I remember my mother having to do that when I was a girl. With hair like this, it was agony.'

Johnnie nods and smiles. 'It might help to remember that every loss brings with it the opportunity for a new beginning.'

'Still, I'd like a break from dealing with death so head-on for a bit.' Karen leans back and looks at the ceiling. 'Hear that, God, if you're up there?'

* * *

'Well I never! It *is* you!' Ali comes to the door of his shop to watch as Michael chains his bicycle to a nearby lamp post. 'When you got off that thing, I said to myself, it looks like my friend Michael, and then I thought, no way can that be so. My friend does not ride a bicycle.'

Michael removes his helmet and runs his fingers across the crown of his head. Hat hair doesn't look good on anyone. 'I do now,' he says.

'My, you are looking very fit and trim.'

'Thanks.' Michael doesn't confess it's because he's had to relinquish his car. 'I'm on a bit of a health kick, trying to exercise more.' Regular exercise is part of the programme he's been doing with Leona.

'That is not a "bit" – it is a lot. It is many miles from Rottingdean to here.'

'Only six,' says Michael.

'I could not bicycle six miles for all the money in Rajasthan,' says Ali. 'I blame Mrs A., feeding me too much.' He pats his tummy.

Michael laughs. 'So how is Mrs A.?'

'Oh, she is good, good,' Ali grins. 'A man must not complain when he has a fine lady wife and after so many years that we are still, you know—' he checks left and right to ensure there is no one else in earshot, ' – doing the rumpy pumpy.'

Michael chuckles. Until recently he was so self-conscious about his own lack of libido that he would have changed the subject as fast as possible, but he seems to be getting his mojo back – if last night with Chrissie was anything to go by – and he'd forgotten how much Ali's humour tickles him.

'So how's business?' he says, eyeing the store. The shelves look sadly depleted.

'Don't ask,' says Ali, shaking his head. 'I am OK here for now, but I cannot open any more hours, or lower my prices any further.'

'Sorry to hear that,' says Michael. He has a surge of anger. I should have put a brick through the window of the Tesco Metro, he thinks, rather than smashing up my shed. Though a fat lot of good it would have done.

'Oh, never mind me,' says Ali, clapping Michael on the back. 'Everything will turn out for the best, I am sure, in the long run. So, can I get you a cup of tea?'

Michael's hot from his cycle ride. 'Actually, a glass of tap water is fine.' And as Ali disappears into the back of the shop to fetch one, Michael considers his friend. Ali always was more optimistic than me, he acknowledges. I used to think he was naive, taking on this greengrocer a few years ago. Maybe I've been the one who lacked wisdom.

'What have you been doing these last months?' asks Ali when he returns. 'Have you been working?'

'Truthfully?'

Ali nods. 'Yes, please. I do not wish you to lie. Look at me here.' He shrugs, but his expression is cheerful. 'Please do not feel you have to impress me.'

'I've been thinking, mainly. Yeah . . .' Michael pauses, wondering how best to sum up. 'Initially I just kept going round and round, churning stuff over.' That barely touches on how bad I got, he admits to himself, but it's not this he wants to share with Ali. 'Anyway, I got to mulling about

395

my . . . er . . . life, if you like. I realize I've spent years being rather at sea.'

'It sounds as if you transformed your joblessness into a sort of spiritual retreat,' says Ali. These aren't the words Michael would choose, but the gist is right. 'I believe being spiritual can be a very good use of time.'

'I'm still not sure what I'm going to do next,' Michael continues. 'But Chrissie has a job now, and Ryan and Kelly are earning a bit as it's the university holidays, which helps take the immediate pressure off.'

'I am glad about that,' says Ali. 'It was a lot of responsibility you had. Too much for one man to have on his shoulders.'

I'm glad too, thinks Michael, I'm very glad indeed.

And as he cycles back along the prom to Rottingdean, he recalls something Leona said before she waved goodbye to him that afternoon.

'Sometimes I wonder whether what we call depression isn't depression at all. Instead, like physical pain, it's an alarm of sorts, alerting us that something is wrong. Maybe for you it's been like that, showing you that perhaps it was time to stop, to take time out, and address the unaddressed business of filling your soul.'

Very soppy way to phrase it, Michael thinks, but the sentiment rings true all the same.

48

'Ahem . . . Hello?'

Michael is up a ladder putting the final touches to the display when he hears a voice behind him. He turns and sees a woman he thinks he recognizes, though she looks so different he's not entirely sure.

'It's Abby,' she says helpfully. Little surprise he failed to place her. He's never seen her out and about. Plus it's been *months*. But the child in the pushchair helps – he remembers her little boy being brought to visit her at Moreland's.

'Bloody hell,' he says, before he can stop himself. He can't tell exactly what's changed – maybe her hair is longer, she's put on weight, or perhaps it's simply that she's caught the sun. After such a cold, grey start to the year, it's turned out to be a spectacular summer.

'I saw on Facebook you'd initiated this,' she says.

Michael is caught off guard. That must have been Kelly; his daughter appears to have taken it upon herself to manage the event's social media PR. 'It's not entirely down to me. My son's sorted all the music, and Lillie's sister has helped fund it.'

'Still,' says Abby. 'It's a brilliant idea.'

'Thanks.' Michael is embarrassed, but hopefully she'll just think he's pink from the heat. It is very warm today – and he's been working in the sunshine for hours. It's a good job they're due to start soon, or the flowers will have wilted.

'You're OK,' she says, eyeing the banner he's securing to the highest point of the wrought-iron pillars that hold up the roof of the building. 'It looks straight.'

He climbs down from the ladder and joins her on the tiled walkway that leads from the bandstand to the prom-enade. At that moment there's a fizz of electricity, and the *BOOM! BOOM!* bass of what he now knows is Ryan's fa-vourite Missy Elliot track.

At once Abby's little boy claps his hands over his ears. 'I'm not sure he's going to manage this,' she says. 'He hates loud noise.' She reaches beneath the seat of the pushchair, re-trieves a pair of ear defenders and eases them over his head.

'I think my son's only testing the system,' says Michael. 'We're not due to start with anything that full-on.'

As he says this, the music stops. Thank God, he thinks. I like a bit of volume occasionally, but I still can't stomach rap. He's looking forward to the punk section at 7 p.m.; he's insisted Ryan include that. Michael might not have a full-time job yet, but he's doing one day a week teaching flower-arranging to the patients up at Sunnyvale House, and he sure as hell feels like pogoing.

* * *

Karen is heading along the seafront with Molly and Luke and Lou. Little Frankie is asleep in his pushchair, wrapped in a handmade patchwork quilt Lou says she received as a surprise gift in the post that very morning. As they approach the bandstand the music is getting louder – Frankie's slumber seems unlikely to last.

'Hurry up!' says Molly. She yanks on Karen's sleeve to encourage her, but Karen can feel her mobile vibrating in her handbag, and stops to answer.

'Hold on, darling,' she says to her daughter. She can tell from the screen that it's Abby.

'I'm afraid I'm having to take Callum home, so won't be able to meet up with you.'

'Oh, that's a pity.'

'I thought he'd find it too much, in all honesty. But I'm glad we came down here. I just saw Michael.'

'Michael? You didn't!'

'I did. He was doing the flowers.'

'So you were right, it *was* his idea.'

'I told you I read that online,' says Abby. 'Along with some other people.'

'That's amazing,' says Karen. 'Just shows what you can do if you put your mind to it.'

'Yes, doesn't it? Anyway, I hope you have fun. And I'm seeing you on Saturday, aren't I?'

'Oh God, yes.' Karen winces.

'You promised!'

'I know, I know, we will do it. I told you, my friend Anna has been on at me to for ages.'

Heaven help me, what am I letting myself in for, she thinks.

'Is she the one who met her boyfriend that way?'

'Yes,' says Karen. 'The writer.'

'Maybe she could advise us on our profiles,' says Abby.

'That's a good idea.' Anna would love nothing more than to use her copywriting skills to help us sell ourselves, she thinks. Maybe if we crack open some wine after I've put the kids to bed I'll lose my inhibitions. Yes, Karen can picture them now, the three of them crowded round her computer screen, ogling potential suitors and giggling . . . 'I'll see when she's free.' Molly yanks Karen's sleeve once again. 'Sorry, I'd better go.'

'Who's Michael?' says Lou, the moment she rings off.

Karen blushes.

Lou peers at her closely, eyes narrowed.

'No, no,' protests Karen. 'You've got that all wrong.' But given the event they're going to, it seems more ludicrous than ever that she's not filled Lou in on this properly before. 'Er . . . You know I told you I met Abby on a course?'

'Ye—es . . . ?'

'I met Michael at the same time. She says he's done the flowers for the bandstand.'

'Ah.' Lou appears surprised. 'You did a course in *flower-arranging*?'

Karen has to laugh. 'No. We met at Moreland's, actually.'

Lou looks even more startled. 'What, Moreland's Place? In Lewes?'

Karen nods.

'I didn't know you went there.'

'When Dad died I got really down, so I went as a day patient for a bit.'

'Why didn't you tell me?'

'I'm sorry.' Karen grasps Lou is wounded. 'I didn't want to bother you with it at the time, but it wasn't anything to do with my not trusting you. It's only it was exactly when you were having this little one.' She leans to coo over Frankie. 'I'll tell you the full story later, I promise. Let's go and see what's happening first.'

Karen quickens her pace – Molly and Luke are eager, and she doesn't want to lose them in the swelling crowd.

A young man close by is keenly jangling a yellow bucket of coins. There are several others dressed as he is; all proceeds are going to a mental health charity, according to the jacquards they are wearing. Karen reaches for her purse and is so intent on rummaging for change, it's not until she looks up that she sees who is holding the bucket.

'Colin!'

''Tis I,' he says, and takes a little bow.

'But you're outside,' says Karen.

Colin holds out a foot. 'And in shoes.' He chuckles.

'Oh, I'm so proud of you!' she says, and gives him a hug.

'Took some doing,' he admits. 'Baby steps, you know. This is the first time I've been this far from the hospital, but, well—' he coughs, ' – you know, I had to.'

Karen hugs him even tighter. He's lovely and cuddly, she thinks, reminded for a split second of Simon.

'She was one of the best mates I've ever had,' says Colin, as Karen releases him from her embrace. 'I always found it hard to make friends, but Lillie, I dunno, she just kind of got me, right from the start . . .'

His voice wobbles, and Karen can tell he's finding it hard to hold himself together. *Though I wouldn't care if he bawled his eyes out*, she thinks. 'Colin,' she says on impulse. 'I'd like to be your friend. I can't promise to be anything like Lillie, but I'd love to stay in touch.'

'Really?'

'Yeah, and I see Abby, so maybe we can meet up from time to time. I've got your number.'

'I thought you were just being polite, when you asked for it,' he says.

'And I thought you were just being polite, when you gave it to me.' Karen smiles. 'What are we like?'

Colin grins. 'Rubbish. Hey, you know, Johnnie said some of the staff are coming to this, too. Or he and Beth are, at any rate.'

'That's nice.' *It would be good to say hello to Johnnie again*, thinks Karen.

'And that's Tash, up there—' He points to the promenade up above them, and sure enough, she glimpses a flash of pink frizz. 'I'm sure she'd like to see you too. Maybe we could go for a drink some time: me, you, her and Abby. It's not like we're Bads or anything.'

'Exactly.'

At that moment, the strains of the 'Blue Danube' waltz fill the air.

'Oh, look, Mum, lots of Auroras!' says Mollie, pointing.

Karen follows her daughter's gaze. On the bandstand are a dozen couples, swooping and twirling in time to the music. The women are in floor-length ball gowns; the men in jackets with tails. It's all rather ad hoc, but that only makes it more enchanting, somehow. One of the dancers is more elderly and seems a bit unsteady on her legs compared to the rest, and when Colin nudges Karen and murmurs, 'See who that is?' she realizes it is the snowy-haired Rita. Her gown, a silk sari, is covered in beads, and she's waltzing with Karl, the Mohican.

What a shame Callum missed this, thinks Karen.

And as for the flowers . . . They are like something from a fairy tale. There is ivy entwined round every pillar, and hundreds of white trumpets burst from the roof, as if heralding the talent of each of the performers below.

'Bravo!' As the waltz finishes, Karen claps enthusiastically along with the rest of the crowd and says to Lou, 'I gather we're working through from traditional ballroom to today – and anyone who fancies taking part can have a go. Apparently there's all sorts later – you know, the street dancing Lillie was known for, break-dancing and stuff.'

'I don't think we'll last through all that.' Lou glances down at Frankie. 'We'd better make the most of this tamer bit of the celebration.'

Normally Karen would only stay for the gentler music, too. But today she doesn't give a damn if the tracks aren't to her taste or no one's rehearsed or has any idea what steps they're supposed to be doing. She doesn't care if the kids insist on staying too late or it gets so noisy that the council is inundated with more complaints than they know what to do with. The whole experience of being here right now will be worthwhile, whatever happens.

As they move round the bandstand to get a better view, she can see there's a banner strung high above their heads facing the prom. It's glistening in the sun, so she has to shield her eyes to see it properly. When she reads the words, she's unsure whether to laugh or cry.

A LAST DANCE FOR LILLIE, it says.

A note from the author

People often ask if my novels are drawn from experience, and the honest answer is 'Of course they are.' That doesn't mean my books are autobiographical: they're not. My husband didn't die on a train like Simon in *One Moment, One Morning*, and I've never been through IVF like Lou and Cath in *The Two Week Wait*. Equally, my circumstances are not identical to those of Karen, Abby or Michael in this story. However, I *do* have first-hand experience of anxiety and depression, and it's this that made me want to write this book.

Because the problems of mental illness are very real and immensely painful, I feel passionately that mental health should be taken as seriously as physical health. Yet by and large it isn't. Too often sufferers are told to pull themselves together or snap out of it. This is partly because the symptoms are often not visible, but it's also because the topic is still hard for many of us (myself included) to talk about. And yet mental illness is something that touches all of us. Statistics such as 'One in four suffer some kind of mental health problem' are often bandied about and can be helpful in illustrating how widespread problems are. To view mental illness as something you either have or don't have still boxes people off, however – and makes it easy for others to keep the lid of that box firmly closed. The result is that we live in a world where suicide is rarely spoken of, much mental illness is surrounded by shame and blame, and politicians can make cuts to services whilst we who voted for them turn a blind eye.

Instead, perhaps it's more helpful to see mental health as a continuum – no one is 100 per cent healthy, no one 100 per cent ill – and it's my belief that we all fall somewhere within this range. Moreover, individual mental health is dependent on many variables – our age, physical health, economic circumstances, relationship status and so on. The list is endless and it's different for each of us – so where we fall on that continuum will change over time.

Let me put this another way: *ordinary people get mentally ill*. Michael, Abby and Karen are not bad people or mad people; they're just people. As are George and Callum and Lillie and the rest. They're people on a continuum, who I hope don't seem so very different from me or you. And if reading about them helps lift the lid on the subject of mental illness, just slightly, so that a handful of people feel able to talk a little more freely or others feel a touch more understanding, then the time I've spent writing this particular book will have been worthwhile.

Acknowledgements

Many people have helped shape this novel. I very much appreciate those who shared their experiences with me: Catherine Newell told me of her Aurora-loving son Axel, my local florist Ian Graham helped me understand what goes into running a shop, and it was an honour to chat with Natasha Bevington, Kirsten Bicât and Simon Rattenbury. I benefited from the expert insights of child psychotherapist Dilys Daws (my stepmother), nurse Rhoda McClelland, psychiatrist Sarah Daley, psychotherapist Liz Bubez and the staff at the Priory Hospital in Brighton. Any inaccuracies about treatment, medication or protocol (both private and NHS) are mine, not theirs.

I am also very grateful to agents Vivien Green, Gaia Banks and Lucy Fawcett at Sheil Land Associates. I suspect many people think 'all' agents do is do deals – i.e. sell books, scripts and so on to publishers, film companies and the like. Yet this is only part of what Vivien, Gaia and Lucy have done for this novel; just as vital was their input as keen readers and wise critics, thereby helping produce a manuscript worthy of submission.

Next I must thank my friends. It was over coffee with Nicola Oatham that I first discussed the idea, and she and Zoe Hammel encouraged me from the start. A big hug goes to those generous people who made the time to read the manuscript in advance of publication – Alexandra Addison, Nicola Lowit and Rachel Williamson tackled draft 1, then Mark Dawson and Hattie Gordon gave me invaluable feedback on draft 2, and Emma Hall went through draft 3.

I must also express my gratitude to Francesca Main, my editor at Picador. She has an eye for detail but equally vital is her appreciation of character development and the overarching story – skills which immeasurably helped sharpen, shape and strengthen this book.

I'd also like to acknowledge my father's input, which didn't come in the form of direct feedback, but instead was, if anything, more profound. My dad, Eric Rayner, is now in his late eighties, but he worked as a psychoanalyst for almost fifty years. He was dedicated to his patients and campaigned to make psychotherapy more widely available to all. His passionate interest in mental health rubbed off on me, and his influence permeates every page of this novel.

As with all my books, I'd like to say thank you to my mother, Mary Rayner, for her support and wisdom. Finally, thank you to Tom Bicât, my husband. Throughout the whole process he's listened and advised. He says he doesn't read novels, yet he's read *Another Night, Another Day* more times than I suspect he cares to remember.